**"Do you need me to spell it out, Maggie?"**

Landon's lips creased into a smirk. He grabbed her hand and brought it to his mouth. His lips traced the ridge of her knuckles. "I wanted to get into the good graces of my lady boss."

A blaze ignited in her stomach. Much like the one he'd created in the dark interior of his truck when he'd slanted his mouth over hers in a searing kiss.

"Landon, I don't..."

A storm of fury and lust flared in his eyes. Her heart seized in her chest. Before it jumped back to life again, the emotion in those dark depths vanished.

He lifted his mouth from her hand. "Liar."

# HER UNEXPECTED COWBOY MATCH

*USA TODAY* Bestselling Author

Christyne Butler

Christine Wenger

Previously published as *The Cowboy's Second Chance* and *The Cowboy and the CEO*

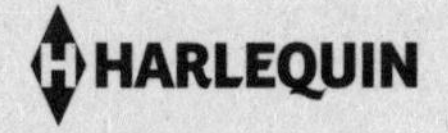

If you purchased this book without a cover you should be aware that this book is stolen property. It was reported as "unsold and destroyed" to the publisher, and neither the author nor the publisher has received any payment for this "stripped book."

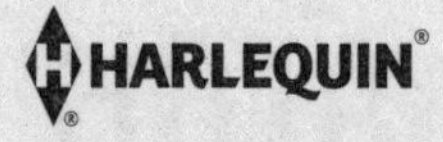

Recycling programs for this product may not exist in your area.

ISBN-13: 978-1-335-18994-3

Wyoming Country Legacy:
Her Unexpected Cowboy Match
Copyright © 2020 by Harlequin Books S.A.

The Cowboy's Second Chance
First published in 2009. This edition published in 2020.
Copyright © 2009 by Christyne Butilier

The Cowboy and the CEO
First published in 2007. This edition published in 2020.
Copyright © 2007 by Christine Wenger

All rights reserved. No part of this book may be used or reproduced in any manner whatsoever without written permission except in the case of brief quotations embodied in critical articles and reviews.

This is a work of fiction. Names, characters, places and incidents are either the product of the author's imagination or are used fictitiously. Any resemblance to actual persons, living or dead, businesses, companies, events or locales is entirely coincidental.

This edition published by arrangement with Harlequin Books S.A.

For questions and comments about the quality of this book, please contact us at CustomerService@Harlequin.com.

Harlequin Enterprises ULC
22 Adelaide St. West, 40th Floor
Toronto, Ontario M5H 4E3, Canada
www.Harlequin.com

**Printed in U.S.A.**

# CONTENTS

**Christyne Butler** is a *USA TODAY* bestselling author who fell in love with romance novels while serving in the US Navy and started writing her own stories in 2002. She writes contemporary romances that are full of life, love and a hint of laughter. She lives with her family in central Massachusetts and loves to hear from her readers at christynebutler.com.

## Books by Christyne Butler

### Harlequin Special Edition

#### *Welcome to Destiny*

*Destiny's Last Bachelor?*
*Flirting with Destiny*
*Having Adam's Baby*
*Welcome Home, Bobby Winslow*
*A Daddy for Jacoby*
*The Sheriff's Secret Wife*
*The Cowboy's Second Chance*

#### *Montana Mavericks: 20 Years in the Saddle!*

*The Last-Chance Maverick*

#### *Montana Mavericks: Rust Creek Cowboys*

*The Maverick's Summer Love*

Visit the Author Profile page at Harlequin.com for more titles.

# THE COWBOY'S SECOND CHANCE

Christyne Butler

Dedicated to my own Nana B...
Margaret Elizabeth Blakeslee, and my aunt,
Carol Ann Baranowski, both of whom continue
to live on in my heart. And to my mother,
Sandra Jean Toms, thank you for your love and
strength!

Extra special thanks to Charles and Gail
for your belief in me, "The Goddesses" at
WriteRomance—Alison, Christina, Jen, Sandi
and Tina—NHRWA and everyone at the
eHarlequin boards for all your support!

# *Chapter 1*

"You no-good, rotten thief!" Maggie Stevens stomped across the trampled grass of the fairgrounds and tried not to spill the frothy beer from the plastic cups she held in her hands. "You're stealing my man!"

Kyle Greeley shot her a sardonic grin and continued to peel bills from the large roll of money. By the time Maggie reached him he'd handed over at least a hundred dollars to the cowboy standing next to him—*her* cowboy.

"Not man, babe," Kyle said. "Men."

"What do you mean, 'men'?"

She shot a look at Spence Wilson, one of the hired hands who'd worked for her for the last few months. Then she saw Charlie Bain step from the shadows, his gaze locked on his boots.

She should've known.

While spending a beautiful summer day enjoying Destiny, Wyoming's, Fourth of July Celebration with her daughter and grandmother, she'd seen neither hide nor hair of her cowboys.

Until now.

"It's nothin' personal, Miz Stevens," Spence said. "We enjoy workin' at the Crescent Moon, but Mr. Greeley's pay is too good to pass up."

Maggie fumed. The dangling carrot of more pay had charmed away ranch hands—at least her young and strong ones—once again. They took the bait like a pair of hungry rabbits.

*You did, too, at one time.*

Okay, so a few candlelight dinners wasn't cold, hard cash, but she'd been enamored all the same by Kyle's smooth-talking ways. Then she'd found out what a scumbag he really was.

Kyle leaned into her. "You know, Maggie, you could be quite comfortable if you'd accept my offer for your land. Buy yourself a place in town, spend more time with your daughter, get yourself a man…"

She glanced at the beer, trying to control her anger and the urge to dump the liquid over his head. She gritted her teeth. "I've told you before, my land isn't for sale."

Movement caught her eye, and she saw her former employees scurry into the shadows of the darkened barns and empty animal corrals.

Cowards.

She looked back at Kyle. "Why stop with those

two? Why not wipe me out completely and go after Willie and Hank, too?"

"Those old coots should've been put out to pasture years ago." He stepped closer, wrapping a finger around a strand of hair that had worked loose from her ponytail. "Admit it, you can't handle all that land, cattle and horses."

Maggie jerked her chin, freeing his hold. "Go to hell, Kyle."

She headed for the bright lights of the raised wooden platform beyond a cluster of cottonwoods. He fell into step beside her.

"I remember a time when you didn't want me to stay away."

She shook her head, barely able to tolerate that she'd once been taken in by his baby-blue eyes, chiseled cheekbones and charming lies. "Three months," she said. "Three months of romancing me to get my land."

He smirked. "Sometimes a man's got to make sacrifices. I never could figure what Alan saw in you. Then I realized he'd stuck around to get his hands on your ranch."

She spun to him, furious. "Well, he didn't. And you can forget about getting your hands on it, too."

They'd reached the trees. Kyle leaned in and grabbed her arms. Whiskey laced his breath. She mentally kicked herself for not noticing sooner. Sober, Kyle was annoying, but after a few drinks, he could get downright mean.

"I can put my hands any damn place I please," he said.

A flash of a buried memory caused Maggie's stomach to lurch. Beer splashed over the edges of the cups and dripped over her fingers. "You bastard," she choked. "Take your hands off me."

"Not until I'm good and ready."

A flicker of panic coursed through her, but anger snuffed it out. "Get ready now or you're going to find yourself with a face full of Budweiser."

"You wouldn't dare—"

With an angry flick of her wrist, she launched the contents of the cups at him. He jumped back, releasing her with a shove. "Goddammit!"

The liquid splashed on Kyle's fancy, snap-button shirt and her sundress, leaving enough for round two. "Don't dare me anything." A step backwards took her deeper into the trees. "Back off."

Greeley seized her again, his blunt nails digging into her arms. "You're gonna pay—"

"She told you to leave her alone."

Maggie froze as a low, commanding voice rumbled over her shoulder.

Actually, it came more from over the top of her head. She was acutely conscious of a man towering behind her. Overwhelming her. The husky tone causing a ripple of…what? Need? Awareness?

Annoyance crossed Kyle's face. "This is none of your business, Cartwright."

"Maybe not, but the lady's made her feelings quite clear."

"Let *me* be clear." Kyle took a step closer, his attention focused over Maggie's head as his hands tightened on her. “If you want to keep your job, I suggest you turn and walk away.”

The man behind her took a step closer. “Let. Her. Go.” His voice grew harder with each word.

Kyle flicked his gaze back to Maggie. “We still got business between us.” He dropped his hands and stepped back. “Don’t bother showing up at the Triple G tonight, Cartwright. In fact, I suggest you leave Destiny. For good.”

Spinning around, Greeley vanished into the darkness.

Oh, boy, that was…she wasn’t sure what that was, other than Kyle being his usual idiotic self. A deep breath helped. Maggie turned to thank her rescuer, but her foot caught on a tree root, and she stumbled backwards.

A pair of strong hands clamped her waist, pulling her back against a solid chest and rock-hard thighs. The man’s jaw brushed her hair, a rush of hot breath flowed over her ear.

Twisting in his grasp, she tipped her head back to look at his face. Intense eyes stared at her from beneath the crown of a black Stetson. Dark stubble outlined his mouth and covered his jaw. A shiver she couldn’t control raced through her. He dropped his hands and took a step back.

Maggie struggled to speak. “Thank you…for, well, thank you.”

“No problem.” He tucked in his chin, effectively blocking her attempt to peer further under the wide brim of his hat. “You okay?”

“Y-yes.” She nodded. “I’m fine.”

"You better get going before he decides to come back."

Before she could reply, her rescuer stepped around her and followed Kyle into the darkness. She watched his tall form disappear, trying to ignore the sudden rush of butterflies zooming around her stomach. Placing the blame for them firmly on Greeley, she glanced at what remained of the beer. Racy and Leeann were waiting for her. She'd better get moving. Mindful of the tree roots, she headed toward the crowded dance area.

Maggie offered a few hellos to familiar faces before she caught sight of her best friend in the middle of the dance floor with her seventy-year-old ranch hand. Willie tried his best to keep pace with Racy, who was four decades his junior, but like everyone else, he was distracted by her flame-red curls and undulating curves.

The dance ended and Racy joined Maggie. "Boy, Willie can still do a mean two-step." She grabbed one of the cups. "About time you got here. Where've you been? And what happened to my beer?"

Maggie poured the remains of her drink into Racy's. "I got sidetracked."

"Doing what?"

Maggie ignored the question, renewing her determination not to let Kyle Greeley's antics spoil her fun. "Where's Leeann? I thought she was meeting us."

"Her beeper chirped about ten minutes ago."

"I thought Gage gave her the night off."

"Yeah, well, being a deputy in a small town means

you're always on call. Besides, you know Sheriff Steele," Racy snorted. "All work and no play makes for a pain-in-the—"

Maggie cut her off, tired of her friend's nasty comments about the local lawman. "High school's long gone, Racy. Let it go."

"I have!"

Maggie raised an eyebrow.

Racy flushed. "Let's not waste time on ancient history. Where's your grandmother and Anna?"

"Nana B. went back to the ranch after collecting her blue ribbons, and Anna's sleeping over at a friend's house."

Racy's face lit up with a bright smile. "So, you're a swinging single tonight. Honey, let's find someone to push that swing!"

Flashes of denim, tanned skin and a black cowboy hat filled Maggie's head. It'd been dark among the trees, but she easily recalled broad shoulders, shirtsleeves rolled tight against strong forearms and long legs encased in snug jeans.

Maggie pushed away the details and focused on her friend. "Don't you ever give up? I told you, I'm not interested. And unless you've forgotten, I've got a few things on my mind. Especially now. Greeley walked off with Spence and Charlie tonight."

"Those low-down, belly-crawlin' snakes! And you thought they had staying power. What are you going to do now?"

What was she going to do? She needed help. Hopefully the ads she'd placed all over town would bring in some fresh faces. "The same thing I've been doing all along," she replied, "keep on keeping on."

"Well, not tonight. Tonight is for fun and what you need is a red-hot cowboy who'll leave you too sore to move and too tired to care."

"What I need is to get home. I've got a pile of paperwork waiting and—"

"Oh, come on. It's a holiday!" Racy finished the last of the beer and tossed the cup in the nearby trash. "We're celebrating our country's independence, not to mention our own. Besides, the place is swarming with hunky cowboys."

"Forget it, I'm not interested."

"Look, I'm gonna find me a dance partner and I suggest you do the same. Then another and another." She offered a quick wink. "Personally, I'm shooting for double digits."

Maggie watched as Racy latched onto the closest cowboy and led him onto the dance floor.

"How long does it take to reach zero?" she muttered.

Zero.

Those were his chances of getting another job in this dot-on-the-map town called Destiny. Great place for an out-of-luck cowboy like him.

Landon walked across the teeming fairgrounds. The sun had set, and clusters of teenagers and families enjoyed the game booths and carnival rides that twirled in bright splashes of neon color.

He sidestepped an excited little girl carrying a prized stuffed animal and a breath-stealing squeeze compressed his chest. Shoving a hand deep into his pocket, his fingers curled around a familiar oval object. His boots shuffled to a stop and he closed his eyes against the memory before it had a chance to bring him to his knees.

It took a long moment, but he succeeded. Breathing deep, he opened his eyes and spotted the sheriff chatting with a group of men. Giving a tug on his Stetson, Landon pulled it lower on his brow. If there was anything he'd learned in the last few months, it was that the law was best avoided.

Hunger gnawed at his belly as he ducked into the food aisle, but he ignored the battling aromas of fried hot dogs and spun candy. The fifty dollars tucked in his pocket would have to last until he was employed again. After standing up for that lady, he was hell and gone from his next possible job three hundred miles away.

But what a lady.

Honey-colored hair and a sweet, fresh scent. Despite a shapeless dress, he could attest, thanks to having her body pressed to his, she had curves in all the right places. He hadn't meant to get so close, but the weight of her body against his and the feel of her hair catching on his whiskers stayed with him.

Then she'd looked at him. A flash of something—longing, maybe—came through the anger and fear. A warning bell had gone off inside his head.

*Leave. Now.*

He'd ignored his own advice long enough to make sure she was okay, then followed his former boss to make sure the jerk didn't come back.

Damn, he needed a job.

Greeley's ranch was the largest in the area. The man meant it when he told him to get out of town. Big ranches and their owners carried a lot of power in small communities.

Landon headed to the far end of the parking lot where he'd left his truck and horse trailer. The dark shadows and relative quiet were the most he could offer his best friend right now. Hell, G.W. was his only friend, and the main reason for pulling off the highway earlier today.

"Hey, boy," he said as he stepped inside the trailer and moved beside the stallion. "How's the leg?"

He crouched down, murmuring softly as he ran his hands along G.W.'s forelimb, checking the area around the shipping boot. The horse snorted softly and shifted away.

"I know you hate these things, but it should help with the swelling."

It wasn't.

Landon had first noticed the horse favoring his leg the night he'd been not-so-politely told to leave his last job. Being on the road the last seven days meant he'd done a piss-poor job of icing the injury. He needed to find a place for the two of them to bunk down for a while, so he could take care of G.W. properly.

Three jobs since his release, three times told to move on.

He'd been foolish enough to reveal his conviction the first time. Never again. Now he did his best to keep to himself, but somehow the news always got out.

His stomach growled again. He opened the chest in the corner and found it empty. The ice packs were only slightly cool.

He leaned his head against the side of his horse. "I'm going to grab some chow and another bag of ice. Be back in a few."

He stroked a hand over G.W.'s smooth coat, then exited and locked the trailer, heading toward the market across the street. Bright fluorescent lights shone on a woman behind the counter when he entered.

Was that wariness on her face?

He offered a quick, polite nod then walked to the first aisle. Five minutes later, he'd moved back to the cashier when a dog-eared piece of paper on a bulletin board caught his attention. The words "Wanted: Cowboys" jumped out at him.

Damn, he must be crazy.

He yanked the paper off the board and shoved it into his pocket. After paying for his stuff, he crossed the road back to the parking lot with a sandwich, a cold soda and a bag of ice. He peeled back the plastic wrapping around the day-old bread with his teeth. It was stale, but he hoped it would cover the bad taste in his mouth left by the store clerk's apprehension.

His hair was too long and he was a week away from his last shave. Maybe that's all it was. Or maybe it was because he was a stranger in a small town. She'd beamed at the two clean-cut cowboys with pressed snap-buttoned shirts and shiny belt buckles who'd come up behind him, obviously knowing them.

Landon shrugged off his mood and finished the sandwich in two bites. He wasn't usually filled with his own thoughts. Not since his release. Before, he'd had plenty of time to think. Now he preferred a hard day's work that left him too tired for anything but sleep. Something he hadn't done much of over the last week.

He moved to the back of the trailer and led G.W. outside, taking the boot off and crushing ice around the injury. Standing in the light from an overhead parking lamp, he opened the soda and took a long draw on it, then yanked the piece of paper out of his jeans pocket and looked at it again.

"Okay, Crescent Moon, you're my last chance."

A soft shuffle invaded his consciousness, then sudden pain exploded between his shoulder blades. Seconds later, he smashed headfirst into his trailer.

Maggie waved goodbye to Racy from across the dance floor. She ignored her friend's answering frown and made her way through the crowd. Unable to find Willie, she gave up and decided to head home alone.

Gave up looking for her cowboy rescuer, too.

"No, not *my* cowboy," Maggie muttered, digging her keys from her purse.

Guilt settled in the pit of her stomach. She'd heard Kyle warn the stranger not to show up for work. She hated the idea he was now jobless because of her.

Offering him a job at the Moon had occurred to

her while she stood on the sidelines of the dance floor. She needed a man—heck, she needed men, and as many as she could afford.

Kyle's words came floating back to her.

"Buy yourself a place in town, spend more time with your daughter, get yourself a man."

Nope. Not that kind of man. She didn't have the time, strength or the emotional energy to deal with that.

Not anymore.

Heading across the full parking lot, she checked her watch. Almost ten o'clock. With her daughter gone and her grandmother probably tucked in bed with a book, she'd have plenty of time to attack the mess on her desk.

Exactly what she wanted to do on a hot summer's night.

The promised relief of an overnight thunderstorm hadn't materialized, leaving the air sultry and thick. No, what she'd love to do was head home to enjoy a long dip in the cool waters of the pond behind the house.

Minus a bathing suit. And wouldn't it be nice if she wasn't alone.

The image of a certain cowboy drifted into her mind. This time Maggie let the fantasy play out, smiling at their sensual image. "Okay, girl, admit it, maybe Racy's right. Maybe it's been too long—"

A high, shrill neigh filled the air, startling her. Maggie froze, heart racing.

The second time the horse cried out she knew it was scared to death. The commotion was coming from the end of the row of cars. She raced toward it and saw a honey-colored stallion tethered to a trailer, its eyes wide with panic. The animal was frantically trying to free itself. She reached out to calm it, but stopped when she saw three men fighting not ten feet away.

Actually, it was more like two bullies beating up the third, but he fought back, twisting and kicking, despite being held by both arms. A fist crashed into his face and the man sagged.

Maggie gasped. "Stop! Leave him alone!"

The two creeps looked at her, breathing hard. Stetsons shadowed their faces. They released the beaten man and took off into the dark. The man crumpled.

She rushed to where he lay face down in the dirt. "Are you all right?"

He groaned and pressed large hands against the ground. The muscles across the wide expanse of his shoulders tightened beneath his shirt as he attempted to get up.

"That was a dumb question. Of course you're not all right." Maggie's fingers hovered between his shoulder blades, inches from long strands of hair covering his collar. "Don't move. I'll get help."

"No," he said, low and determined.

Maggie dropped to her knees. She wrapped a hand around his upper arm to steady him, her fingers small in comparison to his muscular bicep. Heat radiated from his body into the humid summer evening.

"You're hurt. Please, let me—"

*"No."* His refusal left no room for argument. "That's the last thing I need."

A zing of awareness raced through her.

The cowboy twisted and rolled onto his back. A cloud of dust rose as his head lolled to the side, away from her. A string of curses followed another moan. Dark hair fell across his forehead and blood trickled from the corner of his mouth.

She grabbed her purse and pulled out a handkerchief. "Look, I don't know why you and your buddies got into a fight—"

"They're not my buddies," he muttered.

"Then we need to call the sheriff." Forced to lean over him to press her hankie to his mouth, her fingers scraped the whiskers on his jaw. It reminded her of the dry stacks of summer grass in her barn. "Did they steal something from you?"

"No. I did a good deed and got my ass kicked for it," he growled through clenched teeth as he pushed himself up on one elbow. "Typical, always doing the right kind of…"

His voice faded as he turned toward her to shove her hand away. Two black eyes, one swollen shut, collided with hers. Steely fingers clamped around her wrist.

"You."

# *Chapter 2*

"You!" Maggie echoed, her heart pounding in her throat.

His fingers seared her skin and she tugged free. He grabbed at her handkerchief, held it against his mouth. His denim shirt, ripped open to his waist, was covered in dirt and spatters of blood. A black Stetson sat on the ground nearby.

"Ohmigod, this wasn't—" She hadn't recognized the other men as they scuffled in the dirt, but now… Greeley's foremen. "They jumped you because of me."

"No." Looking away, he wiped at the blood on his mouth.

"I don't believe you."

He rolled onto his hip, one leg bent at the knee,

and gave his head a quick shake as if trying to clear it. "I don't care what you believe," he rasped, pushing unsteadily to his feet. "Where's my hat?"

Maggie rose, ready to catch him if he fell. She grabbed the dusty Stetson, and held it out to him. "The fight was because you helped me."

"Let it go, lady."

He grabbed the hat, slapped it on the back of his head, and grimaced. The horse whinnied. The man swayed, but managed to steady himself before staggering to the animal. "Easy, boy…it's all right."

Maggie grabbed her purse and followed. "Did they hurt your horse?"

"G.W. is fine. Go away."

His harsh words stung, but she didn't give up. "The horse may be fine, but you're not. We should get some help—"

Maggie stopped talking as he untied his horse and led it inside the trailer. She leaned against the cool metal surface, tucking a strand of hair behind one ear. The smell of stale hay teased her nose.

Poor baby, the stallion must have been so frightened. Inside, the cowboy's muted cadence soothed the skittish horse. Soothed her, too. Gradually his words faded away. She pressed an ear to the trailer. Nothing.

Was he okay? Had Greeley's men hurt him so bad he'd passed out?

"Damn you, Kyle," she whispered. "Haven't you done enough?"

"You still here?"

Maggie whirled around to find him standing behind her, so close the brim of his Stetson brushed against her hair. His height blocked the overhead glow from the parking-lot lights, casting his face into shadow. His presence overpowered her, but somehow made her feel safe, too.

Safe? Where in the world had that come from?

"The medical clinic is down the street," she said. "You should have someone take a look at your injuries."

He took a swig from a bottle, grimaced and spat bloody water on the ground. Then he splashed a palm full of water over his face and wiped it away with his shirt sleeve. "Why?"

Maggie planted her hands on her hips. "Look, you need to—"

"I don't *need* to do any…"

The cowboy swayed again. She laid a hand against his chest to stop him from crashing into her. "I can't leave until I know you're okay."

His gaze dropped to her hand, then returned to her face. "We're fine."

His whispered words belied the uneven beat of his heart beneath her fingertips. She jerked her hand away. "Your lip's stopped bleeding, but one eye is swollen shut, and you've got a nasty bruise at your temple."

"What? You wanna play doctor?"

His deep whisper sent a flush of heat fanning over Maggie's cheeks. She swallowed hard against the lump lodged in her throat. "I'll play operator and dial 9-1-1."

"No thanks." He moved past her, shuffling toward the truck cab.

She followed. "I don't think you should drive. You could pass out and kill yourself and your horse. Never mind what you might do to someone else."

He tugged on the door, cursing when it wouldn't open. Finally he got it free and crawled into the cab. "Been in enough fights—not hurt bad—not going far, anyway."

Maggie put her hand on the door before he could close it. She stepped up on the truck's running board, and watched him aim for the ignition.

He missed twice before he paused to squint at the keys. "Was planning to look for…a place to sleep."

The low tone of his voice, mixed with a hint of southern twang, grabbed at her in a place she thought long dead. "This is my fault. Please let me help."

He shook his head then his eyes rolled closed, his hands fell to his lap and he slumped against the seat.

"Are you—hello?"

Silence.

Maggie hesitated then gently removed his hat to get a closer look at his face. She braced one hand on his thigh to keep from falling into his lap. Soft denim and powerful muscles lay beneath her fingertips. Her pale-blue handkerchief sat clutched in his hand, the lace trim out of place next to his large, tanned fingers and the coarse texture of his skin. A deep shudder rumbled through his chest, the warm rush of his breath falling against her cheek. His eyes remained closed.

"I'm going to get help." She'd seen enough injuries on the ranch to know he needed medical attention. "I'll be back."

"Don't." She jumped when his fingers tangled with hers. He held tight for a moment then his grip loosened. "I'll…be fine. Please don't…"

The quiet desperation in his voice struck at the deepest part of her heart. Why was he so against letting someone help him?

"Girly, what in hell's bells are you doing?"

Maggie gasped and pulled her hand free. She swung around and looked into a pair of startling blue eyes framed by a shock of white hair. "Willie! You scared me half to death. What are you doing here?"

"Your grandmother took my ride. I saw your truck in the parking lot, and figured on hitching back with you. Darned surprised to find you getting all frisky in a stranger's pickup."

Willie's sharp gaze peered around Maggie. "And with a drunken cowboy. Hoo-wee!"

"He's not drunk." Maggie stepped from the cab. "There was a fight. I've been trying to convince him to let me get help, but he keeps refusing."

"Yep, right up to when he passed out." Willie shoved his hands in his pockets. "You sure he ain't tanked tight?"

Maggie frowned. "I'm sure. Can you take a look at him?"

The old man, more a member of the family than an employee, stared at her for a long moment.

"Please?"

Willie sighed, then nodded and Maggie stepped out of his way. He gently poked and prodded the unconscious man with a sure touch. Finally, he turned, thumbing up the brim of his hat.

"Well, he ain't dead."

"I know that. Should we take him to the clinic?"

"He's got a lot of bruises and took a good clock to his left eye. He's gonna be hurtin' in the morning." Willie stepped away. "But nothing's broken from what I can tell, and his ribs appear okay. His pupils look fine, too, but that don't explain why he's out cold."

"Exhaustion?" Maggie offered. "He said he needed sleep. He's not from around here and doesn't have a place to stay."

"Oh, boy, I know where this is going."

"Willie—"

"Don't 'Willie' me. I've known you all your life, and if it's one thing you can't resist, it's a hard-luck case." He pointed his finger at her. "Don't matter if it's a four-legged or two-legged creature, you've given away more hot meals and places to sleep than anyone I know."

"Yeah, and then they take off for greener pastures. Look, I'm not out to rescue anyone, but we can't leave him here."

Willie crossed his arms, pulling his starched shirt across his bony shoulders. Age stooped his once-tall frame, but he could still look her in the eye. "There's something more going on here."

Maggie sighed. It took a few minutes to fill him in on losing Spence and Charlie, as well as Kyle's sleazy behavior—until this stranger stepped in.

Willie's features hardened as she spoke. He looked at the cowboy again. "So, they paid him back?"

"Yeah. The least I can do is give him a place to sleep and a decent breakfast in the morning. And I'm not going to get the sheriff involved over something as trivial as Greeley jerking me around."

"What about this guy getting the crap kicked out of him?"

Maggie dropped her hands to her sides, the cowboy's Stetson banging against her leg. "He was adamant. He doesn't want help from the sheriff or anyone else."

Willie grunted. "You check the trailer. I'll move him to the far side of the truck."

Maggie protested, but he cut her off with a wave of his hand. "I ain't gonna let you drive him to the ranch alone. And it's no good if he wakes up and finds a stranger behind the wheel. So it's the three of us."

"Fine," Maggie handed over the cowboy's keys. "My truck can sit here overnight. I'll pick it up tomorrow."

She checked the trailer then climbed into the cab. The cowboy leaned against the door, his face toward the glass. Willie joined them, forcing her to scoot into the middle, pressing her body into the unconscious man from shoulder to knee. His heat radiated through her dress to dance along her skin. The warm night air jumped up another degree as she watched his chest rise and fall in a steady rhythm.

"Margaret Anne, I hope you know what you're doing," she muttered, dropping his hat into his lap.

Willie pulled out of the parking lot and headed for home as fireworks lit the night sky. A half hour later, they turned off to the ranch. Despite his breathing, the cowboy hadn't uttered a sound. If he didn't wake soon, she'd place a call to Doc Cody.

The headlights gleamed over the bunkhouse and barn as they pulled into the drive, and Willie jolted the truck to a stop. "Sorry 'bout that, the brakes on this thing seem to be as old as me." He opened the driver's door and stepped out. "You stay here with sleeping beauty. I'll get the barn doors."

A gentle rocking caused Landon's head to loll back and forth. He became aware of soft, feminine curves pressed against him and realized for the first time, in a long time, he wasn't alone.

This was a dream. It had to be.

Unlike the nightmares of the past, he welcomed the heat against his body. Desire to nestle closer stirred deep. He was desperate for her scent, her touch. Desperate to believe this was real. He wanted her next to him, on top of him.

Then the warmth and curves moved away and a hard bounce caused his head to snap backwards. A ricochet of piercing light sparked inside his brain near one eye, and then spread to fill his entire body. He tried to move away from the pain, but his legs protested.

Was he sitting up?

He shifted again and pain exploded in his chest. A groan threatened to erupt, consuming every inch of air in his lungs as he forced himself to focus.

Did he hear voices? The sound of a truck door closing? His truck?

The familiar stale odors from the trailer filled his nose and he tried to slow the merry-go-round spinning inside his head.

*Think, dammit! What's the last thing you remember?*

The sweet scent of fresh linen. No, that didn't make sense. He hadn't slept in a real bed in over a week. But the fragrance managed to make its way through the smells of his truck.

He curled one hand into a fist, crushing cool cotton against his palm. The same whiff of clean sheets, fresh from drying in the hot sun and a cool breeze, washed over his face as the gentle touch of a woman's hand covered his.

Her curves were back, but it wasn't enough. He wanted to feel her against him. This time his body obeyed his silent command, and his hand found a delicate shoulder.

He pulled her toward him, need rushing through him as he breathed in her cry of surprise. He drew her closer, swiping his tongue over his dry lips before he covered her mouth. Breath rushed inward between supple lips, and his tongue followed.

He didn't care if he was hallucinating. It was too perfect to stop—and he concentrated on his first kiss in four long years.

A minty flavor greeted him as he explored her mouth. He traced the edge of her teeth with his tongue then slipped out past her lips to dart at the corners of her mouth, sweet like a summertime rain.

His hand stole across her upper back, sliding across cool, soft fabric until silky hair tangled with his fingers. He angled her across his chest. Her lips moved against his, and a small stab of pain made him groan. She retreated and this time he let her go.

Consciousness pulled at him, and Landon forced his eyes to open.

One obeyed, the other managed only a slit. His hair fell forward, partially blocking his view of feminine fingers lying over his fist. Clutched inside was a lacy handkerchief. Looking up, he focused on the outline of a woman. For a long moment, a pair of wet lips held his attention. Those lips trembled then the tip of her tongue stole out across her bottom lip.

"Oh…are you okay?"

Despite the shakiness of her words, Landon recognized the voice. Soft, sexy and sweet. The same voice that had sucker-punched him the first time she'd offered a breathless token of gratitude. The lady at the fairgrounds. The same lady who'd interrupted him getting his ass kicked and then refused to go away.

Was it a dream? Had he really kissed her?

Landon ignored her question and the pain shooting through his body. "What are—where am I?" He straightened, tunneling his fingers through his hair.

They sat in his parked, idling truck. He peered into the darkness. Thanks to the glow of a porch light, he could make out the outline of a house.

"My place."

He swung around to face her, and the throbbing intensified. Landon cradled his forehead in his hand. "What the hell am I doing here?"

"You needed a place to sleep."

"Lady, are you crazy? You don't know me."

She withdrew to the steering wheel, her face now hidden in the shadows. "Was I supposed to leave you in the parking lot for the sheriff? I guarantee I can provide a more comfortable bed than the local jail."

The image of a barren room with bars flashed before his eyes. It was quickly pushed aside by another image, springing fully formed in his head before he could stop it.

The two of them, in a bed this time, tangled in crisp, clean sheets. Him flat on his back, her hands spread across his shoulders as he cradled her hips. She leaned forward and her curtain of blond hair hid them from the outside—

Landon squeezed his eyes closed to erase the fantasy. Another sharp ache pounded in his head—as demanding as the one pressed against his fly.

"I know I keep asking, but are you—"

"I'm fine." It was a lie, but he sure as hell wasn't going to tell her what was in his mind.

The truck started to move. Landon opened his eyes, and watched her back toward a large barn that loomed out of the darkness.

She slowed to a stop. "Willie's opening the barn doors—"

"Who's Willie?"

"He works here for—"

"I'll help him."

Landon tugged on the door handle and nearly fell out the cab. He grabbed his hat before it hit the ground and slammed the door closed.

The last thing he needed was this angel of mercy asking him again if he was okay. He wasn't. Wasn't close to being okay after the vision he had of the two of them together.

Where in the hell had that come from?

He'd had plenty of chances to be with a woman since his release. Every town he'd worked in had bars and honky-tonks filled with ladies who didn't care where you came from or where you were going. Women who wanted the attention they weren't getting at home. He'd never been attracted to any of them. Hell, long before his conviction he'd lost any desire to be physically close to the opposite sex.

Amazing what deception could do to a man.

Burying the memory, Landon reached for the barn doors. He shoved, and they opened easily, thanks to the elderly cowboy on the other side. Had this old timer seen what'd happened in the truck? Did he care?

The man offered a curt nod. "Nice to see you on your feet."

Landon nodded in return. "Thanks. You must be Willie."

They moved aside when the trailer crossed the threshold.

G.W. Damn!

He'd started for the barn's interior when another wave of dizziness hit him. Pressing a hand to his forehead, he fought off the unsteadiness and noticed the square piece of blue cloth in his grasp. A deep breath pulled in the smell of fresh linen and a hint of something spicy. It made him feel…peaceful.

He shoved the handkerchief into his jeans, next to the locket, and entered the barn at the same time as his lady rescuer. She flicked a switch and a circle of light sprang to life overhead. The occupants responded with low neighs.

"Hush, now," she said, then turned to him. "Okay, let's get your horse out of this trailer."

Landon watched the woman, still not understanding how he'd ended up with her and this antique cowboy in the first place. He pinched the bridge of his nose, willing away the pain behind his eyes. "Ah, I'm a bit confused—"

"Not surprising considering the blow you've taken to the ol' noggin," Willie said with a hint of mockery. "You look like you've been rode hard and put up wet."

"You told me no sheriff," the woman said, opening the trailer's gate. "But someone had to look you over, and both you and your horse needed a place to sleep. Willie took care of the first, and the second will be done as soon as we get this animal into a clean stall."

Landon dropped his hand and watched as she lowered the ramp to the floor. She put a foot on the edge, but Willie stopped her.

"Some cowboys think of their horses like they do their women." He pulled the lady a few steps back. "Don't want nobody else touching 'em. The first couple of stalls are empty. Take your pick."

Landon stared hard at the old man then nodded and walked inside the trailer. He ran his hand along G.W.'s coat and dropped his head to rest against his warm mane. He drew in the familiar comfort of his friend before backing him out of the trailer and into a stall.

Grabbing his duffel bags and ice chest, he dropped his stuff on a low bench outside the stall. Another bout of dizziness hit him, but he pushed it away.

"She does this a lot."

Landon looked up, surprised to see it was only him and Willie in the barn.

"Can't resist helping someone who's downtrodden," Willie continued. "Been that way since she was a little bit. Doesn't matter if it's a rangy dog or a broke-down cowboy, she's always there to offer a hot meal and a warm bed."

Landon didn't know which the old man considered him to be. "Is that so?"

"She doesn't expect anything in return and that's usually what she gets, but I've been here since God was a boy, and part of my job is looking out for my boss. I don't want her hurt."

Wait a minute.

Landon blinked. Did he say *boss?*

# *Chapter 3*

"Yeah, you heard me right. She's the one in charge around here. We haven't been properly introduced. Willie Perkins." He stuck out his hand.

Landon took it, not surprised at the strong grip. "Landon Cartwright."

"At least you know who ya are. Come on, I'll fix ya up in the bunk—"

"No, thanks. I'll stay here."

Willie's bushy white brows arched high. "In the barn?"

Landon pulled his hand free. "Yeah, I've slept in worse places. Believe it or not, I've been in fights before, too."

"Now, why don't that surprise me? We got enough trouble around here, you hear?"

"Look, old man. I didn't ask for her help. Or yours. And trouble is the last thing I'm looking for."

Willie stared back at him for a long moment, then nodded. "Fair enough. I'll park your truck by the house. You get the doors."

He didn't wait for a reply. Minutes later, Willie walked by and tossed him the keys before disappearing into the bunkhouse. Pocketing them, Landon closed one barn door, then stopped. His eyes drifted across the yard to the light spilling from a window in the main house.

Who was this lady? Did she own this spread? Alone?

Willie hadn't mentioned a husband, and she seemed pretty upset with Greeley back at the carnival. He couldn't remember if she wore a wedding ring, not that a piece of jewelry kept someone faithful.

And this ranch.

Other than the outlines of a few buildings, including a one-story house with a wraparound porch, he couldn't see much in the darkness. The quiet surprised him. The barn sounded as if it was full of horses, but except for Willie, there weren't any other cowboys in sight, and only one other pickup besides his own.

Unusual for a Saturday night and a holiday…

*Stop thinking so much.* Landon shut the other barn door. *You've got more important things to worry about.*

His body was wracked with sharp twinges of pain as he moved toward the stalls. After closer inspection of G.W.'s leg, he was happy to see the swelling under control.

"Wish I had some liniment to help you out, boy." He kept his voice soft as he rewrapped the leg with firm pressure. "We'll have to rely on good ol' cold and hot therapy until I can get more cash."

G.W. responded with a flick of his ears. A twinge of guilt twisted through Landon as he watched his horse feed. After a week of foraging on the side of the road, it was clear the palomino was enjoying the fresh hay and water.

Landon left the stall and walked to the bench. A low groan escaped as he pulled off his boots. It took a minute for another wave of dizziness to pass before he emptied his pockets into the duffel bag. He kept the tarnished silver locket. It took all his strength not to open it and look inside.

Rubbing his fingers over the inlaid scrollwork, he stared at it for a long moment then shoved it back into his jeans. Not now. He couldn't deal with any more pain tonight.

What was left of his shirt hung free and he undid the few remaining buttons before releasing the top button of his jeans. His shoulders and arms ached as he reached around to rub the scar tissue on his lower back. He could get the crap kicked out of him and the injury didn't flare up. Then something as simple as changing a tire and—

*Injury. Yeah, right.*

Injury implied healing. Not this. This he would carry for the rest of his life. He peeled the shirt off his shoulders. A low creaking caused him to spin around.

"I'm sorry. I didn't mean to startle you." She walked from the shadows, her arms filled with blankets, a pillow and a glass of water. "Willie called me from the bunkhouse and said you'd be staying…"

A rush of heat spread across Landon's skin when her gaze trailed from his face, past his open shirt to his feet, then back again. Brightness shone in her emerald eyes. The pink on her cheeks matched her full lips and the memory of their imaginary kiss came rushing back.

He didn't know if she was married or not, but the intensity of her stare was enough to start the pressure building behind his fly for the second time tonight.

"I guess I should've knocked first."

Landon forced himself to relax. He tugged his shirt back onto his shoulders, thankful he still wore his hat. "It's your barn."

She held out the bedding in her arms and frowned. "Why sleep out here?"

"I already told your cowboy. The place is clean and the hay's fresh. Better than where I've slept the last few days." Landon's heart pounded as he took the blankets, warm from her body. The now-familiar scent of fresh linen drifted around him. "Besides, most cowboys don't welcome sharing a bunkhouse with an outsider. And I'm sure your husband isn't too crazy about you bringing home a total stranger."

He placed the items on the bench then turned to find her holding out the glass in one hand, two pills in the other and a faint blush on her cheeks.

"You might be right about the cowboys, but not the husband. I don't have one." She pushed the glass and pills at him. "Here, you must have one heck of a headache."

No husband.

He ignored the jolt the news gave him, looked at the pills instead. He hesitated, hating how three years in prison had colored his view of people. He doubted the pills were anything other than pain medication. How could he refuse? She'd done more for him, a total stranger, than anyone else since he'd gotten out.

"You said your ranch hand checked me out?" He took the glass. "How did he do that exactly?"

"Willie served in the Korean War as a medic." She dropped the medicine into his hand. "He has a bit of medical school under his belt, too. He's helped a lot of people around here over the years."

Landon nodded before he tipped his head back and pretended to take the pills. Instead, he slipped them into his pocket and washed the dryness from his mouth with the cool water.

"So, you all set?" She moved past him toward the horse stalls. "Got enough pillows, blankets… liniment?"

"Excuse me?"

"You told me those men didn't hurt your horse." She stood at G.W.'s stall and grabbed the top edge of the split door. "But I saw him favoring his forelimb when you brought him out of the trailer."

He joined her, but stayed at arm's length. "They didn't hurt him. His injury happened about a week ago. Tonight's excitement didn't help."

She took the glass from his outstretched hand. "Neither did riding in your trailer."

G.W. shook his head and offered a nicker in response. She grinned and held her hand flat for the horse's inspection before laying her palm on his nose and gently rubbing.

Another stabbing pain pierced Landon's chest. This one didn't hurt like the others. Laced with an edge of something carnal, it curled inside his gut.

He put more space between them and crossed his arms over his chest. The sawdust covering the concrete floor was cool against his feet. "He's okay. I've got it under control."

"I've got Dermcusal, but it might be too late." She offered the horse a final pat before moving away. "Warming liniments might help. There's a refrigerator and warmer in the tack room."

"Lady, what are you—"

"Wait right here." She disappeared through a door in the corner of the barn. He could hear the jingling of keys, then she returned with a jumble of small boxes and tubes that she handed to him. "Here, these should help. If you want, we can call Kali Watson in the morning. She's the local vet, well, the practice is her and her husband, but he's gone at the moment—"

"No."

Landon's reply was stronger than he intended, evident by how she skittered backwards. He looked at the medicine he'd been hoping for a moment ago. Medicine he couldn't afford.

"Ah, no thanks." His voice was softer this time. "I can care for him."

"How? You said you didn't have anywhere to go tonight."

"I did? When?"

"Back at the fairgrounds when we debated whether you were fit to drive." She took another step toward the side door. "That's how you ended up here."

Geez, he needed to clear the fog swirling in his head. What else had he said?

He again looked at the tubes of ointment and swallowed hard. "I appreciate this, but I'm passing through. I can't… I don't have the money to pay you."

She waved off his words. "Don't worry about it."

Pride filled him. He'd always earned everything he'd gotten in life. Long before his time in jail, charity wasn't something he'd ever taken lightly. "And the hay—G.W. can eat like there's no tomorrow. Your hospitality—"

"Consider it a proper thank you for what you did for me tonight." She reached behind her and opened the door. "You know, with all that's happened you never did tell me your name."

"Cartwright." The word was out of his mouth before he thought about it. "Landon Cartwright."

"Well, Landon Cartwright, my name's Maggie Stevens. Welcome to the Crescent Moon. You're invited to breakfast come morning if you're still here."

She hurried through the door, closing it firmly behind her. Landon remained rooted to the spot and stared after her before he dumped the meds on the bench.

Had he heard right?

He pulled the help-wanted ad from his jeans.

Yep, Crescent Moon.

*Bam, bam, bam.*

Maggie allowed one eye to open wide enough to look at the clock on her nightstand. A low groan escaped her lips. Despite the morning light filling her bedroom, it wasn't quite six o'clock. Unlike most nights when she'd fall into bed already half asleep, it'd taken hours before she'd stopped reliving the events of last night. For a day that started so simply, it certainly ended with a bang.

More like an explosion.

She pictured the tall, handsome stranger sleeping in her barn and relived his soul-stirring, stomach-dropping kiss. The memory made Maggie's insides plunge all the way to her toes.

The same as they did last night when Landon had grabbed her and pulled her close in his truck. She had seen his head snap back against the seat rest when Willie had hit the brakes. Her first instinct had been to make sure he was okay. His first instinct, evidently, had been to cover her mouth with his. She'd been so surprised by his actions and her response that it had taken a groan from him to make her pull away.

Racy was always telling her she needed a little excitement in her life. Nothing like breaking up a fight and bringing home a not-so-conscious sexy stranger to liven things up.

A stranger who cared very much for his horse.

Intuition told her the cowboy and G.W. were best friends, despite the sad conditions of both his truck and trailer. Maybe it was because he'd wanted to stay in the barn. Or the relief in his eyes when he'd first seen the medicine. A relief quickly hidden behind a mask of pride.

*Bam, bam, bam.*

Maggie groaned again and crawled from her bed. She crossed to one of the windows facing the barn. It had to be Hank. No matter how many times she'd told him it was okay to start the workday a little later on Sundays, he was always up at dawn. Thanks to ranch hands disappearing and the list of chores growing daily, she was up with the sun most days, too. Hank had agreed to do something away from the house until everyone else was up and moving. But not this morning. No, it sounded as if he was right beneath her window.

White eyelet curtains ruffled in the cool morning breeze, obscuring her view. She pulled them to the side and squinted at the cloudless blue sky and the promise of another hot summer day. She scanned the swimming hole in the backyard and the empty foreman's cabin until her eyes came to rest on the tall figure wielding a hammer at the main corral.

That wasn't Hank.

There was no way anyone could confuse her ranch hand, a shorter, solid, fatherly type, with the man outside her window. A lean, muscular body poured into a black T-shirt and matching jeans, stood tall in the morning light. His long hair was tied at the base of his neck under a black Stetson.

"Landon Cartwright," Maggie whispered against the windowpane.

He dug into a pocket before dropping to a crouch. Her next breath came out in a low hum as the denim covering his backside pulled taut. His shirt did the same over muscular arms and shoulders as he lifted a wooden slat. He braced it with his knee, and then—*bam, bam, bam*—three blows of the hammer sank three nails to secure the board in place.

Okay, that was impressive.

He rose and circled the corral, stopping to test each section, making quick work of an important job she hadn't had time to tackle in the last month.

Thanks to the work she'd done with a horse for Destiny's mayor and the fact that his wife was a cousin of Tucker Hargrove, she'd won first crack at taming a horse purchased by the A-list movie star for his talented but spoiled daughter. Black Jack, a wild mustang who fit his name perfectly, was due to arrive the day after next.

Landon stopped and turned, his gaze narrowing on her window.

Maggie dropped the curtain and scooted to the side, bracing herself against the flowery wallpaper. Her heart raced.

"He's a man doing ordinary chores," she chided, ignoring the butterflies in her stomach. "Get over it."

She wished it were that easy. His dark eyes and calloused yet gentle touch had haunted her deep into the night. Willie was right. She'd brought home another stray. Without a second thought to the pile of bills on her desk, she'd handed over medicine she should've kept for her own horses.

But she couldn't stop herself.

The palomino was a beauty, with its golden coat, dark eyes, and white mane and tail. Its owner was a cowboy who'd stepped in when most would've minded their own business, and got the crap kicked out of him for his troubles.

A cowboy who was now finishing one of the many chores at her ranch.

A cowboy who'd kissed her, but likely wouldn't even remember.

It was for the best.

With all last night's excitement, she hadn't given a second thought to what the loss of her ranch hands would mean until long after she'd crawled into bed. Once again, she toyed with the idea of talking to this stranger about the job. Lord knows she needed the help, but should she take the first cowboy that sashayed down the road?

The air remained silent. Maggie glanced past the edge of the curtain in time to see his knees hit the ground as he grabbed on to the side of the corral.

She raced from her bedroom, out the back door and across the cool, green grass and the dusty, dirt-packed drive. When she reached him, he was back on his feet, but bent at the waist.

"Are you all right?"

He took his time rising to his full height. One hand rubbed his stomach, pulling the fabric of his shirt tight across his chest. The other hung at his side, the hammer clenched in his fist. His dark eyes roamed over her, from her bed-head hair to her naked toes.

"Is that Clint Eastwood?"

Maggie followed his pointed gaze, and let loose a low groan, her face and neck growing hot. Her pajamas consisted of a tank top, emblazed with a head shot of the legendary actor, and matching loose cotton pants, covered with horseshoes and saddles, that hung low on her waist.

"They were a gift." She fidgeted. "Are you sure you're okay?"

He tugged his Stetson lower. "Tired. I was up most of the night with G.W."

"How is he?"

"Fine."

Maggie waited for him to go into detail, but the firm press of his lips told her he was finished.

"But you're not."

He stared at her for a long moment. Maggie returned his gaze. With his dark skin and hat pulled low, it was hard to see the varying shades of the shiner around his eye, but at least he was able to open it. Her toes curled into the dirt under his steady gaze.

"I'm fine, too," he said at last.

"Better than fine the way you wielded that hammer."

"I didn't know I had an audience."

A flush of heat stained Maggie's cheeks. "Things are pretty quiet around here on Sunday mornings."

"Well, after waking to find a shotgun in my face—"

"What?"

"I think I surprised one of your ranch hands." He shoved a hand into the front pocket of his jeans. "I told him I had permission to camp in the barn. I guess he believed me because he let me help muck the stalls and feed the horses. He then saddled up and left."

Maggie heaved a sigh. "Hank Jarvis. He's my other hand. Did he say anything else?"

Landon cleared his throat. "He mumbled something about a soft-hearted do-gooder."

"That would be me." Maggie crossed her arms, conscious she wasn't wearing a bra. "So, you want to explain why you're fixing my corral?"

"I figured since I was awake I'd do something to thank you for the meds, putting me up last night… everything."

"Last night was my way of thanking you for helping me with that pain-in-the-ass Greeley," Maggie countered, "and getting beat up for your efforts."

"I told you—"

"Yeah, you told me." Maggie propped her hands on her hips. "Don't let the fact I'm a natural blonde fool you. I'm not as dumb as I look. Not anymore, and—"

"Margaret Anne Stevens! What in the blazes are you doing out here half-naked? And talking with a stranger, no less!"

Maggie jumped and spun around. Her grandmother, five feet of wiry enthusiasm and pure white curls, stood on the back porch. "Nana B., you scared me!" Then she sighed, and turned back to Landon.

"My grandmother. You might as well come meet her before she goes for her shotgun, too."

His mouth twitched at one corner.

Maggie started across the yard, a hot prickle dancing across her skin. As much as she wanted to blame it on the July sun, she wondered if it was Landon's heated gaze on her back.

And her backside.

"I'm not half-naked and this isn't a stranger...well, not really." Maggie pushed her hair from her eyes as she reached the porch. Turning, she found he'd stayed at the foot of the stairs. "This is Landon and he—ah, he and his horse needed a place to crash last night. Landon Cartwright, my grandmother, Beatrice Travers."

"Ma'am." He hooked one finger on the brim of his Stetson and nodded.

"Call me Nana B., everyone does." Her grandmother shot Maggie a quick look then continued. "So, you're the noisemaker. You look right at home with a hammer. We're lookin'—"

"Nana B.!" Horror filled Maggie at her grandmother's words. "Mr. Cartwright isn't looking for work."

"I'm passing through, ma'am."

Nana B.'s back stiffened, then a bright smile danced over her aged features. "Not without washing up and some breakfast." She headed back inside. "I'll get started on the food, you two get wet."

Get wet.

The two little words sent Maggie's heart racing again. Last night's fantasy of a midnight skinny-dip, present company included, flashed inside her head. Mortified, she bit her bottom lip, glancing toward Landon. "Ah, there's a half bath inside if you want it."

His gaze dropped to her lips. Something hot and powerful flashed in his dark eyes. Her nipples tightened against the soft cotton of her tank top. His eyes flickered to her breasts for a moment before looking away.

A muscle ticked in his jaw as he focused on the horizon. "I should be heading out."

A voice deep inside, frantic and desperate, cried out for him to stay.

*Good Lord, where'd that come from?*

"N-not without breakfast. My grandmother would skin me alive if I let you leave before tasting her blue-ribbon muffins." She backed up until her butt hit the door. She pulled it open and stepped inside. "Besides, your horse is going to need—"

"I know what G.W. needs."

The screen door banged closed between them at his abrupt words. Maggie didn't know him from a hole in the wall. Her gut told her he was a good man, but hell, she'd been wrong before. Her body's reaction was a poor barometer. She had her family and ranch to protect. Besides, it was clear he wanted to leave.

"Fine…do what you want."

She forced herself not to look back as she made a beeline for the bathroom. The phone on the hall table rang. She grabbed the extension before it stopped. "Crescent Moon."

"Mama?"

Joy flooded Maggie at the sound of her daughter's voice. "Hey, sweetie."

"Are you okay? Did I wake you?"

"I'm fine, honey, and no, you didn't wake me." *A tall, sexy-as-sin cowboy who's no doubt packing his truck as we speak, did.* "Why are you calling so early?"

A long pause filled the air. "I wanted to check on things."

*Oh, Anna.* Maggie leaned again the wall and pressed a hand to her forehead. *Eight years old is too young to be such a worrier.* "Everything is fine here."

"No accidents while we were at the carnival?"

"You know Hank stayed at the ranch while we were in town." Maggie straightened and forced a smile into her words. "Did you and Julie have a good time last night?"

She listened to her daughter's excited chatter for a few more minutes before ending the call. After lingering under the spray of the shower, she grabbed her robe and headed to her bedroom. Once inside, she paused at the door. Despite the nearness of her room to the kitchen, she didn't hear a word of conversation.

Not her grandmother's lilting pitch, which still carried a hint of her Irish heritage, or Willie's gravel-filled murmur that reminded her of aged leather. And certainly not the low, smoky tone of her rescuer-cowboy.

*Girl, you've got more important things to worry about than a cowboy and his lame horse.* She closed the door and moved to her dresser. *Like the financial standing of your ranch.*

*Financial leaning* was a better way to put it.

After pulling on her boots, she used the hair dryer to blast her shoulder-length hair then pulled it into a ponytail as columns of figures from her so-called budget flashed through her mind. An upcoming vet payment to the Watson Clinic loomed, and her credit line at the feed store was near its limit. Not to mention the final balloon payment on the loan she'd had to get to buy her ex out of the Crescent Moon.

Balloon payment! What a stupid term for a financial dealing. Made it sound like something connected with a birthday party instead of a way for her to lose everything.

*Lose everything? Over my dead body.*

Maggie marched into the kitchen, drawn by the aroma of her grandmother's cooking. Weaving her leather belt through the loops on her jeans, she walked right into a heated wall of muscles.

# Chapter 4

"Watch out!" Landon cried out. "Hot coffee!"

"Oh!" Maggie grabbed on to the front of his shirt.

With one arm clamped around her waist, he swung her in a neat circle. He held a mug away from them, managing not to spill a drop. "You're in a bit of a hurry, aren't you?"

She looked up. Despite the height difference—he easily carried six or more inches on her—she noticed how perfectly they fit together. Without his hat and his dark hair pulled back from his face, the sharp angles of his nose and cheekbones were more prominent.

Maggie's stomach zoomed for another roller-coaster ride. She forced herself to look away, her eyes centering on his chest. Her blood ran cold.

She pushed, and he released her. "Where did you get that shirt?"

"I gave it to him." Nana B. set two plates of food on the table. "No sense waiting on Willie. The old coot probably can't pull himself away from the mirror. You two eat."

Landon grabbed an empty chair, but remained standing. Maggie stared at him until she realized he was waiting on her. She fumbled with her belt, getting it tight against her stomach, before she pulled out her chair and sat.

He followed. "It was either this shirt or nothing. All of my stuff is wet."

"What?"

"I started his laundry." Nana B. placed another plate of food on the table as Willie entered the kitchen. "It's about time, Handsome."

Maggie's eyes shifted from Willie's cheeks, marked by embarrassment, to her grandmother. "You did what?"

Landon put his napkin on his lap. "After washing up I walked out of the bathroom and found your grandmother waiting with a steaming mug of coffee in one hand and this shirt in the other."

"One whiff of the duffel bag he'd brought in told me he needed his skivvies cleaned, and cleaned good," Nana B. said. "So, I dumped it all in the washer. Then I demanded his T-shirt, too."

"I've been on the road the last week and haven't—she said I wasn't going to eat until I changed." Landon offered a careless shrug. "After catching the scent of eggs and bacon, I did what I was told."

"Which is usually best when dealing with my grandmother," Maggie said, staring at the older woman.

"Makes sense to help him out." Nana B. offered an arched brow in response as she joined them. "If he's gonna work here."

"I told you he's not—"

"I told you I'm not—"

Landon's words collided with Maggie's, and they both stopped short.

"Mr. Cartwright fixed the corral in less than an hour," Nana B. said while buttering her toast. "Isn't that amazing? Maggie's been after Spence to get it done for a week now. Speaking of that youngster, think we might see him and his sidekick crawl outta the bunkhouse anytime soon?"

Maggie set her coffee mug on the table. "Ah, Nana, I should've told you before you started cooking. Spence and Charlie quit last night. They're working for Greeley now."

"They're what?" Nana B. cried out, her knife clanging against her plate. "Those no-good, snot-nose saplings! What are we going to—"

Maggie cut her off. "Let's talk about it after breakfast, okay?"

Silence filled the sunny country kitchen. The only sound came from Willie, who seemed determined to finish his breakfast in record time.

Nana B. frowned, then replaced it with another bright smile. "Whatever you say, dearie. Mr. Cartwright can be on his way as soon as I'm done fluffin' and foldin'."

"Ah, ma'am, I can handle my own laundry—"

"Don't you never mind." Nana B. cut Landon's protest off with a wink. "Considering the quick work you did this morning, we owe you a debt of thanks. Now eat before it gets cold."

Landon glanced between Maggie and her grandmother before he turned to his food and dug in.

Maggie did the same, not completely trusting her grandmother's scheming mind. Not that she could do anything about it now. If the woman thought corralling Landon was a way to help, she'd try to do it.

Not that Maggie wasn't trying to hire more cowboys, but after finding Kyle sweet-talking Spence and Charlie, she'd bet his long reach extended to the whole county, keeping anyone from answering her ads.

Except for his former employee who sat at her kitchen table.

"So, cowboy, where you from?"

Willie's question broke the silence. Maggie gave Landon an expectant look.

"No place special," he said. "I finished a drive for the Red River Ranch in Blakeslee, Colorado. I've never been to this part of the country before, so I decided to head this way."

"How long were you at Red River?" Nana B. asked.

Landon paused for a long moment. Maggie got the feeling if it was anyone else asking, he'd tell 'em to mind their own business. "About a month. Before that the Double Deuce outside of Las Vegas, and the Circle S near Tucson."

"You move around a lot." The words were out of Maggie's mouth before she could pull them back.

His lips pressed into a hard line before he spoke. "There's a lot of country to see."

*He's a drifter.* Maggie put the thought firmly at the front of her brain as she resumed eating.

Landon forced his attention away from Maggie's mesmerizing green eyes and back to his plate. Her folded ad burned in the back pocket of his jeans.

Should he stay or should he go?

The question swirled inside his head, much as it'd done all night. After getting a good look at the Crescent Moon in the daylight, he understood why Maggie and her grandmother were upset about losing two more cowboys. They needed help. A lot of help.

Most of the buildings could do with repairs and fresh paint. He'd found the tools to fix the corral in a shed that looked ready to topple at a strong wind. Here in the kitchen the linoleum flooring curled in places and the appliances were a shade of avocado green that dated them back three decades. He didn't know how many head of cattle or acres of land she had, but he'd tended to almost a dozen horses in the barn this morning.

How was she going to handle it all with her grandmother and two geriatric cowboys?

Two ladies and two old geezers. Too much like family for him. At one time, family had been a big part of his life. The biggest. Not anymore. And he had no one to blame but himself.

"You got another job lined up?"

Another nosy question from Willie broke into his thoughts.

Landon looked up and found all three watching him. He took a sip of strong, black coffee. "On the other side of the Black Hills."

That was a lie. When he'd been forced from his last job, a fellow cowboy had told him about a place, saying they were always looking for help. What he didn't have was enough money to get from Wyoming to South Dakota.

"I guess you'll want to head out soon, seeing as it's a couple days' drive," Maggie said.

His gaze held hers. "Yeah, you're probably right."

She pursed her lips then returned to eating. This time he couldn't look away from the fork sliding between her lips. The memory of his mouth on hers flashed through his mind.

Had they or hadn't they?

He still wasn't sure if the kiss in his truck was real or a fantasy. He raised his gaze, surprised at the quick flash of heat in her eyes. Was she thinking the same thing?

Probably not, he decided when her eyes flickered away and centered on his chest, her lips flattening into a hard line. She'd frowned like that earlier when she'd pushed him away. Good thing, too, or else she would've realized the effect her body had on his.

Another reason to get the hell out of here.

What exactly occurred between the two of them last night was a bit fuzzy, but having her in his arms again this morning made one thing clear. He'd put his hands on her. And not to steady her or keep her from falling. No, he'd held her close, pulled her up hard against him in order to feel the intimate details of her soft curves.

"Bats wingin' around the belfry?"

Landon looked at Willie. "Excuse me?"

"The way you're shaking your head makes me wonder if we should be hearin' a rattling noise or the thrapping of wings."

"Thrapping?"

"Yeah, you know." Willie dropped his fork and knife, tucked his fingers under his armpits, and waved his bent arms. "Thrap, thrap, thrap."

Nana B. frowned at Willie. "Old man, you've taken one too many horseshoes to the head." Then she smiled at Landon. "More food, Mr. Cartwright?"

"No, thank you, ma'am." Her generous helpings had filled his empty stomach. He ignored Willie's question and rose, putting his plate and utensils in the sink. "I wouldn't mind another cup of coffee, though."

"Help yourself." Nana B. pointed to the counter. "The coffee maker runs twenty-four hours a day around here."

He filled his mug with the steaming liquid. He could feel Maggie's gaze on him.

"You need more food, honey?"

Landon turned to lean against the counter just as Maggie's grandmother asked her the question. She snapped her attention back to her plate, a faint blush on her cheeks. "Are you kidding?" she said, jabbing at the remains of her eggs. "There's too much here already."

"Hogwash! You're too skinny, like those girls on that castaway show. Now, finish up."

Willie guffawed behind his coffee mug. Landon did the same, though more quietly. Too skinny? No way.

He'd been right last night about her dress hiding her curves. They were in plain sight today, thanks to a soft, gray T-shirt and faded jeans hugging her in all the right places. A ponytail made her look about eighteen, probably ten years younger than her true age.

"Well, the day's a-wasting." Willie rose, wiping his mouth with a napkin. He placed his dishes in the sink before grabbing a ragged, straw Stetson from a hook near the door. "I'm gonna meet up with Hank and check the herd. Unless you need me here?"

Willie eyed Landon and Maggie followed his gaze.

"No, we'll be fine," she said. "Oh, my truck. I've got to get into town—"

"I'll take you," he interrupted.

Her green eyes returned to his, and he found himself wishing for his hat.

"I thought you were leaving?" she asked.

He was. So why weren't his feet moving?

Placing his mug on the counter, he shoved his hands into the front pockets of his jeans. "I'll drop you off on my way out."

She didn't reply.

"Margaret Anne, where are your manners?" Nana B. chided. "Say thank you."

"Thank you," she dutifully repeated, looking away as she rose.

Landon nodded, not believing she meant it and wondering why he cared. "I'll finish up my laundry so we can head out."

"I told you not to worry about that." Nana B. dried her hands with a dishrag. "It's gonna be a couple of hours before you can leave anyway."

"A couple hours?"

Maggie walked to the sink and dumped her dishes into the soapy water. "The machine's old. It takes a few cycles to get everything dry."

"Dryer-schmryer. I'll put this beautiful day to good use and hang most of it outside. Nothing like the smell of clean clothes fresh from flapping in the sunshine." Nana B. draped the dish towel over Maggie's shoulder and winked before walking into the mudroom.

Fresh linen.

The memory of that scent invading his dreams caused Landon to draw in a deep breath. There it was again, mixed among the lingering smells of frying bacon and lemon dish soap. Since he'd held Maggie in his arms, her fresh, unsullied fragrance clung to his clothes, and his fingers itched at the awakened memory of soft skin.

Willie cleared his throat. "I'll be heading out, then."

Maggie nodded. "See you at dinner."

Willie nodded and moved to Landon. "I guess I'll say my goodbyes."

Landon took his outstretched hand. "Much obliged for—well, for last night."

"No need. You helped Miss Maggie with that jackass Gree—" Willie's eyes darted to Maggie's grandmother busy at the washing machine. His voice dropped to a mumble. "—and we helped you."

"Is he as much of a weasel as he pretends to be?" Landon asked, ending the handshake.

"Yes siree."

"No."

Maggie's disagreement had Landon locking gazes with her across the kitchen. Her eyes held for a moment then broke free, and she busied herself clearing the table. He looked back at the elderly cowboy.

"You didn't take a beatin' for no reason," Willie muttered before heading out. The sound of the back door closing echoed through the kitchen.

Landon moved toward the table, keeping his voice soft. "You told Willie about your run-in with Greeley. But not your grandmother?"

Maggie ignored him as she put things away in the refrigerator.

He leaned closer and asked, "She accepts a stranger who spent the night in your barn and ends up at her table the next morning?"

"Not much surprises my grandmother anymore." Maggie closed the fridge door, pausing to push hard against the handle until it clicked shut.

"Why didn't you tell her?"

She spun around, her honey-colored hair whipping over her shoulder. "What happened last night was no big deal."

Landon crossed his arms over his chest, ignoring the need to brush away the few strands caught at the edge of her mouth. "You get manhandled, break up fights and bring home strangers often?"

First surprise, then anger crossed Maggie's features. She advanced on him until they stood toe to toe. "You don't know me. You don't know this ranch. And you sure as hell made it clear you don't want to work here. So why don't you mind your own business?"

She pushed past him and stomped across the kitchen.

He watched her go, a grin playing at the corner of his mouth. Maggie Stevens had a temper, and she was sexy as hell when riled.

*No, don't go there. You're halfway out the door.*

Still, his gut told him something wasn't right. He didn't know if it was Maggie's refusal to tell her grandmother about last night or the fact she'd brought home a total stranger and treated him like family.

*Forget it. You don't know these people from a hole in the wall, and you've got your own problems to deal with like an empty wallet and a lame horse.*

*Ah, hell.*

He started for the back door, grabbing his hat on the way out. Maggie headed across the yard. He followed her into the cool interior of the barn. "Hold on a minute—"

"I don't have time to hold on." Maggie moved from one empty stall to the next, pausing to open each door and push it flat against the wall. "In case you haven't noticed, I've a lot of work to do."

The words were out of his mouth before he could stop them. "Where do I start?"

She paused a moment, then grabbed a pitchfork and walked into the first stall. "You don't."

He followed, pulling her ad from his back pocket. "I thought you were looking for cowboys."

"You thought wrong," she snapped, turning around. Her gaze zoomed to the folded piece of paper in his hands. "Where did you get that?"

"From the general store in town." Landon stepped farther into the stall. "Right before I got jumped."

Pain filled her eyes at his reminder. "It's an old ad."

He fingered the worn, dirtied edges but kept his eyes trained on hers. "You need help around here. Now more than ever."

"No, what I need is to be more efficient." She turned back to a bale of straw, and attacked it. "And to mind *my* own business."

Landon fought the impulse to walk away. He couldn't. He owed her. She was in trouble up to her neck, but she wasn't asking for help. In fact, she'd opened herself up to more trouble by bringing him home when she should've left his sorry ass in the parking lot.

He watched her toss the straw around the stall with her pitchfork, something valiant in the set of her shoulders.

"I'll take the job," he said abruptly.

She stopped and looked at him. "Why?"

A loud whinny from G.W. prevented him from answering as they both rushed to his stall. Landon got there first and found his horse pawing at the fresh hay on the ground.

"Whoa there, boy." He dropped to his knees and put his hands on G.W.'s injured leg.

"What is it? I thought you said he was okay."

Maggie leaned in to look over his shoulder, her curves pressing against his back. Heat stole through his shirt and he bit back a groan.

"Ah, the inflammation hasn't dropped. G.W. hates these pressure bandages."

"Most horses do." She moved to rub the horse's nose and the stallion quieted. "He's beautiful."

Landon refused to think about the loss of her body heat and concentrated on removing the bandage. "Yeah, he's pretty impressive."

"Where'd you get him?"

His hands stilled. Anger flashed hot inside. "He's mine, bought and paid for. I have the papers if you want to see them."

"What? Oh, you thought I—that's crazy."

She wasn't going to question his ownership of the stallion. The men he'd worked for over the past months always had. Then again, she was no man. Maggie was all woman. Soft, sexy and right here in front of him.

Landon looked up and found her stomach at eye level. The snug fit of her jeans over her hips and thighs registered first in his brain, and then throughout his body.

*She might be your boss now. You'd better remember that.*

He forced his attention back to the horse. G.W.

responded with a gentle nicker that Landon took for pleasure at either losing the bandage or the way Maggie continued to stroke him.

"His name, the initials G.W. Do they stand for anything?" she asked.

"Georgia's Wind, after his mother."

"Have you ever thought about putting him out to stud?"

"I did once. The foal didn't make it." He pushed the memory from his head, and stood. "He's the reason."

"Huh?"

"You asked why I want this job. You can see for yourself he's hurting." Landon latched onto the obvious. "I don't want to move him. We've been through a lot together over the—anyway, he needs time to rest and recover."

"So you're looking for something temporary?"

*Yeah, the shorter, the better.* "Until G.W. is healed."

Her mouth curved into a wistful smile. "The paint in the last stall is mine. Rowdy's my best friend, too. He was born the same month I graduated high school. We've been together for the last twelve years."

Landon understood the pride in her voice. G.W. had been a college graduation present from his folks. They'd hoped he'd forget his dream of the rodeo and return home. Instead, he and G.W. had burned up the calf-roping circuit for three years straight. Until a phone call changed everything.

A familiar sting forced him to blink hard and look away.

"Well, I guess that settles it," Maggie said. "Hey, you all ri—oh!"

Landon's eyes flew open the moment the warmth of Maggie's hands and then her body, landed solidly on his chest. Grabbing her upper arms, he braced his legs to keep them both from tumbling to the ground.

Over Maggie's shoulder, G.W. bobbed his head. Landon realized his buddy was playing an old game. He found himself grinning in response, until his gaze returned to the woman in his arms.

Her eyes, wide with surprise, collided with his. A rush of warm breath caressed the bare skin at the open collar of his shirt. He swiped at his lips, his gaze firmly planted on the enticing mouth before him.

He shouldn't. She was his boss. Despite his wonderings over what had happened last night, this wasn't a good idea. In fact, it was a real wrong idea. Her lips parted and he dipped his head—

"Well, well, what's going on here?"

Landon jerked away from Maggie at the sound of the silky-smooth male voice. Releasing his hold, he immediately tucked her behind him.

"A bit territorial, aren't we, Cartwright?" Kyle Greeley stood in the center aisle of the barn and grinned. "Well, it seems I'm not the only one who enjoys spending time with Maggie Stevens in deserted barns."

# *Chapter 5*

Kyle's words caused the faded scar at Maggie's hairline to burn as if still fresh.

Six months ago a dinner date ended with Kyle giving her a tour of his new state-of-the-art barn. Minutes later, he'd cornered her, expecting something in return. Her knee barely missed crippling him, and his ring caught her high on the forehead. He claimed it was an accident. Too humiliated, she kept her mouth shut and ended the budding relationship.

Maggie shoved the memory away and moved out from behind Landon. "What are you doing here, Kyle?"

"What the hell is *he* doing here? And wearing a Crescent Moon shirt?"

Landon took a step toward Kyle.

Maggie moved between them. "What do you want?"

Kyle's eyes moved from her face to stare over the top of her head. "Do you mind? We'd like a little privacy."

"What do *you* want, Maggie?" Landon's words whispered hot over her ear.

"Why don't you do something useful," Kyle said. "Like take out the trash."

"With pleasure."

Landon moved from behind her. Maggie's restraining hand shot out and landed on a denim-clad, rock-hard thigh.

*Oh, boy, this wasn't good. On so many levels.*

She yanked her hand away, tried to ignore the sensations dancing along her arm and looked over her shoulder. Full lips, pressed into a firm line, made the angle of Landon's jaw appear hard as stone. Faint discoloration around his eye and the slight swelling at the corner his mouth reminded her it was Kyle's men who'd jumped him last night. Because of her.

"Landon, why don't you finish here?" Another display of male testosterone was the last thing either of them needed. "I'll take this outside."

His eyes narrowed in a silent threat. "Fine."

Maggie waved toward the barn doors. Greeley turned and headed out. She followed him into the deep shade of the cluster of cottonwoods near the pond.

"Well?" she asked. "What is it? I've got a lot of work to do today."

He jerked his chin toward the barn. "Yeah, I can see."

Maggie turned away. "You can see yourself out."

"When I heard you'd brought that drifter home, I figured you were looking to fill some lonely hours. Don't tell me you've actually hired him."

His words stopped her. "You heard what?"

"Oh, come on, Maggie. You know what a small town Destiny is. It doesn't take more than a whiff of something nasty to start the local rumor mill."

Yes, she knew better than most. Two years ago, Alan had walked out on their ten-year marriage, their daughter and the ranch after realizing he'd never get total ownership of the Crescent Moon. The news kept the town buzzing for months. Had someone seen her and Landon last night in the parking lot before Willie'd shown up?

"You stopped by to gossip?"

Kyle closed the gap between them, pulling off his Stetson. "No. I came for two reasons. The first is to apologize for last night."

Suspicious, Maggie stepped back. In the two years since Alan had headed for greener pastures, Kyle had tried everything to get to her. She'd fallen for it until she discovered the devious snake coiled behind his charismatic smile.

"Fine," she replied, borrowing Landon's word.

"Good. The second is you left before the big announcement. I thought it was best you heard it from me."

She had no idea what Kyle was talking about. She eyed his western-cut suit and shiny cowboy boots with barely a scratch on them. The whole outfit probably cost more than what she'd paid in vet fees for the last six months.

"Don't tell me." She offered a phony smile. "You're selling your holdings and leaving town?"

A grin pulled into a deep dimple. "No. As of this morning I'm the newest board member at Destiny's First National Bank."

Her world shifted. It took all Maggie's strength not to close her eyes. Kyle Greeley a board member at her bank? With his influence, he might as well own it. Like he now owned her ass.

The gleam in his blue eyes, tinged red from partying last night, had her wanting to slap the patronizing look off his face.

"I understand you have a meeting later this week with the branch manager." Kyle twirled his hat in his hands. "About rolling the balloon payment on your loan into extended financing?"

This time her world completely stopped. The air stilled, every sound vanished and it was impossible to catch her breath. She forced the words from her mouth, praying she wouldn't choke on them. "What about it?"

"It's been cancelled. I don't think the bank can afford to..." His voice trailed off as he looked around, his gaze stopping to rest on each of the buildings.

Maggie followed his pointed look, seeing her home as he did. Run-down, the list of needed repairs, both seen and unseen, too numerous to count.

"...take a chance on such a risky operation as

the Moon," he finished. "My fellow board members agree."

"You son of a bitch." Maggie's voice was low. Anger fueled her defense of the land that had been in her family for generations. "You know how great the Moon was, and can be again. That's why you're so desperate to get your greedy hands on it."

"You sound like the desperate one here."

"Bull—" Maggie cut off her reply when her grandmother appeared with another basket of wet laundry and Maggie's straw cowboy hat sitting on top. "Nana, look who stopped by for a visit."

"Yes, I see. Hello, Kyle." The older woman wrinkled her nose in Kyle's direction. "My, you're looking more like your daddy every day. I'd add 'God, rest his soul,' but as you know, there's been some debate as to which way your pappy headed after he passed on."

Kyle's mouth thinned. "Hello, Ms. Travers. I see your tongue's as sharp as ever."

Nana B. turned her back on Kyle and nudged the basket in Maggie's direction. "You forget something?"

"Obviously." Maggie grabbed her hat and stilled at the sight of the cell phone lying underneath. She never left the house without either one. Until this morning. She caught the mischievous twinkle in her grandmother's eye and slapped her hat on her head. "Don't say a word."

The crunch of tires against gravel filled the air. Maggie watched a metallic-red, four-door pickup with a matching trailer pull into the drive. She could make out Will Harding, the mayor of Destiny, in the passenger seat.

"Honey, I forgot to tell you the mayor called when you were in the shower," Nana B. said. "He said he'd be out this morning instead of Tuesday."

Great. Black Jack had arrived. And none too happy about it by the banging on the sides of the trailer.

"What's Harding doing here?" Kyle said. "Sounds like a pretty unhappy animal. You aren't trying your silly hocus-pocus stuff, are you?"

Kyle's question reminded Maggie he was still there. Locking away her panic at the cancellation of her meeting with the bank manager, she focused on the horse. Right now, her entire future lay inside the trailer.

"That's none of your concern," she said, silently rearranging her to-do list. She'd have to ask Nana B. to pick up Anna.

Dammit, she wasn't ready for this. Despite Landon taking care of the corral, she'd hoped for a day or two to mentally prepare for the volatile horse. But at least the first installment of her fee would be in her bank account this morning. It wasn't enough to pay off the loan, but once word got out about her success with the horse, she was sure more offers would come.

"I'll go over and say my hellos while you finish here," Nana B. said. "Good thing Landon got busy this morning and fixed the corral, isn't it?"

"You actually hired that cowboy? Are you crazy?"

Kyle demanded after Nana B. left. "You know I fired him last night."

Maggie noticed the trailer stop shaking when the truck halted. A good sign? Or was Black Jack resting before round two?

She refocused on Kyle. "I was there, remember? And who I hire is none of your business."

"Well, I do have half interest in this land—"

"Wrong. If I don't make the last payment on my loan, the *bank* gets half interest. But that's not going to happen. This ranch is going to be one hundred percent mine. I want it all."

"You're getting it all, thanks to that cowboy. Cartwright sure is making himself at home. Hell, I tried for months and never got invited back here."

No, he hadn't. In the midst of the pain and disillusionment of her divorce, Maggie never had the desire to be intimate with Kyle. Thanks to Alan's extramarital activities the last few years, she'd had no desire to be physically close to any man.

Unlike last night when a total stranger had kissed her—a kiss she'd started to participate in—before he'd pulled away. And thanks to a not-so-subtle nudge from his horse, it looked as if Landon had intended on a repeat performance.

Did that mean he remembered what happened last night?

Maggie yanked the brim of her hat low over her eyes. "I think it's time you left."

"You sure do rile easily." Kyle trailed the back of his hand down her bare arm. "Maybe I was too quick to accept Alan's word you were an ice queen. Makes me wonder what it'd be like to see you fired up—"

She shook off his touch, disgust filling her. "Goodbye, Kyle."

"I'll see you again…soon."

Maggie propped her hands on her hips and waited until he climbed into his glossy, oversized pickup. Pulling in a deep breath, she looked up at the bright-blue sky, and blew it out. Straightening, she adjusted her hat then froze. Landon had stepped from the barn, and was staring at her. He turned and headed for her visitors.

What the hell was he doing?

She started toward him as he shook hands with the mayor. Quickening her pace, Maggie forced a confident grin and said a quick prayer. She hoped that's all she would need. The last thing she wanted was Kyle's disparaging hocus-pocus comment, or the memory of her father and ex-husband sharing the same sentiment, getting inside her head.

"Good morning, Will." She greeted the mayor with a handshake. "Good to see you."

"You, too, Maggie," he replied. "What was Greeley doing here?"

"He stopped on his way into town." Maggie raised her voice over the ruckus Black Jack created inside the trailer. She had to get these men away from the horse for this to work. "I must say that was quite a celebration yesterday."

Will Harding's chest puffed up at the praise, as Maggie knew it would. "I think it was the best Fourth of July we've had in years," she continued, backing away from the rocking trailer. She looked over her shoulder, caught Landon's gaze and tipped her head toward the house. A puzzled look came over his features, but he, too, backed away.

She focused again on Will. "You were right to bring in more rides for the younger crowd. The kids stuck around instead of going off and getting into trouble like teenagers tend to do—"

"Don't you want to get the horse out of there?" Will asked, jerking his thumb over his shoulder.

"All in good time." Maggie maneuvered the group until they reached the grassy area surrounding the house. "Why don't you go inside and get some coffee? I think Nana B. has some cranberry muffins cooling in the kitchen."

"How long is this going to take, Maggie?" He glanced at his watch. "I've got a late-morning meeting. Your cowboy was about to get a rope—"

"I think Black Jack is a bit upset," Maggie interrupted with what she hoped was a reassuring smile. "Let's give him a few minutes to calm down."

*Calm down?*

Landon looked at the shaking trailer. Hell, if the horse kicked any harder it was going to topple the damn thing over. Anger radiated from the vehicle and hung in the air like a dark thundercloud ready to explode. Much like his new boss as she glared at him from beneath her straw cowboy hat.

Curiosity at the sound of an approaching vehicle had had Landon stepping from the barn, but the sight of Greeley standing close to Maggie had started a low burn in his gut. The rush of annoyance had surprised him, and he'd quickly doused it with a hefty dose of common sense.

What'd happened earlier was him thinking purely with the lower part of his anatomy. Not a mistake he'd make again. She was his boss, for the time being at least, and he needed to keep his hands, and his thoughts, to himself.

"Kyle told me I was nuts to recommend you for this." The mayor, built more like a pro wrestler than a politician, followed Maggie onto the porch. His words pulled Landon from his thoughts. "If you hadn't done such a great job with that beast of Trish's..."

Landon watched Maggie's smile slip. Was this guy going to give her a hard time, too? He moved to stand behind her. She took a deep breath and relaxed her shoulders. Good girl.

"Working with your daughter's horse was a challenge, but with a great outcome," she replied, "that's why Tucker Hargrove hired me to work with Black Jack."

"Well, that and my wife really talked you up to him. Did I tell you he's looking to build a home near Destiny? He's still a real cowboy despite just playing one in the movies for the last two decades."

"Which is why I want him to have the best horse—"

"Black Jack is the best," Will interrupted.

"Not if he can't be ridden. Hargrove's daughter has been riding since she was a child, but a teenager needs an animal she can handle. A horse she can teach, as well as learn from."

"And you've got a magic spell that'll turn an ornery creature into a winner?" Will asked.

"Yes."

Landon heard the assurance in her voice, but the second of indecision before she spoke kicked his trainer senses into full gear. He closed the distance between them. "You need any help?"

"No." Maggie looked at him, her smile more natural and easy now. "Not at the moment, thanks."

Nana B. opened the back door and took over occupying the mayor with chatty conversation. Within minutes, she herded them inside. Maggie sighed in relief, then headed for the trailer.

"Hey, wait a minute—"

"Back off, cowboy." She whirled toward him, but continued walking backwards. "I know what I'm doing."

Landon followed as far as the end of his truck and stopped. He doubted she was crazy enough to open the trailer and let the wild animal loose, but hell—who'd have thought she'd bring him back to her ranch?

She slowed when she approached the vehicle, circling the entire truck and trailer a few times. Then she started to trace a path back and forth from one side of the horse trailer to the other. Landon had no idea what she was doing, but by her third pass, the horse had stopped his persistent banging. Maggie's lips moved, but he couldn't hear what she was saying.

Was she talking to herself? To the horse?

He braced his hands on his hips and shifted his weight to one foot. The desire to go to her remained powerful. Then it merged with confusion as to why. Both battled inside his head while he watched her.

She retraced her steps, moving closer to the vehicle each time until she paused on the side facing him. She slowly leaned against the trailer, crossed her arms over her chest and bent her head as if studying the ground, not moving.

Landon checked his watch. Fifteen minutes later, she waved him over. He followed her hand signals to take a wide berth. She moved in the same direction, but stayed closer, her hand gliding along the trailer's smooth surface.

She motioned him toward the pickup. "Start it up." Her voice was low and soothing. "Can you maneuver this thing back to the main corral?"

He nodded.

"Good. Go slow and easy and no matter what, don't stop," she said. "I'll be where you can see me in the side mirror."

Climbing into the pickup, Landon settled behind the wheel and cranked over the engine. He glanced in the mirror. Maggie continued to talk, but he was too far away to hear her. He inched the truck into reverse, using both side mirrors to guide him and keep an eye on the backside of a certain lady rancher. A very nice backside.

"Keep your mind on your work," Landon muttered to himself, focusing his eyes somewhere else.

He got the vehicle in place and shut off the engine. Exiting the cab, he took the same wide circle as he headed for the corral. The lilting tone of Maggie's voice called to him and he watched her open the main gate. The trailer was still ten feet from the opening. They'd have to move it back farther.

She must have read his mind and shook her head. He opened his mouth to protest, but she waved him off. Somehow, she'd gotten the horse quiet again, but there was no telling how the animal would react once the trailer's gate opened. He took a step toward her, but she glared at him.

Damn, she was crazy! He went to his truck, grabbed a length of rope and fashioned it into a lasso.

"Trust her, Landon. She knows what she's doing."

Nana B. and the mayor stood on the porch. How long had they been there?

"It's the horse I don't trust," he said.

"Smart move," Will said. "It took four men to get the damn thing into the trailer. Don't tell me she's going to—"

"Not by herself, she's not." Landon rolled his shoulders and headed to the far side of the trailer.

He wished his muscles were less sore, but no matter. He heard the bolt slide and the creaking of the gate. Rounding the corner, he found Maggie lowering the ramp to the ground. She looked his way, her gaze climbing the length of him. He planted his feet, the rope hanging loose in his hands. He could see in her eyes she wanted him to leave.

No way.

She frowned and turned her attention back to the trailer. Landon didn't know if she was accepting his defiance or not.

He didn't care.

"Okay, boy, you're free." Her voice remained calm as she spoke to the horse, who, except for pawing at the metal flooring and a swish of his tail, remained quiet. "Now, I want you to back out of there and follow me straight into the corral. You hear me, Black Jack?"

She had to be kidding.

Landon fought the urge to roll his eyes, and instead concentrated on the horse's first step. Maggie repeated the commands as the mustang slowly emerged. The animal remained peaceful as it followed her inside the corral, stopping in the center. She stepped out of its way and scooted outside the fence.

"You can burn off some of that energy now," Maggie called after firmly closing the gate.

The horse responded with a loud whinny and a toss of his head before he galloped with wild abandon around the enclosed pen.

Awe rippled through Landon. "Hands down, that is the most amazing thing I've ever seen."

"Thank you." She didn't look at him, but continued to stare at the horse. "You can put your rope away and move the truck."

He did as he was told. The mayor headed out, looking a bit shell-shocked and Nana B. returned to the house. Landon watched Maggie talk to the still-nervous horse. He'd been around animals all his life and he'd never seen anyone handle a horse, especially one with such a surly disposition, the way Maggie had.

Before he could start toward her, Nana B. appeared with his clothes neatly folded and stacked. "This is the first bunch. You got more coming."

"I appreciate you doing this." Landon opened the driver's side door and reached for his empty duffel bag.

Nana B. nudged him out of the way and deposited the stack into the open canvas bag. "Why don't you let your horse get some fresh air, before you load him inside your trailer?"

Landon just nodded in reply, having already decided it was Maggie's place as ranch owner to let her family know she'd hired him, at least temporarily.

He waited until Nana B. headed back inside. He kept his back to the open cab of his truck, then yanked the Crescent Moon ranch shirt over his head without bothering to undo the buttons. He grabbed a light blue T-shirt and pulled it on, tucking the hem into his jeans while he walked.

When he reached the corral, he copied Maggie's posture with one foot on the bottom rung of the fence. His elbows rested next to hers on the top railing, and he eyed the midnight-black horse prancing back and forth inside the corral.

"He's a beauty, isn't he?" she said.

Her soft words invited him to look at her. "A beauty and a beast rolled into one. I can't figure out how you got him to walk out of the trailer."

"All I did was give Black Jack time to relax, get used to the smells of his new surroundings and one person to focus on." She bumped up the brim of her cowboy hat and smiled. "I also threw in a bit of mag…"

Her voice trailed off and her eyes widened, skimming over his chest and shoulders. His skin grew hot under the intensity of her stare. A desperate need to know what was going on inside her pretty head filled him, but he pushed it away.

"A bit of what?"

"I'm sorry?"

"You were telling me how you got the horse to listen."

"Oh, ah…" Maggie's smile came back, full and natural. "A bit of magic."

"I don't believe in magic," he said.

"Well, I guess I'll have a chance to change your mind."

Landon opened his mouth to protest, but Maggie pushed on. "Oh, I know you're probably a man who sets his mind to something and that's that. My other cowboys thought the same, too, but I converted them."

"Then they walked out on you?"

Maggie's smile faded. A warm breeze caught the end of her ponytail and chased it into her face. "Which is why I'm looking for more help. Willie and Hank are the best and have been here forever, but they can't handle the work alone."

He nodded. "I wondered why it was so quiet."

"When you interrupted me and Greeley last night…well, he'd just hired away my last two hands." The smooth column of her throat rippled as she swallowed before turning back to watch the horse.

"Something he's been real good at over the last six months."

The image of her and Greeley flashed in his head again. "Why?"

"That's another story—" she stopped and pushed out a deep breath "—for another time. Look, we didn't talk about pay. It's not much, but it includes feed and board for your horse. Thanks to Nana B., the food for us humans is good, too." She pointed to the far side of the yard, past the pond. "The foreman's cabin is empty if you prefer privacy."

Landon glanced over at the structure. "You haven't had a chance to talk to your family about me. Maybe you should clear things with them first—"

She cut him off. "I make all the hiring decisions around here. Not my grandmother or my cowboys. Not even my daughter, okay?"

"Who?"

"My daughter, Anna."

Maggie's words barely registered as Landon's world spiraled into numb, bitter darkness. Memories charged him and he was powerless to fight them off.

Memories of *his* daughter, Sara.

Of the day he'd entered the nursery in the predawn hours, drawn by her soft cries. Tiny hands outstretched and big tears clinging to her dark lashes, she'd leaned against the railing of her crib. After he'd changed her diaper and warmed a bottle, he'd held her as she ate. Once she'd fallen asleep again, he'd placed her back in the crib, and watched her small chest rise and fall in a steady motion.

"I'll always be here for you, little one," he whispered. "I know I wasn't for a while. I blamed you for the mistakes your mother and I made. I was wrong. But I'm making things better now. You can count on me."

He'd lied to his daughter that day. He hadn't been there for her. He'd had back-to-back meetings all day, and it was dark before he'd returned to the ranch. A mile from the main house, he'd seen a deep orange-and-red glow over the treetops. His foot had stomped the car's accelerator. He'd arrived to find the main barn engulfed, his brother and the ranch hands desperately trying to save the horses and the rest of the outer buildings. He'd joined them, but no one realized the fire had spread to the main house where Sara and her mother were trapped—

"Landon? Landon, are you all right?"

He jerked from the warmth of Maggie's touch, unable to escape the stench of burnt wood or the feel of hungry flames licking at his skin. Reminders of his own private hell. A hell he visited repeatedly in his dreams. A hell that had branded him a murderer.

"My God, what is it? What's wrong?"

"Nothing." Struggling to catch his breath, Landon forced air to move in and out of his lungs. Staring straight ahead, he pushed away the memories and locked them into the dark recesses of his heart. "Leave me alone."

"You're as white as a sheet. What did I say?"

"You didn't—it has nothing to do with—" Landon clenched his jaw so hard his teeth ached. "Please, Maggie, let it go."

"Can I help—"

The walkie-talkie anchored at her hip crackled to life. "Crescent Moon, this is Willie…come in, Maggie."

Maggie's eyes flew from him to the radio and back again.

"Come in, Moon, Willie here. Darn it, girl, where are you?"

"Answer your cowboy," Landon said.

Grabbing her radio, Maggie never broke eye contact as she brought it to her lips. "This is Maggie, what's up, Willie?"

"It's 'bout time. We got ourselves a mess. The front end of Hank's wagon came off the lift."

Confusion filled her eyes. "Can't he wait until after lunch for help?"

"Darlin', Hank's under the wagon."

# Chapter 6

Maggie yelled for her grandmother and bolted for the house, Landon close behind. From the moment she'd brought him home, it had seemed as if he was never far away—except for a few moments ago when he'd been lost in a different world. The look of utter misery on his face was heart-wrenching.

Nana B. rushed outside. Maggie filled her in on Willie's call. "We're heading out. Call Doc Cody and ask him to meet us there."

"He's gonna bring that darn ambulance," Nana B. said. "You know Hank isn't going anywhere near it, much less the clinic."

"He might not have a choice this time." Maggie's heart hitched in her chest. She couldn't lose Hank. A quick prayer raced through her before she returned her attention to the walkie-talkie. "Willie...we're on our way."

"Copy that. Got a piece of railing jammed in there for leverage, but I gotta drop this gosh-darn contraption before I drop the railing."

"We'll be there in ten minutes. Don't do anything foolish." Maggie whirled around, and froze. Damn! Her truck was still in town. She held out her hand to Landon. "Give me your keys."

He ignored her request. Instead, he jumped into his pickup and cranked the engine. "Get in. You told Willie *we* were coming."

Had she? She was so used to using the singular *I* it didn't seem possible she'd have automatically included him. Maggie marched over to the open door. "Move over, I'm driving."

"I can drive."

"I know where I'm going and you're arguing with your boss."

He slid across the seat and Maggie jumped in. Slamming the door shut, she threw the truck into gear and tore out of the driveway. Cutting between the barn and the foreman's cabin, she headed across the open field. Landon braced one hand against the dash when she swung onto a dirt road, never touching the brakes.

"What did you mean when you told your grandmother Hank might not have a choice about the ambulance this time?"

Maggie kept her eyes glued to the wide expanse of land ahead. "Hank's been hurt a lot over the years. Life of a cowboy, I guess. Sometimes we take care of it, sometimes we call the doc. I think Hank would rather fight the devil himself than see the inside of an ambulance."

Her fingers tightened on the steering wheel. "Meredith, Hank's wife, fell sick one winter. I was young, I don't remember her." A lump formed in Maggie's throat, but she pushed her words past it. "I'm told she refused to see a doctor. A storm had dumped a couple feet of snow by the time Hank convinced her to get medical attention. It took the ambulance two hours to get there. She died on the way to the hospital."

Maggie glanced at Landon. His face could have been made of stone for all the emotion he displayed.

"I can see how that would change a man."

"It's been twenty-five years and Hank's never found anyone new. He used to say he's not likely to find love again. Can you imagine feeling like that about someone?"

"No."

Her eyes flickered to rest on him for a few seconds and she again noted how he was no longer wearing the ranch shirt. It'd shocked her when she'd found him in the faded, denim button-down at breakfast. The sight brought back a powerful and hated memory with such force she'd tripped over her own feet to get away.

Her father had loved those shirts. She'd hated them.

She focused her attention back on the dirt road. A small cabin and barn appeared on the other side of a hill. Maggie stopped in front of the barn. "Willie!" she threw the truck into park and jumped out at the same time. "Where are you?"

"In here," came the muffled reply from deep inside.

Maggie and Landon raced into the cool interior in time to hear the cry of splitting wood and a string of colorful curses. Willie's lips were pulled back from his teeth and cords stood out in his neck and arms. With all his weight on one end of a long wooden lever jammed under the end of the wagon, he'd managed to keep it off Hank's chest long enough for the man to breathe.

Another crack from the railing propelled Landon forward. He maneuvered backward under the wagon, feet on either side of Hank's chest. Bracing his hands on his knees, he took the wagon's full weight on his back as the railing split.

"Hank!"

"Landon!"

Willie and Maggie called out when the wagon fell on Landon. His knees gave a few inches, but he pushed upward, creating space over the fallen cowboy. He closed his eyes. "Get Hank out…now."

Maggie crouched on one side of her cowboy and Willie did the same. They pulled him out of harm's way.

"Willie, grab—hay bales and drag—" Landon grunted the words through clenched teeth "—drag them—"

"Gotcha." Willie grabbed a set of metal bale hooks, dragged the hay and shoved them under the corner of the wagon, kicking aside pieces of the now-useless wooden wheel.

"Let it go, Landon," Maggie begged, "before you get hurt."

Landon's gaze crashed into hers and held for a moment, then he dropped to all fours, his knees hitting the dirt as his Stetson fell from his head. The wagon rested on the makeshift jack created by the bales of hay.

Maggie forced her attention from Landon to Hank. Willie crouched beside him, checking him out. Relief filled her chest when he offered a quick nod of assurance he was okay. "Hank Jarvis! You should be ashamed of yourself. Why in God's name did you get under the wagon?"

"You know why," Hank whispered, his eyes closed against the obvious pain wracking his beefy body. "A promise is—"

"A promise." Maggie cut him off, knowing Hank was talking about the promise he'd made to his wife, when she was on her deathbed, to fully restore the antique Texas buckboard wagon they'd bought together. A promise that had taken a quarter of a century to keep. "I can't lose you, too, Hank. I can't."

"I'm not going anywhere, honey." Hank opened his eyes. "It's a couple of bruised ribs."

"You're probably right." Willie rose to his feet. "You need checking out all the same. We should call Doc—"

"Maggie, come in, Maggie." The walkie-talkie again came to life, this time with Nana B.'s voice coming over the airwaves.

Maggie pressed the talk button. "He's okay. We got here in time."

"Saints be praised! Doc's out at the McIntire place. He's on his way."

Landon moved out from beneath the wagon. "Tell her we'll meet them at the house." Waving off Willie's outstretched hand, he rose to his feet and grabbed his hat. He placed it back on his head and brushed off his clothes. "Hank should stay flat. We can put him in the truck bed. I'll bring it around."

Landon headed out of the barn, walking stiffly, but not limping. She couldn't believe what he'd done. "Nana, we're bringing Hank in. Have Doc meet us there."

"I heard," her grandmother said. "I'll be waiting."

"I'll get some blankets." Willie ran out behind Landon.

Maggie's gaze went back to Hank, air pinching in her chest at the pain etched on his weathered face. My God, if they hadn't gotten here in time. If Landon hadn't been with her—

His truck appeared inside the barn doors. Willie returned and jumped in the back, arranging a makeshift bed. Landon got out and moved toward them. The brim of his hat was pulled so low Maggie couldn't see his face. It struck her he always wore it that way.

"Ready to move him?" he asked.

"I'm hurt," Hank groused, "not dead."

"Lay still, you stubborn fool," Maggie said.

"This'll work a lot easier if you don't help," Landon said to Hank, sliding his hands under the cowboy's shoulder and hips. Maggie followed suit on her side while Willie supported his friend's legs. "On three..."

Muscles flexing in his arms and shoulders, Landon took the majority of Hank's weight. They put the cowboy in the truck bed, his boots hanging off the tailgate and his face three shades paler than before.

"You stay with him." Landon started for the cab. "I'll drive."

Maggie grabbed his forearm. "Can you drive? Are you hurt, too?"

"I'm fine."

He tried to pull away but she held on. "First the corral and now this. All I keep saying is 'thank you.'"

His dark eyes focused on her for a long moment before he nodded and stepped back. She released him and sat next to Hank. Willie joined Landon in the truck. They headed back to the main house and found Nana B. pacing in the driveway.

Willie jumped out after Landon parked. "Need bandages for his ribs," he told them. "If the doc wants to take him in, it's gonna be a long ride to town."

"I ain't going."

"Oh, pipe down, old man." Nana B. hovered nearby.

"Hank, please." Maggie looked at the man who was more a father to her than the man who'd raised her. "How about I take you in the truck? Will you go if I drive?"

"Is it...necessary?" Hank breathed.

"If you ever plan on getting back on a horse, it is," Landon said, moving toward them.

Maggie's gaze collided with his, seeing the gravity in his eyes. Was he right, or only saying that to scare Hank into getting help? The thought of Hank never being able to ride again tore at her.

Willie returned and climbed up next to Maggie with the bandages. "I see our newest boarder is here. Isn't Black Jack a bit early?"

Hank tried to sit up. "That wild horse is here? You shouldn't have taken him on all alone—"

"Lie still," Maggie ordered when Hank winced in pain. "I—ah, we took care of him."

"Let's get these thingamajiggers on you." Willie held up the bandages.

"Here, let me help." Landon gestured at her. "You need to get out of there. Not enough room for all of us."

"But your back—"

"I told you I'm fine." His response was as firm as his touch when he reached for her.

Maggie grabbed his hand, her pulse racing as she allowed him to help her down. She moved to stand next to her grandmother as Landon climbed in.

"I'm not made of glass you know," Hank grumbled. "I won't break."

"You're already broken," Nana B. shot back, her hands tightly wringing. "How did this happen?"

Maggie filled her in, her eyes drawn to Landon as he crouched behind Hank's shoulders and lifted. Willie worked quickly, wrapping ace bandages right over Hank's shirt.

"And if Landon hadn't taken the weight of that old wagon on his back the moment the lever gave way…" Maggie paused, emotion clogging her throat, "I don't know what would've happened. We could have lost—"

"It's all right, Magpie," Hank said, using her childhood nickname. "I might be useless for a while, but I'm not ready to punch my ticket to the pearly gates yet."

Useless for a while…*ohmigod, what was she going to do now?*

Maggie's fear transformed into panic. The sharp sting of tears bit at her eyes. Hank would be out of commission for at least a few weeks, and Landon only planned to stick around the same length of time. Her help-wanted ads flashed through her mind, the word "wanted" morphing into "desperate" with a capital *D*.

"I should've known better." Hank's face contorted in pain as Willie continued to work. "I heard about those two losers walking on us. Maybe—damn, that hurts—ah, we have about a million miles of fence line to deal with, and I'm gonna be laid up like a fat bass at a fishing tournament. Maybe you should talk to Greeley about borrowing help—"

"No!" Maggie bit hard at her bottom lip to stop her outburst. She jammed her hands into the back pockets of her jeans, eyes glued to the ground. "I can handle it."

"We can handle it."

Her head jerked up at Landon's words to find him staring at her.

"Maybe you should tell them."

Maggie saw resignation mixed with torment in his eyes before he looked away. He didn't want to work here. When he'd offered to take the job she thought she'd seen something—familiarity, acceptance—in the dark depths of his eyes. And after her work with Black Jack, she'd reveled in the respect she'd read there.

However, when she'd started talking about the job, assuring him she did all the hiring at the Crescent Moon, an expression of such desperation and pain came over his face it'd astounded her.

She realized four pairs of eyes were staring at her. "Ah, Landon's offered to stick around for a while. His horse is laid up and he's agreed to work for a few weeks until G.W. is better. Or until I hire more help."

The shock on Willie's face and her grandmother's pleased expression didn't surprise her. Hank's expression was a mix of confusion and pain, but he held out his hand to Landon.

"Thanks for sticking around, and for saving me back there."

An overwhelming need to repeat her cowboy's gratitude filled Maggie as Landon shook Hank's hand. She spun away, needing to put some distance between herself and the truck before the words spilled from her mouth.

What was the matter with her?

Landon was simply another cowboy, not the second coming of her salvation. Or her sex life. So, okay, she was attracted to the man, but she had more important things to worry about than kisses and—

"Do you still want me?"

His heated words caressed the side of her face. Maggie whirled, her face flaming. "Yes, I want—ah, yes of course, you're hired. Are you sure you're okay? You didn't hurt yourself?"

He squared his shoulders and took a step back. "Aren't you getting tired of asking me that?"

A white SUV spun into the yard, stopping Maggie from answering him. Seconds later, a little girl with braids raced across the gravel driveway.

"Mama! What happened? Are you all right?"

"I'm okay, sweetie." Maggie drew her daughter into a long hug, breathing in her sweet smell. Doc Cody got out of the truck and headed their way. "Thanks for coming, Doc. What's Anna doing with you?"

"Julie's mom heard in town about your call for help. Anna insisted on coming home. I ran into them at the crossroads and offered to bring her the rest of the way."

Maggie nodded, knowing the call must have frightened her daughter. She put her arm around Anna's shoulders and gave a quick squeeze. "Sweetie, everything's okay. Hank got knocked around a bit—"

"Hank!" The little girl wrenched free and ran to the back of the truck. "What happened? What did you do?"

"I'm—I'm fine, Little Bit," Hank whispered, lifting his head to look toward her. "Don't worry about me."

Anna looked at Maggie with wide, trusting eyes. "Is he gonna be all right?"

"Yes, Anna, he is." She ran her hand along her daughter's blond hair, giving a small tug on the end of a braid. She pulled her away from the doctor, who was already speaking with Hank. "And we have someone special to thank for saving Hank. I want you to meet our new cowboy, Landon Cartwright."

She didn't think it was possible, but he'd tugged his Stetson even lower on his brow. His hands braced on his hips, fingers spread wide and digging hard into the denim of his jeans.

"Landon, I'd like you to meet my daughter, Anna." Maggie wondered if he was in more pain than he was letting on with his rigid posture. "Anna, this is the man who saved Hank's life."

Landon opened his mouth as if to protest, but before he could say a word, Anna flew at him and wrapped her arms around his middle.

"Oh, thank you! Thank you!"

"Gotta admit this is a good idea, camping out to deal with the fence line repairs."

Landon glanced over at Willie. The old man continued to look straight ahead, his thin frame rocking naturally with the movement of his horse.

They'd left the main house a half hour ago, each on horseback, with enough supplies to last at least a week.

Maggie had convinced Hank to go to the hospital after all. He'd be home later and staying at the main house while he nursed what the doctor had figured was four cracked ribs.

With Hank on bed rest for the unforeseeable future, Willie filled Landon in on his and Hank's daily trips to repair the broken fence line. Camping out instead of returning back to the main house was something Landon had used at his own ranch in the past.

And it would keep him away from a certain little girl and her mother.

"Course, that leaves the womenfolk with just Hank to look out for 'em," Willie continued. "No matter. Laid up or not, he's still a pretty good shot."

Landon eyed the shotgun holstered on the side of Willie's saddle. "Is there a reason he needs to be?"

The old cowboy didn't answer him, but said instead, "I take it sweet little girls ain't your cup of tea?"

"What are you talking about?"

"Saw the look on your face when Miss Anna wrapped you in a bear hug." The old cowboy cackled like a wet hen. "Would've thought someone had come at you with a red-hot branding iron."

Landon tugged on his Stetson. Damn! At this rate, he was going to punch his head right through the top of it. He shifted, trying to get used to the new mount he reluctantly accepted, as G.W. was in no shape to be involved in ranch work.

The memory of the little girl's arms wrapped around his middle stuck with him long after Maggie, face flushed with embarrassment, peeled her daughter away. Four years since his daughter's death. In the nine months since his release from prison, he'd taken great pains to stay far away from children.

Finding out Maggie had a child, and the flashback

to the night he'd lost his own baby girl, was a blow he still hadn't recovered from.

"She surprised me, is all," he said.

"Yeah, I figured." Willie removed his hat and wiped at his face with a faded bandanna. "Mind if we stop by Hank's place first? We flew out of there like our tail feathers were burning. Wanna make sure things are locked up tight."

"More problems with your neighbor, Greeley?"

Willie's head snapped around, his gaze sharp. "What makes you ask?"

Landon quickly filled Willie in on the man's visit to the ranch earlier. "It doesn't take a rocket scientist to figure out he sees this place as easy pickings."

When they arrived at Hank's cabin, he stopped his horse next to Willie's. Both men dismounted.

"Other than stealing her cowboys, what else is Greeley doing?" Landon asked.

"You struck me as a person who minded his own business."

"Look, old man, I work here now." Landon admired Willie's loyalty, but he refused to be kept in the dark. "Part of my job is looking out for our boss and this ranch. Like you said, I didn't get jumped last night for nothing."

Willie nodded, but remained quiet as he went inside the cabin. Moments later, he closed the door behind him, double-checking to make sure it was secure. He returned to Landon and the horses. "Let's check out the barn."

Landon followed.

"Maggie's daddy died five years ago. A bastard

to the end, he left half interest of the Moon to that sorry excuse for a husband of hers." Willie's gravelly voice filled the interior as he checked each stall on one side of the barn. "When Alan Stevens walked a few years back, Maggie bought him out."

"You mind telling me what we're looking for?" Landon asked, grateful the old man was talking, but not sure how Maggie's father and ex-husband played into what was going on with her neighbor.

"Anything that looks like it doesn't belong."

"I guess that makes sense." Landon mirrored Willie's actions, but neither of them found anything out of place.

"Gonna check the loft." Willie headed for the front end of the barn.

Landon walked to the center and stood next to the wagon on the hay bales. "What else is going on?"

"Well, ranching is a dying art. Nowadays, it's about dollars and cents instead of cattle, cowboys and common sense." Willie's voice echoed from the loft. "The ways that blowhard ex of Maggie's handled the books barely left us breathing. Now, she's trying to keep all our heads above the rising waters. Thanks to equipment failing or disappearing, cowboys walking and damage to the fence line no one's got a good explanation for, we're busier than a one-legged man in a butt-kickin' contest."

Landon shook his head at Willie's analogy. "And you think Greeley's responsible?"

"Well, like you said, the slimy weasel's got his eye on this place."

"Isn't his ranch, the Triple G, the biggest in the county?"

"Sure is. In fact, it butts up against our land on the east. That's a section of fence line that never has any problems."

Landon nudged at the broken pieces of a shattered wagon wheel with the toe of his boot, his gaze falling on the smooth edges of what he figured were the spokes. Dropping to a crouch, he studied them. "Hey, Willie?"

"Yeah?"

"How did Hank get stuck under the wagon?"

"He said he was attaching the wheels, but something must've gone wrong." Willie left the loft and joined him in the center of the barn. "Why?"

"Look at these pieces. When wood breaks, it splinters. The edges on these pieces are smooth, as if they were cut."

"Well, I'll be a suck-egg mule." Willie rose and scurried toward the barn doors.

"Where are you going?" Landon said.

"To call the sheriff. This is gonna stop right here and now."

# Chapter 7

Landon eased himself into the claw-footed tub. A moan of appreciation for the hot water on his aching muscles rushed past his lips.

Working two weeks straight on the fence line had meant camping out nightly beneath the stars with Willie. It also meant washing up in an ice-cold stream. Despite daily temperatures in the nineties, those encounters had grown old quickly. He'd dealt with downed barbed wire plenty of times in the past, and he and Willie fell into an easy teamwork pattern of repositioning the posts and restringing the wire. The last pole this morning had caused the familiar shooting pain to rip right through him. Thankfully, the throbbing receded as he and Willie had ridden back.

They arrived around suppertime to find only

Nana B. and Hank at the main house. Willie asked if there'd been any trouble. Nana B. assured him things had been quiet, with nary a sight of Greeley in days. Not wanting to analyze why he was relieved at the news, Landon'd checked on G.W., glad to see his buddy back to form.

Sliding down, he immersed himself completely in the steaming water. He sat up again, shoving his hair back from his face, unable to push Maggie out of his head.

Damn the woman.

Out of sight, out of mind.

That had been his plan for stamping out the tight coil of emotion she'd caused him. It hadn't worked.

He grabbed the soap lying on the shelf next to the tub, and created a sudsy lather. He rubbed at his scars for a moment before letting his eyes close. He leaned against the cool porcelain and let the weariness of two weeks of hard work slowly take over his body. Shutting down his mind wasn't as easy. In order to survive working here, he'd have to stay as far away from Maggie as possible.

If he got the chance to stick around.

His mind flew back to the morning in Hank's barn when Willie was talking to the sheriff on the phone.

The last thing Landon had wanted or needed was to get anywhere near the local law. A wave of shame hit him. A man had been hurt, and if his gut feeling was right, and it usually was, it hadn't been an accident. A deputy sheriff, who looked barely out of high school, showed up. Landon answered as few questions as possible, but didn't flinch when the kid looked him straight in the eye. Neither he nor Willie offered Greeley's name, but Willie did tell the deputy about the ranch's troubles. Then they headed out again with Willie relaying word of the deputy's visit to Maggie. She wasn't happy with the news.

Later that night, and many nights after, Willie had shared more stories about life on the Crescent Moon. Maggie's father had been a bastard, and her ex wasn't much better.

Landon thought about what she'd gone through most of her life, living with men who did little or nothing to build her self-esteem. The woman he'd come to know, thanks to Willie's nonstop chatter, amazed him. He found himself wanting to work harder, pushing harder to get the job done, and done right.

For her.

A sudden pounding came at the front door. "Landon! Are you in there?"

Maggie.

"Landon, can you hear me? I need to talk to you and it can't wait."

He looked around and found the towel lying on the bed. He started to rise. "Just a minute," he called out.

The front door slammed open. "Landon! How could you..."

He dropped back, splashing water over the edge of the tub. Muscles tensed as Maggie's wide-eyed gaze roamed over him.

A long minute passed. Her presence filled the one-room cabin. He tried his damndest to keep his eyes on her face and not the miles of tanned skin displayed by her short denim skirt and sexy, red cowboy boots. It wasn't hard to do with her hair flowing around her shoulders, smoky makeup emphasizing the bright green of her eyes and the red stain on her lips. She looked ready for a night on the town.

A heated emotion slammed into his chest. Jealousy? Whatever the feeling, he squashed it. "Is there something you wanted?" he asked instead.

"You're in the bathtub."

Breaking free of her gaze, Landon stared at the fabric privacy divider standing uselessly at the foot of the tub. "Not much gets by you."

"What are you doing?"

*Growing harder by the second.* Landon slammed closed the thought and decided to go for the obvious. "Taking a bath."

"Why?"

"Because I'm dirty, tired and I thought it might relax my sore muscles."

*Not every sore muscle, pal.*

This was the closest they'd been in two weeks. He'd heard her daily over the walkie-talkie he carried, but she'd only spoken to Willie. Her voice had sounded throaty and sexy over the device. It'd stuck with him, haunting his waking hours and his dreams—

He pushed the thought away. Her voice was having the same effect on him right now. He placed his elbows on the tub's edge, using his hands to create a screen between Maggie's gaze and the lower half of his body, despite being chest-deep in soapy water.

Where was his damn hat when he needed it? "Do you mind? It's a bit drafty in here."

Pink stained her cheeks. She stepped inside and slammed the door closed.

He raised an eyebrow. "You're on the wrong side."

"Too bad. I know what you did, Landon." She marched to the edge of the tub. "And I'm pissed as hell."

What in God's name was she talking about? His prison record?

She waved a fistful of papers in his face. "What the hell gave you the right to sell those horses?"

Realization dawned. "I didn't sell them."

"Don't split hairs with me." She crossed her arms under her breasts, pushing them against the snug T-shirt. "I know it was you who called the Still Waters Ranch in Texas."

It'd taken a ten-minute call to his brother's foreman to convince him Maggie's horses would fit in perfectly on the ranch. "Hank made the sale—"

"Hank closed the deal because he has the authority to do so, but neither of us had ever heard of Still Waters. Did you think I would accept this sale as a stroke of good luck without checking into it?"

He should've known she wouldn't. Landon had seen the quality horseflesh his first morning at the ranch, and again when he'd checked on G.W. last week. When Willie said he suspected Greeley was somehow keeping Maggie from getting a good deal in the local market, he'd made the call.

"How are you connected to Still Waters?"

Landon was pulled from his thoughts. "What?"

"I spoke with a Storm Watkins. He told me a former employee contacted them." Maggie again waved the papers. "Then he double-talked his way out of giving any more information."

"You're fishing."

"Is it true? Did you work there?"

Yeah, he'd worked there. Since he'd been able to walk. It was his family's ranch. And except for a few years on the rodeo circuit, right up until the day they'd led him away in handcuffs.

Rippling waves of bath water competed with Landon's rippling muscles for Maggie's attention, but the intensity in his coal-black eyes made it impossible to look anywhere else.

"You haven't answered me. Did you work on the Still Waters Ranch?"

"Does it matter?"

Hell, yes it mattered. When Hank told her about an offer coming from a ranch in Texas, Maggie went from shocked to suspicious in a matter of minutes. At first, she thought Greeley was somehow behind it, conjuring a bogus deal to tie her up in endless paper work. Then a fax arrived with a fair-market amount, a bit over her asking price.

Talking to the ranch's foreman had been like talking to a brick wall, but when she'd threatened to cancel the deal despite the money being wired to her bank, he'd relented enough to tell her the initial contact came from a former employee.

It'd taken all of thirty seconds before she was out the door.

It had to be Landon.

She'd spent the last fourteen days convincing herself Landon was another temporary cowboy who'd do his job, collect his paycheck and soon be on his way. Willie's reports of Landon's hard work hadn't surprised her, but his expertise with time-saving techniques on the fence line had.

Now with him arranging this sale, she didn't know what he was up to. Did he think she couldn't handle things here at her own ranch? Could he actually be positioning himself to take over the Moon? Damn, she had enough to deal with when it came to Kyle and her ex-husband. The last thing she needed was another man seeing her as a helpless—

"Hello? Maggie? Cat got your tongue?"

Startled from her thoughts, Maggie focused on Landon and the water beading over his body's hard planes. Soapy water lapped around bent knees, rising and falling over the brown, pebbled nipples on a muscular chest.

She blinked and directed her gaze to the paper work in her hands. "I don't know what you're doing, but taking care of this ranch is my responsibility."

"Who said it wasn't?"

A frustrated sound escaped. "What made you call Still Waters? I didn't see it on the list of references you left with Nana B."

"So? Didn't my former bosses say enough glowing things about me?"

"I don't know. I didn't call them."

A shocked look crossed Landon's face. Maggie kept flipping through the paper work, the printed words nothing more than a blur. "I learned a long time ago to trust my instincts. To listen to the little voice inside my head, inside my heart. It's something I've ignored in the past, and I'm still living with the consequences."

A ragged breath escaped her lungs. The next words popped from her mouth before she could pull them back. "But I trusted you."

Landon sighed and kept his hands in a tight grip over his chest. "Yes, I worked there. And before you get to the page that lists the owner, I'll tell you right now he's..." His eyes closed. "His name is Chase Cartwright. He's my brother."

Maggie gasped. A look of anguish came over him. Not the intense pain she'd seen two weeks ago, but enough heartache that it squeezed her own heart.

Unable to stop herself, she dropped to a crouch next to the tub and laid one hand over his clenched fingers. His skin was hot and wet. The scent of clean man filled her head as she focused on the impossibly long, dark lashes across his skin. "Landon, what is it?"

He jerked from her touch and opened his eyes, but didn't look at her. "It's nothing." A muscle ticked along his jawline. "It's no big deal."

"It is a big deal." Maggie laid her fingers along his chin, and pressed until he looked at her. "I can see it on your face. Please, let me help—"

An invisible door slammed shut in his eyes, and Landon yanked from her touch. He leaned as far away from her as the tub allowed. "I don't need help."

Her hand fell away and landed on the tight muscles of his arm. "Landon—"

He opened his eyes again, and a flatness, devoid of any emotion, stared at her. "You don't want to sell the horses, fine. I don't give a damn."

"Yes, you do. What I don't understand is why you're doing this—"

"Do you need me to spell it out, Maggie?" Landon's lips creased into a smirk. He grabbed her hand and brought it to his mouth. His lips caressed the back of her hand before tracing the ridge of her knuckles. "I wanted to get into the good graces of my lady boss."

A blaze ignited in her stomach. Much like the one he'd created in the dark interior of his truck when he'd slanted his mouth over hers in a searing kiss. Now, that same mouth sucked at her skin, that same tongue tracked the crevice of her clasped fingers.

"Landon, I don't..."

A storm of fury and lust flared in his eyes. Her heart seized in her chest. Before it jumped back to life again, the emotion in those dark depths vanished.

He lifted his mouth from her hand. "Liar."

She reared back, stumbling as she forced her legs to obey her silent command to move. Was her desire so obvious? Could he see the fantasies that haunted her dreams in her eyes? Humiliation filled her, and she bolted for the door. She grabbed the handle and twisted, but powerful arms shot past her to slam it closed again.

"Maggie, wait."

His deep voice whispered her name and the wet

heat of his body surrounded her. A wild craving raced through her veins. Did he bother to grab a towel or was he naked behind her?

She pictured the long length of him pressing into her and bit back a moan. Forcing the words out, she said, "Let me out."

"No."

"You did me a favor with the sale, okay? I'll stay out of your business..." She let her voice fade as embarrassment crept over her.

"Maggie, listen to me," he said with quiet emphasis.

"No!"

He leaned closer, his breath warm against her neck. "Why not?"

"Because I won't play games with you."

"Games?"

"One minute you're looking at me like you want to crawl on top of me, slip inside my skin. The next, you shut down and pretend I don't exist. I won't do it, Landon. Let me out."

"No."

His calm refusal twisted her discomfort into anger. Maggie spun around. His eyes brimmed with tenderness, and her angry words died in her throat. His hair hung around his face, droplets of water falling from it, dampening the front of her shirt.

The tenderness in his gaze melted into the raw yearning she'd seen earlier. The change matched her own battling emotions. How could he look at her this way? Make her feel this way?

"This isn't right." Her words were halfhearted.

"I know."

She raised her hands to push him away, but he captured her wrists in his strong grip and pulled them over her head, gently shackling them against the door. She closed her eyes to hide the desire spinning through her. He moved closer, and she jumped when the heat of his lips set her neck aflame with soft, wet kisses.

"Landon, please let me go."

"You asking for my permission?" he rasped, trailing the tip of his tongue down her jaw until it skimmed along her lower lip.

"What are you—"

"Go ahead, Maggie. Let...go."

He accepted the open invitation of her mouth and swept inside, his tongue seeking hers, demanding she take part. More water fell from his hair, landing on her closed eyelids and cheeks, the coolness sizzling against her skin.

A low moan filled her chest and rumbled through her. Landon released her lips and buried his face against her neck. Then he freed her wrists and dug his fingers into her hair as he pressed his forehead to hers.

"Touch me, Maggie. Please touch me."

A shudder coursed through him as her hands slipped through the wet strands of his hair and brushed across his shoulders. His muscles flinched and tightened beneath her fingers, his flesh rising in goose bumps as she discovered the outline of his biceps and the undersides of his arms.

Maggie wasn't satisfied. She wanted to feel

more—to feel all of him pressing hard against her. Arching against him, she trailed her hands down the side of his body, curving around his hips when suddenly he vanished from her touch. She landed hard against the door. It took a moment to open her eyes.

Landon stood three feet away with nothing but a white towel clenched low against his flat, hard stomach, partially covering a path of dark hair and the erection beneath.

"I can't do this," he punched out between breaths.

His free hand tightened into a fist at his side. His other squeezed the terry-cloth fabric, revealing more of the angled planes of his hipbones, accentuating the raw power of his body. His face was devoid of any emotion except regret.

"You're right, this shouldn't be happening."

Clawing at the door, Maggie yanked it open. She ran from the cabin, half-blind by tears, not waiting to hear the rest of his rejection.

"Isn't the tray a little light?"

Racy's voice rose above the deafening music of the Blue Creek house band. It was a typical Saturday night at the local roadhouse where Maggie's best friend had hired her as a waitress three months ago. Maggie hated the time away from Anna, but she needed all the extra money she could get. Today's horse sale notwithstanding.

Maggie leaned across the bar. "What did you say?"

Pointing at the empty bottles on the tray, Racy lifted replacements from the cooler. She popped the tops before setting them on the bar. "Call it the bartender in me, but I think a paying customer would rather have a full beer than an empty."

"Sorry." Maggie switched the bottles. "I guess my mind isn't here tonight."

"If I had a gorgeous hunk of cowboy waiting at home for me, do you think I'd be wasting time behind three feet of wood?"

"He isn't gorgeous, and he isn't waiting for me," Maggie shot back, surprised both her voice and hands remained steady.

"Oh, please. I ran into Anna and Nana B. last week at the ice-cream shop, and they sang his praises." Racy refilled the drinks for a couple of cowboys in front of her then turned her attention back to Maggie. "So, is he back from 'banging the barrier'?"

Maggie tucked a long strand of hair behind one ear. "If you're asking if he and Willie are finished working the fence line, the answer is yes."

Racy winked. "I like my way of putting it better."

"I know."

"According to your daughter and your grandmother, this guy is a walking, talking, card-carrying member of the Justice League."

"Anna barely knows Landon. She only met him for a few minutes. What did—" Maggie lowered her voice when the band switched to a country ballad. "What did they say?"

"More than you." With an air kiss, Racy thanked the cowboy who insisted she keep the hefty change from his tab, and tucked the money into her cleavage. "The guy is saving people left and right, making repairs with a single blow of his hammer, and to top it off—"

"No, there is no top." Maggie steadied her hand beneath the tray. "Landon Cartwright isn't a super hero. He isn't a saint. He is just another cowboy."

"Hmm, he certainly has blown your skirt up," Racy mused. "Since I haven't laid eyes on him yet, let me add if he can kiss as good as he does everything else, I'll move his rating from superhero to scrumptious demigod."

Maggie recalled Landon's mouth on hers and flushed, reliving the intensity of his kiss. Scrumptious? No, it far surpassed that and zoomed right into decadent.

She didn't know if he remembered kissing her—mouth gentle, touch hesitant—the night she'd brought him home. Nothing like this last time. The power in his hold pinning her hands to the door, the sureness of his lips on her neck. His mouth strong against hers. His desperate plea for her to touch him.

Right up until he backed away.

After racing from the cabin, she'd gone straight to her truck. Her family probably wondered why she hadn't said goodbye, but she couldn't face their inquisitive eyes. The sight of Landon in her rearview mirror, standing in the doorway in a pair of jeans and pulling a T-shirt over his head, stayed with her long after she'd gotten to the bar and hastily fixed her makeup.

Had he been coming after her? For what? To apologize?

Maggie didn't think she could take it. The regret

in his dark eyes when he'd stared at her from across the cabin was clear enough.

Shaking off the memory, she lifted the tray.

*Let it go, girl.*

It was…hell, she didn't know what it was other than the best kiss of her life. The honest assessment made her arms shake like jelly. She struggled to balance the tray, and the bottles clanked together.

"Hey, you okay?"

Steadying herself, Maggie backed away before Racy could see her telltale blush. "I got it. I'm okay."

"You deliver those beers and get your butt back here." Racy easily twirled a bottle of whiskey on the palm of her hand before filling the glasses in front of her. "We need to talk."

"Last time I looked it was Max who signed my paycheck."

"He may be the owner, but I'm your boss." Racy tossed the bottle over one shoulder and caught it at hip level. "And that's an order."

Maggie stuck out her tongue and walked away. She made her way through the mob of thirsty revelers to one of her assigned tables. It didn't take long for the bottles to disappear and dollar bills to take their place.

Willie sat at a corner table with his regular group of cronies, all fellow senior-citizen cowboys. Maggie returned his wave and forced a smile. She'd purposely eavesdropped earlier when she'd heard him extolling Landon's hard work and list of ideas for the ranch.

*I tell ya, boys, if Cartwright ain't once owned his own spread I'll eat my hat.*

His words rang again in her ears. Had Landon once owned his own place? Maybe with his brother in Texas?

Maggie made her way back to the main bar. After cashing in, she found Racy at the far end.

"Jackie, take over," Racy called to the leggy brunette whose Daisy Duke cut-offs and lingerie-inspired corset made her a favorite among the cowboys. She then dragged Maggie to a shadowed back hallway. "Okay, girlfriend, spill it."

Maggie hugged her tray to her chest. Thankfully, the band was taking a break and the bar's sound system filled in with rowdy, but quieter, country rock. "Spill what?"

"Something's got your panties in a twist and I think it's your new hired hand. Weren't we talking a few weeks ago at the fair about you needing some fun? I think Cartwright might be the guy."

"Mess around with one of my employees? What about Anna? What kind of example would that set for her?"

"I'm not suggesting you do the wild thing in the middle of your living room. Come on, you know how to be discreet. And I know you're on birth control—"

Maggie pressed her hand over her friend's mouth, cutting off her words. "I'm on the Pill because it regulates me, not because of sex."

"Whatever. It's still not an issue." Racy leaned forward. "Maggie, this guy is temporary. He's gonna be gone once Hank's feeling fine and frisky again. Why not enjoy his company while he's—"

Racy's eyes flickered over Maggie's shoulder, her grin downright wicked. "Well, lookie here. I think you've already got someone checking you out."

"Who?"

Maggie started to turn, but Racy grabbed her. "Two o'clock, dressed in black from head to toe. My, that's a good-looking, tall drink of water."

Maggie frowned. "What are you talking about?"

"Well, isn't that what they always say about a handsome stranger in those westerns you love?" Racy smiled, then her eyes widened. "Ohmigod, is that him?"

# *Chapter 8*

Maggie spun around. Landon stood at the wall, apart from the crowded tables and swarming mass of people, his arms crossed over his chest and his booted feet crossed at the ankles. He was staring straight at her.

Oh, Lord, what was he doing here?

She didn't know what she'd say to him, but she'd hoped to have until tomorrow to think about it. She whirled back to Racy, her fingers gripping the tray.

"It *is* him!" Racy let loose a low wolf whistle. "Oh, yum. Take that cowboy, and the horse he rode in on, for a wild ride."

"Will you give it a rest?" Maggie groaned. "Not having sex isn't a crime, ya know."

"It is in my book. It's been so long for me, I consider it a class A felony."

"Then I'm your man."

Maggie gasped. For a moment, she thought the words might have come from Landon, but then she realized the deep, masculine voice came from over Racy's shoulder. She watched her friend's dark brown eyes widen. Shock filled her face, but it quickly disappeared with a toss of her flowing red hair as a tall man emerged from the shadows.

Maggie smiled at Destiny's sheriff. "Hi, Gage." His knowing grin told her he'd listened in on her and Racy. Had he heard everything? A wash of heat roared over her. "What brings you to the Blue Creek tonight?" she asked.

"Checking on things," he said as he tipped the brim of his Stetson. "How are you, Maggie?"

"Embarrassed to the tips of my toes, but otherwise I'm fine."

A teasing smile creased into deep dimples. "Don't worry, I didn't hear what you ladies were gossiping about." Then his grin disappeared. "How are things at the ranch?"

"Ah, good. Quiet, and have been for the last couple of weeks."

"I talked to Deputy Harris. You know we still aren't sure how Hank's wagon came apart. There's no evidence the wheel was tampered with, and Hank said he boned the spokes so they wouldn't chip."

"Which could result in the clean breaks when the wheel came off," Maggie said. "Leeann filled me in earlier today when we met at the station."

The sheriff nodded. "Kyle told me he'd fired Cartwright two weeks ago after his references didn't check out."

*No, Kyle fired him after he rescued me.*

Maggie forced herself not to look at Landon. "Really?"

"But I'm guessing his references checked out for you?"

Certain she could feel Landon's eyes boring into her back, Maggie shot a look at Racy, refusing to return her smirk. "Yes, everything is fine. Perhaps Greeley had another reason for letting Landon go."

"Could be." The sheriff nodded, then addressed Racy, his voice dropping to a low whisper. "Evening, Ms. Dillon."

Racy crossed her arms under her breasts, causing the ragged neckline of her black tank top to reveal more of her ample cleavage and red satin bra. "Sheriff Steele."

Maggie had to give Gage credit. His eyes strayed only for a moment before he focused on her face. "Any chance of getting a cup of coffee?"

"We aim to please at the Blue Creek." Racy offered an arched brow as she brushed by the sheriff to step around the end of the bar. "Can I add a shot of something to improve your mood?"

"My mood is fine," Gage replied. "Any problems tonight?"

"Nothing I can't handle."

Gage frowned and took the mug. "Earlier this week—"

"By the time your boys appeared, I had the situation well in hand."

"I bet you did."

"Ah, Gage, I've been meaning to ask," Maggie cut in before Racy could respond. The fire flashing in her friend's eyes warned of another round of scathing comebacks—a favorite pastime of these two over the last fifteen years. "Nana B.'s birthday is next month. I hope you're free the last Saturday of August? You, too, Racy."

"Sorry, hon, no can do." Racy whisked away empty beer bottles and wiped at the wetness they left behind. "Got plans that weekend."

Gage took a swallow from the mug emblazoned with the Blue Creek logo before lowering it to the bar. "Me, too. I'll be out of town."

Racy wiped at the wetness the bottles left behind, her hand moving closer to where the sheriff's hand rested. So close, her electric-blue fingernails grazed his skin. Her friend was playing with Gage, and Maggie suspected the sheriff knew it.

"Oh?" Maggie persisted. "Where are you going?"

"Vegas."

Gage and Racy's eyes locked as they answered in unison.

"You're going to Vegas the last weekend of August?" Racy said.

Gage nodded. "For a law-enforcement forum."

"Great, the town will be overflowing with cops. I'm going for the Midwest regional in the All-American Bartending Challenge."

Maggie smiled. "Bartenders and cops? Sounds interesting. You think the town is big enough for the two of you?"

"I guess we'll find out." Gage took a step back and tapped the brim of his Stetson. "Maybe Ms. Dillon can get an Elvis look-alike to help with that *felony* problem of hers."

Racy's jaw dropped. She quickly regrouped and leaned over the bar. "Yeah, it'll take both of us to remove the stick you've got shoved up your—"

"Racy!" Maggie grabbed her friend's arm, and the sheriff walked away as if he hadn't heard. "Geez, the two of you never stop, do you?"

Racy pulled free. "Gage Steele is the most arrogant, condescending—"

Maggie cut her off with a grin. "Brave, sexy, honorable—"

"You think Gage is sexy?"

Maggie yanked hard on one of Racy's red curls. "Say it a little louder, why don't ya? Come on, you got to admit the man does great things to a pair of jeans."

"Oh, no, you aren't distracting me." Racy grabbed a beer and when one of the waitresses waved in their direction and pointed to her watch, she picked up the microphone. "Here, take a beer to your cowboy before I make you get your dancing boots on this bar."

She shoved the bottle at Maggie. "Go on, he won't bite. If I'm wrong, trust me, you'll love it."

Maggie's fingers tightened on the ice-cold bottle. She forced a deep breath, squared her shoulders and turned around.

*Just another cowboy.*

The words echoed in her head as she searched for Landon. Racy's voice called out over the bar's sound system, her announcement bringing cheers from the crowd. Both sounded very far away.

Maggie made it through the maze of revelers to the back wall where Landon had stood.

He was gone.

The beer slid down too easy.

Sitting on the front porch of the foreman's cabin, Landon hooked his finger around the bottle's neck, balanced the bottom half on his knuckles and tipped his head back. Another long swallow of the cold liquid poured into his throat.

He hoped it would wash away the bitter taste he got remembering Maggie, standing with a cold one in her hand, looking for him.

He'd walked away from his spot against the wall when he recognized the man talking to Maggie and her redheaded friend as the sheriff. At the exit, he'd looked back. Confusion, and if he wasn't mistaken, hurt, flashed in her eyes when she'd scanned the crowd. Then her bartender friend had made an announcement he couldn't hear. He did see a group of Maggie's fellow waitresses climb on the bar as the band broke into old-time country rock.

When she'd walked away, he'd hightailed it out of there. Yeah, like he was going to stick around and watch those long legs of hers dance across the bar…

*Dammit! Don't go there!*

Hell, she'd probably gone back and told the local lawman to lock his ass up for laying that kiss on her earlier tonight. A kiss he could still feel.

Landon took another long gulp, mindful of his

empty stomach and the two bottles he'd already finished. He'd hit the local market, bypassing the ready-made sandwiches for an ice-cold six-pack of America's finest, and headed home.

*No, not home. This place isn't home no matter how relaxed you're feeling.*

Landon grabbed the prepaid cell phone he'd picked up along with the beer and a pack of cigarettes. He punched in a familiar number and waited.

"Hel—Hello?" The greeting was hoarse and low.

Damn, Chase Cartwright sounded exactly like their father. A voice created from hard work and long hours spent outdoors. Landon's earliest childhood memory was his old man's voice. A voice silenced over ten years ago.

He washed away the memory with a long swallow of beer. "Hey, bro."

"Landon?"

"Yeah, it's me."

"Wh—what time is it?" A rustling filled the airwaves. "Damn, it's two in the morning. Is something wrong?"

*Wrong? Yeah, I've got the hots bad for my boss.* "Sorry, it's only going on one here. And does there have to be something wrong? Am I taking you away from someone?"

"If you were, I would've hung up on you by now." Chase yawned in Landon's ear and cleared his throat. "It's good to hear your voice, big brother."

Landon sighed, an ache in his chest. "Yours, too. It's been a while."

"Three months. How'd you end up in Wyoming?"

"How'd you know—oh, Storm told you." Landon realized the ranch's foreman must've filled him in. "It's a long story."

"Nothing with you is a long story," Chase said. "Tell me."

Using as few words as possible, Landon relayed his misadventures with G.W. and Maggie Stevens and how they led to the Crescent Moon.

"Boy, you never take the easy way." Chase chuckled. "This place doesn't sound like the others you've worked at."

"You don't know the half of it."

Landon dropped his hat to his side. He leaned against the porch railing, one boot on the top step, the other on the gravel path. With only moonlight to see by, he could easily spot a half-dozen needed chores. Not to mention the total rebuilding of the tool shed, his focus for tomorrow.

A warm breeze ruffled through the trees. It brought with it a feeling of comfort, a sense of home and family he hadn't felt in years, before his life was turned upside down. Nana B. and Anna were tucked safely in the house. Hank, too, who was sleeping in the study. Willie should be strolling in soon, and he guessed Maggie wouldn't be far behind.

They all belonged in this place. He was the outsider.

Another swig emptied the bottle. Landon realized he was missing much of what his brother was saying. Or maybe the beer was hitting him faster than he realized.

"And a lady boss, another first. Any easier to work

for?" Chase continued. "I know how you like to take things over and run 'em your way."

"Storm tells me the ranch is doing well. You've done a great job taking care of the place, Chase."

A long pause filled the air. "Thanks, bro. It means a lot coming from you. I'm doing this for both of us."

Landon knew his brother wanted him home, but he couldn't go back. He never planned to set foot again on Still Waters. The ranch had caused him to lose the most precious thing in his life, leaving him with a shattered heart and burned soul.

He grabbed beer number four and wrenched off the top, the sharp edges of the cap tearing into his skin. "You approved the purchase of the horses?"

"Sure did. Storm was impressed with the information. It'll be a month or so before we can send someone to get them. No additional training needed?"

"They're superb. Maggie has a touch I've never seen before." Not counting Black Jack, who was being as obstinate as a creature could be.

"This Maggie sounds pretty special."

A long silence covered the miles between the two brothers.

"Look, I know Jenna carved you up pretty bad, long before you lost her and Sara," Chase said. "But you've got to stop blaming yourself for not being able to save them. You need to move on with your life. Find someone to heal—"

Landon gripped the phone so tightly he was sure it was going to shatter in his hand. "Don't go there, Chase. Not tonight. Please."

His brother must have heard something in his voice. "If that's what you want."

"I've got to go."

"Okay. Keep in touch."

Landon promised he would and ended the call. Special? Yes, Maggie was, but not for him. He didn't deserve anything special in his life.

Not anymore.

Landon tossed the phone on the porch floor and tilted the bottle to his mouth, draining half of it in seconds. He put it down and grabbed the pack of cigarettes. Placing one in his mouth, he dug into his pocket for matches.

His fingers found them and the smooth warmth of another object. Despite his silent command to leave it alone, his hand pulled out the silver locket. He stared at it, turning it repeatedly in his fingers.

Weeks had passed since he'd looked at Sara's picture, but he knew it by heart. Every curve of her sweet cheeks, the dark hair curled around her face and the trusting dark eyes, so much like his own. His baby girl. Taken from him only a few weeks after her second birthday.

He struck a match and opened the locket. The flame's glow danced over her features. Harsh, biting memories of a terrifying night crept out of the darkness. He closed his eyes against them and the sharp sting of tears.

"Don't burn yourself."

Landon's eyes flew open.

Maggie stood in front of him, her skin dark and smooth in the shadowed moonlight. She'd released her T-shirt from its tight knot, the hem loose at her waist. The short jean skirt made her legs appear long and lean. His gaze traveled the length of her, surprised when he saw her bare feet.

"Those things were killing me." She gestured at the pair of boots on the ground. "I didn't know you smoked."

"I don't." The cigarette bounced against his lips with his words. A raised eyebrow had him snatching the butt from his mouth. "I did, for a while... I quit."

"Yeah, I can see that," Maggie said. "When?"

He snapped the locket shut, curling it inside his fist, and dropped the match and the cigarette in an empty bottle. "About nine months ago. It's a nasty habit I picked up in—"

He clenched his jaw shut. *Way to go, genius.* Why not tell her the best way to survive the hellhole of prison was to have a cache of cigarettes because they were like gold?

Landon tucked the locket back into his jeans. The rest of beer number four disappeared as he looked out at the inky darkness of the nearby pond. "Ah, bad habits die hard, I guess."

He watched her from the corner of his eye. She nodded, but didn't reply. She didn't walk away either. Unable to stop himself, Landon looked at her. Was she waiting for him to offer to share the front stoop?

"What are you doing here?" he asked.

"I live here."

"I mean what are you doing *here?*"

She bit on her lower lip. "Do you mind if I join you?"

The effects of the alcohol fueled his curiosity. He waved at the porch. “It’s your ranch.”

She sat beside him. Dropping her purse to the ground next to her boots, she stretched her legs with a sigh. A sigh that could mean she was either glad to be off her feet or she wasn’t looking forward to whatever she planned to say next.

Fisting her hands in her lap, she said, “We need to…ah, we need to talk.”

# *Chapter 9*

The sight of her naked feet inches from the toe of his boot sent a stab of need through him. His body responded for the second time tonight.

No, make it the third.

"Landon?" Maggie's voice was soft. "Did you hear me?"

Talk. Yeah, she wanted to talk.

He braced himself. This was it. When he'd gotten back to the ranch, he'd waited to crack open the beer, sure the sheriff was on his way after Maggie told him how the hired help man handled her earlier. Then he figured it didn't matter if he was drunk or sober when the law came to haul his butt into town.

But time had passed. Now she was here. Alone.

She wasn't going to have him arrested. No, she was going to fire his ass.

But at least now he knew—the first kiss had been real. The ones they had shared on the other side of the wooden door behind them was all the proof he'd needed. He'd known the moment his mouth crashed down on hers.

"Yeah, I heard you." He looked at the bottle in his hand. Damn, these things were going too fast. He hoped she'd let him sleep it off before he had to hightail it off her land.

He returned the empty to the cardboard container and pulled out the last two. "Want one?"

Maggie hesitated. "I don't want to take your last one."

"This is my last one." He gestured with the bottle in his left hand. A smirk he couldn't stop pulled at the corner of his mouth. If he was out of here, he wasn't going to make it easy for her. Not when she'd wanted the kiss as much as he wanted it. "Come on, Ms. Stevens, aren't you in need of a little liquid courage?"

Annoyance flashed in her eyes. Good.

"Why not?"

She grabbed the bottle. Her fingers brushed across his and fire danced through his veins. He watched her pop the top, her lips cradling the opening as she tipped it. Eyelids fluttered closed, neck arched and breasts pushed out against the faded words on her T-shirt.

*Down, boy.*

Landon inhaled deeply, pulling in Maggie's magical scent of a summer's day and clean, fresh linen.

Mixed with a trace of smoke from the bar and her sweat from a hard night's work. It intoxicated him.

When she lowered the bottle, a drop of liquid hung on her bottom lip. She brushed it away with the tip of her finger. "Mmm, tastes good. I'm usually the one handing beers to people, not the other way around… except for you. Where'd you go tonight?"

He busied himself opening his own beer. "I don't do well in crowds."

"How'd you know I worked at the Blue Creek, anyway?"

"Hank told me it was the best place to get a cold beer on a Saturday night. I didn't know you'd be there until I saw you with your friends."

"Oh." Maggie took another sip. "Why didn't you join us instead of staring from across the room?"

"Like I said, you were with friends." Landon mirrored her movements with a long swallow. He wasn't about to tell her he avoided the law. "I don't mix business with pleasure."

A slight frown creased her brow. "Neither do I."

*Here it comes.* Landon swallowed hard and looked away. "Yeah?"

"Ah, I never—I need to thank you for the sale to your brother's ranch."

It took a second for him to process what she'd said. A thank-you before she kicked him to the curb? "I told you I didn't—"

"But you started the ball rolling," Maggie interrupted. "More than I've been able to do in the last few months. Thank goodness I got the offer to rehabilitate Black Jack."

"Willie said your work has been hit-or-miss with the beast."

"True, but it's part of the process. Just one more thing to do around here." Maggie's voice faltered before she continued. "That's what I need to talk to you about. I've got too much on my plate to…ah, to…well, to add anything else."

Relief flooded his veins. She wasn't firing him, she was warning him off.

He didn't understand the sudden desire to stay on this little scrap of land, but hell, at least he acknowledged it, if only to himself. It sat hard in the pit of his stomach. He didn't want to leave.

A sense of dizziness overwhelmed him. He closed his eyes and let his head drop back against the porch post. "Like what?"

"Excuse me?"

His eyes remained closed. "You said you've got a lot on your plate?"

"Well, there's Anna and the rest of my family."

"And Kyle Greeley."

"Yes, Kyle, too." She paused and he could feel her studying him. His skin prickled as if she'd touched him with her fingers instead of her gaze. "I suppose after you talked to Tommy, Willie told you about my dealings with Greeley."

Landon swallowed the bad taste her neighbor put in his mouth with another mouthful of beer. "Tommy?"

"Tommy Bailey, the sheriff's deputy."

Ah, right. Another reason for him to keep his distance. "Yeah, Willie loves to talk. His voice was the last sound I heard each night and the first I woke to each morning."

"What exactly did he tell you?"

Did the temperature drop a few degrees? Landon opened his eyes to find her staring out into the darkness. "He told me about your divorce and Greeley hanging around ever since. I guess that's why he's part of your crowded plate."

"Because the jerk has managed to steal away every cowboy I've hired in the last six months." Her voice had risen sharply before dropping again. "I'm not dating him."

A streak of protectiveness ran through him. His fingers tightened on the beer bottle. "Who said anything about dating? I was talking about your land, your horses—"

"Yes, he's after both, but he's not getting either. How could I put a price on this place? My family has been here over a hundred years. It's a part of me, a part of my history. If I didn't have the Moon I don't know where I would go, what I'd do."

The powerful love in her voice caused a band to tighten around Landon's chest. How easy would it have been for her to sell out? To start over away from the one place that must carry a heavy load of pain and heartache thanks to the way her father treated her?

*Like you did?*

He'd made the choice to walk away from Still Waters years ago. And he hadn't missed it. Not once. But when he tried to imagine what it would be like to know his family's ranch wasn't there, wasn't a part of him, he couldn't.

"I don't think Kyle understands," she continued, her voice softer. "He doesn't have the same connection to his land."

"Why?"

"Richard Greeley, the original owner of the Triple G, was a bachelor, but I guess he was quite a busy man in his youth. Rumor has it he's got a few kids scattered around the country. Kyle showed up about eight years ago when Richard got sick. It took a blood test before the old man would accept him as his son. When he died, Kyle took over."

"So why is he interested in this land?"

"I don't know. Greeley's sunk a lot of money into his own place and into the town, which is good for Destiny, but it inflated his already oversized ego. It's like he's trying to buy his way in."

"Including the sheriff's office?"

"No." Maggie's denial was absolute. "I've known Gage—Sheriff Steele—since we were kids. He's one of the good guys."

Landon wasn't so sure, considering the way Steele's deputy gushed about Kyle, but he kept his opinion to himself.

"Anyway, old man Greeley died five years ago, around the same time as my father. When my husband walked out, Kyle started sniffing around. Romance didn't work, so now he's trying to use the local bank—"

She broke off her tirade and tipped the bottle to her lips. She finished her mouthful of beer with a swipe of pink tongue. He watched, unable to pull his gaze from her mouth.

He forced himself to look away. "Do you think Greeley's behind all the problems you've been having?"

"There's no proof, despite Willie's ramblings. Maybe its bad karma… I don't know, but I can't work on what-ifs, I have to go with what I do know. And I know I can't take any chances right now. I can't get distracted." Maggie's words rushed out of her mouth. "What happened between us tonight wasn't anyone's fault, but it can't happen again. I need you, at least until Hank is back on his feet. You must see me as some desperate-divorcée-slash-lonely-single-mother out for a quick roll in the sack, but I'm not. I'm—"

"Okay."

She blinked. "Okay?"

Did he read hesitancy in her gaze? Her speech came out rehearsed, as if she'd repeated it all the way home. Was she second-guessing herself now?

It didn't matter. She was right.

He guessed he should thank her for reminding him he was still a man with a man's desires. Nevertheless, the two of them were as different as people could be. No, he had to stay away from Maggie for reasons much deeper. Giving into his craving would only end in heartache for her because that's all he had to give. Passion, desire, lust. He could describe it half a dozen ways, but none had the word *forever* attached to it.

And Maggie was a forever kind of woman.

Too bad his body wasn't listening. Landon

grabbed his hat and jammed it on. It took what was left of his strength—and he was about empty—to look her straight in the eye. "I said okay. As in, 'You're right. It'll never happen again.'"

"Yes." Her breath rushed out with the word. "Never again."

An overwhelming urge to blow her words to hell with one kiss rose from deep inside. He ignored it and stood. A white-hot ripple of pain shot across his back. He grabbed the porch railing. *Dammit, not now!*

Maggie jumped to her feet. "Are you all right?"

*No, I'm horny, hurting and halfway to hell.*

"I'm fine. I'm going to bed." He placed a foot on the bottom step. The pain exploded, and his knees buckled.

"Whoa, not on your own, you're not." Maggie caught him with her body and wrapped her arm around his waist. She grabbed his hand and held it when his arm landed across her shoulders. "Thought it would take more than a few beers to topple you."

Landon let her believe it was the alcohol incapacitating him as they hobbled to the front door. Her scent filled his head and her body heat branded him from his chest to his knees. He didn't think it was possible, but his erection pulled his boxer briefs tighter. The only light in the room came from a small bedside lamp. When they got to the quilt-covered brass bed, he let go and sat on the edge.

"Wait here a minute," she said.

As if his body would allow him to go anywhere. Landon dropped his hat to his lap, his eyes glued to her backside. She faded into the dark shadows of the kitchen. He heard water running and a cabinet door open and close.

"Here, this will help." She started back toward him, holding out a glass of water. "Drink all of it. You'll be thankful in the morning."

After doing what he was told and handing her the empty glass, he leaned back and braced himself with locked arms. He had to lie down, the sooner the better, but his damn boots had to come off first. He tried to toe one off while Maggie refilled the glass and put it on the table.

"Thanks," he muttered. He agreed with what she'd said on the porch. Anything between them would be one hundred percent wrong, but it was killing him to have this woman and a soft bed so close together. "I've got it from here."

"Sure you do."

Before he could protest, she dropped to her knees in front of him. The air was sucked from the room and his chest. His fingers fisted into the aged quilt beneath him as he looked at the top of her blond head.

"Real cowboys don't sleep with their boots on." She pulled each boot free and set them on the floor. Standing, she grabbed his hat off his lap. "Or their hats."

His breathing returned to normal when she rose, but the brush of his Stetson across the front of his jeans had him scooting backwards. Ignoring the pain, both the good and the bad, he lay flat and yanked the quilt over his midsection. "You'd better go before we both forget the speech you made, boss lady."

He saw her hand freeze for a moment as she reached for the light. One click and the room dropped into darkness, leaving the moonlight streaming through the windows and open doorway.

She stepped onto the porch. "Are you going to be okay?"

No, but he was used to not being okay. He closed his eyes.

"Maggie, go."

Burning heat. It surrounded him, clung to his skin like a layer of plastic he dragged with every step. It coated his eyes, his tears doing little to assist in his desperate need to see what lay in front of him.

He fell to the floor, stretched out his hands and pulled himself along. It felt like hours, his voice raw from calling out, his ears straining to hear the slightest sound that would tell him which direction to turn.

All around him were the cries of dying wood. His rational side screamed at him to leave this place. His irrational side forced him forward, muscles twisting in agony. Without warning, he found what he'd been searching for. It singed his fingers, but he refused to let go.

Dragging himself inch by inch, he retreated from the heat, refusing to give in to the exhaustion, moving toward the blessed fresh air. At last, he gulped in life-giving breaths.

He heard whispers, but didn't understand them. There was no time to reason, to think, he must keep moving. Then a scream roared from deep inside and the hand of the devil captured his soul and dragged him back to the fire—

Landon vaulted upright in the large brass bed, a silent scream on his lips. His wide, unseeing eyes blinked rapidly. His fingers clenched at the sweat-soaked sheets. Forcing himself to breathe deeply, he began to recognize his surroundings. It was only a nightmare. A nightmare he'd thought was out of his head. Out of his heart. A shuddering breath filled him. It'd lasted longer tonight than ever before. This time he'd heard the whispers, but couldn't make out the words.

*What was she trying to tell him?*

He raised his hands to cover his face. Sleep wouldn't come again. Hell, he didn't want it to. He shoved back the blankets and sat on the edge of the bed. At least the pain in his back was gone. Too bad he couldn't say the same about his head. A shower helped, and the aspirin he took would kick in soon. Thankful for no signs of life from the main house despite the sky beginning to lighten with the coming dawn, he stepped outside and found the cell phone sitting on the porch railing.

He wished he could say he didn't know why the nightmare was back, but he did. A thought had come to him before he fell asleep. And it meant another phone call home. He hesitated calling this early but he knew his friend's private line went to his office. He could always leave a message, but he had a feeling Bryce would be awake.

"Powers." A strong voice answered immediately.

"Hey, Buckshot."

"Well, I'll be damned," the low voice said, then chuckled. "It's the Cartwright Kid."

Landon wanted to grin at the familiar use of their childhood nicknames, but the heaviness in his heart wouldn't allow it. "How you doing, Bryce?"

"Same as always. Living large, loving life, thanks to the triplets up at this godawful hour. Geez, it's been forever since we talked. Don't tell me you're home?"

"No, I'm not."

A long pause filled the air. "Okay, at least tell me you've talked to your brother recently. We're meeting for lunch later today."

Landon went on alert. "We talked last night. Is something wrong?"

"No, strictly a social thing. MaryAnn wants to show off the girls and try to fix up your brother with one of her friends. Now, you want to tell me why you're calling at the butt-crack of dawn? Is it dawn where you are?"

Landon watched as the sun broke over the horizon. "Yeah, it is. I'm sorry I called so early. I don't have any right to ask, but I need your help."

"Hey, no time or distance—"

"Or evil varmint or wanton saloon girl can come between the Daredevil Duo." Landon's words joined Bryce's as they recited their childhood oath together. The reminder of their lifelong friendship had him blinking away a sudden stinging in his eyes. He quickly blamed the bright sunrise.

Bryce Powers, one of the winningest lawyers in

the state of Texas, had refused to give up on him after he was found guilty. He'd worked tirelessly to prove the fire that took Sara and Jenna wasn't an act of arson, but a horrific accident, resulting in Landon getting his freedom back.

A freedom he couldn't convince himself he deserved.

"So, what's up?" Bryce asked.

Landon told him about Maggie, the ranch and Kyle Greeley. "It's probably nothing, but I need to know how much of a threat Greeley is to the Crescent Moon—see if anything strikes you the wrong way. If you could keep this as quiet as possible, I'd appreciate it."

"How do I get a hold of you if I find anything?"

Landon gave him the cell phone number and said goodbye. He headed for the barn, questioning why he'd made the call. Because Maggie didn't fire his ass when she had every right to? Or because he didn't want to see another woman and her little girl hurt on his watch?

Black Jack stood quietly at the open doorway of his stall, which connected to the large corral. The moment Landon moved from under the trees, the wild mustang raced outside.

"Are you coming to say good morning?" He moved to the edge of the corral. "Or warn me off?"

Black Jack galloped back and forth behind the fence. The closer Landon got the more agitated the horse became. He stopped, giving the mustang a chance to catch his scent. "See, boy, I'm not out to hurt you. No one here is."

The horse reared and shook his head as if he didn't believe him.

"Yeah, I know. But you've got a good thing here if you're smart enough to realize it. A nice place to sleep, plenty of grub and if you'd get over yourself, there's a couple of pretty fillies inside who'd like to get to know you."

Black Jack offered a loud snort in reply and backed away.

"Who am I to be giving advice?" Landon mumbled as he made his way into the barn. He checked on G.W., the words he'd said to Black Jack ringing in his head. Hell, was he talking about the animal or himself?

Refusing to allow his mind to go down that road, he let G.W. and the rest of the horses free in the paddock on the other side of the barn, glad to see his friend fully healed.

As he mucked out the stalls, the whispered words from his nightmare returned.

It was Jenna. She was trying to tell him something with her dying breath. He could hear the husky tone of her voice, but couldn't make it all out. More likely, he didn't want to understand what she was saying.

*Your...fault... Sara...not...me...*

He gripped the rack, the veins in his hands pushing tight against his skin.

"Stop," he whispered between clenched teeth. "I know it's my fault. I know I didn't… I couldn't…"

With a pile of dirty hay covering his boots, he gave in and yanked the locket out of his pocket.

Opening it, he looked at the words engraved opposite the picture.

*To My Daddy, Love Sara.*

Jenna had given it to him on their six-month anniversary, the night their daughter was born. Back then he'd thought their shotgun marriage might work. Too bad he'd found his wife in bed with one of his ranch hands six months later. He didn't let on he'd seen them, but she knew. The fact he'd moved into another bedroom and sent the cowboy packing had been enough of a clue. He'd spent the better part of the next year as far away from Jenna and Sara as he could. Until he'd realized he was punishing his daughter for something she'd had no part of. He'd vowed on her second birthday to be the kind of father she needed.

A vow made too late.

"Good morning."

Landon spun around. The locket fell from his hands into the pile of straw, dirt and manure at his feet. "Sh—ah, hell, what are you doing here?"

A pair of green eyes widened. "You're lucky my mama didn't hear you." Tiny fists jammed into her overalls. "Do you know how yucky a bar of soap tastes? Besides, I live here."

Like mother, like daughter. Other than the first day when this pint-sized version of Maggie had flung her arms around him in a surprise hug, Landon hadn't seen Anna Stevens, thanks to spending the last two weeks camping out with Willie. Oh, he knew all about her. Willie's ramblings made sure of that.

He didn't talk about Maggie without talking about her little girl.

And how Alan Stevens had walked out on the two of them.

Landon had gone to sleep many nights wondering how a man did such a thing. Lord knows, his marriage to Jenna was over long before her death, but he never would've walked out on his daughter. Had Sara lived, she'd be a few years younger than the girl in front of him.

Tears burned at the edges of his eyes. He looked away. "Ah, sorry. You surprised me."

Landon turned his back to her, blinked away the stinging and stared at the ground. The locket was gone. He bent down and started to search.

"Whatcha looking for?"

He froze at the sound of Anna's voice. Closing his eyes, he willed the little girl to go away. "Nothing. Something I dropped."

"Can I help?" She plunked down beside him and started tunneling through the hay. "Mama always says four eyes are better than two when you've lost something."

Her hair, blonder than her mother's, hung loose over her shoulders. A deep breath drew in the mixture of baby powder and stale hay. Tightness seized his chest. When she turned and peeked at him through her hair, his heart told him to look away. He couldn't.

"Ya know?" She offered a grin with two missing teeth. "I'd be a whole lot better at this if I knew what I was looking for."

Forcing his gaze from her, Landon focused on pushing around the hay and dirt. "Ah, you should go back to the house."

"Why?"

"Because your mom might be looking for you."

"Why would she—oh, I found it." Anna jumped up, the open locket cradled in her palm. "Is this what you're looking for? Wow, what a pretty baby. Is she yours? What's her name?"

Landon jerked to his feet. He took the locket and shoved it back into his pocket. A throat cleared behind him softly. His body turned to stone.

"Mama!"

Anna raced across the barn and Landon forced himself to face Maggie, who squatted to return her daughter's hug. His throat closed, choking off his breath.

"Are you bothering Mr. Cartwright?" Maggie asked, voice low as she smoothed her daughter's hair.

"Nope." Anna squirmed away. She offered him a bright smile. "Am I?"

He could do nothing but shake his head.

Maggie rose to her feet, eyes still on her daughter. "Well, you better get back inside, young lady. Since you insisted on being up so early, you can help Nana B. get breakfast on the table."

The little girl pouted, but after a gentle swat on her backside, she left the barn. Maggie followed, not once looking Landon in the eye.

# *Chapter 10*

"No, I didn't ask him yet."

"One reason." Racy's voice rang loud through the phone above the noisy din of the Sunday afternoon crowd at the Blue Creek Saloon. "Give me one damn reason why you haven't asked Landon about his daughter. And it better be good."

"I've been busy." Maggie tucked the cordless phone between her ear and shoulder and reached for another pillowcase to fold. A week had gone by since she'd come across Anna and Landon in the barn in time to hear—she wasn't sure exactly what. "Besides, I'm not clear on what he said."

"Bull. You're scared."

"Language!"

"Stop mothering me and ask the man."

"It's been crazy around here. I have a ranch to run—"

Racy cut her off by clucking like a chicken.

Maggie didn't respond. From her window, she could see Landon on his hands and knees, finishing the repairs to the deck next to the pond. Jeans, faded in all the right places, showed off his backside and muscular thighs to perfection. The plain white T-shirt pulled tight across his back emphasized the width of his shoulders and darkness of his skin. His black cowboy hat covered his hair except for the ponytail lying between his shoulder blades.

"Hello? Girlfriend? Did I lose you?"

"I'm here."

Her gaze moved to Anna, who stood nearby with Mr. Darcy, her oversized orange tabby, in her arms. Anna said something and Landon paused, resting back on his heels as he responded. He stroked the cat's fur then directed Anna to step back when Mr. Darcy began to squirm. Anna willingly complied.

Maggie smiled.

Her daughter had become Landon's shadow from the moment he'd given her a ride on G.W., allowing her to circle the corral a few times after he'd quizzed her about her riding experience. She'd followed him everywhere since then, peppering him with questions and little-girl chatter. At first, Landon had looked shaken and avoided her whenever possible. Two days later, he'd waved off Maggie's latest apology for her daughter's persistence and appeared resigned to Anna's presence. Now, it looked like he actually enjoyed it.

"You're certainly quiet," Racy chimed in. "Let me guess. Mr. Tall, Dark and Positively Yummy is providing a distraction?"

"Racy…"

"Oh, please, like you haven't enjoyed working with him, and the man does like to work. Hell, other than to say hello, he didn't look twice at me when I was there for dinner the other night."

"Lord knows, that rarely happens." Maggie tried to ignore the thrill shooting through her at Landon's immunity to her best friend's considerable charms.

"Ha-ha. His eyes certainly followed your every move."

"So you keep telling me, but except for meals, we've rarely seen each other. Hank is feeling better now, leaving me free to concentrate on the horses, especially Black Jack." Maggie's gaze flittered toward the black mustang in his corral. "He's accepting the saddle and I spent some time riding him yesterday. I'd never be this far along if Landon didn't start work long before sunup. It's like he's driven to get this place in tip-top shape."

Racy snorted. "Something you're not used to seeing in a man under age fifty."

Yes, but it was something else, too. She hadn't confided in Racy about the passionate kiss they'd shared last week, or about when she'd made it clear she wanted nothing from him but an honest day's work. He was sticking to their agreement and staying as far away from her as his job allowed.

But he did watch her. She could feel his eyes on her all the time, and to be fair, she spent a good part of each day watching him, too. And the nights. Oh, she couldn't think about her wild dreams without blushing all the way to the tips of her toes.

"Imagine what he could do if he put those muscles to work on you," Racy continued. "Say, in the hayloft or by the creek? Oh, I know—how about the porcelain tub your great-great-grand-whatever dragged out West decades ago."

"Racina Josephine!"

Landon glanced over his shoulder, and despite the sun reflecting off the window Maggie swore she could feel the heat of his gaze. She spun away, clutching the pillowcase she was folding to her breasts, the pang of squashed desire so strong it ached.

Racy laughed. "Okay, I'll stop. So, how come I had to hear about your horse sale at the bar instead of from you?"

The air rushed from Maggie's lungs. "Who told you?"

"What? Is it a secret?"

"No, not exactly."

She'd wanted to keep the sale under Kyle Greeley's radar as long as she could. Of course, he probably had ways of finding out about the sizable increase in her bank account. Along with the fee for training Black Jack, the sale would put a nice dent in the final loan payment due the end of next month. She was already trying to secure another loan from a bank in Cheyenne to pay off the remainder.

"Like I said, I've had a lot on my mind lately."

"Sexy cowboys notwithstanding. So, are you coming into work early to help me with this crowd?"

"I shouldn't. It'd serve you right to be stuck alone with all those thirsty, NASCAR-loving cowboys. Do you think Leeann will stop by?"

"Doubtful. I told her Bobby had the pole position and everyone was gathering to cheer on the hometown hero. You would've thought I was talking about the weather for all the reaction I got, but what else is new."

Maggie had also noticed the difference in Leeann since she'd come back to town. Long gone was the vivacious girl they'd known, who'd always persevered despite an overprotective father and beauty-pageant-obsessed mother. "I'm not surprised. We had lunch together last week and she was—I don't know. I can't describe it, but she sure has changed from the girl she was twelve years ago."

"We all have—" Racy's voice dropped away. "Hey, cowboy! You touch that bottle of tequila, and I'll chop off the protruding parts of your body and serve them to you on toast."

Maggie grinned. "Not all of us have. You're the same sweet, loving girl you've always been."

"Damn straight," Racy said. "And you better bring some 4-1-1 with you when you come in later, or I'm gonna corner that cowboy myself. I know I'm not the only one with questions."

Maggie ended the call. Racy was right. She did have questions for Landon, but in light of her "I'm the employer, you're the employee" speech, she didn't feel right asking about his personal life.

*This is what you wanted. Space and separation.*

*You made it clear. He's being paid to do a job, not romance you.*

And what a job he'd done. The tool shed, rebuilt from the ground up, stood strong with a fresh coat of red paint. Both the bunkhouse and the foreman's cabin sported new, dark-brown paint. A second, smaller barn was almost finished in the same color, and the main house was next on the list. Gallons of bright-white paint waited in the cool shade of the porch.

Together with Willie and Hank, he'd completely reorganized the inside of the main barn, including the addition of a new watering system for each of the stalls. She didn't think she could afford it until Willie showed her Landon's cost-effective plans.

"What would I do without—" Maggie bit hard at her bottom lip, stopping her words. She blinked, refusing to acknowledge the freshly folded clothes on her bed appeared watery and out of focus.

She couldn't do this.

So what if everyone treated him like he was family?

Nana B. had gone out of her way to make apple cobbler after she'd discovered he loved it. Hank and Willie easily followed his lead on the never-ending list of ranch chores. Her daughter had a serious case of hero worship, and if Maggie let herself, she could easily fall in—

The slam of the screen door made her jump. Her heart thumped in her chest, and she brushed away the moisture on her eyelashes. Scuffling noises told her someone was searching for something.

She headed to the kitchen. "What are you looking for, munchkin?"

Anna opened and rummaged through cabinet drawers in quick succession. "Nothing."

"What does this nothing look like?"

"Mama, please. I'm in a hurry."

Maggie smiled and leaned against the counter. "I've got to go into work early tonight. I know we planned to christen the new deck when Hank and Willie got back, but we'll wait until tomorrow, okay?"

"Sure, mama, whatever." Anna slammed the last drawer shut and raced out of the kitchen, her blond braids bouncing against her shoulders.

"Honey, what are you—" Maggie stopped when Anna came back in with a pair of scissors in her hand. "Anna?"

"I'm walking, Mama," she said, moving slowly toward the back door and holding the shears correctly. "I'm walking."

"Walking where?"

"To Landon's." Her voice carried through the screen door when it shut behind her. "I'm gonna give him a haircut."

It took a moment for the words to register. When they did, Maggie bolted after her daughter. Anna had quickened her pace and was at the cabin's steps by the time Maggie caught her.

"Hold on a minute, honey." She latched onto her daughter's arm. "What do you mean by 'haircut'?"

"Landon says his hair is getting in his way and he's going to the barber's," Anna explained, wiggling from Maggie's fingers. "I told him I could cut it, and he said okay."

For a moment, the woman in her mourned the loss of her cowboy's thick, black hair. The first time she'd seen it, loose and flowing, it had touched off a yearning so deep she immediately attributed it to the teenage rebellious side she'd thought long dead.

Her more mature adult side had Maggie reprimanding her child. "Anna, what have I told you about telling fibs—"

"Honest, Mama." Anna's eyes widened. "He said I could."

"You must have misunderstood—"

"She didn't." Landon stood in the doorway of the cabin with a towel over one shoulder, a wooden chair in one hand and a stack of newspapers in the other. "You ready, Miss Anna?"

Anna walked up the steps. "Yup!"

Maggie was right behind her. "Landon, you can't be serious. She's—"

"Going to cut my hair," he interrupted, his full attention on Anna as he set the chair in the middle of the porch. "Here, I'll hold those scissors while you put the newspapers down so we don't make a mess."

"Okay." Anna grinned, and laid the newspaper around the chair. "How much should I use?"

"It's not like you're shaving a polar bear. I'm just a man."

A man who'd paid more attention to her little girl in the last week than Anna's father had in the last two years.

Anna giggled. Maggie smiled as she crossed her arms over her chest.

"You sure about this?"

He looked at her. A heart-tugging tenderness filled his eyes. She'd seen that emotion before. Long ago in Alan's eyes when Anna was first born. Was Landon thinking of his own—

"It's hair, Maggie." He paused, as if he was going to say something more, but he pressed his lips closed. The pained emotion in his gaze disappeared. "It'll grow back. Besides, she's only cutting off the pony tail."

Unable to trust her voice, she nodded. They were alone for the first time in a week, as alone as one could be with an eight-year-old chaperone, but Maggie's heart raced all the same.

He turned and spoke directly to Anna. "All set?"

"All set." Anna took the scissors he held out to her. "My mom cuts mine, Hank's and Willie's hair all the time. I know what I'm doing. Have a seat."

Landon sat and arranged the towel so it lay flat over his shoulders. He shook out his hair, then gathered it at his neck with a piece of rawhide. "Cut above the string, okay?"

"Gotcha."

Anna went to work. Maggie sidled past Landon, a shimmer of electricity grazing her skin where their arms brushed. "I'll watch from back here."

"I'm doing fine, Mama," Anna said, her tongue tucked into the corner of her mouth. "I'm—oops!"

A chunk of black hair and two pieces of rawhide dropped to the newspaper.

"Oops?"

Landon's voice sounded calm, but the muscles across his shoulders tightened.

Maggie stared at her daughter's handiwork and hid a smile behind her fingers. Anna looked at her with wide, pleading eyes. "You better answer your customer, young lady."

"I, ah… I cut below the knot."

"So it stayed right where I put it," Landon said. "Do you want to try again?"

"What in tarnation are you three up to?"

Maggie whirled at the sound of Willie's voice. He and Hank were heading for the cabin, a large cardboard box in Willie's arms quivering on its own.

"I'm giving Landon a haircut," Anna said proudly. "Who's next?"

"I think I'm all set, Little Bit," Hank replied.

"Me, too," Willie said, "but we've got somep'n—ah, a few somep'ns for ya."

"Me?" Anna handed the scissors to Maggie and scrambled down the steps. Willie dropped to one knee and put the box on the grass.

"What's going on?" Maggie asked. "How'd your appointment with Doc go?"

"Ah, fine. It went fine." Hank cradled his ribs with one hand. "But I've got to wear these blasted bandages for a while longer. Ain't that right, Willie?"

"Ah, yeah," Willie piped up. "Maybe another week."

"Or two," Hank quickly added.

"Or three. Looks like we need you around here a bit longer, Cartwright."

Hank nudged Willie with the toe of his boot, an action not lost on Maggie. She glanced at Landon, and followed his gaze to Anna and the writhing box she was helping Willie open. "What's in—"

"Kittens!" Anna's gleeful cry filled the air along with cries and meows from tiny balls of fluff. "Wow, look at them!"

Maggie groaned inwardly as her daughter fell into the box. "William Howard Taft Perkins." She eyed the cowboy who managed to look chagrined and prideful at the same time. "Are you out of your mind?"

Hank backed away with a wry smile on his face. "I better take a few of those pain pills before I head to my place. Doctor's orders."

*Doctor's orders, my ass.* Hank knew when to hightail it to safety. Maggie crossed her arms and stared balefully at her other cowboy.

"Now, you know Ms. Kali's office is right next to the doc's office." Willie tried to keep the squirming kittens inside. "Her assistant found the kittens by the side of the road. They're all healthy, and she was taking them to a shelter in Cheyenne. No telling where they'd end up."

"Oh, they are so cute." Anna picked up two of the kittens, one white and the other black. She buried her cheeks in their fur.

Maggie knew she was in trouble.

"Here, hold one." Anna offered the black kitten to Landon who caught it just before it wiggled off his lap. He let out a sound Maggie could've sworn was laughter as he held the kitten close to his chest.

"Hey there, little one." He easily cupped the animal in one large hand, its tiny claws sinking into the towel as it nuzzled his neck. "Where are you going?"

"Not sure how your Mr. Darcy is going to feel about these intruders," Landon said to Anna as he stroked the kitten's back.

"Mr. Darcy can be their mamma."

Maggie choked back her own laughter.

Landon's eyebrows rose. "Ah, I thought Mr. Darcy was a boy cat."

Anna tipped her head to one side. "So?"

Landon shot a questioning glance at Maggie. "You want to handle this?"

"Oh, no, you're doing fine," she said, then grinned.

"I think I'll show Mr. Darcy his new babies." Anna put the kittens back into the box. "Can you carry them for me, Willie?"

"Whatever you say, little lady."

Willie scrambled to his feet and made a hasty retreat with Anna on his heels. Maggie watched them go. Her head told her she needed to make a few phone calls to find good homes for the kittens. Her heart? That was something different. She doubted Mr. Darcy would have any interest in the miniature versions of himself, but Anna was a nurturer, like her.

"I think I've been abandoned." Landon crossed his arms over his chest, pulling the T-shirt snug against his muscular arms. "Guess I've got nothing compared to a couple of balls of fluff."

*Oh, I wouldn't say that.* Maggie forced her gaze to stay on his face and away from those tanned, rippling muscles. "Sorry. You know the attention span of little girls."

His jaw hardened and his gaze flattened. "No, actually I don't." He dropped his arms and started to rise. "I plan to restock the tool shed this afternoon. I'll get to it after I head into town—"

"Stay put." Maggie pushed his shoulder and at first he resisted, his body hard and unmoving. Then he dropped back into the chair. She yanked her hand away, willing herself not to rub it against her jeans in an attempt to erase the tingling sensation. "I'll finish your haircut."

"You don't have to—"

"I want to, I mean, it's the least I can do after your bravery at letting Anna give it a try. Do you mind—" She motioned to the open cabin door.

"It's your ranch."

"Be right back."

Maggie went inside, heading for the bathroom. She tried to ignore the rumpled bed sheets and Landon's personal care items on the sink.

His closed expression at her comment about little girls had her wondering again about his daughter. How old was she? Where did she live? Had Landon been married? Not that that was a requirement to have a child nowadays. Did she dare ask him about this?

"Maybe you should mind your own business," Maggie muttered, a packet of new combs in the cabinet catching her eye. *Ah, success.* Heading back to the front porch, she half expected to see the taillights of Landon's truck pulling out of the drive, but he sat still in the chair.

She moved behind him and pulled the remains of the rawhide from his hair. His shoulders stiffened again and she couldn't stop herself from pressing her knuckles gently into his rigid muscles. "Relax, I'm good at this."

He didn't reply, but his upper body did soften a bit, if it was possible for solid muscle to do so. Maggie pulled the comb through his shorn locks. A giggle escaped her as she surveyed the ragged edges falling below the neckline of his shirt.

"That bad, huh?"

"Nothing I can't fix. How short do you want it?"

"Whatever, I trust you."

His words made her pause.

*Don't be silly, it's a haircut. Don't make anything more of it.*

She started cutting, his hair sliding through her fingers like smooth silk. The heat of the day lifted his natural scent—one part hay, one part hard work—and it enveloped her. She brushed the back of his neck and he hummed softly.

"You've got a soft touch, Maggie."

She clenched hard on the comb and scissors at the rumble of his voice.

*Concentrate, girl, concentrate.*

# *Chapter 11*

The air was heavy with the sudden quiet. Landon shifted in his seat, his shoulders taut as he crossed his arms over his chest. "I found your ranch shirt in my latest batch of laundry. Don't let me forget to give it back to you."

Anger and pain Maggie had thought long gone rushed through her, erasing any thought of Anna. "I don't want it. Keep it, toss it, I really don't care."

"This from the ranch's owner?"

"I'm sure Willie shared with you the history of the Moon and my less-than-stellar relationship with my father. Those shirts were his toys, prizes he gave out to his favorites."

"But not to you."

"On my sixteenth birthday I found one of those

shirts in the bathroom and I foolishly thought my father had left it there as a gift," she said, as she dropped her hands to his shoulders, angling the scissors into a safe position. "I didn't have it on ten minutes before he hauled me into his office and told me no woman would ever wear one of his shirts. I never did. I thought I got rid of them all after he died."

She took a deep breath and trimmed his hair, catching sight of Hank and Willie as they drove away in Hank's truck. She didn't know what she would've done growing up if not for those two stand-in daddies. They'd bandaged more cuts, dried more tears and showered her with way more love and affection than she'd ever received from her real father.

"I was four when my mother ran off with one of my daddy's cowboys," she continued, the words rolling off her tongue like a conveyer belt. "It took a while to figure out I was a constant reminder of my mother's betrayal."

Her words hung in the air for a moment before Landon spoke. "I take it Nana B. wasn't here then?"

Maggie pulled in a breath and remembered the day she'd found the petite, white-haired woman on her front porch. "No, she didn't come to the Crescent Moon until I was a newlywed. Nana B. is my mother's mom, and she'd lost contact with her daughter years before. She found us thanks to a private detective."

"Your dad was okay with her?"

"He welcomed her once he got a taste of her cooking. I'm better with horses than I am in the kitchen." Finished with the back and sides, Maggie moved to stand in front of him. She didn't want to think about how her father had mellowed after she and Alan had married. Of course, Alan was the son he'd always wanted. "Ah, can you tip your head to the left a bit?"

Landon shuffled his feet, making room for her between his thighs and tilted his head. "Like this?"

She placed her fingertips on his chin. "A bit more..."

His gaze latched onto hers, and she was powerless to look away. Coal-black eyes framed by equally dark lashes roamed her face before pausing on her mouth. Then he looked back into her eyes.

"Being a single parent isn't easy."

Maggie flushed and straightened. She could only imagine what Willie had said about Alan, considering the old man had never seen her ex-husband as anything but, to use his own words, a flannel-mouthed blowhard.

Since Alan had left, his contact with Anna had dwindled. During their early marriage, he'd been a fun-loving, attentive dad. But now Anna and she were on their own.

"I'm not raising Anna by myself." Maggie returned to cutting his hair. "I've got Nana B. and my extended family and friends."

"You're a great mom, Maggie."

His soft words sank into her soul and tears sprang to her eyes. She was embarrassed at how much his simple words meant to her. Even with her family to help, Maggie thought, Anna was her responsibility. And her joy and proudest achievement.

Taking a step back, she couldn't help looking at

Landon's face. A sigh of relief bubbled in her throat. His eyes remained closed.

"Something wrong?"

"Ah, no."

"Black Jack has started to behave," he said. "Guess you found the right mumbo jumbo, hocus-pocus, voodoo thing?"

Now, why when *he* said it did she hear respect instead of ridicule?

She moved to the back of the chair again and layered the top. Tamping down her frantic pulse, she concentrated on his question. "No magic spell. I think Black Jack has just realized I'm not out to hurt him. He knows he's safe here and it's okay to trust me."

Landon pulled in a long breath, his shoulders widening. A long silence stretched between them while he slowly released it. Her words replayed in her head. Was she talking about the horse or Landon?

"Enough about me. Why don't you tell me about you?" Maggie asked.

"There's nothing to tell."

"Oh, there must be something. All we know about you is that you've traveled around a lot and your best friend is a horse. What about your family?"

"My folks are gone."

"You mentioned your brother's ranch—"

"Are you finished yet?"

Her hands stilled, then she stepped away. "All done."

Landon rose and headed into the cabin. "Thanks, appreciate it."

Maggie doubted he meant it and bent to retrieve the scattered newspapers.

Should she follow? Hell, it was her cabin, and she needed to put this stuff in the trash. Marching inside, she laid the scissors and comb on the table and found the garbage can, then went to stand in front of the sink. He caught her staring while he looked at himself in the mirror. His gaze returned to his reflection and he pushed his hair back over his ears. "It looks great. I haven't had it this short since—" His lips pressed together. He swallowed before his eyes again met hers in the mirror. "—since I left home more than four years ago."

Maggie stepped in behind him. "You've been moving from ranch to ranch for the last four years?"

He leaned against the sink, his hands braced on his hips. "Must be hard for a homebody like you to understand, huh?"

"I think you're a homebody, too. I think you miss Still Waters—"

"What makes you think that's my home?"

"Okay, so it's your brother's," she conceded. "But I think you miss it, and your family."

He froze. "What family?"

"Your brother." Maggie paused, swiping her tongue over dry lips. "Your daughter?"

A tortured look filled his eyes. "You heard me in the barn with Anna."

She nodded then moved closer. "I'm sorry I made you think I didn't—"

"You heard wrong." Landon pushed away, and skirted past her. "I don't have a daughter."

"But Anna was looking at something." Maggie grabbed his arm, stopping him. "A picture? She asked you who—"

"Sara." The word was choked and grief stricken. "Her name was Sara. She's dead."

Shock and anguish rose inside her, bringing with it a fear only a parent could understand. "Oh, Landon, I'm sorry. I don't know what to say. I didn't mean to… I can't imagine how it feels to lose—dammit, this is none of my business. If you want me to shut up, just say so."

Landon spun back, sorrow etched over his face. He pulled her hard against his chest. His mouth hovered over hers and his fingers dug into her waist. "Maggie, shut up."

His gentle yet desperate words washed over her. Going on instinct, she didn't stop to think. Comfort. She wanted to comfort this man for what had to be unfathomable heartache. She cradled his face in her hands, and he closed his eyes. Her heart teetered on the edge of something sharp and painful. Her eyelids lowered and her lips moved to his—

A petrifying scream filled the air. Their eyes flew open. Puzzlement, then understanding filled his dark gaze.

"Anna!"

Landon and Maggie bumped into each other as they ran from the bathroom, racing onto the front porch, scanning the backyard.

"Anna!" She grabbed his shirt, repeating her daughter's name. "That was Anna!"

Another shrill cry filled the air, this time more animal than human. A cloud of dust billowed at the edge of the barn and Landon ran toward it. Raw, primal fear grabbed at him, making it feel as if he were pushing his way through waist-deep water. He arrived at Black Jack's corral with Maggie just behind him. The wild mustang charged in a circle around the enclosure, kicking up dirt and rocks over himself and the scared little girl frozen in the middle. The tiny kitten in her arms wasn't faring any better.

"Stay back," Landon shouted at Nana B., who burst from the house.

Anna spotted Maggie and cried, "Mama!"

Maggie started forward, but Landon stopped her. "Anna, be quiet," he called out to her daughter.

"I'm—I'm scared." Her high-pitched voice crawled inside him, twisting his gut.

"I know you are, honey," Landon said.

Maggie's hands dug into his arms in a desperate need to be free, but rushing the corral would only make matters worse. "But you have to stay real still, like a statue."

"B-but the horse—"

"Shhh, no words, no movement, okay?"

Anna's head jerked in what he hoped was a nod. Landon doubted she'd be able to do what he asked for long. He looked at Maggie, the fear and shock in her eyes tearing at him. "Go to the far side, talk to Black Jack."

He gripped her arms. He had to make sure she understood. "Listen to me. Do your magic, cast a spell, hypnotize the beast, I don't care. Give the horse something to concentrate on besides Anna."

Maggie's eyes cleared except for the unmistakable gleam of unshed tears. "What are you—"

"I'll get Anna." He pushed her away. "Go."

Landon waited until Maggie headed in the other direction, her singsong voice wobbling as she called to the agitated animal. Black Jack reared in her direction, but he continued to dart between Anna and the railing.

With the horse's attention diverted, Landon crouched low and inched toward the corral. He froze when Black Jack whipped in his direction, nostrils flaring as if catching his scent. Maggie's lyrical voice continued. The stallion turned his attention back to her, and Landon had to move.

Now.

Staying out of the animal's line of sight, he crawled to the fence and slipped between the posts. Maggie's voice caught, but his focus stayed on Anna.

He had to get to her. Save her.

In three steps, he grabbed her and the kitten, pulling both to his chest. The kitten's tiny claws dug into his arm. Anna's squeal alerted Black Jack again. The animal whirled.

Landon locked eyes with the creature, then raced back to the fence. He beat the charging horse by a heartbeat, diving through the posts. Hitting the dirt with his shoulder and hip, he rolled to his back, keeping his small charges safely tucked in his arms.

"Anna!"

"Mommy!"

Seconds later, his arms were empty as Anna hurled herself at Maggie.

Landon stared at the bright-blue sky. His breath came in short, hard gasps. He pushed up to a sitting position, ignoring the dig of pebbles and dirt in his skin. The kitten was safe in Nana B.'s hands and Anna in Maggie's.

Sharp throbbing pain shot across his lower back. Tears stung his eyes. He brushed the moisture away, blaming it on the swirl of dust covering him. He refused to believe it was the sight of three generations of a family in a tight huddle, Maggie's and Nana B.'s hands fluttering over Anna, from her ponytails to her sneakers.

She was okay. One child saved.

One child lost.

The feminine voices, fragile and shaking, faded into a loud buzz. A wall of darkness closed in. His heart pounded against his rib cage, threatening to explode. Panic rioted within, and one thought raced through his head.

Get out.

Now.

Ignoring the blinding pain in his back, he stumbled to the rear of the barn, feeling the lick of a searing inferno on his skin—flames engulfing wood, the snap and crackle screaming in his ears, soot blanketing his eyes, making it impossible to see.

Desperate to rid himself of the heat and pain, he wrenched on the outdoor faucet. The hose sprang to life. He bent over, braced a hand against his knee and doused himself in the cold spray.

He squeezed his eyes tight and water rushed over his neck and head, soaking the collar of his shirt and flattening the sleeves to his arms. It wasn't enough. His skin still burned. He yanked the shirt off and icy water bathed him in coldness, numbing him from the outside until it matched the deadened interior of his soul.

"I'm sorry, Sara," he cried, the useless apology falling from his lips. "I'm sorry, baby. I couldn't save…"

"Landon."

He heard her call his name, but it was too late. He didn't get to her in time. Either of them.

"Landon."

The heat of a hand on his arm jerked him upright. Water flew from his hair as he stumbled backward. He tunneled his fingers over his scalp, sending cold rivulets down his chest and back. His eyes, wide and unblinking, stared at nothing. "Don't—don't touch me."

"My god, are you all right?"

"I'm sorry." His voice cracked, and he struggled to get the words past the burn in his throat. "I—I couldn't do it. I couldn't save her."

"Landon, what are you talking about? You did save her. You saved Anna."

He blinked and saw his wife's cropped black hair plastered to her head, the light fading from her dark eyes, their child cradled in her arms.

*I'm sorry,* she whispered, *I'm sorry.*

"No." He brushed away her apology. "It's my fault.

The flames, the smoke—it was too hot. I couldn't… I didn't get to you in time—"

"Landon, stop! I'm fine, Anna's fine." She grabbed his arms and tried to shake him. "What's the matter? What's wrong?"

"A-Anna?"

"She's fine. She's with my grand—Landon?"

He blinked again. The image before him shifted. Long, blond hair and green eyes came into focus. Bright sunshine on a hot summer day replaced the smoky gloom. "Mag—Maggie?"

"Yes, it's me. You saved my daughter—"

"But not mine." The words tore from his throat. "I couldn't save Sara."

"What are you talking about?"

The hose fell from his hand into the large puddle at their feet. He tore free of her hold. His chest heaved, drawing in life-giving breaths, while his mind allowed the nightmare to fade.

Three steps had his back against the corral. "Leave me alone."

"Landon, please." She advanced, concern in her eyes.

He spun away. It was a mistake. Naked to the waist, he'd bared his scars to her, the constant reminder of his failure.

"Ohmigod, what—Landon, what happened to you?"

He grabbed the top railing, the wood biting into his palms. His muscles flexed and pulled at the tight skin, the pain gone. Still, he flinched when her fingertips pressed lightly between his shoulder blades.

"There was a fire."

The words fell from his mouth, but it was as if someone else were speaking. He tried to stop, but they continued to flow. "It was nighttime, dark…so dark. My wife and d-daughter were trapped. I tried to find them, but by the time I got…got them out…it was too late. They died and it was my fault."

She put both hands on him as she moved up behind him. The softness of her hair caressed his skin, and a deep shudder coursed through him. The light touch of her lips to his back almost dropped him to his knees. He couldn't make out her murmured words, but he knew what she was offering.

Sympathy.

He didn't deserve it. Not now. Not from her.

He pushed her away, vaulted over the fence and started across the field. He whistled for G.W., who raced toward him.

"Landon, wait!" Maggie cried. "I want—I want to help."

"You can't." He swung onto his horse bareback, refusing to look at her. "No one can."

It was midnight when Maggie pulled her pickup to a stop at the house. All was dark but for the familiar back-porch light and the full moon.

She'd called home a few times during her shift at the bar to check on her daughter. Nana B. assured her Anna was fine and was more concerned about Black Jack being punished. Maggie knew it wasn't the horse's fault. She prayed the commotion hadn't set back the stallion's progress.

She had no idea if she could say the same about Landon.

She'd watched him take off across the open field, G.W. jumping the fencing to disappear over a hill. Nana B. had checked the foreman's cabin a few times, but it remained empty. Willie had stopped by the bar after dinner and told her Landon still hadn't returned. Maggie had been so worried about him, she had a hell of a time keeping her mind on her work. She'd screwed up more orders than she could count. All she could think about was Landon.

His reaction to saving Anna had scared her. He'd stood before her like a man possessed, eyes wide and unseeing. She'd assured him Anna was okay. Then his second shocking confession fell from his lips when he said both his wife and child were dead—and he was to blame.

She had to find him. She had to tell him he was wrong. Landon was not a killer. There was no way he was responsible for anyone's death.

She stepped from the truck, untied the tail ends of her button-down, sleeveless denim shirt, and eyed the dark cabin across the pond. Relief filled her at the sight of his trailer and pickup parked along the side. Maybe he was home. If not, should she wait for Willie and then go looking for him?

Shoving her keys and wallet into the pocket of her miniskirt, she headed for the barn. First things first. She'd check to see if G.W. was back. If he was, she'd check on Landon.

Her boots crunched against the gravel as she

walked inside the barn. A single overhead light cast a warm glow, but the stalls remained dark.

Caring so deeply about this wandering cowboy was wrong. In a matter of weeks, maybe days, he'd be heading down the road. Too bad her heart wasn't listening to her head. The same heart that was now lodged in her throat.

*Please. Please let G.W. be here.*

Tears of relief stung her eyes when the golden palomino swung his head over the stall door. Maggie wrapped her arms around his neck. "Oh, it's so wonderful to see you. Are you okay, sweetie? Where's your friend?"

"Right behind you."

# *Chapter 12*

Maggie whirled around. Landon stood near the hayloft stairs, his white shirt hanging loose, hands shoved deep into the front of his jeans.

"You looking for me?"

His voice was low, but carried across the silent barn. The insolent tone changed her relief to anger.

"Damn straight, I am. What happened to you?"

"What do you mean?"

Maggie stomped across the floor. "I mean we were worried. The way you took off this afternoon. How could you do that?"

"Easy. I've been riding G.W. bareback for years." Landon uncrossed his boots and straightened. His cowboy hat cast a dark shadow over his face. "It's been a while, but you know what they say about never forgetting—"

"That's not what I'm talking about, dammit." Maggie smacked his chest with the palm of her hand. "How could you disappear? And for so long? There's a lot of desolate land out there. You or G.W. could've been injured with no way to call for help—"

Landon shrugged. "Who cares?"

"I do!"

Maggie smacked him again and this time he wrapped his hand around her wrist. The heat of his firm touch was her undoing. Tears filled her eyes. She wrenched free and flung herself at him, wrapping her arms around his neck.

"Oh, Landon, please tell me you're all right."

He stiffened, but Maggie refused to let go. A thrill raced through her as the hard planes of his body leveled against her curves. His hair was damp, and the sweet smell of soap and clean skin invaded her senses. It was forever before his hands touched her. A tingling shockwave raced over her skin when his fingertips, tentative at first, caressed her back. Then a groan rumbled in his chest and his hands tightened.

Maggie pressed her face to the warmth of his neck, not caring he'd be able to feel the wetness of her tears. "I was so scared." Her words came out in a rushed whisper. She didn't stop to think but spoke from the heart. "I didn't know where you'd gone, if you were okay…if you were coming back…"

Her lips found their way along his jaw, over the hard stubble. It stung and she licked away the pain, tasting heated male skin. Maggie swiped her tongue along the smoothness of his full bottom lip.

A rush of warm breath greeted her. She pushed to her tiptoes and with an unnerving boldness, covered his lips with hers. She explored the recesses of his mouth, seeking him, craving him. He responded, and their mouths collided in a heart-stopping kiss. Then Landon tore free and pushed her away.

"Maggie, stop." His voice was laced with desperation.

Dazed, she rocked back on her heels. The only thing keeping her from stumbling was his tight hold on her hips. "What?"

"You shouldn't kiss me like that."

She looked up, gulping air as she struggled to catch her breath. Damn his hat! She couldn't see his face, but felt his eyes boring into her. "W-why?"

"I'm not into gratuitous sex."

Shocked, she stared at him. "What?"

"You know. I saved your daughter's life. Now you feel obligated—"

"Stop right there." Her hands clutched the front of his shirt. "If you think I want—I kissed you because of what you did today, you're wrong."

His mouth flattened. "Am I?"

"Yes. Landon, I want—my kissing you has nothing to do with saving Anna. I kissed you because of the way you make me feel. Dammit, *because* you make me feel."

He stepped forward, bringing his body back in contact with hers. "Is that all you want, Maggie? Kisses?"

She could see his dark eyes now and the array of emotions swirling there. Desire. Need. Passion. It'd been years since she'd seen this kind of naked yearning in a man's eyes. Not because of a husbandly obligation, or a desire for her land. But because he wanted her.

A tremor of fear coursed through her. She didn't know if she was ready for this. A moment ago, she was running on pure emotion, a need to be in this man's arms. What would tomorrow hold if they took this step tonight?

"Come on, Maggie." He moved closer, pressing her against the stair railing. He dipped his head and trailed his lips from her forehead to her cheek. "Say it. Tell me what you want."

She threw all her doubts aside. "You. I want you."

Landon swallowed the last of her declaration with his kiss.

She wanted him. And he wanted her.

Her hands clutched at his shoulders as she returned his deepening kiss. He tightened his arms in a vise-like grip, needing to get her closer. It wasn't enough.

She was trying to undo his shirt with desperate, frantic movements. But he refused to allow the rest of their bodies to separate. The feel of her cradled between his thighs, against his erection, sent sky-rockets exploding deep inside.

Her fingers yanked at the collar, and her gasp of surprise at how easy the materials parted made him chuckle.

"Snaps, darling," he whispered against her lips. "Go ahead, give it a tug."

Maggie complied and his shirt flew open. The

cool night air hit the heat of his skin. Then the warmth of her touch from his collarbone to the too-tight waistband of his jeans sent his blood pounding through his veins.

"My turn." His fingers went to the top button of her shirt.

"Careful, cowboy. Those are regular buttons," she whispered, while laying soft kisses on his chest.

"I'll figure it out." His fingers fumbled with the first button and again with the second. Hell, it had been years since he'd taken off a woman's clothes. Years since he had been with a woman.

So why now? Why her?

He was saved from answering when Maggie's hands brushed his away. He watched as she undid the buttons herself. The familiar smells of her hard work at the bar drifted from her warm skin, not completely masking the fresh linen scent that was uniquely hers.

She hesitated after the last button, making no move to part her shirt. "Ah, it's…it's been a long time. I haven't done anything like this since my marriage ended. Long before my marriage ended, actually."

A territorial thrill he had no right to feel raced through Landon. He'd wondered if loneliness and need had caused her to find comfort in another's arms after her ex had walked out. The fact she hadn't made his mouth go dry.

"Me, too, darling." He captured her face in his hands, and kept his gaze locked with her. He lowered his head, mixing kisses with his words. "Me, too."

There was surprise in her bright-green eyes as his mouth covered hers in a carnal kiss. Her hands dropped to his hips, her fingers caressing him. He peeled her shirt off her shoulders and pulled it away to see full breasts covered in white cotton.

"I know, it's nothing fancy." The tips of her fingernails bit into his skin as she tightened her grip. "It's plain, serviceable—"

"Perfect." Landon dropped his hands to her waist and lifted Maggie until she stood on the first step of the stairs. "You're perfect."

She grabbed his biceps, unable to raise her hands any higher, her shirt pinning her arms to her side. He let go long enough to push back the brow of his Stetson, his eyes never leaving the deep shadow of her cleavage. Thanks to the step, he had only to bend his head a little to place his mouth on the soft skin. His fingers wrapped around her back, while his thumbs brushed up and down her stomach from the waistband of her skirt to the underside of her breasts. Her heart beat wildly beneath his lips. He kissed a trail to her collarbone, loving how she bent toward him, her hair creating a curtain of privacy.

Was this happening? Did he have this woman—this responsive, amazing, beautiful woman in his arms? She arched into him, a low moan escaping when he covered her breasts with his hands. He swallowed the sound when he kissed her again.

She wanted to touch him. Everywhere. But all she could do was hold on as a whirl of emotions and long-unfed desires whipped her into a summertime storm, complete with thunder-like rumbles and rushing winds. The weight of his hands on her, the callused tips of his fingers as he traced the upper edge of her bra, sent an electric fizz zipping over her skin. His palms cupped and caressed while his mouth ravaged her in an endless kiss. His fingers moved upward, following the path of her bra straps. Her stomach clenched. He worked his way beneath the straps then inched them from her shoulders.

Whistling invaded her ears, an out-of-tune warble of a classic love-gone-wrong song.

Maggie tore her mouth from his. "Ohmigod, do you hear that?"

"What?" Landon's chest rose and fell, his words punched out between deep, gutted breaths.

"Whistling. Do you hear it?" Realization dawned. "Willie! He's heading in here!"

The creak of the barn door sounded like a shotgun to Maggie. Suddenly Landon lifted her into his arms. "Landon! What are you—"

"Shhh."

He took the stairs to the loft two at a time and rounded the corner, stepping into the darkness as Willie appeared below. Lowering her feet to the ground, he pressed her against the rough-hewn post at the landing. "We can't be seen," he whispered.

His body blocked her view, but Maggie could hear Willie's chatter below as he discovered Landon's horse back in its stall. "Let me go talk to him," she whispered back. "I don't want—"

"What's the matter, Maggie?" Landon moved closer, his body hard against hers. She could hear the teasing in his hushed voice. "Never been caught necking in the hayloft?"

"No, and I don't want to start now."

She tried to ignore the heat of his bare skin and the clean, manly smell of him mixed with the scent of fresh hay. Moonlight streamed through the open loft door, but here in the shadows it was dark. The feel of his lips on her neck made her jump, and his touch, high on her thighs beneath her skirt, forced a low, deep moan. "Landon!"

"Shhh, you don't want to be discovered. Remember?" His tongue teased her ear, leaving a wet heat on the edge.

Maggie tilted her head to the side and closed her eyes. She struggled between letting this wonderful craziness continue and doing the right thing. "I still think—"

Before she could finish, Landon stripped her shirt from where it hung at her elbows. Shocked, her eyes flew open in time to see it sail into the dark corner of the loft.

"You think too much. How about just feel, Maggie?" His soft words floated over her. His hands caressed her bare skin from her shoulders to her fingertips. "Feel my lips on your face, my hands on your skin."

He dropped his hands again to her legs and lifted her skirt. His fingers curled around the back of her thighs and pressed his erection against her. "Feel what you do to me."

Maggie let his words wash over her. Delving her fingers into his damp hair, she pulled his mouth to hers, feeling his smile against her lips. Seconds later, she grabbed his Stetson and it, too, sailed across the loft.

"Hey!"

"Shhh." She repeated his words back to him, wishing she could see his face. "You think too much, too."

"That was the best thing you could think to remove?" he groaned, his fingers pressing into her flesh when Maggie's hips rotated against him.

"I want to see your face."

Landon stilled. "It's too dark up here."

"Not for this," she replied, fingers dancing over his forehead, outlining his brows and running over the hard planes of his cheeks. She traced his lips and he nipped at her finger, then soothed the bite with the tip of his tongue.

A snap sounded in the main barn and everything went dark. The creak of the barn door closing told her Willie had left. "Ah, it looks like we're alone again."

"Good."

Landon crashed his mouth on hers. Maggie tasted desperation in his kiss. A swirl of questions invaded her head, but she shut them out and focused on her body and soul. And what this one-of-a-kind cowboy was doing to both.

He didn't want to talk.

He didn't want to think.

He only wanted this woman. All of her.

A fine sheen of sweat broke out over his skin. He didn't know if it was from the summer heat or from having Maggie in his arms. He eased his kiss—the last thing he wanted was to hurt her—but she dug her fingertips into his shoulders and urged him onward.

Unable to stop the desire roaring inside, Landon ravished her mouth. He pulled her closer, his hands pushing her skirt higher until he cupped the bare skin of her backside.

Whoa, he never expected that.

His fingers outlined the barely-there pieces of silky string and a patch of lace. After seeing her bra, he'd figured on the same white cotton. Not that he had a problem with it. Hell, this woman could make a potato sack sexy. A groan ripped from his mouth, and the need to breathe made him pull back.

"Okay, so now you know my secret," Maggie panted, her words hot against his skin.

"You wear these all the time?" he asked.

"I threw out my plain granny-panties the day I signed my divorce papers." She kissed his neck, shoulders and chest. "Helps remind me I'm a woman while I'm mucking out stalls and chasing after horses."

She dragged his shirt over his shoulders, and he reluctantly let her go so she could tug it down his arms. It dropped to the ground. Her hands returned to his body, her blunt nails scraping against his muscles. They caught on his nipples, and a loud hiss escaped his lips.

"You like that?" she asked, repeating the movement, nicking the small nubs as she rained kisses on his chest.

"Yeah, I like it," he replied, one hand cupping the back of her head, while the other moved to her back. With a practiced motion, honed ages ago on the rodeo circuit, he released the clasp of her bra. The tentative stroke of her tongue across one of his nipples made him crazy, and he yanked her bra from her arms. She shivered as he dropped it to the floor and pulled her in tight.

"You cold?"

"No, not really…nervous, maybe."

Her soft words tugged at his heart. It was dark where they stood in the loft, more so now with the light shut off. It was hard to see her. And he wanted to. Wanted to see every inch of her. But first, he wanted her to be sure about this.

No man ever died from not finishing what he'd started, even if the ache took forever to go away. Hell, he'd never forced a woman, no matter how long it'd been. He needed to make sure this was what she truly wanted.

He bent, grabbed his shirt and shook it out. Pulling in a deep breath, he wrapped it around Maggie's shoulders, helping her to slide her arms into the sleeves. He pulled it closed over her breasts, his heart stopping in his chest when his hands brushed against her lush curves.

"Landon? What are you doing?"

"Taking a deep breath." He tried to smile, then realized it didn't matter. She couldn't see his face. He gave her fingers a squeeze. "Taking a few deep breaths."

"You're stopping?"

Was that disappointment in her voice? "We need a minute—"

"You've changed your mind." Her voice fell away and he could tell she'd dropped her chin to her chest. "You don't want me. I get it."

Anger surged through him. What in the hell was she talking about? How could she honestly think that? He grabbed her hand and gently pressed it over the rigid flesh straining against his jeans. "Not want you? Does this feel like a man who doesn't want you?"

Cradling her chin with his other hand, he forced her to look at him. Damn, he needed her to see his face. He rubbed his thumb back and forth across her lips, then gave in to the need to kiss her doubts away. He pressed his mouth to hers, easily pushing past her lips to deepen the kiss.

Maggie responded instantly, returning his kiss with a matched eagerness. She fervently stroked him through his jeans. Then her hands went to his waistband, and she tugged on the top button. It gave way. Seconds later, two more followed.

Landon tore his mouth from hers, his breath coming in harsh gasps. He rested his forehead against her. She freed the last few buttons. His hands met hers as they moved to the elastic waist of his briefs.

"I need to know you want this," he panted, "that you're sure."

"I want this, Landon." She punctuated each word with a tug on his jeans. They slid from his waist to his hips.

His knees buckled at the delicate touch of her fingertips as they inched inside his briefs. She reached low and captured him in the palm of her hand. Then she released him and skimmed the sides of his body until she wrapped her hands around his neck.

"I'm sure."

He pulled her hard against him. Her skin melted into his and he backed her farther into the loft among the towering stacks of hay.

He stopped when they were bathed in moonlight, and with one hand, forced her to look at him. "Say it again."

"I want this," she repeated, looking at him. "I want you."

Her blond hair, silver in the moonlight, shaded her eyes. But not enough to hide her certainty. Along with something else. He didn't have time to decipher it before she closed her eyes and arched her back, her breasts sliding over his skin. "Landon, please..."

He caught her plea in a quick kiss, then bent and captured the beaded tip of one breast in his mouth. He suckled, nipped and wet it with the heat of his tongue. His hands pushed her skirt up to her waist, covering the tight perfection of her backside. She rocked against him, hot and wet through the scrap of lace covering her.

He needed that wetness on his hands, his fingers inside her.

They tangled in the strings of her panties, and he pushed the lace aside, his thumb exploring the soft curls until he found her center. The slightest pressure brought forth a sweet moan from Maggie and both their knees buckled.

He released her nipple with a reverent kiss. He had to get them horizontal. "I don't know how soft the hay is—"

"Behind you," Maggie gasped, pushing at his shoulders. "A horse blanket."

Landon turned. The faded quilt lay over a short stack of hay. He pulled her to the bale and tumbled down, tugging her with him.

She grabbed his shoulders as he pulled her onto his lap. With a hushed squeal, her knees collapsed, the toes of her boots catching at the edge of the hay bale. "Landon, I'm going to fall."

"No way," he growled against her skin as he caught her, his mouth caressing the swell of her breasts. "I won't let you."

Too late.

She'd already fallen hard and fast. There was nothing she could do to stop it. And she didn't want to. She had no idea what was going to happen after tonight, and—for once—it was okay she didn't care. She was determined to live in the here and now, in this moment, with this man.

Maggie stretched higher, cradling Landon's head in her hands. He covered her breasts in more wet kisses and his fingers continued to caress her. She trembled under his touch, her breath disappearing from her lungs. The cotton material of his shirt clung to her sweat-dampened skin. She wanted it off, but at the same time loved the feel of it wrapped around her. The denim of his jeans scraped her inner thighs.

When he slid one finger deep inside her, she arched off his lap. Her body convulsed and a tightening curled in her chest, ready to explode. It had been so long. She wasn't going to last.

She forced Landon to look at her. "No, not like this."

"Yes." His lips brushed over hers. "Yes, like this."

Her fingers gripped the powerful muscles of his shoulders. It was too potent, too overwhelming, but every inch of her body reveled in it. She'd never felt this way before. Strong and weak, generous and needy. She wanted to give all of herself and take everything. His lips left a trail of kisses over her collarbone, his uneven breaths matching hers. He found his way back to her mouth. His tongue stroking and demanding, mimicking his fingers on the most intimate part of her, creating a burning intensity that rose higher and higher, thrusting her to the edge of a cavernous void.

Then his hand was gone and he filled her with his hard length in one smooth motion. She had no idea how he'd managed it, but he was inside her. His arms encircling her, his kiss swallowing her cries when she shattered around him. She tore her mouth from him, her head dropping back as her body leapt into the emptiness to find it filled with explosions of fire and heat.

She welcomed his commanding thrusts, and his raw, passion-filled moans thrilled her inexperienced heart. He drove them deeper into a passionate haze until his guttural groan filled the air and he found his own release. Shivers, sparked by uncontrollable joy, danced along her skin. Catching her breath was impossible until the wild race of her heart slowed to a powerful thump, thump, thump. She cradled his head in her arms and dropped a tender kiss on his sweat-soaked forehead.

He pulled her close, then stilled. His viselike grip on her back eased.

"I..." Chest heaving, he struggled to catch his breath. "I guess this is where...where I should apologize."

# *Chapter 13*

Maggie went still in his arms. Then she was off his lap in a shot. She yanked her skirt down around her sexy backside and silky thighs before finding her shirt and bra.

He licked his suddenly dry lips. "Let me explain—"

"Not necessary," Maggie interrupted. "I think your need to apologize says enough."

Damn, how could she walk? He couldn't even stand—his legs were like jelly. Settling instead for tucking himself back into his briefs, he managed to get his jeans up to where they belonged. He stopped fighting with his fly to grab her as she marched past him.

He forced her to sit on the bale of hay and knelt at her feet. "Maggie—"

"No explanation needed." Avoiding his eyes, she

grabbed at the shirt she still had on—*his shirt*—and pulled it tight over her breasts. "I get it."

"No, you don't. I know what's running through your head, and you can stop right now."

"You have no idea what I'm—"

"I didn't use protection."

Maggie froze. The clothing in her hands fell to her lap, eyes wide.

Damn, damn, and double damn!

This wasn't like him. Since his first time, barely into his teens, he'd never forgotten. Hell, it was years before he knew what it felt like to be inside a woman, flesh to flesh.

Landon stood up. He realized he had Maggie's torn panties in his grasp and shoved them in his pocket then backed away. Her eyes followed his every move.

A sudden desire to find his hat filled him. He spotted it nearby, grabbed it and shoved on his head. "I'm sorry, it never crossed—but you don't have to worry. About me, I mean. I meant it when I said it's been a while. I'm clean. I got a complete physical before I got—" He saw the shadow of a smile on her face. "Are you laughing at me?"

"No." Her gaze flew to his. "No, I would never laugh. I thought… So, you weren't going to apologize because I wasn't—because it wasn't good?"

"Maggie, it was so good, I'm already hard again."

Desire flashed in her eyes.

Landon yanked his hat farther down his forehead, not wanting her to see the same mirrored in his. "But that's not important—"

"It's okay."

"You're damn right it was. Better than okay."

"I mean *it's* okay. You don't have to worry about me getting preg—" One hand flattened low over her belly, the other fisted at her side, bunching the faded quilt. "I'm on birth control."

A one-two sucker punch crashed into Landon, knocking all the air from his lungs. An image flashed in his head. Maggie pregnant with their baby. His child growing inside her.

No.

He slammed his eyes closed, shattering the picture into a thousand pieces. Another child was the last thing he needed. Or wanted. He'd already learned his lesson, in the most gut-wrenching way possible. He wasn't cut out to be a father. He never wanted to be responsible for another human life ever again.

"Landon?"

He jerked when the warmth of her hand landed against his bare skin. He opened his eyes to find her standing in front of him. Her other hand held the quilt tight around her shoulders. It covered her completely from her chin to her boots. His body blocked the moonlight, leaving her face in shadow.

"Did you hear what I said?" she asked.

Her words blew hot across his skin, and his need for this woman roared back to life. He jammed his hands into his back pockets to keep from reaching for her. "Ah, yeah…birth control. I heard you."

She nodded, her long hair, mussed from his hands, swaying against her cheeks. "You don't have to worry about the other thing. I'm clean, too. I mean,

I haven't been with anyone since Al—after I learned about my ex's numerous affairs. I made sure I got tested."

A rage, nothing to do with sexual want, pressed hard in his stomach. "Your ex is the biggest jackass in the county. Hell, the whole state of Wyoming."

A smile came to her full lips. "You know, talk like that will get you..." Her voice held a teasing hint before it trailed off.

"What?" Landon pushed her jerk of an ex-husband from his mind. He took a step toward her, forcing her to tilt her head back in order not to break eye contact. "What will I get, Miss Maggie?"

Her shoulder squared and she lifted her chin. "Me. Again. Now. If you want—"

He whipped his hands out from behind him to cup her face, his kiss cutting off her words. *He did want.*

He pushed his tongue past her open lips, the heat inside adding to his spiraling need for this woman. She stilled under his assault and he immediately pulled back. The last thing he wanted was to scare her.

Sipping softly at the outer corners of her lips, he struggled to clamp down on his intense passion. He had no idea where it came from. He should tell her no. He should walk away.

He couldn't.

"I want you," he whispered, the hoarseness in his voice betraying his hunger. "Again. I want to lay with you between the cool sheets in that big old brass bed. I want to feel your body draped over mine. I want to be so deep inside you, we won't be able to tell where I end and you begin."

She swayed into him and he scooped her into his arms, blanket, clothes and all, and started for the loft stairs.

"I can walk, you know." She released the blanket, letting it fall from her shoulders as she wrapped her arms around his neck.

Her shirt parted and the feel of her breasts against his chest made him almost miss the last step. He tightened his hold as they exited the barn, thankful the moon had skipped behind the clouds.

"I can walk faster," he said roughly.

He wasn't sure, but Landon thought he'd felt her lips curve into a smile against his neck.

Maggie snuggled into the pillow. She pulled in a deep breath, filling her head with the sexy smell of pure man. The man beside her asleep on his stomach, his face half hidden by the silkiness of his hair.

She smiled. His scent covered her everywhere. Her hair, her skin—

She closed her eyes and relived the past hours with him, making love in the hayloft and twice more after they got to the cabin. The memory of the passion between them caused her to shiver. She burrowed beneath the sheets, blaming the cool breeze that came through the window.

Maggie opened her eyes again, noticing how the light of the coming dawn was slowly chasing away the darkness. She should get back to the main house. But she didn't want to leave. Not yet.

She concentrated on Landon again. Using her fingertips, she traced the corded muscles of his bicep, followed the hills and valleys to the bend of his elbow. She moved to his back, his strength evident even as he slept, her fingers slipping toward his tapered waist. The hard ridge of puckered scar tissue made her pause. Tears filled her eyes as his words returned to her.

*A fire.*

*Wife and d-daughter trapped inside.*

*They died.*

*My fault.*

Her eyes overflowed and the tears ran down her cheek, disappearing into the fabric of the pillowcase. He'd been hurt trying to save them. The thought of losing her family stabbed Maggie deeply.

How had he survived? Was he still in pain?

Of course he was.

Flashes from the past few weeks filled her head. The morning he'd fallen to his knees after fixing her corral. The stiffness in his walk after he saved Hank. The time he'd stumbled after his sudden rise from the porch. It had nothing to do with the beers he'd drunk and everything to do with scars her fingers massaged.

"Don't."

Maggie's gaze flew to Landon's face. His eyes remained closed, mouth pulled tight. "Am I hurting you?"

After a long moment, he shook his head.

She rose on one elbow, holding the sheet to her breasts. Leaning closer, she kneaded the inflexible scars. They stood out against the darkness of his skin, but she could tell they weren't new.

How long had he carried the physical and psychological pain of that horrific night?

"Tell me," she whispered, refusing to let him pull away despite his attempts. Moving the sheet low on his hips, she continued to stroke his skin, feeling the hard muscles beneath begin to respond. "Please, tell me what happened to you…to them."

Long minutes passed before he spoke. "After my parents died, I was in charge of running my family's ranch—"

"Still Waters." Maggie's breath caught as she realized the ranch his brother worked for, one of the biggest and most profitable in Texas, belonged to Landon. To him and his family.

He nodded and continued, "Business took me away a lot. Meetings, deal making, contracts…hell, I spent more time in office buildings than on the land. And it wasn't going well. The weather, a couple of stupid moves on my part—"

His shoulders expanded as he pulled in a deep breath before slowly releasing it. "To top it off, my so-called marriage wasn't a happy one. We married because of…circumstances, not love. Jenna wanted more of my time than I could give, so she found company elsewhere. Not hard to do on a ranch full of cowboys."

Landon's hands clenched the pillow beneath his head, crushing its softness in his tight grip. "I was going to end it. Then she told me she was pregnant. I didn't know if the baby was mine, and after Sara was born, I insisted on a paternity test. She was a Cartwright. I tried to make the marriage work, but Jenna didn't care…about me or the baby."

Maggie's eyes closed, trapping more tears. Her heart broke for him and his little girl. She didn't want to judge the woman, but how could Landon's wife not be satisfied with him? He was strong and hardworking, patient and kind.

"One night I was late getting home. I saw the fire from the main road. By the time I got there, one of the old horse barns was completely engulfed. My men and I were so busy trying to save the horses and control the flames no one noticed it had spread to the second story of the main house. By the time we did, the top floor was… I raced inside. It took me forever, but I found her…them—"

His voice broke and Landon jerked from the bed.

Maggie's eyes flew open. She watched silently as he yanked open a dresser drawer and pulled out fresh clothes. Pain and sorrow emanated from him as he tugged on his underwear and jeans. She wanted so badly to go to him, to hold him in her arms.

"I am so sorry for your loss," she said, knowing it was inadequate.

"Yeah, my loss." Landon paced in front of the long table separating the main room from the kitchen. "I brought it on myself. I did this!"

"Landon, no!" Maggie grabbed at the T-shirt he'd tossed on the bed. She pulled it over her head, thankful it fell past her naked backside. Turning on the bedside lamp, she went to him. "You can't blame your—"

"I should've been there." He pulled from her touch and walked to the window, his gaze focused on the outside world. "It was my fault. It doesn't matter how it started, or what any damn report said. I was—" He crossed his arms over his chest and faced her, his expression lost in the darkness. "I am responsible."

Maggie ached for him. His grief was so powerful it surrounded him like a living thing, sucking all the life from the room. The tragedy explained so many questions that had been swirling inside her since she'd met him.

Only he wasn't a wandering cowboy, despite what he'd told them about working at other ranches. He was the owner of a spread five times the size of the Crescent Moon, and he'd walked away from it all.

"When did it happen?" she asked.

"Five years ago," he answered in a hushed whisper. "Sara would have been seven come November."

"So you walked away? Left your home?"

His gaze dropped.

She sensed that something deep inside him kept him from telling her the full truth. He'd already said too much. "Yes… and no."

"What does that mean?"

He stared at the floor for a long time then drew in a deep breath before looking at her again. "It means it doesn't matter. It's in the past."

"Landon—"

"Look, you wanted to know about my scars and I told you." His voice became hard. "I've satisfied your curiosity about my past. You know every—all you need to know."

* * *

He heard the words coming from his mouth, and while he silently cursed every one of them, they had to be said.

He couldn't believe he'd spilled his guts to her. What the hell had made him—no, he knew why. Maggie. She was getting too close. Her, her family and this whole damn place.

He moved past her, waving at the rumpled blankets on the bed. "Don't think what happened here changes anything. I made it clear from the beginning this was a temporary job."

Her face paled as she grabbed her clothes and boots and disappeared into the bathroom. Landon cursed. He never should've gone to the barn tonight.

He never should've touched her.

Hell, it was inevitable. He'd known the moment he offered to work here something like it would happen. But a wild, uncontrollable coming together in the hayloft was one thing. Then he'd brought her here, and it had changed from sex to something more. Holding her, loving her, letting her love him. He'd never felt this way in his entire life. And he didn't deserve it.

Plus, Maggie and her family didn't deserve to have an ex-con in their life. Being cleared of the crime didn't free him of the responsibility. He'd failed to protect his family and he could never take that chance again.

Fully dressed, Maggie walked from the bathroom and held out his T-shirt. "Don't worry about the sheets. As you know, we do the laundry around here on Mondays."

He took the shirt. "Maggie—"

"Don't." She stopped at the door, her hand on the knob. "I don't know what switch I pulled or why talking about your past is causing you to be this way—"

Her voice broke, and a hard knot of guilt settled in Landon's stomach. He couldn't stop himself from walking up behind her. The stiffness in her shoulders told him not to touch her. He twisted the shirt in his fists, using every ounce of his resolve to obey.

"I know I should agree with you and say this doesn't change anything between us. Not that there is anything..." Her voice was so low it was barely a whisper.

Landon tried to concentrate on what she was saying, but something—something was wrong. "Maggie, stop talking."

She whirled around. "How dare you—"

Landon silenced her. His head buzzed with memories of that horrific night. That had to be it. That had to be why the crackle of flames filled his ears and a deep breath brought with it the rancid smell of—

*Smoke!*

He pushed her out of the way and yanked open the door, eyes flying over the main house, the barn and bunkhouse. Nothing. He scanned the area again, another deep breath bringing with it the taste and smell of a smoldering fire. The predawn lightening of the sky mixed so well with the swirls of gray and white he missed it the first time.

"The tool shed." He spun around and grabbed

his boots. He pulled them on and yanked the shirt Maggie had worn earlier over his head. "It's on—"

"Fire!"

Willie's hoarse cry carried across the yard. Maggie raced outside, Landon right behind her. He wanted to tell her to stay back, but it would be useless. He watched as Willie, dressed in a wrinkled wife-beater, boxers and boots, grabbed the hose attached to the bunkhouse.

Racing for the hose behind the barn, he gave a quick prayer, thankful the tool shed stood apart from the other buildings. He twisted the spigot and aimed the rushing water at the engulfed structure.

The heat licked at his skin and he was transported instantly to the scorching inferno of another fire. Another night.

He snapped back to the present, and the seductive dance of the flames, twisting and spiraling into the sky, taunted him as they devoured every square inch of the shed. The crackle of the wood jeered his inability to advance, to breathe, to fight back.

He couldn't move.

# *Chapter 14*

"Willie, wet the grass," Maggie yelled, her hands covering Landon's unmoving fingers. She twisted the hose, stealing it from his grasp and shoved him out of the way with her hip.

"Get a shovel from the barn," she shouted over her shoulder. "We need a firebreak to keep from losing the paddocks."

She stared into his wide, dark eyes. The fresh memory of what he'd told her about his family was all over his face. Bottomless pain and sadness contorted his features. She hoped he understood the compassion and empathy in hers.

"Go," she added softly. He blinked hard and pulled himself from the blaze's hypnotic hold.

"Don't get too close," he said. "You're not dressed properly—get yourself wet."

Maggie's heart tripped at the concern in his voice. She turned the hose into the air and doused them both with a spray of cold water before directing it at the base of the fire.

Landon ran for the barn, reaching it just as Hank's pickup circled around from the back. "What the damnation is going on?" he asked, hopping from the truck's cab.

"Come with me," Landon commanded.

Within minutes, the two of them emptied the barn, setting the horses loose in the pasture. Then they went to work creating a circle of turned earth around the burning structure, ensuring that it would be the only thing on the ranch consumed by the flames.

Nana B. appeared on the side porch, her arms around Anna, both in their pajamas. Hank took the hose from Willie with orders for him to get inside and get some clothes on his skinny bones.

"Here, give me that." Landon reached for the hose in Maggie's hand.

She stepped away, her gaze focused on the burning embers and spots of flame. "I'm fine. I can do this."

"I know you can." He grabbed the hose. "Please… let me. Besides, I saw Nana B. with the phone to her ear. I bet your friend the sheriff is going to show up any minute."

Maggie looked over at the porch, her heart breaking at the fear on her grandmother's and Anna's faces. She longed to go to them, but she had to be certain Landon was okay, too. "Are you sure?" she asked.

"Yes, I'm sure." His hand covered hers, his touch cool and wet for a moment before he pulled away and took the hose. "It's pretty much under control anyway."

What he said was true. Hank stood on the far side of the structure, still dousing the wood with rushing water. The fire was more smoke than flames now. She could see through the smoldering building to her cowboy's ragged features.

"And you might want to get out of those wet clothes," he said distantly. "Before your grandmother figures out you didn't sleep in them or your own bed last night."

His tone of voice was a stark reminder of what he'd said inside his cabin. He'd shut down, physical and emotionally, for reasons she couldn't comprehend. And now that another crisis had been averted, he was doing it again.

Maggie gave a powerful tug with the crowbar and blinked back the fresh sting of tears. She wouldn't cry. Not out here in broad daylight. At night, alone in her bed, was another story.

It had been three days since the fire. By the time Destiny's volunteer fire department had arrived, the shed was a total loss. Gage had called this morning and confirmed the initial findings. An electrical short in the new wiring. He then gave her the okay to clear the site.

She was determined to start the rebuilding right away. It was going to put a dent in her savings, but she didn't have any choice. Besides, it felt good to destroy what remained of the charred wooden structure. Anna said it was giving her nightmares. Maggie had to admit the blackened skeletal remains made it tough for her to get any rest as well. Better to blame the fire than the real reason for her sleepless nights.

A six-foot walking tower of stone silence.

Landon had gone from passionate lover to distant employee in a matter of just a few hours. She'd tried to find a private moment to talk, but she wasn't sure what she'd say if she found it.

*I'm sorry? Sorry for asking about your past? Sorry for throwing myself in your arms? Sorry for being stupid enough to give my heart to a man who can't—or won't—take it?*

Yes, she'd fallen in love with the wrong man. Again.

A man who'd effectively shut her out, willing to suffer her presence only when she was talking about the ranch. He rarely looked her in the eye, his damn hat always pulled low over his brow. When he spoke, it was all business, with barely a "yes, ma'am" or "no, ma'am" to her questions.

One final tug and the shed's last corner stud fell to the ground at her feet. There. Much better.

Liar.

She didn't have any idea how to make things better. Around the ranch. Or with Landon.

"Lord, it's said you never give a body more than they can handle." Maggie spoke the prayer softly as she added the dead wood to the pile. "But if it's all the same, I think I'm at my limit."

"Excuse me, Miss Maggie?"

Startled, Maggie whirled around at the voice. Surprise filled her at the sight of Spence Wilson and Charlie Bain, her former employees. She hadn't heard the sound of Spence's battered pickup. Both stood with their hats in their hands and sheepish looks on their faces as they tried to keep their gaze off the pile of burnt rubble.

"What are you doing here?" Thankful she'd remembered her bandanna this morning, she used it to erase the moisture from her eyes.

"We've been talking it over and well…these are for you." Spence thrust a bouquet of yellow roses wrapped in green tissue at her.

Maggie dropped the crowbar and grabbed at the flowers before they landed in the dirt. "Oh, ah… thank you."

Spence glanced over at Charlie who looked very interested in the toes of his cowboy boots. "We'd like to come back to the Crescent Moon. If you'll have us."

Maggie gripped the flowers, schooling her features not to reveal her shock. Almost a month since they'd walked out and no one had answered any of her ads. Except for Landon.

She pushed the thought aside. "Why?"

"Greeley's money was nice, but lately we've heard talk. How he's looking to break you and take your land." Spence's gaze shot to the pile of rubble from the shed and then back to Maggie. "What Greeley's doing ain't right, and we don't want any part of it."

"Besides, the cook at the Triple G doesn't come anywhere close to Nana B.'s fixings," Charlie added with a small grin.

Optimism welled inside of her. Spence and Charlie knew how things worked around the ranch. It wouldn't take long for them to learn the changes

Landon made. They could take on some of the heavy work he tended to keep from Hank and Willie.

"We know you got yourself a new foreman," Spence said, putting his hat back on his head. "The place is looking good. But your ads are still up around town, so if you're interested—"

Another truck rounded the corner and pulled to a stop near them. Hank was at the wheel with Willie and Landon next to him. Landon opened the passenger door and stepped out, his gaze firmly planted on Spence and Charlie.

Maggie ignored the crazy jump her heart took at the sight of him, standing there in dusty jeans, sweat-soaked T-shirt and familiar black Stetson.

"What's going on?" he said.

She quickly made introductions, telling herself it didn't matter Landon couldn't look at her.

Willie climbed out of the truck, leaving the passenger door open. "What are you young pups doing here?" he said. "Got yourselves free of Greeley's leash?"

"Spence and Charlie work here…again," Maggie said, pleased to see the happiness on their faces.

"Since when?" Landon asked.

"Since now."

Landon crossed his arms over his chest. His gaze never left the younger men, both of whom tried their best not to squirm under his direct stare.

"Why don't you two go into town with Hank?" Maggie said to Spence and Charlie. "You can put away your gear later."

"Yes ma'am," they said in unison and headed for the pickup.

Willie moved away, but Landon stood his ground, forcing them to walk around him. Irritation cut through Maggie, but she kept her mouth shut until the pickup pulled away and disappeared down the drive.

"Want to explain your behavior?" she demanded.

Landon remained silent. A muscle twitched in his cheek.

"That is, if you can put together more than a two-word sentence."

Willie ducked his head and headed for the barn. "I think I'll find something to keep me busy."

"Well?" Maggie asked, after Willie was out of earshot.

"You sure about this?"

*Wow. Four words strung together.* She struggled to rein in her temper, knowing her reasons for being angry with Landon went much deeper than the way he was questioning her hiring skills.

"Yes. I've known those guys a long time and they're good people. I'm glad to have them back because now I can concentrate on Black Jack."

"I thought things were going okay with the beast."

"They are—they were—before the fire. He's been a bit skittish since then. It's gonna take some time for him to trust me again." Maggie knew she was talking about Landon as much as the horse. Would he see that?

He nodded. "You've been busy this morning."

"Gage called. He said the fire was due to faulty wiring. They're sending a report to the manufacturer." She had to make sure Landon didn't think this was his or Willie's mistake. "I know you two installed it, but it passed inspection."

"I'm sorry about the fire."

"It's nobody's fault."

"I know." Landon paused. "You want it rebuilt right away?"

"Yes, especially now with Spence and Charlie back." Maggie waved the flowers at the bunkhouse. "Keeping the tools in the bunkhouse was a temporary solution, and with three full-time cowboys living there now—"

"Temporary isn't going to work, is it?"

She stopped and looked at him. "No, it isn't."

"Maggie—"

A Jeep rounded the corner and pulled into the drive, cutting off whatever Landon was going to say. The sheriff's emblem on the door gleamed in the bright sunlight. It came to a stop near the house and Leeann stepped out, dressed in her summer khaki uniform.

"You were saying?" Maggie pushed.

"You've got company." Landon turned and headed for the cabin.

"What in tarnation are you doing?"

Landon paused at the sound of Willie's voice then continued to shove his clothes into the duffel bags on the bed. "Packing."

"So I see." The old cowboy leaned against the doorway. "What I can't figure out is why."

"It's time I was moving on."

"Mov—you're leaving?"

He ignored Willie's surprised look and headed for the bathroom to gather his stuff. Toothbrush, toothpaste, shaving cream—he refused to allow his eyes to stray to the shower. Hell, it didn't matter. Every morning and every night, he stood there, icy water raining down his body. He'd hoped it would stop the memory of him and Maggie showering together that night, enveloped in a world of steam, soap suds and sex.

It didn't. Nothing did.

He returned to the main room, not surprised to see the old cowboy still there. "I thought you had something to do in the barn?"

"Seems I've got my work cut out for me right here, dealing with a stubborn jackass." Willie slammed the door shut behind him. "What in hell's bells do you think you're doing?"

"What I have to." He shoved the items in one of his bags, his fingers colliding with the cell phone. He was out of minutes after Bryce's last call yesterday. He'd relayed pretty much the same information Maggie had told him the night they'd shared a beer on the cabin's front porch. Greeley was a weasel of a man, but he wasn't into anything illegal. In fact, he'd backed off lately on bothering Maggie altogether. "Things are running fine here and with those two returning cowboys, you've got plenty of help. You don't need me anymore."

"Bull-hockey."

"This was temporary. I took the job to help G.W. and fill in while Hank healed. Both are doing well. It's time to move on."

Landon was surprised to feel Willie's hand on his shoulder. "You can't outrun it, boy. Take it from someone who knows."

His hands stilled over the bags, and he was glad

Willie stood behind him. "I don't know what you're talking about."

"Yes, you do, son. I've been where you are, done what you're doing."

Landon looked up. In the reflection of the dresser's mirror, he watched Willie walk to the kitchen table, and stop, his battered cowboy hat in his hands.

"When I got back from Korea, I walked away from my schooling and a pretty young thing wearing a promise ring. I couldn't get what I'd seen over there out of my head." The natural grittiness of the old man's voice faded to a rough whisper. "The faces of those young boys, their desperate cries for help, the smell of death—whoever said 'war is hell' knew what he was talking about. Living with the hell afterwards…that's the real trick. After all these years, I still sometimes wake up reaching for my medical kit."

Landon dropped his gaze. The bags blurred and he had to swallow hard. "Does it ever go away?"

"Nope. But you find your way. You learn to live with it."

"That's what I'm doing." Landon cleared his throat when his words came out with a rough edge. "Learning to live with it."

"Don't wait too long to get it figured out, boy. I went back East a decade later, but life had moved on without me."

Landon turned around. "You're happy here, aren't you? With your life?"

"Sure am, being a cowboy is the life I was meant to live." Willie slammed his hat back on his head.

"But there were times when I'd think about—" The old man rubbed his hand across the gray whiskers on his chin. "Sometimes memories are good friends, and sometimes they'll rub ya raw over what might've been."

"Do me a favor, will you? Hitch the trailer to my truck?" Without waiting for an answer, Landon went back to his packing. Soon, the clomping of boots told him Willie was heading for the door.

"You best not drive out of here without saying goodbye," Willie said. "She deserves that much."

Which *she* was the old man referring to? Nana B.? Anna? Maggie?

All three had found their way into his heart. A heart that didn't have room. All of them, especially Maggie, deserved so much more. He wasn't the man to give it to her. Not now. Not ever.

"How well do you know this new cowboy of yours?"

The coffee mug shook as Maggie handed it to Leeann. She'd been surprised when her friend said she was here on official business. Maggie had ushered her into the house, glad her grandmother and Anna were shopping in Cheyenne.

"Why are you asking?" She busied herself with putting the yellow roses Spence had given her in a glass vase. She cursed her shaking hands and placed the flowers in the center of the kitchen table. "I told you last week at lunch how great he's been around here."

"I know you did." Leeann took a seat at the kitchen

table. "Right after you told me how he stepped in when Kyle Greeley was giving you a hard time at the fair and how he saved Anna from that wild horse, but that's not what I'm asking. What do you know about his past? Where he came from? Where he worked before showing up in Destiny?"

Maggie grabbed her own coffee mug. "He gave me a list of references."

"Which you never called."

She bit her bottom lip before answering. "How do you know that?"

Leann sighed. "I know you. Despite your jerk of a father and an ex-husband who couldn't keep his pants zipped, you're still the most trusting woman in the county."

Her friend's words stuck hard. "Don't be shy, Lee. Tell me how you really feel."

"I feel like you're being taken for a ride, Maggie. I know things have worsened since Alan took off. Your ongoing war with Greeley over cowboys is the least of it, but you hire this total stranger and allow him to take over the running of the Moon?"

"Hey, I run the Moon."

"You said yourself he's come up with some great ideas—"

"He has, but nothing was put in place without my approval."

"And where do you think he got those great ideas?" Leeann pulled in a deep breath and set the mug on the table. She laid her hand on the folder in front of her. "I've got the official report for the fire here. You're going to need it for your insurance company. There's also a background check on Landon Cartwright."

Maggie set her mug on the table hard. "What?"

"It's standard procedure. We ran it when he and Willie reported their suspicions about Hank's wagon."

"You told me it was an accident."

"It was, but the report on Cartwright was misfiled. I found it today." Leeann opened the folder. "Do you know he's a one-third owner of a ranch in Texas called—"

"Still Waters."

Leeann looked up. "He told you?"

Maggie nodded, her hand gripping the back of the chair. "Yes. He arranged a horse sale to his brother, who runs the ranch."

"And you don't think it strange the man is working a thousand miles away from his home—" she paused to look over the report "—a place five times the size of the Crescent Moon, as a hired hand?"

"He told me—" A loud knocking on the back door interrupted Maggie. She answered it, surprised to see Kyle Greeley and two men standing there. "Kyle, I don't have time for a visit now."

"You better make time. I need to talk to you."

"If this is about my cowboys walking out on you, there's nothing to discuss," Maggie said, fuming. "It's a free country and men can work for whomever they want."

"This isn't about them. It's about you. And Cartwright."

Maggie's hand fell away from the doorjamb. "You, too?"

Kyle stepped inside, pausing to send away his men with a quick jerk of his head before closing the door. "What does that mean?"

"Nothing." She watched Leeann rise from the table. "As you can see I've got company. Can you make this quick?"

Kyle nodded at Leeann. "Deputy Harris."

"Greeley." Her voice held a bitter edge, her mouth pulled into a thin-lipped smile.

Maggie went back to the table, grabbed her mug and tossed its contents into the sink. "What do you want, Kyle?"

"I have some information on Cartwright you need to know."

Maggie crossed her arms over her chest. "I know all I need to." *Or I will once I get my hands on the folder.* What more could they tell her? She already knew the most horrific aspects of Landon's life.

"He's married," Kyle said.

How does he know that? "No, he's not. His wife and daughter died in a fire five years ago."

"A fire he was convicted of setting."

Shock flew through her. She was barely able to control her gasp at the bombshell. It mutated into denial. "No, you're wrong."

Leeann moved to her side. "Maggie—"

Kyle took a step toward her. "I'm not wrong. I'm telling you this because I'm worried, and with the fire—I know you hired him to be spiteful. He's a smooth talker. I was fooled, too, but you need—"

"No," Maggie repeated and backed away from his outstretched hand. Her mind raced with Landon's words. *His responsibility. His fault.* "I can't—"

"The conviction was manslaughter," Kyle continued. "You don't want his kind around your family. Let me take care of this. I'll get him off your land—"

"Maggie, listen to me." Leeann stepped in front of Kyle, cutting off his words. "It's true, but there's more you need to know—"

"That's all she needs to know," Kyle bellowed. "She needs to throw that felon off her land."

Leeann whirled around, and jabbed at Kyle's chest with her finger. "I think you should leave. You've accomplished what you've set out to do here."

"Hey, I'm trying to help."

"No, you're not," Leeann said. "You want me to make this official, fine. Kyle Greeley, you need to leave this property right now or I'll arrest you for trespassing."

Maggie shook her head and moved away from them. "Both of you get out. This can't be true. It can't be."

"It is."

Her head whipped around. Landon stood there, his black hat cradled in his hands.

"It's true, Maggie. All of it."

# *Chapter 15*

"Leeann, Kyle." Maggie's voice was soft. "I think it's best if you leave now. Don't ask me if I'm sure, because I am."

"I'm not going anywhere," Kyle sputtered.

A heated flash sparked in Landon's eyes, but he didn't look away from her. "Deputy Harris," she began, praying no one noticed the wobble in her voice, "will you please escort Mr. Greeley off my property?"

"Let's go, Kyle," Leeann directed.

Kyle stomped toward the back door, pausing when he neared Landon. "It's all over for you, cowboy."

Landon tightened his grip on his Stetson, but didn't reply.

Leeann gave Kyle a push on his shoulder, forcing

him to move. "If you need anything, Maggie, call me. I won't be far away."

Maggie nodded. They walked out the door, leaving her and Landon in the kitchen.

*He lied to me. He lied to me. He lied to me.*

The words echoed in her head. The room started to spin. She closed her eyes to get her bearings. Bad idea. She swayed and grabbed for the table.

"Maggie—"

Her eyes flew open. Landon had crossed the room in a heartbeat. Her gaze focused on the tanned, smooth column of his throat revealed by the three open buttons of his shirt.

Why would she notice something so simple at a time like this?

"Don't." She backed away. "Don't touch… I… I need a minute…"

No, she needed more. She needed the truth. And air. And space. The kitchen was too confining. Landon filled it completely with his height, his scent and the memories of shared meals with her family.

*Her family. How was she going to explain this to them?*

"Come with me." She headed for the back door. Once outside, she didn't stop until she stood in the cool shade of the cottonwood trees. "Now, I think you owe me an explanation."

"What Greeley told you is true," he said. "I was tried and convicted of second-degree manslaughter and second-degree arson."

Her stomach rolled, and she had to swallow back

a vile taste in her throat. "What exactly does that mean?"

"The fire was my fault."

Jagged pieces of his past fell into place. "That's why you left home four years ago. You haven't been roaming the country. You went to prison."

Landon nodded.

"But now you're out? Those sound like serious charges. How did you—" Maggie stopped when Willie led G.W. out of the barn and tied him to the end of the horse trailer, hitched to the back of Landon's pickup.

*Ohmigod, he's leaving.*

She marched to the truck while Willie made a hasty retreat. Landon's duffel bags were inside. She spun around. "It doesn't matter, does it? That I know the truth. You're leaving."

"It's time for me to go. We both knew this was temporary."

"And temporary isn't going to work anymore?"

She threw his words back at him, pain and anguish tearing at her heart. She'd never hurt like this in her life. Neither her father's harsh child rearing nor Alan's leaving cut as deep as this man's words. It'd taken her a long time to come to terms with her father's lack of parenting skills and realize she had to use her childhood as an example of how not to raise Anna. She'd always be grateful for her daughter, but her shock at Alan's departure had over time boiled down to the belief they'd married too young and it was for the best.

This was, too.

It would take a while—who was she kidding, it would take forever—but she would get this man out of her head and out of her heart.

Maggie suppressed the throbbing pain, allowing rage to take its place—rage at her foolishness for letting this man past her defenses. "So, all you did, all that happened here…it doesn't mean anything to you?"

A muscle twitched along Landon's jaw. His hands curled into tight fists as his dark eyes looked at her. "No."

"Get off my land." Her voice was quiet, but held a cold contempt. "Now."

She pushed past him and headed for the barn. She had to get away from here. A hot rush of tears blinded her as she stumbled toward Black Jack's corral. Thankful to find him fully saddled from their earlier workout, she swung open the gate, jumped on his back and took off.

Landon called out her name, but she didn't stop. She didn't want to hear anything else from him. She couldn't watch him drive away.

Landon had to plant his feet in the dirt to keep from going after her. He'd hurt her. Deeply. He wondered if it matched the bottomless ache in his gut. "Don't think about it," he lectured himself. "You're doing what's best. For her, for everyone."

The sound of a vehicle pulling into the driveway caught his attention. He braced himself before turning around. If it was Maggie's deputy friend, he'd assure her he was on his way out. If it was Greeley, he could do the same thing, but it might include a hard right to the arrogant man's jaw.

"Laudsakes," Nana B. called out from the driver's side of Maggie's truck. "You look like you're heading out of town."

"Yes, ma'am, I am."

The smile fell from her face. "You want to tell me what for?"

"It's time I was moving on."

"Does Maggie know?"

"She knows."

A ball of energy leapt over her grandmother and raced to him. Landon dropped to one knee in time for Anna to rush into his arms. "No, Landon, you can't leave," she cried. "We need you here."

"Out of the mouths of babes," Nana B. muttered, stepping from the truck.

Closing his eyes against the powerful longing that surged inside, Landon found himself holding on to Maggie's little girl when he should be letting her go.

He waited for the ache that would compare this little angel to the daughter he'd lost, but it never came. Over the last few weeks, it had slowly ebbed away with each moment spent with Anna. He was dangerously close to letting her, and her mother, inside the hollow remains of his heart.

That couldn't happen.

"Sorry, Little Bit, but I'm needed elsewhere." He set her away from him. The sight of tears on her cheeks made a hard lump form in his chest. "Besides, you've got all the help you need right here.

Your mom hired back Spence and Charlie this morning, and Hank is right as rain now."

"But I don't want you to go."

Landon rose, clearing his throat. "Well, darling, sometimes we don't get what we want."

"Sometimes a body is too much a fool to see what's right in front of them."

Landon looked at Maggie's grandmother. "This is for the best, Nana B."

"I can't say I agree." Nana B. handed two bags to her great-granddaughter. "Anna, take these into the house, please. I'll be right behind ya. We've got a truck to empty."

"I'm gonna miss you, Landon." Anna took the bags and headed for the porch stairs, her sneakered feet dragging across the dirt. "Real bad."

The lump in his chest moved to his throat. "You take good care of those kittens."

"I will."

Landon turned away to find Nana B. standing there.

"Well, I thank you for all your hard work. And for the sale of our horses to your brother's ranch." Nana B. smiled then continued. "Yes, Maggie told me about you and Still Waters. I hope between the sale and the fees she's pulling in from Black Jack it's enough to keep Greeley happy."

"What are you talking about?"

"Maggie didn't tell you Greeley took over a board position at the bank?"

Landon shook his head.

Nana B. frowned. "Well, maybe it's not my place

to say anything, but hell, I never did learn to hold my tongue. With his position, Greeley has power over the note the bank holds on the ranch. Maggie had to use the land as collateral in order to pay off that good-for-nothing ex-husband of hers."

"She never said anything."

"I understand, but she's been fretting about a final payment—don't you never mind." She waved her words away and grabbed a box from the truck's back seat. "You've got your own plans."

"Need any help with that?" he asked.

"You best head out now you've said your good-byes." She looked at him. "It will break her heart more, the longer you stick around."

Landon was surprised to see tears in her eyes. He knew Maggie would tell her what she'd learned about him. There'd be no tears then. She'd be happy he was out of her granddaughter's life. "Take care of her, of them."

Nana B. nodded. He leaned inside the truck, pulled out the last half-dozen bags and followed her onto the porch and set the bags inside.

"Thank you, Landon," she said, without looking at him. "Now, shoo."

"Yes, ma'am."

He went to G.W., pausing to take what would be his last look around the Crescent Moon. It was a different place than a month ago. He'd had a hand in the ranch coming back to life, and it was a good thing. He was confident things were moving in the right direction for Maggie and her land.

Greeley notwithstanding. Landon didn't think he

could take over the Moon just because he was part of the bank's board of directors. Of course, if Greeley had them in his back pocket—

*Knock it off! It doesn't matter. You can't be what Maggie and her family need. Besides, you were told by the boss woman herself to get off her land.*

A racing pile of dust coming in from the back pasture caught his eye. Someone was riding fast, too fast. It had to be Maggie. Guess he didn't get out of here quick enough to suit her. He yanked on G.W.'s rope. Ten minutes, fifteen tops. Then he'd be gone.

What the hell?

The horse got closer, its path uneven, as if—dammit!

Fear, harsh and vivid, raced through his veins. He ran to the corral as Black Jack raced by the barn. He stepped in front of the horse and waved his hands in the air. "Whoa, boy, easy there, easy."

The horse reared backward. The sight of the empty saddle sent a riot of panic inside Landon. He forced it back. "Easy, Black Jack, calm down. No one's going to hurt you."

Sweat soaked the animal, and he noticed a trail of dark liquid coming from beneath the saddle. Blood. Black Jack darted past him. Landon lunged for the reins, allowing the horse to drag him toward the corral.

Once the stallion was inside, Landon slammed the gate closed. "Willie! Nana B.!"

Both came running.

"Call the sheriff and the vet." He rushed back to his trailer and easily leapt on G.W.'s bare back.

"Maggie took off on Black Jack, but something went wrong. I'm going after her."

"I'll go with ya," the old cowboy said.

"No. Black Jack means everything to Maggie, and he's hurt bad. Take care of the horse. I'll take care of Maggie."

He didn't stick around to see if they'd listened. He didn't have time. Two quick nudges into G.W.'s flank was all the animal needed. The horse took off, and Landon was thankful for the halter and lead rope. They raced off in the direction Black Jack had come.

Where was she? The Crescent Moon had over twenty thousand acres. She could be anywhere. He followed the trail the horse had left, praying the beast hadn't gone off on a wild tear through the countryside. Landon urged G.W. faster, his gaze moving back and forth between the ground and the horizon, praying he'd come across a pissed-off Maggie walking back to the house.

Nothing.

He realized they were heading to the northwest section of the ranch, an area that ran into the foothills of the Laramie Mountains. One of Willie's stories filled his head. How, when Maggie would run off as a child, she'd always head for the dense, cool forest of the foothills.

Had she gone that way again?

G.W. slowed as the low, scraggy shrubs gave way to towering ponderosa pines and sprawling junipers. Landon checked his watch. Twenty minutes since he'd left the house. Depending on where the sheriff was, it could be another half hour before any help arrived.

He reached for the cell phone in his pocket, then realized he'd left it back in his truck. The walkie-talkie was on the cabin's dresser. Hell, he'd never felt more useless in his life. He had to find her.

G.W. struggled to find solid footing in the soft earth. They made their way up a ragged trail that went to the edge of a ravine, then headed back to where the hills met the flatlands again. The trail wound back to the ravine and away two more times, until they came to the last foothill, the largest so far, with a sharp drop-off at its peak where the ground fell away.

Then he saw it. A straw cowboy hat caught on an outcropping of rocks.

"Maggie!"

He called out again as he slid from G.W.'s back, a sick feeling in his gut as he made his way to the ravine. He flattened his body on the ground, and leaned over the edge. His breath stopped when he spotted Maggie lying motionless ten feet below on a ledge.

"Maggie!" He forced his words from his throat. "Maggie, honey, can you hear me? Maggie?"

Leaving his hat next to hers, he slid over the edge, making his way down the serrated cliff, mindless of the rocks cutting into his skin. Seconds later, he was next to her. He gently turned her face to him and leaned close. Relief filled him as the gentle rush of her breath caressed his cheek.

"Maggie, honey, it's going to be okay. I'm here." Landon spoke softly, his hands checking her arms and legs. "Come on, honey, please wake up."

His fingers brushed her hair off her face then carefully circled her head, encountering a large, wet bump. He pulled back, his hand tangled in blond hair and blood.

*Oh, God.*

He looked up and let out a sharp whistle. He could hear G.W. pawing at the ground in response. "Home," he ordered his horse, and let loose a series of short, shrill blasts. "Home."

After a quick prayer his buddy would both remember the old trick and consider the Moon's barn home, Landon listened as G.W. took off. They had to be out looking for them by now; he hoped they'd find his horse.

He returned his attention to Maggie. The bandanna she usually wore at her wrist was gone. Then he remembered the folded cotton and lace handkerchief in his pocket. The same one Maggie had offered to him the first night they met. He'd meant to return it earlier when he'd gone to the kitchen to tell her goodbye.

"Baby, wake up and show me those pretty green eyes." He pulled the pale blue scrap of cloth from his pocket and held it against her head. "Get angry I'm here, I followed you, anything."

He continued to lean over her, shielding her from the hot sun. "You've got to wake up, Maggie. Your ranch and family can't survive without you. Things are heading in the right direction now. Your cowboys are coming back and you'll have Black Jack eating out of your hand no matter what happened today. All you needed was new ideas and some help..."

The threat of tears choked off his words, but he

pushed through them. "You're the heart and soul of the Moon. This land would be nothing without you."

*I would be nothing.*

It was true. The coincidence of their meeting, of her needing help and his needing to take care of his horse wasn't an accident or a twist of fate. Their meeting had led to him feeling alive, truly alive for the first time in years. The fire at Still Waters had taken more than his family. It had killed his spirit, hardened his heart and blackened his soul. He'd ceased to do more than exist.

Until this woman. Until she, her crazy family and her rundown ranch had found a way to bring him back to life.

"But I can't…no matter how much I want—" He dropped his brow to her forehead. "I can't let myself love you…"

The thunder of hoofs and people calling out filled the air. Landon jerked upright. "Hey! We're here! Down here!"

Moments later three heads peered over the edge of the ravine. Hank, Willie and Sheriff Steele.

"Damn, how is she?" the lawman barked.

"Unconscious, but no broken bones, I think," Landon said. "She's got a good-sized lump on her head, and it's bleeding. We've got to get her out of here."

"I'll get my EMTs—"

"There's not enough room for all of us down here."

"There will be when you come up."

"Forget it. I'm not going anywhere. There's

enough room for one more person. Send him down. We'll strap her in and you can pull her up."

The sheriff stared at him. Landon had no idea what he was thinking, but he disappeared and began shouting out orders. A few minutes later, a rope came over the side, then a pair of black boots. Landon shielded Maggie with his body as the medical technician with a rescue basket scrambled to join them.

They got Maggie secure in the basket and latched to the ropes. Both held the basket steady as she was lifted. Landon kept his hands on her as long as he could, then let go.

The rope came back and the technician climbed up, then Landon. At the top, a large hand stretched over the edge. He grabbed it and the sheriff pulled him up. "Thanks," Landon said.

Steele nodded in reply. "They're stabilizing her. How long has she been unconscious?"

"I don't know." Landon tried to watch the EMTs work, but he couldn't see much with Willie and Hank hovering over Maggie. "Forty-five minutes? Maybe an hour. How'd you find us?"

The sheriff motioned to G.W., who stood nearby with the other horses. "Willie saw your palomino—"

"Okay, we're ready to move her." The technicians moved to either side of the basket. "We need to carry her to the flats, then get her to the hospital. I don't think anything's broken, but the abrasion on her head and being unconscious—"

A low moan sounded and everyone focused on Maggie. Landon couldn't stop himself from moving closer. Willie knelt on one side, Hank on the other. He had to be content with leaning over Willie's shoulder.

"Come on, Maggie," the technician cajoled as he took her hand. "Wake up, cowgirl."

Landon bit back the same words as Maggie's eyes fluttered and she slowly opened them.

"What—what's going on?" she asked.

"Easy there." The technician laid a hand on her shoulder. "You took quite a tumble. Can you tell me your name?"

"Ronny, it's me, Maggie," she mumbled, then she said more clearly, "I gave you your first black eye during a game of spin-the-bottle back in the fourth grade."

The technician smiled. "You're right, you did. I think you're going to be just fine."

Relief rushed over Landon as Maggie's beautiful green eyes looked at each man. When she got to him, they widened in shock. "What are you doing—" she tried to lift her head. "I told you…to leave."

"You rest." Ronny covered her with a soft blanket. "We're going to get you to the hospital."

"We'll help," Willie and Hank said in unison.

Pain lanced through Landon when Maggie closed her eyes and turned away.

"You better stay with me," the sheriff said to him. "We need to talk."

"About what?"

Steele motioned for Landon, Willie and Hank to move away from Maggie and the medical technicians. "Kali radioed to say a chunk of metal was found embedded in Black Jack's backside. It was stuck beneath the saddle. As long as Maggie leaned forward, the animal was okay. As soon as she sat back—"

"It cut into the horse." Fury built inside Landon. "And you think I did this?"

Both Willie and Hank protested, but the sheriff held up a hand. "I need to talk to everyone connected to the ranch." He looked at Landon. "Starting with you."

Hank and Willie left to help with Maggie. Forced to do nothing as they carried her away, Landon punched out deep breaths, squashing his desire to jump on G.W. and race after them. Once they were out of sight, he turned and found the sheriff holding out Landon's battered Stetson. He took it and placed it on his head, shocked to see the lawman's hand extended in greeting.

"Gage Steele. Sheriff," he said.

Landon took the hand. "Landon Cartwright. Ex-con."

They let go, and the sheriff swung onto a big black gelding, reaching for the reins of Hank's horse. "I know who you are, Mr. Cartwright. I read the report. An overturned conviction means you're a good man who got a raw deal. My sympathies for your family."

Landon ducked his head to hide his surprise and climbed onto G.W., taking control of Willie's mustang.

"So, you have any idea of how the metal got under the horse's saddle?" asked the sheriff.

Landon tipped up the brim of his hat and looked him in the eye. "What would you do if I said to ask Kyle Greeley?"

# Chapter 16

*I can't let myself love you.*

Landon's whispered declaration came back to Maggie during her overnight stay at the hospital. The words woke her from a restless sleep, as if he'd spoken them right there instead of hours earlier. Now home and tucked in her own bed under Nana B.'s care, she couldn't get his words from her head.

Maggie gingerly touched the bandage that covered the sutures.

She closed her eyes. The events were a bit fuzzy, but she recalled being upset and taking off on Black Jack. She'd pushed the animal into a fast run and it was only when they reached the foothills that she sat back full in the saddle. The next thing she remembered was the poor animal's pain-filled squeal and being thrown from the saddle. Then the sound of Landon's voice.

"Hey there, you up for company?"

Maggie's eyes flew open. She pushed herself up against her pillows and smiled. A balloon bouquet filled the doorway, almost obliterating Racy behind the array of color. "You're a nut."

Racy pushed the balloons into the room. "Takes one to know one." She released the ribbons and they floated upwards, then she dragged a wicker chair to the bed. "See, they made you smile."

Maggie looked from the balloons against the ceiling to her friend. "Thanks. Anna will love them."

Racy sat, tucking one jean-clad leg beneath her. "So, how are you doing? Really?"

"I'm fine. A cut on the back of my head and some bumps and bruises. Thank goodness Black Jack is going to be okay, too. If we could only find out who tried to hurt him."

"I bet you talked to Kali as soon as you got home."

"Being the wonderful vet she is, she didn't balk when I called last night from my hospital bed," Maggie said. "Then I called Tucker Hargrove."

"Yeah? How'd the two-time Oscar-winner react to the news about his daughter's prized horse?"

"He didn't blame me," Maggie said, sighing, "and he wants me to continue working with Black Jack once he's healed."

"I think the man needs to worry more about his daughter's behavior," Racy huffed, tossing a long curly strand of hair over her shoulder. "Hailey Hargrove spends more time in the tabloids than on movie sets."

"She's eighteen. I remember a couple teenagers who weren't above having a good time now and then."

"Oh, please. Bonfires at the lake and a few cases of beer are small potatoes compared to what that young lady has done."

"Speaking of daughters…" Maggie's smile expanded when her daughter peeked into the room. "Here's my favorite."

Anna smiled. "That's 'cause you've only got one." Her eyes grew wide when she noticed the balloons. "Golly! Where'd they come from?"

"The balloon fairy." Racy grinned.

Giggling, Anna came in and raised her hands, brushing her fingertips through the ribbon tails of the balloons. "I like the pink ones."

"You can take a few and put them in your room after dinner," Maggie said.

"Okay. Nana said to tell you everyone's ready to eat."

Maggie's stomach tightened to a hard knot. "Everyone?"

"Yep. Nana's done cooking, Hank set the table and Willie, Spence, Charlie and Landon are washing up."

"Ah, sweetie, I'm feeling a bit tired. Can you please ask Nana to fix me a tray and I'll eat in here? Racy, too."

"Okay."

Anna skipped from the room, closing the door

behind her. Maggie looked at her friend and saw the suspicion in her eyes. "Don't ask, Rac."

"You're avoiding him?"

"Yes."

"At least you aren't denying it."

Maggie sighed, pleating the sheets with her fingers. "I don't understand why he's still here."

"Maybe for the same reason he was outside your hospital room all night."

Maggie's eyes widened. "What?"

"I stopped by when I got off work. He was there."

"It must have been after two o'clock in the morning."

Racy shrugged. "I snuck in. Anyway, I found his six-foot-plus frame propped up in one of those waiting-room chairs."

*Landon at the hospital? All night? No one had told her.*

Her mind reeled. It was too much.

Discovering he'd spent time in prison, that she and her family meant nothing to him, that making love meant nothing. But then he'd saved her, said he couldn't fall in love with her, stayed at the hospital all night…

Fresh pain stabbed at her heart.

"Maggie." Racy took her hand. "What is it?"

"Noth—nothing." She shook her head. "I'm fine."

"You want to tell me what's going on between you and your cowboy?" Racy sat back in the chair. "We haven't talked in a while, but I can hear something in your voice whenever you say his name."

She closed her eyes against her friend's inquisitive

stare. "There's nothing between me and Landon… anymore. It doesn't matter. It's over."

"Is that the reason he's got a horse trailer attached to his truck?"

Maggie's eyes shot to her friend. "You don't miss much." Then she sighed. "I fired him and he should already be gone, except for—"

"He saved your life?" Racy cut her off. "And what do you mean you fired him? Why?"

A knock at the door saved Maggie from answering. "Come in."

Her grandmother opened the door. "I thought you'd like to know the sheriff and Leeann are here."

"Well, that's my cue. I'm outta here." Racy grabbed her bag and stood.

"Honey, I'm afraid you can't," Nana B. said. "The sheriff pulled in right behind you, blocked your car."

Racy let out an exasperated breath. "Of course he did! You have room to park twenty vehicles and where does he put his Jeep? Right on my ass!"

Nana B. smiled, then became serious. "Maggie, something tells me this isn't a social call."

"You're probably right." She kicked away the blankets. They had to be here because of Black Jack.

"Are you feeling well enough to get out of bed?" Racy handed her a pair of jeans and a shirt. "A minute ago you were determined to stay there."

Maggie ignored her and shimmied off her pajama bottoms.

"You know the boys will insist on hearing what the sheriff has to say."

Maggie's fingers faltered on the zipper of her

jeans. Her grandmother was including Landon when she said *boys*.

She breathed deeply, then released it, doing little to settle the butterflies in her stomach. "They have a right to know what's going on, but if you could keep Anna distracted—"

"Don't you worry, she and I will be in the garden picking veggies. But I expect a full report later."

Maggie agreed and slipped on a pair of sneakers. She glanced at the mirror. It was useless to try to do anything with her hair. Not with the large compress and bandage wrapped around her head.

*You worried about impressing someone?*

Pushing aside the thought, she headed for the kitchen with Racy at her heels. They stepped into the sunny room as Hank opened the back door for Gage and Leeann. She tried to keep her gaze away from Landon, but it was impossible.

Dressed from head to toe in black, he stood in the corner closest to the back door, his attention on Gage. As if he knew she was watching, he turned and locked eyes with her. Spence broke the spell by stepping in front of him to join Charlie at the table.

"So, did you smell Nana B.'s steak sandwiches all the way into town?" Maggie asked, thankful her voice came out unruffled. "Or is this an official visit?"

"It's official." Gage removed his hat. He took a moment to look over the crowded room. Maggie noted his gaze lingered a second longer on Racy, who was leaning against the counter. "If you prefer, we can talk in private."

Maggie moved to the table and rested her hands on the back of a chair. "If this has to do with Black Jack then please go ahead. We're all family—" Her hands tightened on the wood, as this time she succeeded in not looking at Landon. "We're all in this together."

"Maggie, maybe you should sit," Leeann said.

"Why?" The faint pain in her head took a sharp jump. "Did something happen to Black Jack?"

"No." Her friend rushed to her. "You look like someone—"

"Who fell over the side of a cliff and cracked her head open on a rock?" Maggie interrupted. "I know. Now, tell me what's going on."

Leeann glanced at Gage, who nodded. She looked back at Maggie. "We arrested Steve Walker and Butch Dickens a couple hours ago."

Greeley's foremen. "Why?"

Gage stepped forward. "It started with what Spence and Charlie told me—"

"Hey, we didn't know anything about this," Charlie protested.

Spence nodded in agreement. "Mr. Greeley made it no secret he wanted the Crescent Moon, and he boasted how he had the means to get it. We never figured he was doing more than hiring cowboys away from you."

"It's all right," Maggie said. "I believe you."

"Like I was saying," Gage continued, "I spoke to Spence and Charlie after I talked with Landon."

"Landon?" Unable to stop her gaze from flying across the room, Maggie noted his clenched jaw and the tight press of his mouth. His dark eyes revealed nothing as they fixed on her.

Gage cleared his throat. Maggie looked back at him. "Ah, you said you talked to Landon?"

"I talked with everyone connected with the Crescent Moon, and then I spoke with Kali Watson. She brought me the piece of metal she'd taken out of Black Jack."

"What was it?" Maggie asked.

"A rowel from a handmade set of spurs. We put out a few calls and did some checking on the Internet. We found a designer who'd been in town for the Fourth of July carnival and matched the style to him. He said he only sold three sets while here. Two were to locals and one to a cowboy who was passing through."

Gage slapped his hat against his thigh and continued. "One of them was Butch Dickens. As soon as I showed Dickens the rowel, he offered to talk if we cut him a deal. He confessed he and Steve have been causing trouble around here, everything from cutting your fence line to messing with Black Jack. They claimed not to have had anything to do with your tool shed, that the fire and Hank's wagon wheel giving way were just accidents that worked in Greeley's favor. But we may reopen our investigation of those incidents."

A chorus of gruff, hushed curses filled the air. The strength left Maggie's legs and she dropped into the chair. "Why would he tell you all that?"

"Because everything they did was on orders from Kyle Greeley. We've just arrested him. He's in custody on a variety of charges from harassment to animal cruelty. The county district attorney is still considering attempted murder."

Disbelief filled Maggie. Kyle had made it no secret he wanted her land, but to go this far? The disbelief turned to guilt. She should've realized the events happening around the Moon, events she'd chalked up to bad luck, were actually part of something more sinister.

She closed her eyes, and felt Leeann grabbing one hand. Seconds later, Racy gripped the other. Pulling in a deep breath, she returned their touch with a quick squeeze. "I'm—it's okay. I'm okay."

Willing back the tears, she opened her eyes. "Kyle did all this because he wants my land that badly?"

"He didn't say anything, just demanded his lawyer," Leeann said. "We need to get an official statement about what's happened between the two of you."

Maggie nodded. The effects of her inner turmoil slowly ebbed away. It was going to be all right now. With the ranch, anyway. For the first time in a long while, relief filled her. She still owed the bank, but she was sure she could work out something. She had her contract to work with Black Jack and the ranch was running better than it had in years.

Thanks to Landon.

Her gaze roamed to the men who worked for her, purposely avoiding Landon's tall frame at the door. "I'm sorry you all had to go through this. I should've known something—someone was doing—"

"Magpie, there's no way you could've known,"

Hank assured her. "None of us realized the depth of Greeley's greed. We're sorry we didn't push the issue and get the law involved before you were hurt."

Tears bit at the back of Maggie's eyes, but she blinked them away.

"Seems to me we're letting a perfectly good meal go to waste," Willie chimed in. "Let's chow!"

Maggie shot Willie a grateful look, then insisted Gage and Leeann join them. Hank called in Nana B. and Anna from the garden. Racy went to work with her usual efficiency and served a platter of sandwiches and ice tea for everyone.

Leeann leaned in. "Hey, Maggie, you got a second?"

Maggie nodded and followed her into the living room.

"I didn't want to say anything in front of the crowd, because I don't know what you've told them, but I'm glad Landon was here for you yesterday. After Greeley showed up spouting about Landon's past, I think he was planning to use the man's history against him. To try to get everyone to believe Landon was connected to what happened to you. I think you did the right thing keeping him around."

A dull ache settled in Maggie's chest. Yes, things were looking up for her. Except where he was concerned.

"Leeann, I fired him."

"What?"

"The only reason Landon is here is because Black Jack came back to the barn before he left."

"You mean you fired him after he told you about

his conviction being—" Leeann paused "—wait, he didn't tell you, did he?"

"Tell me what?"

"Damn! I swear, when it comes to men and secrets—" Leafing through the folder in her hand, Leeann pulled out a sheet of paper. "Read this. You deserve to know the whole truth about Landon Cartwright."

He forced himself to keep walking toward his truck when all he wanted to do was march right back into the house.

Maggie's house.

It'd taken every ounce of strength not to react when the sheriff had told them what had happened over the last twenty or so hours. He'd wanted to push his way past her family and friends, pull her into his arms and make sure she was okay.

But he couldn't. He didn't have any right. She'd be fine now that Greeley's plan was stopped and the man was behind bars. She had everything and everyone she needed right inside her kitchen.

He whistled softly and G.W. came to the corral's edge. The horse waited patiently as Landon opened the gate and led him to the trailer. It took a firm nudge and a verbal command to get the animal inside. He tossed his head and neighed sharply, telling Landon what he thought of the idea.

"Yeah, pal, I hate leaving, too, but it's time for us to be going." Landon closed the trailer, slapping the heated metal sides as he headed back toward the truck's cab. "Past time."

"Without saying goodbye?"

Landon's hand froze on the door handle for a moment, letting the light breeze carry her words and her clean, sweet scent to him. Then he grabbed the handle in a tight grip and opened the door.

Settling himself behind the wheel, he pulled the door shut with a hard tug. "Seeing how you fired me yesterday, not once but twice, I thought it best to get on my way."

She moved to the side of his truck, and thrust a sheet of paper through the open window. "It doesn't matter I know the truth?"

The paper shook so hard, he could barely make out the Texas state seal on the letterhead.

*Ah, hell.*

He reached for it, but she yanked it back. "How can you leave with me thinking what you said was true?"

"Because it is true." He tightened his grip on the steering wheel. "It doesn't matter what some judge determined. My wife and child are dead, and it's my fault."

"It's not your fault," Maggie cried. "You can't shoulder the blame for a stupid, tragic accident. It never should've happened, but it did, and you suffered a loss no one should have to endure."

"It was my job to keep them safe." Ignoring the need to look at her one last time, Landon forced himself to stare straight ahead. "I failed them. To be responsible again for someone else… I can't do it."

"You can't live in the past. Do you think your

wife or daughter would want you torturing yourself this way?"

Landon swallowed hard, but didn't speak.

"Landon—"

"You're going to be okay, Maggie," he said, feeing as if he had to push the words from his mouth. Jamming the keys into the ignition, he gunned the engine to life. "The ranch is safe, and you've got plenty of help to keep things running smoothly. There's nothing more I can do for you."

"You can stay."

Her soft plea floated into the interior of the truck and branded him deeply. His heart pounded unsteadily. The flicker of desire to stick around flared to life again, but he pushed it back. He was doing what was best.

For everyone.

"I can't."

He slowly released the brake, and the truck inched forward. Maggie backed away. He opened his eyes and glanced in the side mirror, determined to look just long enough to make sure she was a safe distance from the vehicle.

The sight of her standing there, arms wrapped around her middle, made it almost impossible to look away.

Slowly she faded into the distance and he lost sight of her completely.

# *Chapter 17*

The crowd gathered in Maggie's backyard raised their voices in unison as they sang "Happy Birthday" to Nana B. Blinking back tears, Maggie watched Anna help her grandmother blow out the candles on her cake. All forty of them. Actually, there were two cakes, thanks to the large crowd of neighbors and friends.

Anna had wanted a candle for every year of her great-grandmother's life, but Nana B. had convinced her one candle for every two years would be sufficient. Curly puffs of smoke lingered over the cakes as Maggie moved them to a side table to cut them up. The sound of a fiddle and guitar tuning told her the festivities would be going on long after sunset.

She wouldn't get much sleep, but why should tonight be different than any other night since…

"Knock it off," she lectured herself. "You know what you have to do. And in two days you're going to do it."

"It's about time."

Maggie turned to find Willie standing there. "What did you say?"

"This place hasn't been the same since he scattered to the wind. It's time you did something about your cowboy."

"He's not my cowboy." Maggie stared at the cakes.

She didn't have to say his name aloud. They both knew whom they were talking about, and Willie was right. Landon's leaving had created an emptiness at the ranch. At first, she'd been angry at his unwillingness to stick around. Then she realized she'd never given him a reason to stay.

"At least not yet," she continued. "But I'm taking those horses to the Still Waters Ranch at the end of the week."

"Don't come back empty-handed."

"Empty-hearted is more like it." The knife stilled over the white frosting as fresh tears filled her eyes. Maggie brushed them away with her free hand. "I was such a fool, Willie."

"Don't be so hard on yourself, darling. That man is carrying a lot of baggage, and he's got to get it packed and stored away. Else he'll never be any good to anyone, least of all you or Anna."

"I never should have let him leave without telling him how I felt."

"You said yourself you weren't sure what was thumping around in your heart until a little while ago. Maybe he needs more time."

"Well, he's got as long as it takes me to drive to Texas." And she had as long as that to figure out exactly what she was going to say. Maggie looked at the cakes. "Now, I trust you to behave while I get the ice cream."

"Me?"

Maggie laughed at the innocent look on the old man's face. She knew as soon as her back was turned, he'd cut himself a big slice. Heading inside, she yanked open the freezer and took out several cartons of ice cream.

She shoved the door closed and caught sight of the notice held to the fridge with a homemade magnet. In three weeks, she'd give a formal deposition against Kyle Greeley.

The man was out of jail, back on the Triple G, and keeping a low profile. The biggest shock of all was who'd bailed him out. Mick Lofton, a former rodeo star and another son of Richard Greeley's no one knew about, appeared a week after Kyle's arrest. Mick was now officially in charge of the Triple G Ranch and all of its holdings.

The deep rumble of a truck engine had her walking to the kitchen counter and peeking out the window. She froze.

A late-model, shiny black truck with a dual horse trailer pulled to a stop in the crowded drive. Her breath caught. It couldn't be Kyle. He wouldn't dare show his face here. But who—

The driver's side door opened and the setting sun danced off a black Stetson. Shocked, she watched the tall cowboy come around the front of the truck. Dark slacks and polished cowboy boots emphasized long legs. A white dress shirt drew attention to wide shoulders, while the rolled-back cuffs revealed tanned forearms.

Landon.

He'd come back.

Anna ran across the yard and flew into his arms when he crouched to one knee and held her close. They spoke for a few moments, before he gave a gentle tug on one of her braids and rose. The crowd parted as he headed toward her grandmother.

Maggie walked to the screen door, and pushed it open with her hip to see Landon present a gift to Nana B. Her grandmother didn't look at it, instead asking a question Maggie couldn't hear. Whatever he said had her grandmother beaming. Then Willie and Hank joined them and she lost sight of him in the crowd.

Maggie hurried down the steps. She dumped the ice cream on the table and wrapped her arms around herself. Frantically rubbing her skin, she tried to rid the chill seeping to her bones.

*No, this wasn't right. She wasn't ready.*

She wanted to be the one to surprise him. To catch him off guard when she arrived at his ranch. To blurt out what was in her heart before he had a chance to shut down and send her away.

Grabbing an ice cream scoop, she dug into the closest half gallon and started scooping it into bowls. She made quick work of one container, making a mess in the process. She raised a hand to her mouth and licked the vanilla ice cream from her fingers.

"Need any help?"

Maggie spun around. Landon stood in front of her.

His gaze moved slowly from her head to her sandaled feet, igniting a fire inside that effectively erased the coldness. She allowed herself to do the same to him. He'd removed his hat and needed a haircut. Deep, tired lines were etched around his eyes.

He looked perfect.

"What are you doing here?"

A grin tugged his mouth as he nodded toward the crowd. "I wanted to bring your grandmother a birthday gift."

Maggie looked at Nana B. prancing around the yard, lifting her white eyelet skirt to show off her present. "Cowboy boots?"

He looked at her, smile wider now. "I'll have you know those are white quill ostrich and purple alligator-skin boots. I brought a pair for each of the men, too, but they're not purple."

"So, you thought you'd stop by and drop off some gifts?" Maggie heard the anger in her voice. Maybe she hadn't gotten over him walking away. "You think it fixes everything? Makes everything better?"

The smile left his face as his dark eyes stared at her. "No."

"Damn right, no. Why are you—"

Excited squeals from the driveway cut off Maggie's words. She watched her daughter dance around the trailer attached to Landon's truck. Willie slowly led a young, chocolate-brown horse down the back gate.

"Her name is Sunshine and she's the sweetest, most gentle filly a young girl could want." Landon leaned forward, his whispered words caressing her ear. "My brother's been working with her for a month now, but I'm sure you can perform the same magic on her as you did with Black Jack."

He took her arm and turned her to face him. "And with me."

"I—" Maggie struggled to find her voice, lost in the warmth of his hands. "I didn't do anything—"

"Mama! Mama!" Anna raced around the end of the table. "Did you see her? Did you? Her name is Sunshine and she's mine. All mine!"

"I saw her, honey." Maggie pulled from Landon's touch to stroke her daughter's hair. "She's a beauty, and I think you owe someone a thank you."

Anna twirled toward Landon with her arms raised. He put his Stetson back on his head and lifted her. She wrapped her arms around his neck. "Thank you so much, Landon. This is better than the Easter Bunny, my birthday and Christmas combined."

The sight of Landon closing his eyes as he returned her daughter's hug had Maggie pressing trembling fingers to her lips. He had to be thinking about his own little girl, and that he'd never be able to hold her like this. She waited for the pain and anguish to cross his features, but today there was only peace.

"You know, you're lucky you came today." Anna leaned back to look at his face. "Another couple of days and you would've missed my mom."

"Oh, really?" Landon perched Anna on his hip but stared at Maggie. "And where was your mom going?"

"Texas," Anna chirped. "She was taking the horses with her, but Nana B. said she was delivering something more important. Her heart."

Surprise flashed in his dark eyes. "Is that so?"

"Did you bring a gift for my mom, too?"

"Anna!" A fiery blush crept over Maggie's cheeks, both at her daughter's question and what she'd revealed to Landon. "You don't ask something—"

"I sure did." Landon stuck his hand in his pocket and pulled out a black velvet box.

"Wow." Anna reached for it. "Can I see it?"

Landon closed his fingers around the gift. "How about I show it to your mom first? If she likes it, she can show you."

Anna's brow furrowed for a moment. "I guess so. Then can we have cake and ice cream?"

A hysterical laugh at her daughter's words bubbled inside Maggie's throat. It matched the dizzying current that raced through her the moment she saw the small box in his hand.

"I don't think the ice cream is going to wait, Little Bit." Hank appeared and Anna went willingly to him. Spence and Charlie were right behind him. "We'll take over, Magpie. Why don't you two find a quiet place to talk?"

Before she could respond, Landon grabbed her hand and pulled her toward the back steps. He marched across the covered porch to the front of the house, not stopping until they reached the hanging porch swing.

Another one of Landon's projects, Maggie thought, as the noise from the party faded to a muted resonance. She looked at the faded patchwork quilt where she'd sat many nights over the last month reliving every moment, every emotion, and every memory of this man.

And now, he was here.

"I'm not trying to buy my way back into your life, Maggie."

She knew he wasn't. Why had she said those things?

He released her hand. Maggie could do nothing but drop into the softness of the swing.

"Leaving here, leaving you was the hardest thing I've ever done." He paced back and forth in front of her. "I thought I was doing the right thing, but I wasn't home more than two weeks when I realized—"

"You went home?"

Landon stopped, yanked off his hat and tunneled his fingers through his too-long hair. "Yeah, I went home. Not right away. I stubbornly held on to the things I'd been telling myself for years. But at the oddest times, in the smallest moments, your memory would come to me. You made me realize I wasn't doing the right thing—I was running from the past. My past. I needed to come to terms with that part of my life, and put it to rest before I could think about moving on."

She tried not to stare at the box clenched his fingers. "Are you ready to move on now?"

"Yes."

He dropped beside her, controlling the swing's movement with his powerful legs. Tossing his hat down, he stretched one arm across the back of the swing, and leaned in close. "I used to dream about the night my daughter died. I could hear my wife saying something, but it was never clear to me. When I got back to Still Waters, the nightmare came back, night after night, but instead of fighting it off, I lived it again. Listened to her words...she was blaming herself."

"Oh, Landon."

He pressed his finger gently beneath her chin until she looked into his eyes. "But she was wrong. I was, too. I know that now, and I know I hurt you when I left. I'm sorry. I'll never do it again. I love you, and I want you in my life forever."

He released her and opened the jewelry case. Maggie gasped. Nestled on a cushion of white satin sat a trio of emerald-cut diamonds in a platinum setting.

"Marry me."

Her gaze flew from the ring to Landon. Her girlish heart had leapt at the sight of the box, but she'd never expected this. "But what about your ranch in Texas?"

"My brother is running it, and he's got more help than he knows what to do with." He moved his arm around her back and pulled her closer.

"I want to be here at the Moon with you. I know what this land means to you, the connection it gives to your past and future. I want to share that connection. That future. Maggie, please say you'll marry me."

"Landon, I come with a ready-made family. I don't know how you feel about having more children, but I've always dreamed of—"

"I love Anna and the rest of your family. And I'll always have a place in my heart for Sara." Landon placed his lips at her temple, leaving a gentle kiss. "But I want more kids, plenty of brothers and sisters for Anna, as long as you're their mother. Marry me."

This was the moment. Now or never. She didn't have time to prepare a speech of what was in her heart, her soul. When it came to this man, she wanted him in her life, in all their lives. Nothing else mattered.

"Yes."

He captured her answer with a kiss that seemed to go on forever. Finally he pulled back, took her left hand and slid the ring onto her finger. "You know, one thing would make this moment perfect."

Maggie didn't try to stop her tears this time. "What?"

He raised her hand to his mouth and softly pressed his lips to it. "You could tell me you love me, too."

She cradled his face in her hands and looked into the eyes of the man who would work beside her, love her and support her—all her life. The right kind of man for her. "Landon Cartwright, I love you more than words can possibly say, and I'm going to spend the rest of my life showing you how much."

His smile was deliberate and sensuous as he wiped away her tears. "Starting right now?"

She crawled into his lap and wound her arms around his neck. "Well, after our guests leave, and we convince Anna she can't sleep in the barn with Sunshine, and clean up after the party and—"

Landon pulled her tight, pressing their bodies together. Any thought in her head flew away.

"Sounds like a plan, Miss Maggie. Count me in. Forever."

* * * * *

**Christine Wenger** has worked in the criminal justice field for more years than she cares to remember, but now spends her time reading, writing and seeing the sights in our beautiful world. A native Central New Yorker, she loves watching professional bull riding and rodeo with her favorite cowboy, her husband, Jim. Visit Chris at christinewenger.com.

## Books by Christine Wenger

### Harlequin Western Romance

#### *Gold Buckle Cowboys*

*The Cowboy and the Cop*

### Harlequin Special Edition

#### *Gold Buckle Cowboys*

*The Rancher's Surprise Son*
*Lassoed into Marriage*
*How to Lasso a Cowboy*
*The Cowboy Code*

#### *The Hawkins Legacy*

*The Tycoon's Perfect Match*
*It's That Time of Year*
*Not Your Average Cowboy*
*The Cowboy and the CEO*
*The Cowboy Way*

Visit the Author Profile page at Harlequin.com for more titles.

# THE COWBOY AND THE CEO

Christine Wenger

To the bull riders who chase their dream and to the bullfighters who protect them in the arena. Please be careful! A heartfelt thanks to Silhouette editors Leslie Wainger, Susan Litman, Gail Chasan and Paula Eykelhof, who made this writer's dream come true.

# *Chapter 1*

"I can't spare the time to fly to Wyoming," Susan Collins said to her administrative assistant, Bev Irwin. Susan held up the clipboard that was packed with papers. "Many of these orders require my personal attention."

"It's nothing that we can't take care of." Bev shook her head. "You haven't had any kind of vacation in ages. This would be a good compromise. You can fly to the Gold Buckle Ranch, enjoy their new spa and do a little business."

Susan didn't even look at the pamphlet Bev shoved in her hand, and began to pace. "Look, Bev, I appreciate your concern, but I have a business to run. I'll send one of our salespeople to the Gold Buckle to handle whatever Emily Dixon needs in sportswear for the campers. I'll only charge her half of our cost, or I'll donate whatever she wants. Anything for the kids."

"Mrs. Dixon didn't ask for any donations. All she asked for was you," Bev insisted. "She's heard of the fund-raising you've done for physically challenged children, and wants to see what you can do for her program."

That was flattering, but she didn't raise the money for any accolades. She did it in memory of her sister, Elaine. The money went for research, for any special equipment the kids might need, for tutors and books while they were in the hospital, and for fun. All children needed to have fun. She could help a little with the fund-raising, but she didn't have time for more.

Susan sighed. Surely whatever the owner of the Gold Buckle Ranch wanted could be done by phone, fax and e-mail. She flipped through the papers on her clipboard and paced. Where was the order for uniforms from that high school marching band?

Bev handed Susan another colorful pamphlet. "You're exhausted and you know it. You need a change of scenery, Susan. You need to *relax*. Besides, Emily Dixon seems like the nicest lady. You'd love her."

"How on earth did she hear about me out in Wyoming?" Susan asked, stopping her pacing long enough to lean against her desk.

Bev smiled. "Mrs. Dixon also liked the fact that your company is called Winners Wear. And she loved our motto—For Those Who Try Their Best. She said that's the very philosophy of the Gold Buckle Ranch.

They try to reinforce the same goal to each of their campers—to do their personal best in spite of their handicap. Isn't that terrific?"

Susan nodded. Clearly, Emily Dixon got it.

Bev slid an unopened brochure across Susan's desk and began to unfold it. "You should see all the programs they have for children with different disabilities—Wheelchair Rodeo, the Gold Buckle Gang, Cowboy Quest for emotionally troubled kids who are facing legal troubles..."

Susan barely listened to the litany of programs. She didn't want to turn Mrs. Dixon down, but she had plenty of competent salespeople who could handle this project.

As she looked at her to do list on the clipboard, the page began to blur. Her eyes were tired, scratchy, and she was having a hard time focusing. She didn't panic. Small things. Easily correctible with a squirt of eye drops and another cup of high-octane coffee.

Bev continued to push. "Why can't you just let your very talented staff do their thing and take a break?"

Because Winners Wear was *her* company, and she had to be involved in every detail, that's why.

But maybe Bev was right.

Bev snapped her fingers. "Uh-oh. None of the other salespeople are free to go to Wyoming. They'll be at the big trade show in Orlando that week."

The twitch under Susan's eye returned. "I forgot about the trade show."

"Susan..." Bev took a deep breath and held up the brochure. "Emily wants you to experience the essence of the ranch so you can develop a meaningful logo. She also wants cowboy-style shirts and jeans to give to the campers for each program. Then she'd like all kinds of other gear to stock a little camp store. She thinks it'll be a good fund-raiser and that the parents, caregivers and all their donors would want to buy that kind of merchandise."

Susan rubbed her forehead, feeling the start of a headache. She liked the fact that Emily Dixon chose her company, and *really* liked the fact that Emily was so dedicated to helping children.

Her sister, Elaine, would have loved to spend time at a place like the Gold Buckle Ranch.

Susan stood and leafed through the clipboard again, not remembering what she was looking for. "A week is too long."

Truthfully, she *was* exhausted. If she had enough energy to stand at the window and look down at the street, she'd see people pushing clothes racks from building to building. Vendors would be hawking goods from tables on the sidewalks, and shoppers looking for bargains would be haggling with them for better deals.

There was no place like New York's Garment District, and Susan loved the hustle and bustle and the energy of it all.

She'd started Winners Wear seven years ago, after her mother died. She'd bought this century-old building with the money her mother had left her, her entire savings and a huge bank loan. Then she'd hired the best employees she could find, mostly eager young graduates from the city's fashion and design schools.

It had been a big gamble for her financially, but

her sales staff started bringing in contracts—*big contracts*—immediately.

For most of the past seven years, she'd felt overwhelmed, but it had paid off. She worked hard, but she couldn't take all the credit. Everyone worked hard.

She hated to admit how tired she was. She couldn't do her best when she felt like a pile of scrap material.

Maybe she *should* go to Wyoming.

"Go and breathe some clean mountain air, boss," Bev said. "You'll come back nice and refreshed and raring to go. Don't worry about a thing here. We'll take care of everything while you're gone."

Susan took in a deep breath and let it out. Maybe it would be a good idea—before she ended up in the hospital herself.

No thanks. She'd had enough of hospitals when her sister was alive.

"Okay. I'll go," Susan mumbled. "Not for a week, though. I'll leave this Thursday and return on Saturday. Then I have to get back here and take care of business."

Clint Scully meandered through the parking lot toward the front doors of the Mountain Springs Airport. Every now and then, he'd slow his pace even more and take a gulp of strong, black coffee from a white take-out cup.

Nothing like a perfect Wyoming day. Not too hot. Not too cold. A warm breeze and a lot of sunshine. A perfect July day to drag out a lawn chair and take a snooze in the sun. He yawned in anticipation of doing just that.

Mrs. D had promised to bake him a blueberry pie if he picked up Susan Collins at the airport. His buddy Jake Dixon had warned him about his mother's matchmaking tendencies and reminded Clint that she'd sent Jake to pick up Beth Conroy, who became Mrs. Jake Dixon, just last year.

Clint swore under his breath. If Mrs. D had any ideas about matching him up with Susan Collins, she might as well spit in the wind.

Been there. Done that. He liked his freedom too much to commit to anyone.

Once inside the terminal, he checked the monitor and saw that Susan's plane had landed a few minutes ago, so he headed for baggage claim.

"Anyone here from the Gold Buckle Ranch?"

He looked around to see who was speaking, and his gaze landed on the prettiest woman he'd ever seen. She was tall, slender and buzzing from person-to-person like a bee in a flower bed.

Clint grinned. That *had* to be Susan Collins.

Her red-brown hair was done up in some kind of fancy braid. Her dark eyelashes fanned out on her cheeks like paintbrushes. She was as pale as an Easter lily—she looked as though she hadn't seen the warm kiss of the sun in years. She had on some kind of black jeans—designer jeans. A red blouse with a vee-neckline worked for her. The vee wasn't very plunging—just deep enough to make things interesting. Strappy black sandals with a slight heel made her legs look long and slender.

He stifled a wolf whistle and approached her.

Clint tweaked the brim of his hat. "I'm Clint

Scully from the Gold Buckle." He stared into magnificent purple eyes. They must be colored contact lenses, he decided. No one had eyes like that. "And you must be…?"

"Susan Collins." She held out her hand, giving him a strong handshake. "Are you here to drive me to the ranch?"

He enjoyed warmth of her touch and the sureness of her handshake. "At your service."

"Thank you." She studied her luggage. "Where's the skycap for these bags?"

"I can get them. There's only two," he said, flexing.

"Oh, no. They are terribly heavy, especially that one." She pointed to the bigger black suitcase. "It's stuffed with samples and a couple of my catalogs."

"No problem," Clint said, lifting up the suitcases. Damn, they *were* heavy. What else had she brought from New York, the Statue of Liberty?

He managed a smile instead of a groan.

"No problem, darlin'. No problem t'all." He laid on the Texas accent. Ladies from the East usually loved his drawl.

"My name is Susan," she snapped. "And they wheel."

Mmm… Seemed like she wasn't the Texas-drawl type.

"Right this way, Susan. My truck's out front."

He wheeled her luggage and tried to keep up with her pace. She was walking fast, like she was late for a meeting or something.

"I'd like to get a massage after that dreadful flight," she said. "I'm *really* looking forward to the spa."

The words came out in a rush. She walked fast. She talked fast.

"The spa hasn't been inspected yet. Should be soon, though."

"Inspected?" she asked.

"A father of one of our campers donated the hot tub to the ranch. He said that it'd be good relaxation for the caretakers of the children. Mr. D had it installed on the deck of the Caretaker Hotel by the baseball diamond."

She raised a perfect eyebrow. "A *hot tub?* But what about the spa? Massages? Facials? Wraps?"

He shook his head and looked confused. "Mrs. D is the only one who calls it a spa. Everyone else calls it a hot tub. I think there's a communication problem somewhere."

Susan closed her eyes. "I came all this way for a hot tub by a baseball diamond?" She sighed. "Wait until I tell Bev."

Clint told Susan to wait at the curb and went to get his truck. By the time he returned, three cowboys were talking to Susan—hitting on her, really. Bronc riders, he assumed, probably on their way to Cheyenne for the Frontier Days festivities. Bronc riders thought they were hot stuff.

"Toss those suitcases in the back, boys," Clint said, interrupting their conversation. They did so, and then went back to ogling Susan.

"Thanks for your help." He shook their hands, in an effort to send them on their way. "Goodbye now."

One of the cowboys pointed at him. "Hey, aren't you…?"

"Yeah," Clint said, always flattered by the recognition. "Yeah, I am."

Clint opened the door for Susan to get in.

"Just who do they think you are?" she asked.

"Just myself." He grinned. "They've probably seen me around—either fighting bulls or hauling my stock to rodeos."

"I see."

She gave a big sigh and checked her watch. She got into the truck, and so did he. He aimed the pickup toward the mountains.

"Mr. Scully, how long will it take to get to the ranch? I'd like to meet with Emily tonight and show her my samples."

"I don't think that'll be possible. Emily will be busy with the kids. Then after dinner, it's popcorn and movie night. We're showing one of the Harry Potter movies. You won't want to miss that."

"I didn't think that the program had started yet."

"This is Thursday. Right?"

Susan nodded.

"Our Wheelchair Rodeo program ends on Saturday morning, and the Gold Buckle Gang will be arriving on Saturday afternoon. It's a program for—"

"Kids who use crutches or braces," she said softly, pinching the area above her nose as if she were getting a headache.

"How did you know that?"

"I read it in the flyer," she said. "On the plane."

He wasn't sure if she was really interested in the Gold Buckle Gang program or if she was getting a headache. He narrowed his eyes as he watched her.

"Make sure you don't miss the big game on Sunday night. We use a beach ball and the batter uses a big plastic bat. We have shortened bases and the cowboys do some clowning around and get the kids laughing and—"

"Sounds like fun," she said. "But I'll probably be gone by then."

She sounded remote, disinterested. He wondered why. "It is fun, but it also serves a purpose. The kids develop balance and maybe exercise different muscles, or maybe rely a little less on their crutches. Or maybe they just get to laugh a little more than usual." Clint grinned. "Wait until you see the horseshoe toss, and the relay races and some of the other events we have at the end of the program that make up the Gold Buckle Rodeo. We give out gold and silver buckles for the winners."

"Buckles?"

"It's a western thing. Rodeo winners have always received belt buckles—like this beauty." He gripped the big gold buckle he sported and tapped it. "National Championship Bullfighting—2006." He was proud of that, and he'd won the competition four times in a row. The competition was getting tougher and tougher every year, but he still had the moves.

He smiled at Susan. "Maybe we'll get you to play a little beach ball–baseball with the kids."

But he doubted she would. Miss New York City seemed to be even more distant.

"No. I can't," she said abruptly. "I didn't know that a program would be starting and the kids would be here. For some reason, I thought I'd be here in between programs." She took a deep breath and looked out the window. "Like I said, I'll be leaving on Saturday. I have to get back home."

She was getting downright frosty, but he still pushed. "Well, you'll be staying at least a couple days. You'll enjoy the ranch and the kids. The kids are the best."

She didn't answer, then sighed. "I'm suddenly very tired, Mr. Scully. It was a long flight."

Just before she turned her head to look out the side window, he could swear he saw moisture in her eyes. Now he felt bad.

"Susan, did I upset you somehow?"

"Oh, no. No. You didn't. Like I said, I'm just tired."

That was just an excuse. Something was wrong. She seemed really tense when he talked about the kids. Something was going on.

Clint concentrated on the road ahead, knowing that he'd somehow put a damper on Susan Collins's arrival in Wyoming.

He usually stayed far away from women like her—rich, successful, city women who had plenty of money but no heart. Women who were just like his former fiancée, Mary Alice Bonner. Hell, Susan looked like she could teach Mary Alice a few things.

But for some reason, he wanted to—needed to—see Susan Collins smile. He wanted to get her to relax, to get rid of the burden weighing her down.

And if anyone could do that, it was Clint Scully.

# Chapter 2

Susan didn't want to get involved with the kids. She was afraid it would hurt too much.

She was just supposed to help design a logo and a line of merchandise for the ranch, and that was all she intended to do.

It wasn't that she didn't care. Quite the opposite. She hadn't been thinking clearly when she'd agreed to come here—she wasn't sure she could bear facing a group of children whose pain so reminded her of her beloved sister's.

To this day, she could remember the smells and sounds of the hospital where she visited Elaine, who'd died way too young.

As soon as Emily was available, she'd meet with her to discuss what Winners Wear could offer. Then she'd take her scheduled flight out of Mountain Springs on Saturday morning. Bev had bought her an open-ended airline ticket, thinking that she'd decide to stay and relax and enjoy the spa.

She'd be leaving in two days.

With that decided, she glanced at Clint to see if he was still alive. He walked slow. He talked slow. He even drove slow.

Anyone could see that on this wide-open road without a car or a cop in sight, he could go at least seventy.

She checked her watch. "Clint, how far away is the Gold Buckle?"

"A couple of hours."

"Oh."

He could easily cut that time in half if he'd just step on it. Then again, she doubted that the huge, rusty pickup could go much over the forty miles an hour at which he was currently cruising.

She stole another quick glance at Clint. She had to admit he was handsome in a rugged, outdoorsy way. He had a lazy, sexy smile with a little dimple at the corner of his mouth.

Clint Scully was intriguing.

Maybe it was because he was the first actual cowboy she'd ever met. Certainly, it wasn't because his jeans hugged his strong thighs, or because his legs were so long that he could barely fold them beneath the dash. Or the fact that he smelled like fresh air and warm cotton.

Her cheeks heated, and she rolled down the window a little more. She reached up and swept the hair that had escaped her French braid off the back of her neck, trying to catch some much-needed air.

She stole another glance at Clint and saw the laugh lines around his eyes. His hands were tanned and strong. She studied the sharp crease of his long-sleeved, blue-checkered shirt. His light brown hair stuck out from under his white cowboy hat and brushed the back of his shirt collar. Her eyes strayed farther south.

He sure did fill out those jeans.

"Something wrong?" he asked, glancing over at her and grinning.

"Um…no. Just admiring your truck."

That was a lame recovery, but she'd die of embarrassment if he ever guessed that she was checking him out. She decided to change the subject.

"Why did those cowboys at the airport know you?"

"They've probably seen me working the rodeo events. I'm a bullfighter. That's the new politically correct term for a rodeo clown."

"You mean you toss around a red cape and get the bull to charge you like they do in Spain?"

"Absolutely not." He chuckled. "You've never seen a rodeo or a bull riding event, have you?"

She shook her head. "Not once."

He whistled. "I thought everyone in North America had seen one at one time or another."

"Not everyone."

He made a sharp right turn onto a bumpy road. Susan gripped the lip of the dash so she wouldn't fall over onto him. She thought her teeth were going to rattle loose from her head.

"So what does a bullfighter do?" she asked.

"I protect the bull riders."

"From what?"

"From the bull."

"Just how do you do that?"

"Various techniques, but mostly I'm fast on my feet."

Her heart started to pound as she thought of a huge bull charging him or anyone else. "Are you crazy?"

"Mostly." He shrugged. "But then I think you're crazy for living in New York City, but to each his—or *her*—own." He paused for a bit then added, "Anyone special going to be missing you back in New York?"

Hmm… She didn't know whether or not she liked the fact that he was asking about her availability. He was nothing like any man she'd ever met, and would be interesting to get to know, but that was all. She had no interest in a casual fling.

"If you're asking me if I'm married, I'm not. Marriage isn't for me. I don't have time for relationships. How about you? Anyone worried that you're going to kill yourself saving cowboys from bulls?"

"No. Marriage isn't for me, either. Most women aren't happy living down on the ranch once they've seen what the world has to offer."

"Sounds like you speak from personal experience."

There was silence. Then he raised a finger from

his grip on the wheel and pointed at the horizon. "Bet you don't get sunsets like that back home."

The sun looked like a big red ball stuck between two peaks of lacy black mountains. Slivers of purple and yellow and red shot across the sky, and she wondered how long it had been since she'd taken the time to watch a sunset.

She knew the answer to that—not since she'd gotten too busy building her company.

"We might get sunsets like that," she said, "but there are too many buildings in the way for me to see it from my office or my apartment. Those who live on a high floor can see it."

"What a shame," Clint said, shaking his head. "So what do you do in New York?"

"I make uniforms and sportswear."

"Uniforms? What kind?"

"Everything from high school band to major league baseball and everything in between." She hesitated, and then said with pride, "I own my own company. I call it Winners Wear, and our motto is 'For Those Who Try Their Best.'"

"Nice." He nodded. "I like it. But running your own company seems like a lot of responsibility."

"It is. I really shouldn't have left New York. I have a million things that need tending to."

She fished around in her purse, pulled out her daily planner, slid out a gold pen and reviewed the list of items she needed to discuss with Mrs. Dixon.

She made notes until the light faded. "Could you turn on the overhead light?" she asked Clint.

"Sorry. It's broken. Why don't you sit back and enjoy what's left of the ride?"

She had no choice, now did she? She put her planner away and stared out the window.

They pulled into the Gold Buckle just after sundown. She couldn't see much of the grounds in the dusk, only the welcoming indoor lights of several small log cabins strung along a brook that glistened in the moonlight.

"This looks just like a real ranch," she said.

"It is a real ranch." Clint slowed down and made a right turn. "Mrs. D said to put you in the Homesteader Cabin and that she'll try to come by later to give you a proper welcome, along with something to eat. That all right with you?"

"Fine. Maybe we can have our meeting then."

"I thought you were tired."

"The sooner I meet with Emily, the sooner we can take care of business."

Clint pulled up in front of one of the log cabins, the second one from the end. In the glow of the porch light by the cabin door, Susan could see two rocking chairs. Large pine trees loomed behind the structure. If there were snow, it'd look like a Christmas card. She wondered if the guests in the other little cabins were at dinner or snuggled up inside.

Susan felt a little thrill of excitement zip through her when she caught the scent of horses on the breeze. She remembered the riding lessons she'd taken one summer in White Plains—a gift from her father when she was twelve. Her mother had protested, but her father had insisted.

"Susan needs to have some fun, Rochelle," he'd told her mother in one of his rare moments of strength. "And you know how much she loves horses. I'll take her on the train, wait for her and ride back with her."

Those were the best six Saturdays of her young life. After that, her father was gone again, escorting a tour group to Europe. He never managed to stay with them for very long.

Shaking off the sad thoughts, she gathered up her planner and her purse as Clint turned on the overhead light.

"Must be working after all," he said, giving her a wink.

He'd lied to her. The light never was broken. He'd just wanted her to look at the scenery. He'd manipulated her, and she didn't like that, but if he hadn't, she would have kept her face in her planner and missed the beauty of this country.

Clint got out of the truck. He walked her up the stairs of the cabin, his hand holding her elbow lightly. That was polite and gentlemanly of him. He opened the door with a large key and flicked on the light.

She glanced around the room and spotted a phone. "Can I make long-distance calls?"

"That phone only rings to the main office in case of emergency."

"I can't live without a phone. Thank goodness I have my cell." She flipped open her phone. "Why can't I get a signal?"

"It won't work around here. Too many mountains surrounding us. But Em and Dex have a phone in the office you can use." He gripped the door handle. "I'd better haul your luggage in."

"Where's the bell person?"

"I guess that'd be me. We all pitch in around here."

Susan turned around and found herself forehead-to-nose, toe-to-toe with Clint Scully. He grabbed her elbows to steady her.

His eyes studied her face, and then his gaze traveled down to her breasts. She probably should have been offended, but in truth she was flattered. It had been a long time since a man had looked at her that way. He seemed to see right through her, reaching down to a part of her that hadn't been touched in years. The same heat that had licked at her insides before flared again.

He cocked an eyebrow as if he was wondering what she'd do next.

She held her breath, wondering what he'd do.

It'd been a long time since she'd been with a man, and being so close to Clint reminded her of that fact.

She'd given up on men a while ago. They just couldn't understand that her company came before they did.

Yet Clint was very, very tempting, and very different. If his scorching gaze was any indication, he was as attracted to her as she was to him.

He gave his hat a tug. "I'll go get your luggage. Why don't you relax?"

"Thanks, Clint." She offered her hand, to shake his. "For everything."

He raised her hand an inch from his lips. "My pleasure, Susan."

Surely, he wouldn't… No one did that anymore.

Clint did. A whisper of warm air and soft lips brushed the back of her hand, and she melted like polyester under a too-hot iron.

Clint Scully was one interesting man.

Trying to gather her thoughts, she listened to the dull sound of his boots fade as he walked down the stairs of the porch. Then she explored the cabin.

The walls were tongue-and-groove knotty pine, varnished to a shine. Lace curtains on the window gave it a homey touch. Brightly striped Hudson's Bay blankets slashed bits of color around the cottage. It was open and airy with high ceilings and chunky log furniture with bright cushions in a Native American arrow design.

A huge stone fireplace took up most of one wall, and a pile of wood was stacked on a circular stand nearby. She looked for the switch that would make the fireplace spring to life.

"It's the real thing," Clint said, appearing next to her with her luggage. "I'll show you how to start a fire if you'd like."

"I think I can figure it out."

She thought how nice it would be to sit before a real fire at night and read a book. She hadn't had time to read a book in ages. That was something else she'd been missing.

"I'll leave these here, then I'll see about getting your dinner," Clint said.

She walked him to the door and felt all warm and fuzzy when he tweaked his hat and disappeared into the dark night.

Susan Collins, CEO, hadn't felt warm and fuzzy since mohair was in fashion.

Clint grabbed a frosty cold bottle of Chardonnay from the fridge in his travel trailer and set it on the countertop. In three steps, he was inside his bathroom checking his appearance in the mirror above the sink.

Clint bought the thirty-foot trailer from Ronnie Boggs, a down-on-his-luck cowboy who was quitting bull riding. He remembered pulling out his wallet and handing Ronnie more than double his asking price. Ronnie refused to take all that, but Clint wouldn't take no for an answer and stuffed the money into the tough cowboy's pocket.

Clint towed it from event to event wherever he was working. He liked the privacy and the quiet, and the fact that he could cook his own meals and relax in his own surroundings. Besides, if he stayed in a hotel, the riders would give him the business.

Whenever he was at the Gold Buckle Ranch, which was every summer and whenever else his pal Jake Dixon needed him, he parked it in his usual spot, deep in the woods behind the cabins. His favorite thing to do was to crank out the awning, sit in a lawn chair under it and listen to the brook as it sluiced over the rocks.

As Clint walked over to the boxes filled with jeans, shirts and work gear from his sponsors, he reminded himself to fire up his laptop and transfer funds. He'd heard on the stock contractors' grapevine that a couple of rank bulls might be going on auction with a starting bid of seventy-five thousand each. He'd been waiting and watching for those bulls and would pay any amount for them. They'd make a good addition to his stock.

He grabbed a new shirt from one of the cardboard boxes stacked in the corner. Pulling it out of the plastic wrap, he slid off the little white clips and shook out the shirt. Slipping it on, he could still see the fold marks. He puffed out his chest, and the creases faded. Well, he couldn't do that all night. He'd just have to hope for dim lighting.

He swung by the mess hall and collected a picnic basket loaded with food for Susan's dinner, and soon he was heading back to the Homesteader Cabin to see her again.

Ahh, Susan. She was so tense, so coiled up, she appeared to be about to spring. There was a sadness about her—he could see it in her deep purple eyes. Maybe he could distract her for a while.

He had a feeling that Susan Collins would dig her own subway back to New York when she looked out the window tomorrow morning and saw a couple hundred kids engaged in various activities. She didn't seem the kid type, but then again, he'd just met her. And he wanted to get to know her better.

Clint walked down the dimly lit path from the campgrounds that led to the cabins, a wine bottle gripped in one hand, the picnic basket that Cookie had given him for Susan swaying in the other.

He took the steps of the Homesteader Cabin two at a time and gave a light knock on the door.

"Who is it?" Her voice was slurred, sleepy.

"It's Clint. I brought your dinner."

"Just a minute."

She opened the door and Clint immediately liked what he saw. She'd changed into a dark pink golf shirt. On the pocket was bright embroidery in primary colors—her company logo, a halo of stars surrounding "Winners Wear." Printed underneath that, in bright orange, was her motto—For Those Who Try Their Best. Khaki pants clung to a great pair of hips. On her feet were fuzzy pink socks. Her auburn hair was in a ponytail high on her head, and a pair of gold-rimmed reading glasses were barely hanging on to the tip of her nose.

She held up the latest issue of *Pro Bull Rider Magazine.* "It was on the coffee table. Interesting sport, bull riding."

He set the picnic basket and wine down on the kitchen table. "You'll have to see it in person sometime."

She shook her head. "I don't know about that."

"I guarantee you'll love it."

"Care to wager that bottle of Chardonnay against that?"

He opened the picnic basket and pulled out several items wrapped in waxed paper. "You know, we've had a few bull riding events at Madison Square Garden."

"No kidding?"

"No kidding. Now, grab a chair and let's see what Cookie made for us." He opened one of the bigger packages. "Roast beef sandwiches."

He kept unwrapping and found pickles, a container of macaroni salad, two apples, potato chips and a couple of cans of cranberry-grape juice.

"Cookie thinks of everything," Clint said.

"What's his real name?"

"I don't know, actually. Every cook is called Cookie. It's a throwback to the chuck-wagon and trail-drive days." He held up the bottle of Chardonnay. "Some wine?"

"Why not?"

Clint opened the wine and found a couple of glasses in the cabinet next to the sink. Filling them halfway, he handed one to Susan. "Here's to your stay at the Gold Buckle Ranch."

"Thank you." They clinked glasses. "You like it here, don't you, Clint?"

"I do. I love the kids. They have a lot of heart and what we cowboys call *try*. The volunteers that come every year are special people, and the Dixons are the epitome of *try*. I see that you have the word in your logo."

"Emily liked my logo, too. That's why I'm here, I guess. But I can't take all the credit. My mother and I came up with our motto, theme, mission statement, whatever you want to call it when we were making nurses' uniforms in our kitchen. Trying our best is what got us through some tough years."

"And now you're the CEO of your own company." He shook his head. "That took a ton of 'try.'"

The way her eyes brightened and the way she smiled, he could tell she was proud of herself. She should be. But there was still that haunting sadness in her eyes.

They ate and talked about nothing in particular and everything in general until he noticed that she was trying to stifle a yawn.

He was just about to leave when Mrs. D came up the steps of the Homesteader Cabin.

"I saw your light on, Susan, and I wanted to stop by and welcome you to the Gold Buckle Ranch," Emily said. "Evening, Clint. Did you see to our guest?"

"Yes, ma'am."

"I knew you would." She flashed him a teasing smile.

"Emily, do come in." Susan stood, looking for her sample books. "Would you like to talk about the merchandise now?"

"Heavens no, sweetie. It's late and you must be exhausted. I just wanted to welcome you and make sure you have everything you need."

Mrs. Dixon enveloped Susan in a big bear hug. Susan closed her eyes and looked uncomfortable at first, but Emily didn't let go. Eventually, Susan's tense expression turned into a big grin.

And Clint realized that Susan seemed to need just such a hug.

Emily was about Susan's height, and was one of those women who perpetually smiled. She wore her brown hair short, tucked behind her ears, and she seemed like a bundle of controlled energy.

Emily took a couple of steps into the Homesteader Cabin. "Maybe I will come in for a minute. It's been a stressful day—nothing big—just a bunch of little things."

"Anything I can help you with?" Clint asked.

Emily made her way to the living room and sat down on the couch, clearly exhausted. "I don't think so, Clint, but thanks, anyway. My biggest problem is that my arts and crafts teacher had to leave tonight. She was going to chaperone on the trail ride, too. Her daughter is having a baby, and it's coming earlier than they thought."

"I hope you find someone," Susan said.

"Me, too. I'd hate to cancel the arts and crafts program next week when the Gold Buckle Gang program begins. The kids just love making things and taking them home as presents."

"How about someone from town?" Clint asked.

"I've already put out feelers, but so far, there have been no calls, and I'm running out of time. Beth wanted to help—" She turned to Susan. "Beth's my daughter-in-law, Jake's wife. But she's due to deliver *her* baby in a couple of weeks, and the doctor wants her to stay off her feet."

Susan knew she should offer to help, but she'd be leaving in a couple of days herself. Besides, she truly didn't know if she could handle working with the kids in such close proximity.

She'd kept her charity work at a distance by donating money and by organizing and running fund-raisers. She did everything she could for handicapped children in Elaine's memory. But she had never worked with children on a one-on-one basis. She didn't think she'd ever be able to face that pain.

"Well, this is my problem," Emily said to Susan. "I didn't mean to burden you with it on your first night. You're here to relax and enjoy our spa. It should be operational soon. You're staying with us a week. Right, Susan?"

Susan bit back a smile at the spa reference. She now knew that it was a hot tub on a deck somewhere. "Don't worry about the spa. And, Emily, I'm sorry, but I'm only staying for a couple of days."

As he listened to the women chatting, an idea struck Clint—one that guaranteed him more time with Susan. Clint snapped his fingers. "Susan, why don't you take over the class. You'll be great. The kids will love you. Stay the week."

Emily smiled. "Oh, Susan, that would be wonderful! I don't think the classes would take up too much of your time. Just Monday through Friday—two hour-long classes a day."

Susan's mouth went dry, and she felt an uncomfortable lump in her stomach. She *had* to convince Emily that she wasn't staying for an entire week. That she'd planned on leaving the day after tomorrow.

"I don't know if I'd be that great with the kids," Susan finally said.

"Sure you would." Clint winked at her. "And I really love your company's motto—For Those Who Try Their Best." He raised an eyebrow, pointing to the logo on her shirt. He gave her the thumbs-up sign.

Oh, he was sneaky! She could see through him like cheap gauze. He had thrown her own motto back at her.

"Oh… Emily. Okay. I'll do it," she heard herself say. "For the whole week."

"You are a darling!" Emily gathered her into another big hug. "Thank you so much."

Thanks to Clint and his cute dimple and turquoise eyes, she'd just volunteered. To be a teacher. She didn't know how to teach. She didn't know anything about arts and crafts. She'd made a key chain out of braided boondoggle once, if that counted.

Emily walked to the door. "I'll rearrange my schedule to give us some time to plan. Are you also willing to chaperone on the overnight campout and trail ride, too? If not, I understand. I'm already taking too much advantage of you."

She looked at Clint. "I-I'll do it."

*What was she doing?* The words were just coming out of her mouth. Maybe she was just overtired. She'd never acted like this.

"Susan, do you know how to ride?" Emily asked.

"Not really, but I took some lessons when I was twelve."

"Clint will refresh your memory. All of our horses are very gentle. And I promise that classes will only be for an hour or two each day. That'll leave you plenty of time for yourself."

Emily put an arm around Susan. "I can't thank you enough for volunteering. Now, you get some sleep. You've had a long day, and Clint will be here early to take you to breakfast at the dining hall and give you a riding lesson. Good night—to both of you."

With a wave, Emily was gone from the cabin.

Susan headed for the couch and sat down. She'd never backed down on a promise, and she didn't intend to start now.

Clint sat opposite her on the coffee table. "That was a really nice thing you did, volunteering to help Mrs. D."

"I think *you* were the one who volunteered me, Clint Scully. *My* volunteering would have made more sense if I knew something about arts and crafts and riding." She smiled to take some of the sting out of her voice.

"I believe you'll be a wonderful teacher." He stood and tweaked his hat.

She just loved it when he did that. And how could she be mad at him when his eyes sparkled like that?

She'd be mad enough later when she thought about it. Mad at herself. Clint had outwitted her, and it had been a long time since she'd had the rug pulled out from under her.

Maybe she really did want to stay.

# *Chapter 3*

How could she even think such a thing?

Stay here? She'd been counting on doing business, with a relaxing spa weekend on the side—not playing teacher at a kids' camp. But here she was—trapped. And it was her own fault for volunteering.

"Susan, I'll help you with your classes anytime. Day or night," Clint said.

Now, that was a loaded statement. Clint was a flirt, and she was very rusty in the flirting department.

Standing, she walked to the door. Clint got the message and sauntered over to her. "I'll be sure to call on you if I need you," Susan said, then waited a few beats. "Day or night."

He grinned. Tweaked his hat. "See you in the morning."

She could hear the thud of his boots as he walked onto the porch and down the stairs. She locked the door behind him, then sat down on the couch.

She had to think of something besides Clint. The cowboy was getting under her skin, making her stomach flutter and her heart do little flips in her chest. For heaven's sake, she was a businesswoman, not a freshman in high school.

*Don't think about him. Think about your class.*

She'd just promised Emily that she'd teach arts and crafts, but she didn't have a clue as to how to begin. Or even how to relate to the campers.

She'd never been a child herself.

But she never broke her word, not where kids were concerned. She'd been just about to tell Emily that she was only good at writing checks, when the "I'll do it" had come rocketing out of her mouth—not once, but twice.

So she'd try to make her arts and crafts program a success. She would develop it like a business project with a workable plan, realistic goals; set some milestones and plot it all out.

With that decided, she walked over to the refrigerator, suddenly dying for a hearty gulp of leftover Chardonnay.

Her reflection in the window caught her by surprise. It was so dark outside. No streetlights, no marquees, no car lights or skyscrapers lit for night. No TV. No radio. Just darkness and silence. With this kind of peace and quiet, she'd die of boredom within fifteen minutes.

Unless she had a certain cowboy to amuse her.

Reaching in her purse, she took out her cell phone to call Bev at home and check on things at Winners Wear, but then she remembered the time difference. Bev was probably fast asleep. Checking her cell, she saw there was still no signal. With a sigh, she tossed the cell phone back into her purse.

She paced. She sipped some wine. She paced some more. Sipped. Paced. Sipped. Paced. Sipped.

Finally, she decided that she should try to get some sleep. Maybe in the light of day, she'd find her lost mind.

She checked to make sure the door was locked, then for a little extra security, she pushed a heavy chair against the door. She missed her myriad locks, dead bolts and chains.

Back in the bedroom, she changed into a pair of sweatpants and a long white T-shirt, and eyed the puffy comforter on the bed. Slipping inside the covers, she sighed as the delicious warmth enfolded her. The bed was perfect. Now for some sleep.

She turned the light off and couldn't believe how dark and quiet it actually was.

There was no glare from the streetlights. No angry blare of car horns or revving motors. No shouting.

How did people live like this?

Staring up at the ceiling, eyes wide open, she tried to will herself to sleep, but Clint Scully kept intruding on her thoughts.

Cowboy. Handsome. Turquoise eyes. Boots. Sideways smile. Little dimple on the side of his mouth. Excellent butt.

She smiled and snuggled deeper into the bed when

she heard a fluttering noise and felt the slightest breeze against her face.

*"What?"*

She thought that maybe the noise was a squirrel on the roof of the cottage. Did squirrels come out at night? What if it was a mountain lion or something with lots of sharp teeth? After all, this was the wilderness.

Something fluttered. And then again. Whatever it was, it was in her room.

Holding her breath, she flicked on the light and picked up her purse for protection.

A black bird flew by.

No. A bat!

She screamed. It flew by her face. She screamed again. Then again for good measure.

She sprang out of bed and tried to remember what she knew about bats.

Absolutely nothing.

She swung at the thing with her purse, ducking and dodging. The bat flew into the living room. On shaky legs, she turned on every light that she could find.

She screamed and swung again as it flew by her. She heard a series of knocks at the door—or perhaps it was her heart pounding against her chest.

"Susan? It's Clint. Susan, are you all right?"

What a stupid question. "No, I'm not all right. There's a bat in here!"

The door rattled. "I can't get in."

On wobbly legs, she managed to run over and unlock the door so Clint could squeeze in.

"Where is it?"

"Over by the fireplace."

Clint squinted. "That little thing?"

"It's a bat! Do something!"

"I will."

He moved her away from the door. The bat flew out. He closed the door. "Gone."

Her head became a little woozy and she couldn't stop herself from swaying forward.

Then the shock of something cold and wet splashed on her face brought her around.

She gasped. "W-what are you doing?"

"There was a glass of water on the table, and I—"

"I know what you did, but that was wine."

Clint grinned. His eyes didn't move to meet hers, but were riveted to her chest.

She looked down. The wine had made the fabric of the white T-shirt cling to her breasts.

She rolled her eyes and plucked the material away from her body.

"Thank you for getting rid of the bat. Good night."

She stood up to reach for a blanket, but her knees wouldn't hold her yet. Just before they gave out completely, Clint caught her.

She let him hold her, enjoying how his hands roamed over her back and how warm his chest felt against her wet breasts. How his hard body felt against her.

Suddenly nervous, she stepped back, grabbed a blanket and wrapped it around herself. Disappointment dimmed his eyes.

"How did you happen to be here?" she asked.

"I walked Mrs. D home and was just going back to my trailer when I heard you scream. Actually, I think they heard you up in Canada."

She laughed. "Thanks, Clint. I'm glad you were here. I'll be okay now."

"Do you want me to stay with you? I'll take the couch."

Actually, she did want him to stay, but she just couldn't deal with knowing that Clint was in her cabin. She'd never sleep.

"No, thanks. I'm just going to sleep with all the lights on. It'll make it feel more like home."

He grinned. "Suit yourself."

He walked to the door, opened it, locked it again, and the cowboy disappeared into the dark Wyoming night.

The next morning, Susan awoke with the sun shining through the lace curtains. She swore she could see her breath in the frigid cabin.

She pulled the quilt off the bed and wrapped it around herself. Then she searched the bedroom for a thermostat so she could turn up the heat, but there was none to be found.

From habit, she slipped on her watch and checked the time. Eight o'clock. She hadn't slept this long in years. If she'd been home, she would have already put in about two hours at work.

She'd slept so soundly. Maybe there was something to this "clean mountain air" thing after all.

She tightened the comforter around herself,

yanked on her fuzzy pink socks and walked into the living room.

She found the thermostat next to the fireplace, set it at seventy degrees and sat on the sofa, tucking her feet under her to warm them. It felt like December in New York instead of July in Wyoming.

She looked out the window in front of her and saw a kid go by on a horse. He had braces on both legs, and he was grinning and looking around as he rode, like a king surveying his realm. A cowboy walked beside the big horse, and her heart did a funny leap in her chest, thinking of Clint.

*Control yourself, Susan.*

She heard footsteps on the porch and soon heard a knock on her door.

"It's Clint."

In spite of trying to be in control, she felt her heart do a funny leap anyway. "Come in," she said. She knew he had a key.

The door opened, flooding the room in sunlight. She squinted at Clint.

"It's colder in here than it is outside. Why didn't you open the windows?"

"I never thought of that. That's not the usual way it works."

"That's the way it works around here."

He walked around the cottage and opened the windows. Sunlight and warmth filled the room. She loosened the comforter. He was right. It was warmer outside.

Clint sat opposite her on a big leather chair and

propped an ankle on his knee. "How'd you sleep after the bat?"

"Like a rock. I put the covers over my head and didn't move a muscle."

"Did you forget that we have a breakfast date?"

He studied her with a grin, and she knew she must look a sight. How come he looked so good in the morning? Judging by the crease marks on his long-sleeved pink shirt, it looked like he'd just taken it out of a package. His jeans were dark denim and also looked new, and he sported a belt buckle the size of a saucer.

He looked bright and chipper, and she felt as if she'd been run over by a double-decker tour bus. Life just wasn't fair.

"And don't forget your riding lesson," he said. "I only have one day to make a cowgirl out of you."

She hadn't forgotten, but hoped he had.

"Let's get moving—we've got a long day."

What happened to the check-his-pulse, laid-back cowboy from yesterday?

"Is there coffee in the dining hall?" she asked.

"Buckets of it."

"I'll be ready in ten minutes," she said, springing up from the couch and running to the shower.

She figured she'd just get some coffee to go and maybe a bagel with cream cheese. Her stomach was jittery enough from the bat last night and now she had to get up on a horse and try to ride? It'd been *years* since she'd been on horseback.

When she was ready, Clint opened the door for her and she stepped out into the bright sun. Halfway down the path and aiming for the biggest building, she heard a shrill whistle.

Looking around she realized that Clint hadn't budged from the porch of her cottage. "Something wrong?" she asked.

"I always like the view from here."

Curious, she walked back toward the porch and stood a few feet away from him, following his gaze to the mountains in the distance. Yes, they were beautiful. Not something she'd see back home.

She noticed several more buildings on the grounds. A long, wooden building had saddles hooked over the railing that surrounded it. To the left was a barn with a corral. The smiling boy she saw earlier was brushing his horse there. The cowboy who'd been with him sat on the wooden fence, watching.

"Smell that air," Clint said. He took a deep breath.

She did. The scent of pine drifted on the air, but she'd rather smell coffee. "Which building is the dining room?"

He pointed. "Hang on a minute."

He gave a shrill whistle and waved to the cowboy and the boy. "Morning, Jake. Morning, Tyrone."

They waved back.

"That's Jake Dixon. I guess you could call him the program director of the Gold Buckle. Tyrone is a camper." He walked toward Susan, as if he had all the time in the world.

She groaned. "Coffee. Hurry."

But he didn't hurry. She waited for him and looked around. To her right, almost a city block away, stood a large ranch house that must have been the model for the dozen or so smaller cottages. From the beams of the wraparound porch, fuchsia-colored flowers cascaded from hanging baskets. Pink and red roses climbed on white trellises from a bountiful garden.

On one half of the porch was another set of stairs and a wheelchair ramp. A large sign on the roof proclaimed "Office."

There were still more buildings. Some were weathered, others were whitewashed, and some were stone or brick. It looked like a little village.

Clint arrived at her side, and she felt his hand at the small of her back.

"It's not like New York City, I suppose."

She had to admit it was a pretty setting. "Manhattan looks incredible at night, but here there's such wide-open space and all those trees and mountains. It's breathtaking."

"I never thought you'd notice."

"I didn't, until you pointed it out."

Clint laughed and offered his arm. "Shall we dine?"

She hesitated a moment, then took his arm. "Sure."

He motioned toward a chalet-type building with big picture windows. "That's the dining hall, movie hall and all-round gathering place. And there's always a pot of coffee on, day or night."

The man knew how to get to her—forget the Chardonnay, bring on the caffeine.

"I think I should call my office first and see how things are going."

"You've only been gone a day. Let's eat first."

"But I've never been gone a day before."

He shrugged. "Give them some space. Maybe it would show you trusted them."

Maybe he was right, but she was still going to call.

As they walked, Susan was very aware of his presence. She could feel his taut muscles beneath his shirt. The sound of his boots against the hard-packed ground reminded her of a hundred old western movies that her father used to watch on TV—when he was still around, anyway.

She studied Clint. He was clean-shaven, tanned and fit, and he was making her heart beat double time in her chest.

No one she'd ever dated had excited her this much. Admittedly, she'd always gone for typical Manhattan businessmen—stockbrokers, bankers, real estate developers—yet it was this cowboy who intrigued her the most.

Then again, she didn't really know Clint. Heaven knows that she had more in common with the Manhattan singles. She loved to talk business with them. But none of them were for her. None of them could handle it when she left them waiting at the restaurant or the latest trendy bar a couple of times because she had to stay late at work.

Clint opened the door for her and she walked in. One of the first things she noticed were the long rows of picnic tables lined up end to end. The dining hall was crowded and noisy with a lot of laughter, the clang of china plates and the metallic clicking of silverware.

And full of kids.

Susan's heart started to ache immediately. Yet these kids were smiling and laughing, yelling to one another. She could hear snippets of conversation about the horses they wanted to ride and what they planned to do during the day.

Black cowboy hats bobbed up and down, like a flock of crows pecking at seed. Every once in a while, a white hat could be spotted in the mix—a dove among the crows.

Under the hats were cowboys and cowgirls of all ages, wearing long-sleeved shirts, denim jeans and cowboy boots.

Uniforms. Cowboy uniforms.

She looked down at her designer clothes and her strappy Italian sandals. Maybe she ought to find a phone and give Bev a call, ask her to send a care package of western wear.

Clint steered her toward the back of the huge room to a cafeteria line, just like the one she remembered from high school. He plopped down an orange plastic tray in front of her and nodded to a tall, thin cowboy behind the counter. He had bristly white whiskers and a black baseball hat that read "Professional Bull Riders." He wore a gray T-shirt, and on his arms were tattoos of the Marine Corps.

"She wants the works, Cookie," Clint said.

Before she could tell him that she just wanted a toasted bagel with cream cheese, he handed her a plate heaped with scrambled eggs, bacon, ham and fried potatoes with onions.

"Come back for seconds or thirds if you want

'em," Cookie said, grinning. "We got more than enough."

Clint plucked a potato that had fallen off her plate onto the tray and popped it into his mouth. "Every once in a while, Cookie thinks that he's still cooking for the marines."

She looked down at her breakfast, floating in grease. "I see that he specializes in low-fat cuisine."

Cookie handed Clint an identically heaped plate of food.

"The grease makes your hair shiny," Clint said, leading Susan to an empty picnic table. "How do you take your coffee?"

"Black."

"Have a seat, I'll be right back."

She watched him walk to a round table supporting a coffee urn as big as a silo. Clint could really work a pair of jeans, and she could think of several designers who'd scoop him up instantly as a model, but her major concern was the fact that her coffee would be cold by the time he meandered back.

He finally returned and handed her a steaming mug of the coffee and she took a long sip. The strong, bitter brew slammed against the back of her brain and her eyes watered. She gasped for breath as her toes curled into her sandals.

"Good stuff, huh?" Clint said. "That's cowboy coffee."

She closed her eyes. She couldn't speak.

"You'll get used to it."

She took a bite of bacon. It had a nice smoky

flavor and she guessed it was the real cholesterol-laden thing.

"So what are you going to teach in arts and crafts?" Clint asked. "I'll help you any way I can."

She took a deep breath. She didn't want to think about it yet. "Thanks, Clint. I appreciate the offer and will definitely take you up on it."

He nodded and concentrated on his plate of food.

"How come nobody takes their hat off when they eat?" Susan asked.

"A cowboy never takes his hat off," Clint replied. Then he winked. "Well, maybe there's one thing that I'd take my hat off for."

He winked again, and she felt a tingle in her belly. She might be rusty as to the flirting thing, but it was all coming back to her. "You're bald under that hat, right?"

"Like I said, I only take my hat off for one thing, so if you want to find out..."

There was that annoying flip of her heart again.

Before she could think of a witty comeback, she noticed a little girl on crutches awkwardly making her way toward the table. And all she could think of was Elaine, as a pang struck her heart.

How was she going to survive this trip when she couldn't escape her memories?

# *Chapter 4*

Susan couldn't take her eyes off the little girl. She had blond wispy hair like Elaine's, and Elaine's smile, but that's where the similarity ended. Elaine had been much taller and weighed more than this tiny creature.

As the girl got closer, Susan could see that she had braces on both legs. A piece of paper and a pen were crumpled around the handle of a crutch where she clutched it.

She had a big grin as she made her way over to them. "Can I help you with something, sweetie?" Susan asked, trying to ignore her aching heart.

"I want Cheyenne Clint's autograph," she said.

Susan smiled at her. "Cheyenne who?"

The girl tilted her head. "Cheyenne Clint. The rodeo clown. He's sitting right next to you."

"Cheyenne Clint—" Susan laid her hand on his arm to get his attention "—you have a fan here who wants your autograph."

Clint wiped his mouth with a napkin and swiveled to see who was talking to him. "Well, well, aren't you a pretty young lady." He tipped his hat to her. "Cheyenne Clint Scully at your service, little lady."

The tiny girl giggled. "Will you sign your autograph?"

"I'd be honored." Clint patiently waited as she handed him the crumpled paper and a pen. "What's your name, darlin'?"

"Alisa Constance Pedigrew."

Clint gave a high-pitched whistle as he scribbled on the paper. "That's a name for a princess. Are you a princess?"

She giggled again, cocking her head to the side. "No." Her fine, pale hair skimmed the shoulder of her colorful striped T-shirt and then she tossed her head back. She had on a pair of denim shorts that hid the top of where her braces started. She leaned on aluminum crutches with metal armbands.

"Well, I am going to make you the Princess of the Gold Buckle Ranch for as long as you stay here. That okay with you?"

"Sure!"

Clint made Alisa's face light up with pure enjoyment, and that was a real talent.

Clint took off his hat, and Susan saw that he had short, straight brown hair shot with streaks of gold. Mystery solved.

He placed his hat on Alisa's head and said, "I,

Cheyenne Clint, pronounce you Princess of the Gold Buckle Ranch."

Alisa's giggle got louder and she leaned over to cover her mouth with a hand. She glanced around the room as if eager to see if anyone else might have noticed her coronation. Finally, she glanced at Susan, a certain shyness entering her gaze.

"Hello," she said. "Are you Mrs. Cheyenne Clint?"

*Heaven forbid.*

"No. My name is Susan. Susan Collins." Even to Susan's ears, her voice sounded thin and strained.

The little girl brushed back some of her hair from her face. The crutch dangled from her arm. "You're pretty."

"Why, thank you, Alisa. So are you." She didn't know what else to say. "Are you a camper?"

She nodded. "For a while. I'm an orphan, you know. I'm staying with Mrs. Dixon until I get adopted." A slightly defiant look entered her expressive blue eyes. "But Robbie says that because I'm six going on seven, and I'm handicapped, no one might want me. Do you think that's true?"

Susan swallowed hard, resisting the urge to scoop the girl up and hold her tight. Who the hell was Robbie and what made him say such a cruel thing? But Susan knew the answer to that. Kids could be cruel. They'd been cruel to Elaine. They used to grab her crutches and make her reach for them. No one ever asked her to play with them—it was as if she carried some contagious disease that they were afraid to catch. As her sister battled her bone cancer, all she'd ever wanted was to get better—so she could finally be invited to play with the other kids.

But how was she supposed to answer a question like that? To say, “Oh, that’s not true” seemed so hollow. The girl was probably right. It was difficult to place older children for adoption, and those with medical problems were nearly impossible to find adoptive parents for.

She prayed that whatever was wrong with Alisa could be fixed with surgery, or maybe the braces would help mend her.

Clint reached out and gently tucked the little girl’s wispy blond hair behind her ear. “Tell me, who is this Robbie?”

“Oh, he’s one of the boys in the foster home I was in, but he got adopted. He liked to tease everyone.”

“I might have to have a little chat with Robbie. Can’t have him teasing the Princess of the Gold Buckle Ranch, now, can we?”

Alisa and Clint exchanged grins, and she moved closer to him, her small body leaning up against his as if for protection.

“Thank you,” she whispered.

“My pleasure. So Mrs. Dixon is taking care of you for a while, right?”

“Uh-huh. I was the only one left. The foster parents wanted to go on vacation, so my social worker asked Mrs. Dixon to let me stay here. And Mrs. Dixon said that I could ride the horses and be one of the Gold Buckle Gang. Cool, huh?”

“Cool. And I’ll bet you’ll be the best rider here.”

Alisa looked much younger than “almost seven.”

She was too tiny for her age. Susan guessed that it might be due to her condition.

Her heart turned into a lead weight in her chest. It would be too easy to fall in love with this little girl.

Susan wouldn't—*couldn't*—let herself do that.

"Are you going to be working here?" Alisa asked.

"I'll be teaching arts and crafts."

Alisa's light blue eyes were sparkling now. "Are you going on the campout? Can I ride by you? Will you be my counselor?"

Susan tried to swallow so she could speak, but the words wouldn't come. Elaine, too, had looked at her with such hope and blind trust.

Susan had made Elaine promises that she couldn't keep. She'd said that she wouldn't let Elaine die, but she hadn't been able to keep that promise.

"I'm going to teach Susan how to ride," Clint said.

"Awesome." Alisa giggled, slipping Clint's autograph into the pocket of her shorts. "I gotta go now. I'm supposed to meet my social worker at Mr. and Mrs. Dixon's house."

Clint stood to his full height and bowed at the waist. "I'll see you later, Princess Alisa."

Susan watched as Alisa limped away. It seemed like such an effort for her little body to move, and Susan wanted to pick her up and carry her wherever she had to go.

But it was far better to keep her distance from the girl, and the other campers. Distance allowed her to keep the hurt and guilt from filling her up and choking her.

Distance and hard work. When she was working

and busy, she forgot about Elaine and her parents. About how lonely she was.

Clint put his hand over hers and squeezed. "You look pretty shaken. Are you all right?"

"I'm fine." Susan knew her smile faltered a little, but she hid it behind her coffee cup.

"It's hard to see kids suffer like that."

*More than you'll ever know.*

"You were great with her." She liked the feel of his hand on hers.

Clint leaned in closer and grinned. "I'm even better with ladies your age."

She removed her hand. She didn't want him to think she was interested in a relationship with him, or anyone for that matter. "I didn't know what to say to her after she dropped the bomb about being an orphan." Susan took a sip of coffee, closed her eyes and waited for the bitter aftertaste to dissolve.

"You did fine," he said.

She'd wanted to assure Alisa that things would be okay, that she'd find two parents who would love her and they'd make a family. But Susan knew those kinds of wishes rarely came true. Growing up, Susan had prayed every evening for an intact family, but it hadn't happened. She'd asked Santa and wished upon all the stars in the sky, but still her father never came back to stay for good.

Remembering all those unanswered prayers and dreams, she suddenly lost her appetite, but watched as Clint finished his breakfast. Then he washed it down with a long drag of coffee and didn't even blink.

"By the way, why are you called Cheyenne Clint?"

"Because I was born and raised in Boston."

She chuckled. "Okay, sorry. Dumb question, but you could be a Cheyenne Indian."

"Okay. I'm from Cheyenne, Wyoming. A while ago some announcer started calling me that, and it stuck. Now, are you ready to learn how to ride?" he asked.

She thought again of Alisa and the other kids. Although she wanted to help, she knew everyone would be better off if she just wrote out a check.

"Clint, I'm really not good with kids. Not like you are. Maybe you could teach arts and crafts."

Clint leaned back, his arms crossed. His eyes seemed to bore into her soul. The intensity of his gaze threw her and made her want to take back what she'd said. But the words hung in the air between them.

"What are you afraid of?" he finally said. "They're just kids. You'll do fine."

She almost believed him, but somewhere deep inside her a little voice told her he was wrong. He didn't know her history, her childhood. She wouldn't be fine. She knew this like she knew linen from cotton, jersey from wool. She was headed for a fall and powerless to steady herself.

But sink or swim, she'd live up to her promise.

Clint guided Susan through the open doors of the barn.

Even to her untrained eye, the interior was meticulously clean, in spite of the fact that a good three dozen horses, who had nothing to do except eat and poop, were in residence.

The gray cement floor was spotless, and the sweet smell of hay permeated the barn. Stalls flanked both sides of the aisle, and horses of various colors hung their heads over their half doors to inspect their visitors.

Clint looked at her sandals. “You should have changed your shoes for riding.”

“I didn’t bring any shoes for riding.”

“What about running shoes?”

“I did bring a pair of those.” Susan sighed. “I don’t know about all this.” She looked around the barn, then at Clint. “I don’t belong here.” So much about keeping her promises. So much for doing it for the kids. She was just one selfish woman.

Before she could stop him, Clint took her hand, slipped his arm around her waist and began to dance with her around the barn. He hummed a slow tune, something she didn’t recognize, but oh, she liked it—and she liked being held by him.

“You’re just nervous about riding. Relax a little.”

She looked up into his eyes. He smiled and kept humming his tune. He was easy to dance with, easy to talk to. She didn’t want to get to know him or confide in him. She just wanted out. That’s all.

Instead, all her emotions were bubbling to the surface, things that she’d kept buried in her heart.

Susan knew exactly what had triggered it all: Alisa, the little girl she’d met at breakfast.

She wanted to push her emotions back down into that place where she’d kept them hidden all these years, but here, of all places, they just wouldn’t stay put.

*This must be how people with amnesia feel when their memory comes flooding back.*

Clint must have sensed she was about to pull out of his arms, because he held her tighter and whispered, "Slow down, Susie. Just dance with me."

She swallowed the lump in her throat. "No one has called me that since my mother died."

"Tell me about her."

His soothing voice calmed her as his hand gently stroked circles on her back. As they spoke, he continued to slowly move her around the barn as if it were their own private dance hall.

"She died seven years ago. It was a heart attack. She died in her sleep."

Darn it. There was no holding her back now. She was really going to spill her guts to a cowboy she'd only met yesterday.

Susan took a deep breath. "My father left us periodically. He'd just pack up and head out for months at a time. He worked for a travel agency, and most of the times he was gone he'd be leading groups on tours. Later, he left more frequently and stayed away longer because he couldn't cope with…everything."

She'd managed to gather up enough sense to stop from telling him why her father couldn't cope. She wasn't ready to discuss Elaine.

"Mom was a nurse, so I never saw her much, either. She threw herself into her work to keep busy after Dad moved out for good."

"And then?"

"And then she started to do some sewing—alterations, tailoring, whatever she could do to make ends meet. Then she started making cute, colorful smocks for other nurses, and sold them. She showed me how to pin the patterns to the material. After I did my homework, I'd cut the material. Eventually we had quite a business going. I treasured the time with her. Later, during summer vacation from school, we'd make gowns for the patients. We'd make really fun ones for the kids with wild material and colors. As I got older, Mom taught me how to run the sewing machine."

She felt Clint's hand on her neck, under her hair, rubbing and kneading at the knot of tension. She let herself be boneless, loose.

"When my mother died, I started Winners Wear. It was a dream of ours."

"And you made your company a success."

It was a statement, not a question, and she liked that.

"I have," she said proudly.

"Good for you. And your father?"

"What about him?"

"Did he ever come back into the picture?"

"No." Susan felt the usual apathy and bitterness well up inside her whenever she thought of her father. "Apparently he has a pretty successful travel agency of his own now."

He left right after Elaine died—hadn't even come to the funeral. He was taking a tour group to Greece. Susan had only been twelve years old, and she'd needed her father. Her mother had been inconsolable, wrapped up in her own sadness.

She'd never forgiven her father for deserting them.

What was she doing spilling her guts to a bull-fighter? She'd seen some of the best counselors in New York, and had never blabbed like she did to this man in a barn full of horses.

After a while, it seemed like the most natural thing in the world to dance in a barn and tell a stranger about her life. It was okay, she told herself. She'd never see him again after this week.

She closed her eyes and listened to Clint hum. His chest vibrated with each note, each nuance of the tune. She tried to relax her mind and not think about orders for football jerseys or the Idaho marching band with the potato on their lapels. She tried not to think about her father, or how she missed her mother and Elaine. Or how much Alisa reminded her of Elaine.

She simply closed her eyes and concentrated on dancing with this unique cowboy.

The dancing stopped and Clint still held her in his arms. He studied her face, then drew closer. His eyes lowered as if he were studying her lips.

She could hear his breathing increase as he tipped his head.

She wouldn't object if he kissed her. She wanted him to kiss her. Maybe then she'd stop wondering what it would be like.

Instead, he gave a slight wink, tweaked his hat and let her go.

# *Chapter 5*

He'd almost kissed her.

Normally, he would have, but for whatever reason, he had held himself back. But why? He could tell that Susan was willing.

There had to be something seriously wrong with Clint Scully if he'd stopped himself from kissing a beautiful woman.

Who was he kidding? He knew the reason. Mary Alice Bonner still haunted him. She'd had the same expensive tastes and the same drive for success as Susan, the same determination to prove that they could succeed.

Susan had proved that she didn't need her father.

Mary Alice had proved that she didn't need Clint Scully.

While he'd been waiting for the wedding march to begin at St. Paul's Church in Cheyenne, Mary Alice had been on a plane to Chicago.

She had sent him a note via her sister, Louise, so at least he hadn't waited all day for her, wondering what had happened. The note had read simply, "Sorry, Clint. I want something more than you can give me."

*More than you can give me.*

Mary Alice Bonner was now the president of a Fortune 500 jewelry chain, a member of the jet set and a regular in *People* magazine.

He frequently ran into Mary Alice's sister, Louise. Lou said that Mary Alice wasn't all that happy, and had paid a high price for her success.

Susan Collins was all New York City, from the top of her sleek coppery-red hair down to her pedicured toes with the pink polish. She was a successful businesswoman from what he could tell, too. She was smart, had a bossy side, and yet something still gnawed at her.

He could also tell that when she wasn't comfortable in a situation, she wanted to retreat. She still might bolt yet.

Just like Mary Alice Bonner.

Susan was intriguing—and Clint really liked intriguing—but he couldn't get involved with her. No way in hell. He might have taken a few blows in the head from some bulls, but he wasn't stupid.

"Pick out a horse you like," he said. "All of them are as gentle as lambs and have been trained for the Wheelchair Rodeo kids."

"Therefore, we city slickers can handle them, too?"

"Absolutely."

"Okay."

"I'll have you riding before you can say, 'Big Apple,' so don't worry about a thing." He put a hand on her back and could feel the tension in the set of her spine, tension that had almost dissolved when they were dancing.

She continued walking, then stopped to pet the nose of a pretty palomino. "I like this one. She's smiling at me."

Clint rubbed a hand along his chin. "Yep, she's definitely smiling at you."

"What's her name?"

He pointed to the sign above the stall. "Goldie."

She ran her hand along the horse's neck. "Hello, Goldie."

"Watch how I saddle her up, and from now on you can do it." Clint lifted a bridle from the nail next to Goldie's stall and saw Susan checking her watch.

He tightened the girth on the saddle. "Did you get all that? How I saddled and bridled the horse?"

"Absolutely," she said, shaking her head no.

"Great." He chuckled and handed her the reins. "Goldie will be your horse for as long as you're here. You'll both have to get used to each other. Walk her out to the corral."

She tightened her hands around the reins. "Okay, Goldie. Let's go."

Susan was gentle with Goldie and frequently looked back to see if the horse was still attached to the reins and still following her. A lot of first-time riders did the same thing, and he always got a kick out of it.

He walked beside her out to the corral. “Okay. Now take the reins and put them on each side of her neck and keep them in your hand.” He held the bridle. “Okay. Good. Put your left foot in the stirrup and toss your right leg over the saddle.”

“Um…uh…she’s pretty high up there.”

“Yup.”

“No steps?” At least there had been steps where she took lessons.

“No. And she won’t squat down for you like a camel, either.”

“You read my mind.”

She put her foot in the stirrup and did three hops. On her next hop, Clint grabbed her cute bottom and gave her an extra boost into the saddle.

“Was it good for you?” he asked.

She chuckled and rolled her eyes, then concentrated on the horse. “I never realized that they were this tall.”

He wished he had a dollar for every time he heard that, he thought, slipping a hand under a bridle strap. “I’ll just walk her around the corral for a while so you can get used to her. Just relax and feel the rhythm of her gait. Go with it.”

He walked the horse for ten minutes, stealing glances at Susan. She looked like a queen on her throne, smiling, glancing around and petting the horse’s neck.

Clint stopped. “Are you ready to do this yourself?”

"Sure."

He let go of the bridle and held his hands up as if he were being arrested. "Go nice and slow. Nothing fancy. Just walk her around the corral. Big circle. She knows what do."

He hopped up on the fence, leaned his elbows on his thighs and flagged down a cowboy walking by. "Juan, do you have time to saddle up Brutus for me? I don't want to leave our guest alone here. She's a genuine city slicker."

"Will do, Clint."

"Thanks, *amigo*."

Clint watched as Susan rode Goldie at a slow walk around the corral. It was a beautiful scene with the blue skies, a beautiful horse and a beautiful woman, not necessarily in that order. However, the beautiful woman was about to jar her brains loose.

"Keep your heels down, Susan," he shouted. "Go with the rhythm of the horse."

She did as instructed and the results were much smoother.

He let her do that for another five minutes until she yelled, "Hey, we're getting dizzy here."

"Just lean the reins lightly on her neck, lead her over here and hit the brakes."

"Brakes?"

"Just kidding. She'll stop on her own."

"I knew that," she said.

Juan brought Brutus over, and Clint hopped down from the fence. "Thanks."

Juan couldn't take his eyes off of Susan. Clint

slapped him on the back and lightly pushed him along his way. "Thanks again, *amigo.* Bye, now."

Finally, Juan took the hint.

"How about a ride on the Chisholm Trail?" Clint asked.

"I'm not familiar with this part of the world, but isn't that a little far away?"

"We have what we call the Chisholm Trail right here. It runs behind the cabins and alongside the creek. Shall we?"

He nudged Brutus along. Goldie would follow Brutus, so Susan didn't have much choice but to follow him.

No matter how intriguing her secrets were, he couldn't help but wish that he were on the real Chisholm Trail, far away from her.

He knew danger. He dealt with it every time the chute gate opened and a bull came charging out with a cowboy on his back.

Susan was a different kind of danger. She was everything he wasn't.

She was asphalt and high rises. He was prairie grass and mountains. She was designer clothes and Italian sandals. He was jeans and boots.

Still, she was the kind of woman that made a cowboy think about hanging up his spurs and settling down.

Not that he was that kind of cowboy.

No one would ever get him to settle down and work himself to death. His parents had done that. Susan was doing that.

He liked being free.

Susan wasn't the type who'd ever like the road. She'd never even seen a bull riding event. At least Mary Alice had traveled with him for a while.

He didn't even know why he was even thinking along those lines about Susan Collins. He never usually thought about making a life with the women who crossed his path, let alone anything beyond one night.

In spite of all their differences, it didn't mean that they couldn't enjoy each other for a week. When it was over, he'd just say goodbye.

The way he always did.

Goldie dutifully followed Brutus down the so-called Chisholm Trail, and Susan just sat as if she were in a rocking chair. She kept her heels down as Clint had instructed, and checked her watch to see what time it was back home.

"Clint, can we get back? I really need to make some calls."

"Will you relax and quit worrying about what's happening at your company." He glanced over one broad shoulder, a small smile touching the corners of those magnificent lips—lips that hadn't kissed her in the barn for whatever reason. "Look around you. It's beautiful out here."

Gripping the saddle horn, she did look around, realizing with a certain amount of wonder that he was right. The rays of the sun lit up the pine trees and released their scent. On their right side, a little brook sparkled, its slow-running current meandering over rocks and dips and making cheerful, soothing noises.

She noticed the sun hovering over the peaks and bathing the valley in sunlight—sunlight that filtered through the pines.

She let herself smell the pine-scented air and feel the slight breeze on her face. She listened to the water and the steady clip-clop of the horses. For a while, she was so relaxed that she was afraid she'd fall asleep and fall out of the saddle.

There was no denying the fact that time moved slower at the Gold Buckle. As slow as the laid-back cowboy riding in front of her.

Who would have thought that she'd ever be riding through the woods of Wyoming with a cowboy?

The trail widened, and he slowed down to ride beside her. "Look at those little purple wildflowers up there."

She saw a cascade of purple on an embankment. Above the flowers, in a small clearing, stood a big white trailer.

"Who lives there?" Susan asked.

His horse stopped, and so did hers.

"That is Casa de Clint Scully. My house. I tow it wherever I go. Rodeo to rodeo…wherever."

"You live in *that?*"

His eyes twinkled. "It's a home on wheels. Want to see the inside? She's a beauty."

She nodded. "I see." But she didn't. Why would anyone want to live in such a thing? "Is there a washer and dryer in it?"

"No room. Matter of fact, if I gain five pounds, I can't turn around in it."

"Then who does your laundry? Your shirts are

always impeccable and the crease down the arm is perfect."

"This is the way they come out of the package." He pointed to the logo on the front pocket. "My sponsors send them to me by the case."

"You have sponsors?"

"Several. I wear their stuff, and they get free advertising, especially when I'm on TV."

"You're on TV? Really?"

"Some bull riding events are televised. I told you before that Cheyenne Clint is a bona fide star."

He went up a notch in her estimation. Maybe he actually made a living out of his strange profession. Then she looked skeptically at his trailer.

He grinned, obviously knowing what she was thinking. "C'mon. I'll show you inside."

Goldie followed Brutus up a slight incline. Clint expertly got off Brutus and flipped the reins over a tree branch. He took Goldie's reins from her and did the same.

She started to get down from the horse but felt his hands on her waist, helping her down. She turned toward him, but his hands didn't move. Her body heated where he touched her.

She looked toward the trailer, and he cleared his throat.

"Uh…over here." He pointed.

They walked to a screen door on the other side of the trailer. He hit a button and three steps slid out. "Welcome."

Clint flicked on a switch and she could see that the inside was heaped from floor to ceiling with boxes.

"Your wardrobe?" she asked.

"All free of charge."

She was amazed at the oak cabinets, the granite counter, the microwave and the four-burner stove. A full-size refrigerator with a water and ice dispenser stood next to a dinette with seating for four. A beige leather couch was on the opposite side and a plasma TV and music equipment were positioned in a corner cabinet. All the cabinets were oak, the colors beige and light.

"Clint, this is just beautiful."

"You have to see the bathroom," he said, grabbing her hand and pulling her along.

His bathroom was bigger than the one in her apartment. So was the shower.

"Where's your bedroom?"

"Right here. And watch this."

He pressed a button, and the room slid out several feet. It gave the room much more space. There was a full-size queen bed and closets all around the room, another TV, nightstands and a vanity where he had a laptop and printer.

"This is incredible. It's designed so perfectly. Not an inch of space is wasted."

Later, they sat under the awning outside, sipping some ice water and listening to the water cascade over the rocks. Clint walked the horses to the creek and let them drink.

They spent an enjoyable hour just talking. Susan couldn't believe she just sat for such a long time doing nothing. She noticed everything about Clint—his easy manner of talking, the way he leaned forward and listened intently whenever she was speaking.

She couldn't remember when she had a better time.

"We should probably get going," Clint said.

He helped her back onto Goldie, pushing her butt with an exaggerated grunt.

She laughed. "Oh, stop."

"So, is trailer life for you?" he asked when they were back on the Chisholm Trail.

"I don't think so."

"What would you like?"

She thought about that for a while. She'd liked when her family lived in Tarrytown, New York, when she was growing up in a Dutch colonial with a lot of nooks and crannies inside and a front and backyard. It was a great place to live and to go to school. She'd had friends there, friends who had since all gone their separate ways, but who still got together twice a year for dinner. They always asked her to go, but she was always too busy.

Funny, she hadn't thought about Tarrytown in a long time. She'd been happy there, at least for a while.

"If I ever decided to move out of Manhattan, which I never would, I might like a home with some land and a thick green lawn that needs mowing twice a week. And a garden where I can grow flowers and tomatoes."

"Sounds like a prison to me," he said.

"I suppose it does to someone who has a trailer and no roots."

He chuckled. "Just like a tumbling tumbleweed."

"Just like my father," she said. "Only he had a family that he ignored."

He frowned. "I don't have that problem."

That was true, so he could do what he wanted. So could she.

They walked out of the woods into the meadow that lay like a carpet of wildflowers up to the base of the mountain. She had the urge to see how fast Goldie could go.

"Could we gallop, Clint?"

"No. You're too new at this. But how about a trot? Keep your legs down. Don't bounce."

Brutus went faster, and Goldie followed. Clint picked up more speed.

She laughed. She was a kid again at her Saturday riding lesson. She could picture her father cheering for her. Later, they'd take the train back to Tarrytown.

They'd stop for a cheeseburger and chocolate shake at Casey's Corner. All too soon, the weekend would be over. Monday was school again, and her responsibilities would return. She always had to watch over Elaine in school, protect her from the other kids.

What would it be like to have no responsibility like Clint?

She couldn't fathom it. She had more than four hundred people who depended on her for their income.

Clint slowed down and they went back to a walk. He pulled his horse up next to hers. Clint was born to sit in a saddle. His jean-clad thighs looked rock hard, and he seemed natural and relaxed, as if he could ride all day. Yet underneath that exterior, he was a little wild and untamed, and Susan couldn't picture him living anywhere except under the Western skies.

She was breathing hard and could barely talk. "Before I leave, I'd like to gallop."

"You're a tough woman, Susan Collins."

"You ain't seen nothing yet, Cheyenne Clint."

# Chapter 6

Emily Dixon rushed into the barn while they were brushing their horses.

"You're just the two I've been looking for. Susan, I have to cancel our meeting about the arts and crafts program until later this afternoon. I'm sorry."

"That's okay, Emily," Susan said, although she was disappointed at the news. She wanted to brainstorm some projects.

Emily flipped through her clipboard. "Clint, I noticed that you aren't scheduled for any activities until this afternoon."

"What's up, Mrs. D?" Clint asked.

"Alisa's group is scheduled for a riding lesson, but I can't let her participate. She's inconsolable. It's a paperwork and insurance problem with Children's

Services. She has to be cleared by their doctor, and he's not available. Right now, she's crying on her bed up at the house. She's asking for you both."

"Me?" Susan asked. "I barely know her."

"She has connected with you somehow." Emily smiled.

Clint grinned. "Of course."

"I don't know what to do. All I can think of is that maybe she'd like a picnic and a splash in the river. I don't mean to impose, but I have a lot of things to do and—"

"You were wondering if we could help?" Clint said.

"Please?" Emily asked.

Clint nodded. "I'm in the mood for a picnic and a splash in the river. How about you, Susan?"

She'd rather not. It was obvious that Alisa was already getting too attached to them both, but her heart went out to the girl. She had been excluded, like Susan's own sister had always been, so if a picnic and a swim would make her feel as though she belonged, then Susan would go.

She nodded. "Sounds like fun."

"Let's do it, then." He cracked his knuckles. "Mrs. D, tell Alisa to dry her eyes, slip her bathing suit on and wait for us in front of the office. Susan, you do the same."

Emily let out a deep breath. "I'll get Cookie to pack up a nice lunch." She smiled gratefully. "I can't thank you both enough."

A half hour later, Clint was lifting Alisa into the buckboard. Then he helped Susan in. They jostled and swayed, singing songs at the top of their lungs, until they finally arrived at the picnic area.

Clint pointed to a clapboard building. "That's a combination changing area, shower facility and bathroom. Some cowboys and I built it a couple years ago."

The building had a dusting of old rust-colored pine needles on the roof. It smelled like fresh-cut lumber, and looked sturdy enough to withstand whatever Wyoming weather it needed to. Then she noticed a sign: The Gold Buckle Ranch Thanks Clint Scully.

Susan turned to him. "You donated this…building?"

He nodded. "I told them not to put up that sign, but Mrs. D insisted."

She smiled. "That was very generous of you." It must have cost him everything he had.

"It was nothing. I'm only regretting that we didn't make it bigger, so I figure I'll have to donate another one."

Susan wondered whether he was joking.

She turned to see a wide concrete path that led to a glittering river. Green picnic tables were scattered along the bank.

Susan took a deep breath. "It's a beautiful day for a picnic."

Clint raised an eyebrow. "You noticed?"

"Yes. I've noticed."

He jumped down from the buckboard and tied the horses to a post. "Maybe there's hope for you yet."

He came around to her side, offered her his hand and helped her down.

"Thanks."

"My pleasure."

It *was* surprising that she was noticing anything lately. Clint was occupying her thoughts much too much. He made her laugh like she hadn't in years, and she was relaxed around him. Maybe too relaxed. A part of her regretted telling him such personal things about her life. She'd always taken great pride in being able to keep things about her family safely stored and locked tightly inside her. Here, she had way too much free time to think, to unlock her feelings and look inside.

She needed to keep busy. Needed to concentrate on concrete things, like shipping, filling orders, the payroll, the IRS. Those were tangible things that occupied her days and nights in calm, rational ways. She didn't need these emotional feelings that pulled and tore at her very being. That's why she needed to get back to New York.

Alisa appeared at her side. "Susan, could you tie my bathing suit for me? It came undone."

"Sure, sweetie."

Alisa bent her head, and Susan quickly tied her little halter top in place.

"Great suit," Susan said, trying not to notice the way Alisa's right hip protruded from her skinny body. Her right knee looked a little swollen and pinkish near one of the bars of her brace, but Susan knew that this was common. Elaine had suffered from her braces on numerous occasions. The cold river water would help that.

"Look! There's a bird's nest in that tree," Alisa shouted.

Susan looked up, following the line of Alisa's finger. "I see it. It's a pretty big one."

"Can we look closer at it?"

"Sure."

Just as they were walking over to the tree, Clint appeared at their side.

"What's up?" he asked.

"There's a bird's nest in that tree. I want to see if there are any babies in it," Alisa said.

Clint put a finger up to his lips. "We have to quietly make sure there *aren't* any babies in it, or it'll bother the mother bird."

They crept closer to the nest and leaned over.

"I don't see any babies," Alisa whispered.

"I don't, either," Clint agreed. "I think everyone's moved out."

Susan could feel his breath on her neck and could smell his spicy aftershave. If she turned slightly, she'd be mouth-to-mouth with him.

The thought sent a delicious shiver through her.

"Can I have it?" Alisa asked.

Susan turned to look around for a feathered home owner who might object, and her eyes met Clint's. She could get lost in those turquoise eyes of his, the color of the Wyoming sky overhead.

"I can't ever say no to a beautiful lady," Clint said, gazing into Susan's eyes.

He sure could flirt, and she was rusty, but she

leaned over and whispered in his ear, “Can you reach it?”

She could hear his quick intake of air. He turned toward her, and their lips almost touched. She didn’t move. He blinked and swallowed hard.

“Um…uh…” His voice sounded rough, wheezy. “I’ll get the nest for you, Alisa.”

“Thanks.”

She watched as Clint placed the nest so very gently into Alisa’s hands. Tears welled up in Susan’s eyes as she watched him. It was a little thing, but something shot straight to her heart. Could he be any sweeter?

They waited as Alisa examined every inch of the nest. The look of complete awe on her face made Susan smile.

Had she ever been that young, that happy? When had she ever stepped off her treadmill to notice a bird’s nest in a pine tree?

“Could I have a pinecone, too?” Alisa lifted up a crutch and pointed to a top branch. “Could I have that one, please?”

“Of course, sweetie.” Susan plucked it off and handed it to her.

The girl inspected it carefully just as she inspected the bird’s nest.

“Don’t you guys want pinecones?”

Clint nodded. “Absolutely.”

“Sure,” Susan said, wondering what on earth she’d do with a pinecone.

Susan plucked two more from the tree and handed them to Alisa.

"Awesome."

"Let's put them here for now." Susan pointed to the nest, and Alisa dropped them in. "And we'll put the nest on top of the tote bag."

Clint clapped his hands together and rubbed them. "Let's head for the water."

"Don't forget the picnic supplies back at the wagon," Susan reminded him.

"Well, just call me a pack mule," he said, loping off to the wagon.

"Cheyenne Clint is funny." Alisa looked up at her, her head tilted and her eyes squinted into the sun. "Do you like him?"

"Sure. He's funny and happy all the time. Right?"

Alisa nodded. "My dad was funny, too. Me and my mom were always laughing at him." She looked at the water, and then looked down. "Will you help me take the braces off?"

Elaine used to say that to her. Used to look up at her that way. *"Please, Susie, help me take this stuff off."*

"Of course I'll help you."

"I'll show you how."

"I know how, Alisa. I know."

"You do?"

"My sister Elaine had to wear braces."

"Really?"

Susan nodded.

"Does she still have to wear them? Or did she get better?"

"She didn't get better." Susan took a deep breath, and felt the usual sting in the back of her eyes whenever she thought of Elaine. She looked away so that Alisa wouldn't see the water in them. "Elaine is… uh…no longer with us."

Alisa's eyes grew wide. "Elaine went to heaven?"

Susan nodded, not trusting herself to talk.

Susan felt Alisa's little fingers wiggling their way into her hand. She looked down at the sweet, small face of the little girl who was slowly but surely sneaking into her heart.

"My mommy and daddy are in heaven, too," Alisa said.

Susan closed her eyes. She couldn't allow herself to love another girl who looked at her as if she could rope the moon.

Another little girl she might lose.

Susan didn't want to know if Alisa's condition was terminal. Some things were better left unsaid or unknown, or the pain would be unbearable.

Susan glanced over at Clint, who was still back at the wagon, unloading all the things that Emily had sent. She wished he were here to say or do something funny and ease this sudden sad moment.

Well, he wasn't, so it was up to her.

She mustered a smile, gave Alisa's hand a squeeze and knelt on the grass in front of her. "Let's get rid of all that metal and plastic, shall we?"

She unhooked Alisa's braces, slipped them off, and then removed the girl's shoes and socks.

Looking like the pack mule he had joked about, Clint arrived. He carried a picnic basket, a brightly striped blanket, two big gym bags and another tote bag.

He paused when he saw what Susan had done. She nodded slightly, so he'd get the message that things were okay.

He shook out the blanket and spread it on the grass. Opening a gym bag, he peered in and pulled out a small camp chair and a clip-on sun umbrella.

"Emily packed this for Alisa."

"Perfect," Susan said, taking the chair from him and unfolding it. They could put it in the water for Alisa to sit on. If she got sleepy, she could lie on the blanket under the shade of the umbrella. "She thought of everything."

They watched as Alisa wobbled unsteadily to the shore of the river with her bare feet and crutches.

Clint sat on the blanket and yanked off his boots and slid off his socks. "Hang on there, Miss Alisa. Don't put another toe in the water until we're with you."

"Hurry up, then," she ordered.

Clint unbuttoned his shirt, tossed it on the blanket and hurried to Alisa. Seeing his tanned, muscular chest gave Susan an immediate vision of him taking his shirt off for her as they made love.

She swallowed the lump in her throat, waiting until her heart was beating normally again. Then she kicked off her sandals and slipped out of her clothes, picked up the chair and joined them. She walked out into the cold, clear water, which was only about seven inches deep, but ripe with rocks and stones. She immediately regretted not leaving a T-shirt on over her bathing suit for warmth.

"Yeow! This is cold," Susan said, ready to retreat.

"C'mon, chicken," Alisa yelled, splashing Susan.

Susan turned away from the freezing water only to catch Clint ready to splash her, too. "Don't you dare, Clint Scully. Let me get used to this…melting glacier."

"How about if we put this chair in the water and you can sit and splash as much as you want?" Clint said to Alisa.

"Okay."

Clint took the crutches from her and set them on the grass. They both took one of Alisa's hands, and waded slowly back into the river.

Clint unfolded Alisa's chair. "Your throne, Princess."

"Thank you, Cheyenne Clint."

Alisa sat down and immediately kicked up her feet, sending out glittering droplets of water. She giggled and started singing a song that Susan recognized from the movie *Cinderella*.

Susan waded out farther even though her feet were numb with cold. She couldn't believe how clear the water looked, how lazily it gurgled. At her feet was an outcropping of semisubmerged rocks where the water pooled and swirled.

Clint must have been following her gaze. He gave her a nudge with his shoulder, and pointed. "There's a whirlpool."

"I'm tempted to sit right in it."

"So what's stopping you?"

Sinking into the natural whirlpool was a once-in-a-lifetime thing.

Alisa was singing and splashing not even four

feet from them, and seemed to forget that they were nearby.

"She's having a ball," Clint said.

Susan lowered herself slowly into the froth of water. Gasping, she didn't realize how cold it would be.

"You won't notice the cold after a while." Clint stretched out next to her. "Great, isn't it?"

"Mmm…heavenly." She lifted her face to the sun, took a deep breath of fresh air and smiled at the handsome cowboy sitting beside her.

She couldn't stop her eyes from straying to his chest, so she gave up trying.

Clint was buff. She knew that from their dance in the barn, but she never realized how buff. She wanted to see even more of him.

"Oh," she said, noticing a U-shaped scar that traveled from his tight pecs to his even tighter abdomen. "Clint, did a bull give you that big scar?"

"Yup. A two-thousand-pound Brahman with a four-foot rack got me at the Billings event last year. I had a protective vest on, but he hooked me under it. Lost a couple buckets of blood, got a couple hundred stitches and spent a couple of days in the hospital. No problem."

She could just imagine the pain he'd suffered. "For heaven's sake, Clint. You could have died."

"Nah."

She moved toward him slowly, her index finger outstretched, suddenly wanting to touch the toughened skin of his scar. She stopped when she saw the sparkle in his eyes. "May I?"

"Be my guest." His voice seemed lower, huskier.

She ran her finger from the muscles of his arm to his abdomen where it disappeared into the waistband of his jeans. Her hand lingered there, then she traced the scar back up.

If she wasn't mistaken, Clint was holding his breath.

She followed the path of another scar. This one looked pinker, newer.

"Phoenix, Arizona." His voice had gotten softer and she could see a vein pumping in his temple.

Could it be that just her light touch bothered him? She liked that idea, so she traced the scar back up his arm.

"Did it hurt?"

"Not like the horn I took in Vegas." His hands clasped his zipper, and her mouth suddenly became dry.

He glanced over at Alisa, then his glittering eyes settled on Susan. He chuckled. "Sorry, you'll have to wait for another time to see that one."

She swallowed hard—the temperature had just gone up a few hundred degrees.

His gaze settled on her breasts, and his smile faded. When she looked down, she saw that her nipples were way too perky in the cold water. With her index finger and thumb, she plucked the fabric away from her body, but it didn't help much.

"You are *so* high school," she said, heart pounding.

His eyes twinkled. "You are *so* right."

"Let's get back to your job," she said. "All those scars, Clint. Why do you do it if it's so risky?"

"It's fun and it pays great for about three hours of work on a Saturday night. I can contract for as many or as few events as I want."

"I take it you don't like to work."

"Not when I don't have to."

"I live to work," she said proudly, trying not to notice the beads of water glittering on his tanned skin.

"And I work to live. There's a big difference. My living expenses are nothing much. My sponsors keep me in clothes. I tow my trailer around with my used truck. During the summer, I'm here."

Strange way to live. "But you don't have any roots or benefits or a pension plan. Your medical insurance alone must cost a fortune."

"Roots are overrated, and no legitimate insurance company will insure me for less than a fortune, but I need insurance so I pay for it. As for a pension, I give a good chunk of my money to a bullfighter pal who invests it for me. That should take care of my old age, which is about age thirty in my business, and I'm already pushing that."

"A bullfighter pal invests for you? You must make a fortune." She didn't try to keep the sarcasm from her voice. "At least let me give you the name of someone reliable, someone on Wall Street."

"No way." He shook his head. "I'm doing okay with Cletus the Clown."

"Cletus the Clown. You've lost your mind. Nothing like throwing your money away."

He shrugged. "Clete's done a good job."

Since he didn't care about a place to live or getting a real job, she didn't know why it surprised her that he didn't care about an important thing like investing wisely.

She thought about his lackadaisical attitude as she watched two little rivulets of water trickle down his chest, down his flat stomach, and disappear into his waistband.

She ran her wet hands over her face to cool off. It didn't help when she saw him watching her, smiling…knowing.

She turned and smiled at Alisa, who was still kicking up buckets of water. Alisa grinned back without missing a note of her latest song about fish under the sea.

"Tell me, Clint, what scares you about working?"

"I work hard at what I do."

"You know what I mean. A real job. Don't all cowboys have a ranch?"

His smile faded and he seemed a million miles away.

"I do have a ranch—a very profitable ranch. It sits on more than a thousand acres a couple hundred miles from here. I call it the Lazy S, for Scully. It fits, don't you think?"

*A very profitable ranch.*

"You're not lazy at all, Clint. You've accomplished a lot. And from what you've just told me, you're a rich man."

He took off his hat and stared inside the bowl of it as if it contained a crystal ball. "Money isn't everything. Everyone knows that. It doesn't buy…"

"Health? Real friends? Someone who loves you for who you are? A family to live in your house at the Lazy S?"

He raised an eyebrow at Susan after her last sentence. His half smile was particularly wistful, and she could see the loneliness in his eyes. She wanted to take his hand and hold it, to somehow connect with him and to let him know that she could identify with him.

Because she was lonely, too.

"Yes," he answered. "I'd love my parents back there, my sister and brother and their spouses and all their kids, along with my wife and kids. Everyone—back on the ranch. That'd be a dream come true."

Susan blinked back the tears that threatened to fall. Except for her estranged father, she didn't have a family anymore.

"It'll never happen," he said. "They have their own lives."

She could see how hard it was for him to talk about his family. "You never know," she said, trying to be upbeat.

"I do know." His jaw hardened, and his tone was bitter. "Happiness doesn't come cheap, and my family already paid the price."

# *Chapter 7*

Susan looked at Clint with a mixture of pity and shock.

He didn't want her pity, but she did deserve an explanation. She'd been nothing but kind, and he thought he could see the glistening of tears in her eyes.

That touched him.

Clint looked down at the water, remembering the river that ran alongside the Lazy S. It flowed deeper and faster when the snow melted. About now, he could probably jump it.

"Let me explain," he said. "My parents worked from sunrise to sunset to keep their ranch going. We ran about three hundred head of cattle, a few dozen quarter horses and a couple dozen bulls. My sister and brother and I helped them before school, after school and every damn weekend, but we were fighting a losing battle."

He paused, lost in thought, remembering how he'd wanted nothing more than to rope, drink beer and travel to rodeos with Joe Watley and Jake Dixon, but gave it all up to return home to help his folks.

"They let the hands go to save money. They'd sold off stock, some land, but it just wasn't enough. My parents tried. We all tried. In the end, we all watched the auction sign being nailed up on the barn and the house."

"I can imagine how they felt," Susan said. "I'd hate it if I lost Winners Wear. I came close a couple of times, but then, like a miracle, a big order or two would come in and I could keep it going."

"My folks never got a miracle." He took her hand and stared at it. "I watched the light go out in their eyes. Then I swore I'd never let that happen to me. I was going to enjoy my life. See the world. Not care about a chunk of dirt."

"Are your parents still alive?"

"Alive and well in a seniors condo in Fort Myers, Florida. They play in pitch tournaments and take bus trips to the theme parks and the casinos. I bought them a huge motor home that they travel in when they want to visit my sister and her kids in St. Louis or my brother and his kids in New Orleans. Once in a while, they'll show up at a bull riding event and spend some time with me."

"You bought them a motor home?"

He nodded.

"I'll bet you bought them their condo, too."

He grinned.

"Good for you, Clint. Then it's a happy ending?"

"Yeah. They got off the treadmill they were on. Actually, they didn't have a choice, since the place was sold out from under them."

"Treadmill," she mumbled. She removed her hand from his and rubbed her forehead. She'd used that word earlier to describe her own hectic life. "I'm happy that things worked out for them."

"Me, too."

"Now, tell me more about your ranch," she said.

"I bought my parents' ranch from the latest owner and offered it back to them." He sat up a little taller, and Susan could tell that he was proud of that fact. "But they didn't want it anymore. They were enjoying their retirement."

Susan couldn't believe all that he'd accomplished. "You bought the family ranch back?"

"I did."

"Why aren't you there?"

"Because I'm here, helping out with the summer programs. My uncle Charlie is running things for me, and doing a great job."

Susan was astonished. "And you have sponsors. You also get paid for bullfighting, and—"

"And I'm partners with my friend Joe Watley in some ventures."

"You really have a big empire, cowboy."

He shrugged, never comfortable talking about money. "I do all right."

"Would you mind giving me Cletus the Clown's phone number?"

He laughed. "So, I went up a couple rungs on your ladder of rodeo bums?"

"Amazing." She shook her head. "Amazing… and now I think that we ought to get our singing mermaid to dry land," Susan said.

Clint stood and helped Susan to her feet. "What do you say, Alisa? Time for lunch?"

"Aw…"

"Come on. Picnic time," Clint said.

The three of them walked hand in hand back to the grassy bank.

Clint looked at Alisa sleeping on the blanket. Susan had set up the umbrella to keep the girl in the shade.

Susan looked like she was dozing off next to Alisa, too. Never did he expect that the hyper New Yorker could calm down enough to actually sleep.

The picnic lunch was a hit with ham and cheese sandwiches, lemonade and chunks of watermelon. Mrs. D had even included a deck of Old Maid playing cards that he was currently winging into the bowl of his upturned hat so he wouldn't keep staring at the front of Susan's shirt.

She'd rolled up a jacket and placed it under her neck as she lay on her back. The perfect mounds of her breasts rose and lowered with each inhale and exhale of breath. The fabric of her tank top had molded itself to her damp bathing suit.

He got up from the bench of the picnic table, collected the cards and straightened them into a tight deck. He scanned the area, making sure there weren't any two-legged, four-legged or no-legged creatures in the area that aimed to harm the two lovely ladies on the blanket.

Sitting back on the bench, he resumed tossing the cards. He loved being outdoors, no matter what weather, and liked these quiet times where he could just pass the day thinking…or not.

He was becoming quite fond of Susan and Alisa. Susan, for the obvious reason that she was damn sexy, easy to talk to and fun to be with most of the time. Alisa because she was the sweetest little girl he'd ever laid eyes on. He admired them both, each struggling with things in her own way, both fiercely independent—and both lonely.

He might as well add himself to that mix. Susan didn't have close family ties, and Alisa had lost her parents in a car accident. As for him, he had a lot of good friends, several of them female, but most all of his good buddies were busy with their own lives.

His lifestyle wasn't conducive to settling down or raising a family. He didn't let anyone get that close to him, and certainly not a city gal who had the same thirst for success as Mary Alice Bonner. No thanks.

He shot the last card into his cowboy hat—nothing but net. Stretching, he raked his fingers through his hair and decided Susan needed to realize that life wasn't about working yourself to death.

His parents hadn't realized that. Mary Alice hadn't, either.

Clint Scully sure as hell did.

He wasn't a saint. He liked to have money when he needed it, but what was the point if you didn't take the time to enjoy it?

As if she were having a bad dream, Alisa started to whimper. Before Clint could move, Susan awoke immediately and sat up.

"Wake up, Alisa." Susan gently took her hand and rubbed her arm. "You're having a bad dream."

Clint stood, walked over to Alisa's side and knelt on one knee.

They both helped her to sit up.

Clint reached into his pocket and handed her a red bandanna, still fairly damp from the river. "Princess, dry your eyes. It's only a dream."

She ran the bandanna over her eyes and shuddered. "I was dreaming about the accident."

Susan rubbed her back. "It's okay. You can cry if you want, Alisa."

Alisa shook her head. "I don't want to cry."

She was a tough little thing, Clint thought. She had been through so much.

"I'll get some water," he said, trying to be useful.

He walked to the buckboard where he'd put all the picnic supplies after lunch. He got three bottles of water out of the picnic basket, twisted the top off one and took a hefty sip.

He went over to the horses and absentmindedly petted one as it grazed, giving Susan some time to comfort her. His eyes never strayed from the blanket, watching as Susan hugged Alisa and got her laughing.

Susan might be a greenhorn in a lot of ways, but

she was a pro when it came to dealing with a little girl with leg braces and crutches.

Yet, he'd bet all the money that he'd invested with Cletus the Clown that Susan had a disabled friend or relative.

He heard a scream, then another. He dropped the bottles of water. The adrenaline began to pump through his veins, and in a split second he sprinted back to the blanket as fast as his legs would move.

He scanned the area for trouble. When he got to the blanket, he dropped to his knees, searching for the threat that made Susan and Alisa scream, searching their faces.

Just like he did in the arena, he would put his body between them and any harm. Nothing would hurt them as long as he still had a breath in him.

But they were laughing. Laughing and screaming.

"What the...?" He breathed several sighs of relief.

Susan looked up at him. "Sorry if we alarmed you, Clint, we were just doing a little primal therapy. But thanks for coming to our rescue." She turned to Alisa. "He's just like a knight in shining armor, isn't he?"

"Well, Alisa *is* the Princess of the Gold Buckle Ranch," Clint said, forcing himself to take deep breaths to calm down. "Speaking of which, I think we ought to get back."

Susan nodded. "I have to meet with Emily."

She stood and tugged at her tank top and smoothed the legs of her warm-up pants. Her hair was damp and tangled, her jacket crumpled, but Clint thought that she'd never looked more beautiful.

They waited as Alisa put her shoes and socks on. Susan helped her with her braces, then Clint lifted her up and held on to her as she steadied herself.

"How about a Clint Scully piggy-back ride to the wagon?" he asked Alisa.

"Sure!"

Susan picked up Alisa's crutches, grabbed the blanket, umbrella and chair, and they all headed back to the wagon.

Clint hated to see their picnic end. He enjoyed their company. He'd have to think of something else the three of them could do together. Maybe a trip to town.

But first, he aimed to find time to be alone with Susan.

Emily, Clint and Susan walked toward a long, low building not far from the dining hall. Susan read the lettering on each of the doors: Medical Office, Canteen, Staff Training, Arts and Crafts and Chapel.

Emily unlocked the door to the arts and crafts room and pulled up the shade, letting in the late afternoon sun.

Susan noticed a desk in the front and built-in cabinets around the room. In the middle were two rows of three tables with chairs. The tables were covered with thick white paper.

"Go ahead. Look around," Emily said. "See what you think."

Susan took a walk around the room, opening cabinet doors and drawers, her mind ticking off what she could use.

Susan noticed dozens of boxes of crayons that had never been opened and even more watercolor paint kits. Perfect.

"I thought we could have a contest," Susan said. "Instead of me coming up with a logo, the campers could design one and put it on a T-shirt. The best one wins, and we can make it the official logo for all our merchandise."

Emily grinned. "What a great idea, Susan! I never thought of that."

"We could sketch it out on paper, then on practice fabric. They can paint it and then they can put the final design on a T-shirt. Then what?" Susan paced, brainstorming. She needed more activities to keep them occupied.

"You could make pot holders, too," Emily suggested. "We have hundreds of bags of loops and looms that were donated. It's all in the closet over there." She pointed to the left of the room.

Pot holders? She didn't know how to make pot holders, but she was sure she could find someone at the Gold Buckle who could teach her.

"They could give a pot holder to their mothers," Clint suggested.

"Oh? Men don't cook?" Susan shot over her shoulder.

"Or they could give one to their fathers," he quickly added.

Susan looked around the room. "Maybe we could make mobiles or wall hangings of things that could be found in the forest—dried flowers, pinecones, things like that."

Emily nodded. “I knew you’d have wonderful ideas.”

Susan laughed. Maybe this really was going to be fun. “I’m glad one of us thought that.”

“Thank you again for volunteering.” Emily gave her a big hug. “Your first class starts on Monday. Two o’clock in the afternoon, and another at four. The earlier class will have our younger kids in it. The rest of the week, you’ll have the same schedule.” She pulled out a piece of paper from her pocket and handed it to Susan. “Here’s the list of campers and the times they are assigned. Clint will be on hand to help you. Okay, Clint?”

“Right.”

“Good. That’s settled.”

Susan had ideas going through her mind about other projects, but right now she wanted to ask Emily some questions of her own.

“Emily, what’s wrong with Alisa?” she blurted.

If Alisa’s condition was terminal, she couldn’t deal with it. It’d be like losing her sister all over again.

Embarrassed, Susan waved the air with her hand, as if erasing the question. “Um…never mind. Sorry. Forget I asked.”

Emily motioned for her to take a chair. Clint sat down next to her.

“We have a policy at the Gold Buckle Ranch that all volunteers are briefed on every camper by our resident doctor, Dr. Mike Trotter. Since Alisa just arrived the other day and her situation is a little different, Mike hasn’t had a chance to review her file yet.”

"So we'll wait for Dr. Trotter," Susan said, relieved.

"Hang on, Susan." Clint turned to her. "Let's find out what we're dealing with here. Together, we can figure out how to help her."

*We?*

He was obviously thinking that they shared a partnership. Susan didn't know if she liked that. Lust was one thing, being a couple was another.

Emily looked from Clint to Susan, and her gaze settled on Susan. "Alisa did have some injuries from the accident, but she's healed from those. She actually has a rare disease of the hip."

"Will she improve with the braces?" Clint asked.

"They've helped. But Alisa has what's called Legg-Calvé-Perthes Disease. I wish I understood it completely, but the ball of the hip fractures because of lack of blood flow. It can be treated, but she needs an operation—an osteotomy. Her doctors have been waiting until she got a little older, but apparently, now the time is right."

"Thank goodness." Susan squeezed Clint's hand, feeling relief swirling around her like the whirlpool back at the river.

"Will she be able to walk without crutches and braces?" Clint asked.

"If the operation is a success, she will," Emily said. "And I've been told that the operation is not really involved—four days in the hospital, then maybe casting, or maybe not, and then physical therapy, and she'll be walking fine. So hopefully the operation will be successful."

Susan let out the breath she'd been holding. "She's been through so much."

"And there's going to be more for her to handle." Emily met Susan's gaze. "Alisa's only temporarily with me until she can be placed with a foster family or if she's adopted."

"Alisa did tell us that she was waiting to be adopted, but she said that her foster parents are on vacation," Clint said.

"They are, but those foster parents aren't taking her back. They just told her social worker that this morning. Alisa doesn't know yet."

Susan shook her head. "And it'll be hard for Children's Services to find an adoptive couple for a child on crutches who is facing surgery."

"Sounds like you know," Emily said.

"I do." She didn't want to expound further.

"Perhaps after the operation, it'll be easier to place her," Emily said.

Susan didn't like to hear that. "Any prospective parents worth anything would see past Alisa's crutches and braces and love her for the wonderful, sweet girl she is."

"I strongly second that," Clint added.

Emily looked at Susan, then Clint, and then stayed focused on Clint this time. "She needs parents who'll love her like she deserves to be loved. Parents who'll make her the center of their universe."

"Absolutely. You'll see to it that she gets just those kind of parents, won't you, Mrs. D?" Clint asked.

"I'm afraid it won't be up to me. It'll be up to Children's Services of the State of Wyoming."

"You'll have input, won't you?" Susan asked hopefully.

"Well, I probably won't be able to keep my opinions to myself." Emily checked her watch and stood. "Any more questions?"

"I think you answered everything we were wondering about, Mrs. D," Clint said.

"Thanks, Emily," Susan added.

"If you think of anything else, you know where to find me." Emily handed her a key. "Would you mind locking up when you're done?"

Now that Susan's mind was at peace concerning Alisa's condition, she began to worry that Alisa wouldn't find good parents to adopt her.

But that was none of her concern. She'd be out of Alisa's life in a few more days.

She studied Clint. She wasn't going to get involved in his life, either. The last thing she wanted—or needed—was a fly-by-night man. Her father had that disease.

She just wished she could get him out of her system.

There was a fine line between life and death, health and sickness, loving someone and then never seeing them again. Susan vowed never to cross that line again.

They sat in the room in silence, each one thinking about what they'd just discovered about Alisa and the problems facing her.

Clint had the sudden urge to put on a pair of shorts and go for a ten-mile run. Or find a rodeo and release some of his energy fighting bulls. Maybe he could do some of that screaming that Susan and Alisa seemed to be fond of.

He'd do anything to stop looking at the slump in Susan's shoulders or the bow of her head. Where was his tornado of a New Yorker? He never thought he'd want that woman over this one.

"Talk to me," he said, pulling out a chair opposite her.

Silence.

"Talk to me," he repeated. "Emily laid out some heavy stuff just now. I know how fond you are of Alisa and—"

"Aren't you?"

"You bet, but there's nothing much we can do other than to show her a good time like we did today."

"You're right. Neither of us is in a position to adopt her."

"Hell, no," Clint said. "It hadn't even crossed my mind." He certainly didn't have anything to offer the little girl.

"I can't adopt her," Susan said. "It's impossible. I have a business to run. I couldn't give her the attention she deserves, and what if…?" She shot the words out, rapid-fire.

"Whoa. Hold on just a minute. You don't have to justify why you can't adopt her to me. I'm not the family court judge. Besides, we haven't known her very long. She could be an ax murderer or something."

That got a chuckle out of her. "You're right. I just

wish that the absolute perfect couple would adopt Alisa."

"She needs two people who will be there when she comes home from school, help her with homework and tuck her in at night," he said. "Then there's car-pooling to Girl Scouts, and piano lessons and PTO meetings."

Susan sighed. "Well, that sure isn't me. I'm at my office day and night."

"Doesn't fit me, either," Clint added. "I'm driving around working the rodeos."

"Well, that's decided. Neither of us has anything to offer her."

Clint nodded. "End of story."

"Okay." She looked a little sad in a way. Then Susan the businesswoman reappeared. "I might as well start getting organized for my classes." She pulled out her planner. "I need to break down my class projects by age groups, now that I know I'll have two classes." She paused with pen in hand, as if she were thinking.

Something in the back of the room caught her attention.

"Is that a phone?" She looked at him with a big grin and eyes brighter than a lighthouse beacon. "A real phone?"

"Uh-oh," Clint muttered, watching her hurry to the back of the room.

She picked up the phone and held it to her ear. "It works. Yes!"

"Darn," he mumbled.

She punched in a bunch of numbers as fast as her

fingers would move. "I'll charge this to my phone card."

He got up to leave.

"Bev, it's Susan. Yes. I'm okay. How are things there? Tell me everything."

He'd gotten his wish. The feisty New Yorker was back and running her company from Mountain Springs, Wyoming.

"Susan, tell me everything!" Bev said. "Any good-looking cowboys there?"

Susan laughed. "Several, but there's one in particular."

"Tell me about him."

"His name is Clint, but I can't talk for long. I have a million things to do and I need your help. I want you to overnight some white T-shirts. Five dozen in various sizes."

"Why? What are you doing?" Bev asked.

"I'm teaching arts and crafts."

*"You're what?"*

"Long story. Oh, and, Bev, throw in a couple of cases of fabric paint, too. All colors. Oh, how about glitter paint? Kids like glitter. Oh, and some spools of rickrack, buttons, boxes of sequins—all colors of those, and whatever other notions you can think of. Oh, and needles and thread. No, the bigger needles. For kids. And throw in some needle threaders."

"Will do."

"Ship it overnight with the shirts."

"No problem. But tell me more about Clint!"

She told her about her horse ride with him, his

trailer and their recent dip in the river. As she spoke, she looked out the front window and saw Clint jogging alongside the little brook that ran in front of the cabins. He was shirtless and wore a breezy pair of red running shorts. His legs were all muscle. He was tan and buff and his body already had a light sheen of sweat.

Suddenly, all her nerve endings were on fire.

"Susan, what's wrong?"

"Nothing, Bev. Nothing at all."

She hung up the phone and realized that she'd never even asked Bev about Winners Wear.

As she watched Clint disappear from sight, she realized how badly she needed to find out what it might be like to make love with a certain cowboy.

# *Chapter 8*

Clint jogged to Joe Watley's Silver River Ranch. Joe owned a nice chunk of northwest Wyoming about five miles down the main road from the Gold Buckle.

The path traversed woods, meadow and pasture—the same path that he, Joe and Jake had used to ride their horses, motorcycles, four-wheelers or snowmobiles between ranches.

The three of them had been friends forever, but had really become inseparable the first day of high school when they signed up for the rodeo team.

Jake had gravitated to riding bulls. Clint and Joe took to calf roping and were eventually paired together. Clint was the header, and Joe was the heeler. Collectively, the three of them had won about every high school title offered.

After they graduated, they all hit the professional circuit together. Jake won event after event in bull riding until he finally retired last year just after the Wheelchair Rodeo program began at the Gold Buckle Ranch. After he'd met Beth, Jake had decided that a gold wedding ring was better than a gold buckle.

After his folks lost the ranch, Clint went back to the circuit as a bullfighter and not a contestant because Joe had found another partner, and he didn't want to rope with anyone but Joe.

Joe stayed on the circuit a little longer. With every cent he'd won, he bought horses, bulls and steers. Now his Silver River Rodeo Company was one of the six biggest rodeo-stock suppliers in the United States.

Clint needed to talk to Joe. Jake was way too busy with the Wheelchair Rodeo and getting ready for the Gold Buckle Gang right now, and he wouldn't understand, anyway.

Joe Watley had a Mary Alice Bonner in his background, too, so he would understand completely when Clint talked about Susan Collins. Actually, Clint was hoping Joe would tell him to stay completely away from her.

He slowed down when he got to the barn, remembering his vow that there would be no ties with Susan—just a physical relationship.

The fact that she had to call her office the second she found a phone and couldn't get away from her job—not even for a few days—reinforced to him that they just didn't mesh.

So why was he thinking about her so much?

He walked around the barn, stopping for some small talk with the hands and admiring the horses. He paused for a drink and a soak from the hose that hung on a small outbuilding.

"Well, look what the cat dragged in."

Clint looked up to see the big outline of Joe Watley in the doorway of the barn.

"Hey, cowboy." Clint wiped his hands on his shorts and held one out.

Joe had a strong and meaty grip. He'd gained about fifty pounds since their calf-roping days, all of it pure muscle.

"What brings you by? It's too late for lunch and too early for supper. You must want to check on your investments."

Clint co-owned a couple dozen bulls, broncs and steers with Joe, most of it rodeo rough stock, along with dozens of fine quarter horses, but he let Joe handle the business end. Clint wrote him checks, Joe bought the stock, and eventually wrote bigger checks back to Clint.

Being a partner with Joe Watley was like having a gold mine in the backyard.

"I came for a cold one, and maybe some talk, but first the cold one. Make mine water. I'm on duty tonight at the dining hall and then at the nightly movie."

They walked to the ranch house, a sprawling rustic log home with walls of windows that overlooked the mountains and Joe's kingdom. It was spotless inside, thanks to Joe's housekeeper and all-around warden, Aunt Maggie.

Clint took a seat on one of the rocking chairs on the porch as his friend went inside. He returned with four bottles of water, and handed two to Clint.

Clint nodded his thanks.

"Glad you showed up. You can help me load the horses that I'm loaning to the Gold Buckle Gang."

"No problem."

Joe took a long draw of water. "I'll be there Monday morning. I'm doing two trail rides, one in the morning and one after lunch. I've been looking forward to it."

Clint nodded.

"Are you going to keep me guessing or are you going to tell me what you want to talk about?"

Clint took a long drink then poured some water down the back of his neck.

Joe rubbed his chin. "She must be pretty special for Cheyenne Clint Scully to go to the trouble of running up here."

Clint grinned. "All right, all right. Her name is Susan Collins, and she's a workaholic from New York City."

"New York City?" Joe gave a long whistle. "She's a long way from home."

"Yeah. She has her own company there. Sounds like a big deal. She calls it Winners Wear."

Joe shook his head. "She's a workaholic, and you're a country cowboy. Sounds like a match made in heaven."

Clint swore and shrugged. "There's no match, Joe.

She's heading back to New York in a week. I think we're just going to end up slaking a little mutual lust in the meantime. End of story."

"Then what are you doing sitting here drinking water and looking at my ugly face when you could be slaking your lust?"

Clint laughed. He liked Joe's sense of humor and liked his advice, advice he gave whether or not you wanted to hear it.

Clint stood and stretched. "You know, you're right. Time is wasting. Let's go load the horses."

"Hold on a minute, cowboy."

"Yeah?"

"It's written all over your face." Joe gave him an easy punch on the arm. "You've gone and fallen for an ambitious gal, haven't you?"

Clint almost choked on the water. "I have three words to say to you, pal—Mary Alice Bonner."

"That was decades ago, Clint. Aren't you over her yet?"

"It was just *two* years ago, *cowboy.*" Clint could still feel the anger and disappointment that he'd felt that morning when he read Mary Alice's note. "I'm over her, but that doesn't mean I haven't learned from my mistakes. Unlike you."

"Why are you bringing Ellen Rogers up?" Joe asked, with a white-knuckled grip on the porch railing.

"They're all cut from the same cloth. Believe me. They have the same ambition and drive." Clint shook his head. "City and country just don't mix, Joe."

Joe shrugged. "Maybe you're right. But maybe

you should give her a chance. You might be missing out on a good thing. Obviously, she made a big impression on you in a very short time. Has any other woman ever done that?"

Clint grunted, tossed the empty plastic bottles of water on the rocker and vaulted over the railing of the porch. "Maybe you're right."

Before Clint could take a step, he felt a tug on his arm as Joe yanked him back. They stood nose-to-nose, jogging shoes to boots as Joe got in his face.

"What is big, tough bullfighter Cheyenne Clint really scared of? Certainly not a woman. You've had more buckle bunnies than eight cowboys could handle."

He fisted his hands in Joe's shirt and a button went flying. "Susan's not a buckle bunny. There's just something about her. I don't know, Joe. She's got me all knotted up."

"Woo-ee. I can't believe this is Cheyenne Clint talking." He broke into a big grin. "What else is going on in that thick skull of yours?"

Clint let go of Joe's shirt, picked up Joe's shirt button from the dirt and handed it to him. "There's a little girl, too."

"She has a daughter?"

"No, a little orphan that the Dixons are looking after until she's adopted."

"And you're thinking of hanging up your spurs and adopting her? With Susan?"

"It crossed my mind. Or maybe they'd let me adopt her by myself. I have enough money, that'll work in my favor. But it's too premature for a big decision like that, Joe."

His friend gave a long, low whistle. "Take your time thinking about that, partner. That's a big responsibility, adopting a little girl by yourself. And you can't drag her around to rodeos and bull ridings with you."

"I know. I've visited a lot of hospitals, Joe, and been around a lot of children, but no kid has grabbed my heart more than Alisa."

"All I can say is look at Jake. I've never seen him so happy since he met Beth. Who would have thought he'd get married? But he hung up his spurs and never looked back. It can be done, Clint. But give it more time."

"I know." Clint nodded. "I suppose there are worse things than settling down, huh?"

"Like *not* grabbing on to the best thing in your life and *not* going after her," Joe said.

"Can I join you?" Clint asked.

He placed his orange plastic tray on the table next to Susan's. A mountain of spaghetti and meatballs covered the plate. A huge salad and a piece of chocolate cake topped off the tray.

"Sure." Susan had been waiting and watching for him. Then finally he'd walked into the dining hall looking freshly showered and shaved and surrounded by a bunch of girls and boys. He laughed and joked with them, signed autographs, admired cowboy hats and tipped his own hat to the girls.

The girls giggled and swooned when he did that.

They weren't immune to his charms any more than she was.

There was a sincerity and lightness about Clint that made a person feel better by just being with him. There would be no strings attached if a woman had a fling with Clint Scully, and that just suited her fine. She didn't want any strings, either.

He took a seat on the bench. "You're all alone?"

She nodded. "I needed some quiet time after this afternoon."

He raised an eyebrow. "What happened? You okay?"

"Physically, I'm fine. Mentally, I'm not sure I'll ever recover." She took a bite of a meatball. "Beth Dixon asked me to help get a gaggle of girls settled into cabin A. It was loud. Screaming, yelling, giggling. The mandatory pillow fight." She rubbed her forehead and pinched her nose in an exaggerated motion. "They put on enough makeup to paint the Empire State Building and sprayed enough perfume to kill the ozone twice."

"Ouch. How long did you have to watch them?"

"For about eight minutes."

Clint chuckled. "Then you deserve a nice, relaxing dinner."

"What's the movie tonight?" she asked, thinking that she might watch it.

"Something with John Wayne in it."

"I'll pass. Maybe I can find a book to read. I haven't had time to read in years."

Clint had the tiniest bit of sauce at the corner of

his mouth. She wanted to reach over and just wipe it off with her finger. Or lick it off with her tongue.

She stared at it, then at the side of his jaw and the smooth, tanned skin of his neck. He smelled like peppermint soap, pine and maybe a little starch, probably from his fresh-from-the-package shirt that sported the usual crease marks.

She didn't have much time left at the Gold Buckle. And she intended to make the most of it.

With Clint.

Emily motioned for Susan to sit beside her in the front row of the converted dining room. On the stage, a mix of people set up music stands and tuned up their instruments for a sing-along. Several cowboys were putting together a set of drums. Two others were testing the microphone.

Emily and Susan made small talk, mostly about how Jake started Wheelchair Rodeo, and how they expanded to their current program, the Gold Buckle Gang. They wanted to add yet another program to reach out to troubled kids.

Susan could tell that Emily had something else on her mind.

"I need to talk to you about Alisa," Emily finally said.

She took a deep breath and met Emily's gaze. "Is she all right?"

"She's fine." Emily patted her hand. "Calm down. I'm not going about this the right way. It's just that Alisa has been talking about you and Clint nonstop since yesterday, and I thought you could help her deal with something. I think it's going to be very difficult for her."

"Is it medical? I have money, Emily. I'll pay for whatever she needs. Don't wait for Children's Services if Alisa needs the operation right away."

Emily patted her hand. "It's nothing like that, at least not now. I just found out that there's a couple coming out tonight with Alisa's adoption worker, and Alisa wants to talk to you about it. Dex and I talked to her, as did her worker, but she wants to talk to you. She said you had a sister that's in heaven just like her parents and would know how she feels. Would you mind just spending a few minutes with her? Her social worker told her that she wouldn't be going back to her foster parents, and I think she's afraid of another rejection from this couple."

"Emily, surely there is someone else more qualified than I am to talk to Alisa about such an important matter." She gestured toward Clint, who was talking to someone by the stage. "Even Clint is more natural with kids than I am."

"I suggested Doc Trotter and the child psychiatrist we have on staff, but she wants you because she has found something in you that she likes. There's something about you she trusts, and that's very special to a child."

"I'm flattered. I mean…oh, Emily, if you only knew—" Tears stung Susan's eyes.

While she wanted Alisa to have parents who loved her, they had to be special people, because Alisa was a very special girl with special needs.

Special. What exactly did that mean, anyway?

It meant two people who could put a child first, put her needs above theirs and form a family, accept her and make her happy. Above all, they'd love her and wouldn't leave when things got tough and never come back like Susan's own father had.

Susan would be leaving soon. It wouldn't do for the girl to get even more attached to her.

Who was she kidding? She herself was attached to Alisa.

She looked into Emily's kind eyes. How could she say no?

"I'll do what I can, Emily."

"Thank you. She's a sweetheart, isn't she?"

"She is."

"I'd adopt her myself, but she needs a younger couple than Dex and I."

Susan put her hand on Emily's arm and whispered, "Here she comes now."

Susan waved to Alisa, who was walking toward them. Suddenly Emily got up from her chair, babbling something about having to get ready for her guests.

Emily smoothed Alisa's hair. Her hair didn't need smoothing, but Emily clearly had great affection for the girl.

"Remember, Alisa, after the sing-along come right home."

"I'll remember, Mrs. Dixon." Alisa's eyes lost their glow. "But what if I don't like them?"

Emily made a fist like a hitchhiker and pointed her thumb toward the door. "Then we'll kick them right out."

Alisa giggled uneasily, then turned to Susan. "I'm meeting two people who might adopt me."

Susan nodded and put a hand on Alisa's shoulder. She didn't know what else to do, or say.

"Mrs. Dixon, can Susan and Cheyenne Clint come with me and meet them?"

"This is really none of my business or Clint's, sweetie," Susan said. "It's between you and your adoption worker. But if you need to talk, I'm listening."

Alisa nodded, but she seemed boneless and slumped into the chair awkwardly. Luckily, Clint walked out onstage and started talking on the microphone, and she perked right up.

Emily gave Alisa a little pat on the head, raised her eyebrows and thinned her lips to Susan with a "this is going to be difficult" expression on her face, and left.

Clint sat down, strummed his guitar, and Susan watched Alisa's sweet face fill up with the excitement that she'd lost earlier.

Clint played the guitar and sang like an actual country and western star. He even looked the part, with his guitar slung over his shoulders and his cowboy hat shading his eyes.

Susan felt a rising uneasiness. Alisa was getting too fond of her, and Susan was worried that Alisa wouldn't give any adoption prospects a fair chance.

Alisa slipped her little hand into hers. Susan tried to relax and think of how to give her a gentle push toward the couple that she'd be meeting tonight.

To stop herself from obsessing about Alisa, Susan

tried to listen to the words as Clint sang "Home on the Range."

It didn't seem like the corny song that she'd heard millions of times. It was a song about hearth and home and roots, feeling connected, and yet insignificant, to the wonder of nature.

He poured his heart and soul into each word.

But what did the words mean to Clint? He had a ranch that he didn't even run. He didn't stay in any one place for too long. Did he secretly long for roots of his own?

The song ended and the audience was silent until the last chord of his guitar faded along with the last note of his deep voice. Then they broke out into hoots, whistles and loud applause. Clint took a bow and waved his hat, setting the teen girls to screaming. With a bemused glance at Susan, he laughed.

Clint caught up with them later outside the dining hall, where they were slowly walking to the Dixons' house. "You ladies aren't staying for the John Wayne movie?"

Alisa shook her head. "I have to meet some people who might adopt me. Will you both come with me? Please? Please?"

Clint must have caught the desperation in Alisa's voice. "What's got you so nervous, Princess?"

"I don't want to meet them. What if I don't like them?"

"What if you do?" Susan bent down and took her hands. "Wouldn't it be awesome?"

In the outside lighting, Susan could see a single tear slowly trail down Alisa's cheek.

"I want to go to the movie instead," Alisa said softly.

Susan wiped the tear off the girl's cheek with a finger. She felt like crying herself. "You can watch John Wayne any old time. Go and meet the people. They came all the way here to see you, so right away they think you're special. I think you should give them a chance."

Susan smiled in spite of the sadness clutching her heart. She wanted to wrap Alisa in her arms and not let anything hurt her.

"Remember what Emily said?" Susan made the same hitchhiker pose as Emily had earlier. "If you don't like them, you can boot them out. But I'll bet they'll be terrific."

Alisa sniffed. "Okay, Susan."

"How about a lift, Alisa?" Clint asked.

"I'm okay."

"I know you're okay, but how about a lift anyway?"

She wiped more tears away with the hem of her sweatshirt. "I'd like that, Cheyenne Clint."

Clint squatted down. "Hop on."

Susan took her crutches and helped Alisa onto Clint's back. They walked toward the back of the Dixons' residence where there was a separate entrance to their kitchen.

Along the way, Clint cracked jokes and got Alisa laughing. It struck Susan that this was how she'd always wanted her family to be. She remembered longing to take walks with her parents, laughing with them and wanting to go on a picnic. She'd hated that her mother was always working or her father was always gone.

Just once, she'd wanted to see her father hoist Elaine on his back, and make her feel like a part of the family, not a bothersome burden.

Above all, she'd always wanted him to make Elaine laugh so she'd forget her troubles, if only for a little while.

She was attracted to Clint, and the more she got to know him, the more she liked him.

She needed to stop her brain from working double time, filling her mind with thoughts of Alisa, Clint and her own lonely life.

She should be thinking of production schedules, filling orders, packaging and shipping.

She loved the lights and hustle of the city, but Clint was pure country. She was a workaholic, and Clint's pulse barely registered.

He was fabulous with children, but it was Susan that Alisa wanted to talk to.

She was making herself dizzy.

They reached the main house and a tall, muscular man dressed in the cowboy fashion with twinkling eyes and a big smile answered Clint's knock.

"Howdy, Clint." He grasped Clint's hand in a meaty shake, then his gaze dropped to Alisa. "Well, about time you got home, Cinderella!" He smiled at Susan, then grabbed her hand and started pumping away.

"Susan Collins," she said.

"I'm Dex Dixon, and I'm the foreman of this outfit, but only when my wife lets me be."

He stepped out onto the porch and held the door open for Alisa to have more room to walk through. "Your company's here, Alisa, and they seem like really nice folks."

"Okay," she said in a shaky, thin voice. Alisa turned to Susan and Clint. "Thanks."

"You're welcome, Princess."

Alisa held her arms up, and Susan knew exactly what she wanted. A hug.

Crouching down, she waited as Alisa took a wobbly step and wrapped her arms around Susan's neck.

Susan couldn't help herself. She wrapped her arms around the thin, tiny girl and felt herself free-falling through space and time. She had a gut-wrenching need to protect the sweet, sad Alisa, a child that she barely knew, but who was so like Elaine.

Susan also wanted to look over the two people waiting inside for Alisa, but she didn't have any right.

Clint removed his hat and held it over his heart. "You'll be absolutely fine, Princess Alisa of the Gold Buckle Ranch."

Alisa giggled, and when she walked away, she had the air of actual royalty ready to grant an audience.

Susan looked at Clint and sighed.

"I know," he said, slapping his hat back on his head. "Maybe we can help her—together."

# *Chapter 9*

Clint walked Susan to her cabin after dropping Alisa off at the Dixons'.

"I'm worried about Alisa going through the whole adoption process," Susan said.

"Me, too. But she's strong. My money's on her."

He'd met a lot of kids over the years. Many of them touched his heart, and many of them had him blinking back tears, but something about Alisa made him want to take her home, protect her and never let her out of his sight.

He'd been thinking about his conversation with Joe. If he were married, or had a steady job, he'd seriously think about adopting Alisa himself. He didn't think he was actually falling for Susan; all he knew was that something about her got his blood pumping and turned his breathing irregular. When she touched him like she did in the river, he was ready to explode.

Marriage. He didn't want to go down that trail again. He was a bullfighter and an adrenaline junkie. His primary home was a trailer. Mary Alice Bonner knew that, and she headed for Chicago. Susan Collins had no idea what his life was actually like.

"A penny for your thoughts," Susan said, stopping in front of her cabin.

"I'm thinking that I have to get back to the movie," he lied. "Would you mind if I came by later? I'll bring wine."

"I'd like that. See you in a couple of hours."

Checking his watch, he saw that he had about ten minutes before he had to be on duty at the movie. He walked to the dining hall, grabbed a bottle of water made a little small talk with one of the nurses who cornered him, and slipped out the side door.

He walked back to the Dixons' ranch house, not exactly knowing what bothered him. He just wanted to check on things.

The lights were on and the curtains weren't closed. He could easily see into their living room.

Dex and Emily sat on a brown leather love seat. Alisa sat on a kid-size rocking chair. Her crutches leaned against a coffee table. On the couch sat a middle-aged, impeccably groomed couple holding hands. Another serious-looking woman in a somber gray pantsuit studied a folder on her lap. Clint assumed that she was Alisa's adoption worker.

The couple looked nice enough, he supposed. They were dressed like they had enough money to give Alisa whatever she wanted. He looked at the car parked in front, a brand-new silver-gray BMW. That had to belong to the couple. It certainly wasn't Dex Dixon's car.

Upper-class yuppies. Not bad.

Clint moved back into the shadows when he heard a twig snap. He saw her silhouette even before he smelled her floral scent: Susan.

She stopped in front of the Dixons' living room and looked in. She tried to be casual and studied her nails, not that she could see them in the dark.

He didn't know how he could make his presence known without scaring her.

He cleared his throat. She jumped and began to run.

"Susan, it's me." He grabbed her arm, and she took a swing at him. He ducked and dodged. Nice defensive reflexes. Good for her. "Susan, it's Clint."

She stopped in midswing. "You scared me to death. What the hell are you doing out here?"

He let go of her arm but held on to her hand. "Same thing you are. Spying."

She grinned and they both turned to look at the people talking in the living room. Alisa was smiling and laughing.

"She looks happy. Doesn't she?" Susan asked.

"Yeah. I figure that's the prospective parents' Beemer over there."

She looked at the car, then stared back at the house. "They look nice." Susan sighed. "I wonder what they're like."

"I'm sure Alisa will let us know."

They both watched as the woman handed Alisa a present. "Oh, brother," Susan complained. "Nothing like stacking the deck."

Clint made a grunting sound. "The nerve of some people."

"It's probably a doll. Don't they know she's too old for dolls?"

They both waited to see what the gift would be.

"A CD player." Susan let out a puff of air. "Sheesh."

"And some CDs. Look at her grin. She likes them."

"She likes Disney songs."

"I know."

It felt natural to be with Susan, holding her hand, staring into someone's house. Strange, but natural. They shared a bond between them—concern over a young girl.

"Had enough?" he asked.

"Yes. I just wanted to make sure she was doing okay."

He gave her hand a little squeeze, and she smiled up at him.

That was his undoing. He slipped his other hand around her waist and pulled her to him. She looked beautiful in the moonlight with her big eyes twinkling.

He gave her a second or two to push him away or tell him no, and when she didn't, he kissed her—lightly at first. He lifted his head and smiled. She smiled back.

He kissed her again.

She pulled her hand from his and wrapped her arms around his neck. He fisted his hand in her soft hair, hair that glimmered in the moonlight, and moved her head to give him more access to her lips.

He rubbed her back. She kneaded his neck with her fingers.

He broke the kiss to gather his wits about him before he pulled her down to the gravel and dispensed with her clothes.

They stood forehead-to-forehead, smiling, shuffling to a soundless rhythm.

His hand moved naturally to her waist. They swayed, barely moving. He inhaled her scent, kissed her lightly on the forehead. She put her hand on his cheek, then moved her hands across his shoulders and smiled up at him.

He hadn't felt this good in a long time.

"Clint?"

"Hmm?"

"Don't you have to go to the John Wayne movie?" Her voice was barely a whisper, and it held a touch of regret.

"Shoot." He'd forgotten. "I'd better make tracks."

With a look back, they saw that Alisa was still laughing. Hand in hand, he and Susan walked in the direction of the dining hall.

"I can make it to my cabin alone," Susan said. "You go ahead."

"Still up for that wine later?" he asked.

"Sure."

Her sexy smile made him think of star-filled Wyoming nights and warm summer breezes as they whispered through the pines and meadows. That's when he really felt alive.

He wanted her, and time was running out.

Susan jumped in the shower, then slipped into a pair of pink sweats. She settled into a chair with her planner to wait for Clint, needing something to do to take her mind off him.

She wanted to see him again. She had already decided he wasn't her type, and he certainly wasn't the kind of guy to get serious over. Yet she couldn't help herself.

She had no doubt that he was interested in a sexual relationship. He knew that she'd be gone by the end of the week, so there would be no surprises there. Susan wanted him, too. She'd make it clear that their relationship couldn't go any further.

She was a modern woman, and he was an attractive man. What was the harm in some good, healthy sex?

Then they'd go their separate ways. No strings attached.

To take her mind off Clint, she unzipped her planner. This evening, she actually had to look for where she'd put it. Back home, it never left her hand. She had it stuffed with pieces of paper and other junk, and Bev always joked that some day Susan would have to have it surgically removed.

She jotted down some notes for her upcoming art classes, thinking the kids might enjoy learning how the shirts they were going to sew and decorate were made.

After the designing and decorating was done, they could vote for their favorite T-shirt. She'd give out prizes for the winners and finalists. Maybe certificates to the canteen, if Emily was willing.

It grew chilly in the room, so she decided to start a fire in the fireplace. A fire was always romantic. She twisted paper, piled up kindling, then stacked on a couple of logs. She struck a match and watched the paper catch on fire. Okay, it wasn't exactly a blaze, but it had potential. She threw on more kindling, blew on the flames and watched them grow hotter.

She washed her hands, pulled out two water glasses for the wine and set them on the counter. She peeked out the front window again, but saw nothing but darkness beyond the glow of the porch light.

She actually found herself whistling, and she never whistled.

She picked up the book that she'd signed out of the library in the lobby. "Mmm…a real book." It would be a luxury to be able to read something other than printouts of sales figures, supply catalogs or invoices. She tucked her feet under her and began to read.

Three chapters later there was a knock on the door.

"Yes?"

"It's Clint."

Immediately, her heart started to beat faster, and she felt a nervous excitement bubbling inside her.

When she opened the door and saw all sorts of bugs flying around the porch light, she yanked Clint in by an arm and slammed the door shut behind him.

He let out a short, sharp whistle and made a show

out of returning the crease to his shirt sleeves. "Just couldn't wait to get your hands on me, huh?"

"Didn't want to let any bugs in."

"Ouch." He patted his heart. "You really know how to hurt a guy."

When she turned toward him, his eyes were scanning her body.

"You're a sight for tired eyes, Susan."

"Your tired eyes just saw me a couple of hours ago."

"But that's what John Wayne always says."

"What does Clint Scully always say?"

He rubbed his chin, as if thinking. "He's a polite cowboy. He always asks a lady for a kiss."

"Hmm…maybe I should play hard to get."

"No, don't."

He closed the distance between them and wrapped her in his arms. His hand cut through her hair and cupped the back of her neck. Just before his mouth moved over hers, Susan held him back.

"Where is this going to go, Clint?"

"I think you know. If you've got a problem with that, you might as well let me know now."

"Just sex? No commitment?"

"You're leaving at the end of the week to go back to New York. My life is here, or on the road. How much commitment can we have?"

For some reason, when he said it, it seemed so shallow, but she wanted him, there was no denying that. "Kiss me, cowboy."

He did, and she felt his kiss down to her toes. Before her knees buckled, he lifted her off her feet.

Walking several steps to the couch, he sat down with her on his lap.

Clint wiped his face with a red bandanna that he pulled out of his pocket. "Did you start that fire?"

She nodded.

"Nice job. Sure is hot in here. Where did you learn how to start a fire, city slicker?"

"My grandmother's house had a fireplace."

He kissed her again. Her head rested on the arm of the sofa, and his hand started to travel under the hem of her sweatshirt.

She reached for his shirt. With a few tugs on the snaps, it popped open. She ran her palms over his strong, tanned chest. His scars were there, and she traced kisses down one of them, as if she could erase it.

He looked down at her, and let out a noise that was half breath and half whistle. His hand splayed across her stomach, moved up her midriff and cupped a breast.

"You're beautiful, Susan."

He put his feet up on the coffee table, causing her planner to drop. All the papers she had tucked inside it fell out into a big mess on the floor.

"I'm sorry," he said, moving her feet away. "Let me pick that up."

"That's okay, Clint. Leave it."

But it was too late. He had the picture of Elaine in his hand, the one taken a month before she died. Susan sat up and straightened her sweatshirt.

"Is this Elaine?" he asked softly.

Susan nodded. "Yes."

"She reminds me of Alisa."

"Yes. Me, too. Very much so."

"Who is she to you?" he asked softly.

"My sister."

"That explains a lot."

She raised an eyebrow. "What do you mean by that?"

"At first, you acted a little nervous around Alisa."

"I know."

He studied the picture. "Does she have an artificial leg?"

Susan suddenly couldn't talk. Nodding, she got up and walked to the kitchen. "Would you like some wine now?"

"Sure."

She thought that pouring the wine would give her a little time to calm herself and catch her breath, but not when Clint arrived at her side and helped with the corkscrew. It was nice of him to assist, but he didn't have to do it from behind with his arms around her, his warm chest on her back, his hard body moving against her behind.

He scooped up the glasses and the wine and headed back to the couch. He held out his hand, and she took it.

She had known how she wanted this evening to end, but now her mind whirled.

She didn't want to think about Elaine or Alisa; she'd been doing that enough lately. She wanted Clint Scully. She wanted to make love with him, but she didn't want to fall in love with him. If she did, it would cause too many complications and it'd hurt too much when she had to leave.

Maybe all she'd ever have would be this one time with him, and she was going to make the most of it.

The bedroom was down the hall—cheerful and inviting, with its colorful blankets and array of plump pillows. If she led him there, she'd seem much too eager.

"Something wrong?" he asked.

"Um…no." She pointed down the hall. "The bed is more comfortable. We can talk there."

She sounded like an idiot. How obvious could she be?

He grinned. "Lead the way."

Clint sat on the edge of the bed and put the glasses on the end table, then tugged off his boots. They landed on the floor with a thump. Susan walked over to the other side of the bed.

She'd never been this nervous before. This just didn't feel right—not since Clint found the picture of Elaine.

Clint tossed his hat onto a chair. He patted the bed. "Something's bothering you. Sit back, relax and tell me about it."

Silence. She didn't want to talk. She just wanted to forget.

She slid off her sandals and sat cross-legged on the bed next to him.

He put his hand over hers and played with her fingers. "Tell me about Elaine."

For a while, she couldn't catch her breath. "I… uh… I don't think I can."

"I could tell the way you handled Alisa's braces by the river that you knew what you were doing. Elaine wore braces, didn't she?"

Susan felt the sting of tears when Clint said her sister's name.

She took a deep breath and let it out slowly. "Elaine had bone cancer. She died when she was nine, a couple of years older than Alisa. I was twelve. I did everything I could, Clint, but..." She stopped to find her voice.

He took her hand and sandwiched it between his. "Her death must have hurt you," he said softly, gently. His sincere blue eyes showed his concern.

She'd thought of the day that Elaine died a thousand times. Her father was summoned home from Bermuda, where he was leading another tour, and he and her mother had each held one of Elaine's hands. Susan could only stand at the end of the bed and cry, knowing that Elaine knew that she was there.

Elaine had given her a weak smile. "I'll see you when you get to heaven."

"Don't go," Susan remembered sobbing. "I'll do more for you. I'll be a better sister."

But in the end, there hadn't been any time to be a better sister. Elaine had closed her eyes and the pain twisting her small features had vanished in an instant. At that moment, she had looked like a porcelain angel. Exactly like the angel her mother had put on Elaine's nightstand to watch over her. An angel that hadn't done the job it was supposed to do.

Clint didn't say a word. He just reached over, wiped a tear from her cheek.

"After she died, I went out to the railroad tracks behind our house and waited for the nine o'clock train," she said quietly. "When the train zoomed by, I screamed and screamed until I didn't have a voice left. When I got home, I found that my father had left again, but this time he wasn't coming back. He'd never even said goodbye to me."

"You lost two important people on the same night," Clint said.

She nodded. "And my mother was never the same."

Susan had never been the same, either. On that day she'd vowed she would never, ever get close to anyone again. Loving someone only meant getting hurt and ending up alone.

She sniffed. "I blamed Elaine for my father's leaving, do you know that? Poor kid. I blamed her."

"Susan, you were just a kid."

Clint pulled her into his arms. They lay on the bed together facing each other. He held her to him and rubbed her back.

"I understand. Let it out. Go ahead."

She couldn't keep the floodgates locked in place anymore, and it seemed like she'd been waiting dozens of years to let herself cry, let herself heal. Clint was offering himself to her just for that reason. So she let him. She cried like she'd never cried before.

"Seeing Alisa in the cafeteria… I don't know…it just shook me up. Thank goodness, at least there's a chance for Alisa."

"You were struggling not to get close to her, weren't you?"

"I still am. But it's impossible. She's just adorable and sweet, but I can't help but think she's latched onto us as some kind of substitute parents."

"I know. What are we going to do about that?" Clint asked.

"I don't know. I just don't know. We're going to have to talk to her eventually. Maybe the psychologist can help us."

"Excellent idea."

His eyes were so mesmerizing, and his smile so sweet, it was hard to believe that such a man existed. Throw in the fact that he had a heart of gold, and was great with children along with being a successful entrepreneur and bullfighter—well, Clint Scully was unlike any man she'd ever known.

It was a shame he didn't live in New York, but she just couldn't picture him there. She realized that she was actually going to miss him when she left. But she just wasn't going to fall in love with a man like Clint.

She had first-hand knowledge of how bitter her mother had become with an absentee husband.

She'd never allow that to happen to her.

## *Chapter 10*

Susan slept like she'd never slept before. No dreams. No nightmares. No ticking off long lists in her mind.

Sunshine streamed into the bedroom windows. Clint was gone—a bouquet of purple wildflowers was on the pillow next to her.

She picked it up and inhaled its scent, violets with a hint of mint.

She thought back to last night. Clint had held her tight to his warm, strong body and simply let her cry, whispering words of comfort and punctuating them with sweet kisses. He'd dried her tears and rubbed her back all through the night.

They never made love, but she had never felt more cherished.

Smiling, she held the flowers and inspected their

delicate petals. After all those years struggling to keep her feelings bottled up inside her, she'd dumped them all on Clint Scully, a man she'd known only a couple of days. Go figure.

She stretched, and realized she'd never felt better in her life.

Clint helped her realize last night that she'd never let Elaine go and that she blamed herself for not doing more to help her. Susan had been only a young girl herself, and had done what she could for her sister, but in the end, it had been the decision of a higher power.

A half hour later, she was showered, dressed and walking to the dining hall thinking about a mug of steaming coffee, a plateful of scrambled eggs, fried potatoes and a bowl of cut fruit. She could eat a moose.

Emily walked out of the lobby, said a brief hello and handed her a schedule of events before she ran off. She saw her two craft classes listed for Monday and all through the week.

A rush of anticipation shot through her. Funny, she was dreading it before, but now she had a plan for the contest and some other activities, and was actually excited.

"Hi, Susan."

She looked in the direction of the voice, and saw Alisa sitting on a bench outside the lobby.

"Well, good morning. I didn't even see you there."

"I'm waiting for Mr. and Mrs. Ketchum to pick me up. They are going to take me to see their ranch. They want to adopt me."

So that was their name—the couple with the BMW.

Alisa's crutches leaned against the seat of the bench and she looked like the loneliest little girl in the world. She didn't even look happy to be going.

Susan pointed to the space next to her. "Can I wait with you?"

"Will you?" Her face brightened. "Mrs. Dixon said she'd be right back after she did a couple of things."

"Sure." Susan sat down. "So, how do you like the Ketchums?"

"They're nice. They gave me a CD player and some CDs. They weren't Disney songs, but they're okay."

Alisa lowered her eyes, and Susan suspected that there was more to her unhappiness, and not just because she didn't receive Disney CDs. She put her arm around Alisa and hugged her close to her side.

"I'll bet you'll like their ranch, too. I'll bet they have horses and cows and, uh...whatever else is on a ranch."

"Bulls and goats," Alisa supplied.

"And maybe cats and dogs," Susan added, racking her brain to think of more ranch-related animals.

Alisa brightened at that. "Do you have any animals where you live?"

She shook her head. "I live in an apartment on the sixteenth floor in a big city. There's really no room for pets. Besides, I'm not home much to take care of them."

"That means you couldn't take care of me, either," Alisa said quietly.

Susan's heart raced at that, then sat heavy in her chest. She didn't know what to say, what to do. She had suspected that Alisa was thinking along those lines.

She had to try to make her understand without hurting her. She couldn't figure out why Alisa would want her, of all people, to adopt her. Clint, she could understand, but Alisa wanted them both.

"Why don't you give Mr. and Mrs. Ketchum a chance? Go and see their ranch. Have fun. Just stay away from the bigger stuff like the bulls. Okay?"

Alisa gave a halfhearted smile, and that made Susan feel a little better. She hugged her, tickled her neck and she giggled.

A flash of jeans, a pale yellow shirt and a white hat caught the corner of her eye. "Here comes Clint," Susan said.

They waved and he waved back. When he got closer, he tipped his hat. "Howdy, ladies. You both look as pretty as a summer day."

He stood in front of them, looking uneasy. "Um… Alisa, Mrs. Dixon sent me here with a message for you."

He met Susan's eyes briefly, and Susan could tell that the message wasn't good.

He knelt on one knee to be eye level with Alisa. "Mr. Ketchum had to work today and sends his apologies. He won't be picking you up. Some kind of problem at work."

"Oh," Alisa said quietly. She might not have wanted to go before, but she sure looked disappointed now.

A white-hot anger bubbled inside Susan. How totally inconsiderate of Mr. Ketchum to disappoint Alisa like that. The nerve of some people. Didn't he know that she was fragile enough? And what was wrong with his wife? Couldn't she pick up Alisa?

Susan quietly seethed. She bit her lip and telegraphed her ire to Clint. He nodded. It bothered him, too.

Then it hit her. She wouldn't be any better than Mr. Ketchum. If there was some kind of crisis at the office, she'd have to stay and fix the problem.

Clint snapped his fingers. "How about a trip, ladies? I'm free until six o'clock tonight, when I'm scheduled to run the sing-along. I figure that Susan needs to see a little bit of Wyoming before she goes back to that place she calls home."

That sounded nice. She wouldn't mind Clint's company for the day. Besides, Alisa seemed to be coming out of her funk with just the mention of it.

"I'll let Emily know, and I'll be back to pick you both up."

Clint pulled his rusty truck to the front of the dining hall as Susan and Alisa came out to meet him. He hurried to the passenger side, opened the door and helped Alisa inside. "Buckle up, ladies."

Clint took the road to Joe Watley's farm.

"Is this the right way to town?" Susan asked after a while.

"No. Who said we were going to Mountain Springs?" Clint asked.

"I just assumed."

Clint grinned. "We're going to Cheyenne."

"Cheyenne what?"

"Cheyenne, Wyoming. I want you both to see my ranch."

He made a wide right turn into a field. "Hope you aren't afraid of flying," he said, heading for the small hangar.

Alisa clapped. "Awesome! I've never been in a plane before.

Susan gulped some air. "Who's flying it?"

"I am," Clint said.

*"You?"*

"I am. Don't worry. Cletus the Clown taught me how to fly."

She looked at him, eyes wide and mouth open.

"Just kidding," he said.

"Whose plane is it?" she asked.

"Mine. Well, actually I co-own it with Jake Dixon and Joe Watley. You know Jake, and I'll introduce you to Joe."

Clint turned off the motor and got out. He waved to Joe, who waved back. Susan scrambled out of the truck, and he handed Alisa's crutches to Susan, then helped Alisa.

"So what do you think of *Silverbird?*" he asked Alisa.

"Cool," she said.

He squatted down without saying a word, and Alisa climbed up on his back.

Susan shut the truck door and they walked to the plane. "I think I'm in the wrong business," Susan said. "Are there any openings for a rodeo clown?"

"Bullfighter." Clint grinned, introduced Joe Watley to Susan and Alisa, and settled them inside the plane as quickly as he could.

Clint was about to get into the plane, when Joe gripped his arm and chuckled. "I can see why they both have you tied up in knots, partner."

"The knots are getting tighter. I'm showing them the Lazy S."

Joe gave a long whistle. "You are serious. Have a good time."

The flight was picture-perfect—blue skies, fluffy white clouds and a bright sun. They could see for miles.

"That's the Lazy S down there." Clint pointed. "It runs from about that group of pines, follows the river, cuts over to that little outcrop of hills, and then back to where we are."

He landed with a small bump, taxied down the runway and cut the engine. His uncle Charlie would be along soon with the pickup to collect them.

He helped them out of the plane as a series of sharp barks split the air. Rodeo, his black-and-white border collie, came bounding toward them. Alisa grabbed for his hand. Susan clutched his arm.

"He won't hurt you," Clint assured them.

He let out a shrill whistle, and Rodeo stopped in front of him, wagging his tail. He scratched the dog behind the ears and rubbed his tummy when he rolled over.

"Ladies, this is Rodeo. He herds the cows and bulls, and is better than six cowboys."

The dog licked Alisa's face, and she giggled. He

sniffed at her braces and crutches, sat and looked up at her. Obviously Rodeo had found a new friend.

"I can't wait to see more of your ranch," Susan said.

That was music to his ears. That's why he'd brought them here. For some unknown reason, he wanted them to like the Lazy S.

He had a love-hate relationship with the ranch. He'd loved it growing up, and when he'd bought it back years later, he'd loved remodeling it. He painted, plastered, even decorated it himself. He bought new furniture, including a hand-carved king bed.

The house was going to be a wedding present for Mary Alice. But after she left him at the altar, he could no longer find joy in his childhood home—he just didn't want to be at the ranch anymore.

So Clint hired the best cowboys he knew to work the Lazy S, and he pretty much left them alone. Uncle Charlie lived in a small house of his own on the property and watched over everything.

The pickup appeared, but instead of Uncle Charlie, Sam Diaz, an old cowboy with a heart of gold and several gold teeth to match, welcomed them and opened the doors of the vehicle.

"I'll show you my horses first," Clint said proudly. "I have some of the best quarter horses in this part of Wyoming. Then I'll show you Mighty Max, the rankest bull around. He's the one who rammed his horn through me in Reno and sidelined a couple bull riders for the year. His owner was going to put him down, but I bought him instead."

Clint showed them horse after horse, bull after

bull. He put Alisa sidesaddle on a little pony and he led her around the corral. Rodeo, the border collie, walked by their side and kept looking at Alisa as if to make sure she was okay.

As Alisa enjoyed her ride, Susan looked at the expanse of meadow, the miles of fence, the mountains in the distance and the pretty pond with ducks. The main house, long and low and rambling, sat in the middle of a copse of tall trees. There were pots of flowers hanging from the porch rafters, and a three-tiered fountain in the middle of the brick walk that led to the main house.

She put her hand out and let the water flow over her palm. "I'd love to pull over a chair and listen to this water all day."

"You would?" Clint raised an eyebrow. "That seems too tame for Susan Collins, CEO."

He was right. She never would have thought of such a thing a few days ago. She wondered why now, why here. Maybe there was something to this vacation thing after all.

She knew that she'd thrown herself into her work to make it a success, but there was a price she paid—maybe too high of a price.

Clint was showing her that there was more to life than working yourself to death.

Maybe if she hadn't been such a workaholic, she might have found a husband who loved her. Maybe she would have had children. Maybe… maybe… she'd never know.

Clint tied Wanda, the little pony, to a railing and lifted Alisa off. "I'll show you the main house."

A tall, large man with a white chef's apron and a white handlebar mustache opened the door and waved in welcome.

"Ladies, this is my uncle Charlie. He's chief cook and bottle washer at the Lazy S. He's also the vet, my business manager, the head wrangler, the horse trainer, and he's very, very bossy."

Uncle Charlie took off his white cowboy hat and held it over his heart. "Welcome to the Lazy S, ladies. Your beauty dwarfs the spacious skies of Wyoming, and your smiles outshine the sun."

"He also thinks he's a poet," Clint added.

Susan smiled. "I think he's charming."

"Me, too," said Alisa.

He lumbered down the stairs and enveloped Susan in a bear hug. He smelled of garlic and tomatoes and maybe cumin.

"You must be Susan. Clint radioed me that he was bringing some guests. As luck would have it, you're all in time for my famous beef chili."

Uncle Charlie slapped his hands on his knees and leaned over. He winked at Alisa. "Is this Alisa?" He held his hand out, and Alisa slipped hers into his.

He shook it ever so gently. "Welcome to the Lazy S, darlin'. You look like a young lady who'd like a big bowl of cowboy chili and maybe an ice cream cone for dessert. Come in. Come in."

He slapped Clint's back. "About time you stopped by. You have a half-dozen messages on your desk from hospitals wanting you to stop by and entertain the kids. And the Make a Wish Foundation called.

There's a boy with cancer at the Casper Hospital who's asking for you."

Clint nodded. "I'll make arrangements."

Susan stood motionless. He visited hospitals, too?

She felt Clint's hand on the small of her back. "Let me show you around."

The entranceway floor was made of large reddish-brown tiles with thick gray cement around them. The walls were varnished knotty pine, and Susan wondered if the planks had come from the nearby woods. Large pieces of furniture, heavy with wood and marble, fit perfectly with the vaulted ceilings and skylights. A floor-to-ceiling fireplace with a mantel that looked like half of a redwood tree took up most of one wall. There were windows everywhere.

"This is just beautiful, Clint. My apartment could fit into this room about ten times."

He nodded and looked around as if he was seeing it for the first time himself. "Glad you like it."

She heard the pride in his voice.

"Clint did a lot of work on the place. He's very talented," Uncle Charlie said.

Clint shifted on his feet, obviously uncomfortable at the praise. She smiled her admiration, and could have sworn that his face reddened.

When Alisa had to use the bathroom, Susan's curiosity got the best of her, and she wandered down the hall.

There were three bedrooms, all huge. Clint's was in the back. Three sides of the room held floor-to-ceiling shelves. Hundreds of trophies, pictures and belt buckles of every shape and size decorated the shelves.

Near the remaining wall was a king-size bed made out of round logs. She could picture Clint stretched out and naked, holding his hand out to her to join him. Her body heated and her cheeks flamed.

A light went on and she jumped.

"I-I'm sorry. I didn't mean to—"

Clint held up a hand. "No problem. Look all you want."

"I can't believe all your awards." She pointed to a picture. "I see you roping the little cows."

He laughed. "Those are steers."

He showed her pictures of him saving bull riders named Chris Shivers, Adriano Moraes, Paulo Crimber and dozens of others.

All the while, she tried not to look at his big, comfortable bed.

Then she suffered through pictures of him with several Miss Rodeos, all of whom had long, fluffy hair under white hats, fringed blouses with sequins and sprayed-on jeans.

She could tell by Clint's nonstop chatter and big grin that he liked the rodeo life and was proud of what he'd accomplished. All the people in the pictures seemed like family to him.

"Every year, whatever cowboys can make it come to the Lazy S and help me with round-up. We work all day, then drink beer and eat barbecue and relive every ride and every wreck." He chuckled as he remembered something. "Good friends. Good times."

"Do they work with the kids at the Gold Buckle, too?"

"Absolutely. Some bring their families and camp out in trailers by the river. Some of the single cowboys stay all year long and work for the Dixons. When you have a cowboy for a friend, you have a friend for life."

Susan thought it would be wonderful to have friends like that. She didn't have really good friends, just business friends, and there was a difference. She was the boss, and she didn't discuss her personal life with them to any great length, not even Bev.

Yet she'd told Clint her deepest personal thoughts.

She wanted to thank him for last night, but she had a feeling he already knew how much it had meant to her.

She remembered how he'd held her, how he'd rubbed her back, wiped her tears. His kisses were sweet and caring, his arms strong around her.

Maybe he was right about cowboys and friends.

It made her heart soar that that they were friends, and she supposed that they should leave it at that.

Sex would just mess everything up.

Wouldn't it?

# *Chapter 11*

Susan could hear the phone ring in the distance. Soon Uncle Charlie yelled, "Clint, it's Emily Dixon for you."

"Excuse me," he said to Susan. "The phone's in the kitchen."

"Sure. Go ahead. I'll wait in the living room."

On her way, she listened at the bathroom door and heard Alisa singing. "Alisa, everything okay?"

"Yes."

"Okay."

Susan sat in one of the comfortable chairs in the living room. Alisa and Clint appeared at the same time.

Clint sat on the thick coffee table across from Susan and made eye contact with them both. "Mrs.

D said that there was a change in the schedule. I don't have to be back today and neither does Alisa. So how would you both like to stay overnight here?"

"Really?" Alisa asked, looking at them.

Overnight at Clint's house? Susan immediately thought of joining him in his big bed. Her body came alive with excitement that she didn't know existed within her.

She tried to calm herself and sound casual. "Sounds good to me, but we didn't bring any clothes."

"No problem. There are plenty of my sister's clothes here that'd fit you. My niece's would be a bit big on Alisa, but they'll do."

Uncle Charlie announced that lunch was ready, so Clint led the way to the kitchen.

Wherever Alisa went, Rodeo went, and she constantly reached out to pet him.

"I packed a picnic basket," his uncle said. "Why don't you and Susan have a picnic up on the hill. If Alisa would like, we could eat and then read a book. How about that, Alisa?"

Alisa grinned. "And have an ice-cream cone?"

Charlie laughed. "I knew you wouldn't forget that."

Clint thought of being alone with Susan on a blanket in the shade of the lodgepole pines on the hill. They could share more than just chili.

"Two picnics in two days?" Susan said. "That's more than I've been on in my entire life, unless you count restaurants with sidewalk seating."

"Nope. Doesn't count," Clint said. "My, you're

changing into a country gal right before my eyes. Pretty soon, I'll have you roping and yodeling."

Clint whistled as he slipped his hand into Susan's. They left the house and walked up the hill. He felt happy, alive, and he suspected it was due to being alone with Susan.

Susan shook out the blanket and let it drift to the ground. She looked around, smiling. She was noticing the beauty of his ranch. His cattle were grazing on the silvery green grass in the distance, and the horses were doing the same up on the hill to their left. The pond glittered in the distance.

He never realized it, but he missed the Lazy S. Or maybe he was just seeing it again through her eyes.

It surprised him that Susan was so calm and quiet and observant. He half expected her to whip out a laptop or that overstuffed planner of hers. Her newfound serenity was sexy, and it made him forget about food. He was content to follow her gaze until she arched an eyebrow at him.

"Hungry?" he asked.

"Definitely."

He opened the picnic basket and handed her a wide-mouth thermos.

"Uncle Charlie's famous chili."

He pulled out some slices of sourdough bread wrapped in foil, a bottle of merlot and two wineglasses.

Susan watched as Clint opened the bottle of wine. She liked how his hands moved and remembered how he had stroked her breasts—teasing, touching, tempting.

She wiped the moisture that suddenly appeared on her upper lip. "So, what was it like growing up here?"

"It was hard work, but there was also a lot of fun and laughs. We'd race our horses in the field. We'd swim in the pond. We'd think of tricks to play on the cowboys. In the winter, we'd be up at the crack of dawn mucking stalls and tossing out hay for the cattle. We'd play in the snow. Snowshoe and ski all over the place. Then there was school, sports and studying."

"Were you a close family?" Susan asked.

"Uh-huh. We still are, even though we're all over the States now. If ever I needed them, all I'd have to do is pick up the phone and they'd all come running."

"That's a wonderful thing. You don't know how lucky you are." She looked over at the horses in the corral that were content to stand in the shade and swish their tails. "I have no one to call."

He shook his head. "I'm sorry."

"You think I'm pretty pathetic, don't you?" she asked, not wanting his pity.

"I think you're *wonderful*. You've worked hard to make your company a success. You did it all alone, too."

"My employees are the best."

"You're their leader. *They* followed *you*. Give yourself some credit."

His words made her heart soar. She needed to hear that.

Yet, what had it cost her?

"So in all the years there you've never been married?"

"No. When I was dating and made it clear that my business came first, men made their excuses and never called again. A couple of the men I've dated actually tried to woo me in an attempt to take over my business." She looked at him. "How did *you* do it, Clint? You have a successful operation here from what I can tell, yet you're calm and cool and can do what you want. What's your secret?"

He laughed. "I have great people who work for me, so I leave them to do what they're good at—just what I advised you to do when you first got here."

She'd been mulling that over from time to time. She supposed it was good advice, but she couldn't embrace the concept yet. It was *her* company. She started it and no one could do as good a job as she could. No one cared about the business like she did.

"Tell me the truth," she asked. "Why did you keep the Lazy S when your parents didn't want it?"

He pushed back his hat with a thumb. "I had hoped to settle down with Mary Alice Bonner. I'd dated her through most of high school, and asked her to marry me. When that didn't work out, I guess I just wanted a place to come back to, and this was the only home I knew."

She smiled. "Your home on the range?"

He raised his eyebrows, looking surprised that she got the connection.

"You sing, whistle or hum that song several times a day. Now I know why. But you're not here much, are you?"

"No. But I know it's here whenever I'm ready to..."

"To what?" she pressed.

"To hang up my spurs. It's a cowboy expression," he explained, probably when he saw the baffled look on her face.

"You mean, settle down? Give up bullfighting?" She took another sip of wine and stared up at the clouds. "I can't imagine retiring from Winners Wear. Not in a million years."

He seemed disappointed when she said that. "Yeah, well...me, neither, but bullfighting is a young man's sport. I'm getting past my prime."

He looked fabulously prime to her. Just like he had last night.

"Clint, I want to thank you for last night. I knew that...well...that you had other things on your mind. We both did."

Her smile was shy, and he wanted to kiss her luscious lips.

"But being with Alisa all day, and then seeing that picture of Elaine, I guess I had a meltdown. And you're just so easy to talk to. I've never told anyone what I told you."

He shrugged. "You needed to talk. Glad I was there."

"You'll never know how much you helped. How much last night meant to me."

She moved closer and kissed him on the cheek.

"Mmm...nice." He put his arm around her and

listened to the birds chirp, smelled the fresh air and thought that he'd never felt more content.

"Susan, I hope that someday, you'll realize that you just couldn't protect your sister, and that it wasn't your fault. Elaine knew you loved her and you did your best."

"I know that now." Tears pooled in her violet eyes, yet she smiled. "You helped me figure it all out, Clint."

He took her hand again and kissed the back of it. "You know that your mother wasn't right in laying all that responsibility on you, don't you?"

His arm reached around to her shoulder, and he hugged her to his side. She let her head rest in the crook of his shoulder, and she took a deep, calming breath.

"I guess I always knew that, but it was hard to accept that my mother could be wrong. She knew everything."

"Maybe she didn't after all, huh?"

"Maybe not," Susan conceded. "But she was so strong, so fiercely independent."

Clint raised an eyebrow. "Like you?"

She didn't answer that, but she knew what he left unsaid. Sometimes, she thought now, being strong and fiercely independent wasn't a good thing. It didn't mean being isolated and handling everything on your own. Everyone needed help.

Clint was making her see that. He had released another thing out of that locked box inside her heart. Maybe it wasn't laid to rest yet, but it was out.

The worst still remained.

# *Chapter 12*

"I can't believe that I'm just sitting here outside and talking." Susan raised her hands. "I haven't even felt the need to call Bev. Wonder what's wrong with me?"

"Maybe it's called relaxing," Clint said.

"I don't even know the meaning of that word—although I am feeling the need to plan more for my classes. They start tomorrow, you know. I had Bev send me some notions and T-shirts from Winners Wear. When I see what's there, I think I'll be okay," Susan said, eating the last spoonful of Uncle Charlie's chili. "That was delicious chili."

"He'll love to hear that."

Susan took a deep breath and let it out. "So this is how relaxing feels." She slipped her sandals off and felt the cool grass under her feet, something she'd never be able to do in New York.

"I can't believe you don't spend more time here." Susan looked around at the rolling land. "It's just magnificent. All this land. And no neighbors as far as the eye can see. Everything is just like a picture."

"I do like the quiet," he said. "There might be no neighbors, but there's about a dozen down-on-their-luck cowboys who live in the bunkhouse and in a couple of shacks on the other side of the barn. They wander in by word of mouth, or I find them and send them to Uncle Charlie. They heal if they are injured from rodeo or bull riding. When they're able, they'll pay back by working, then they go on their way."

"So you take in stray cowboys?"

"I guess that's one way to put it."

"You're amazing."

He chuckled. "That's what all the women say."

She raised an eyebrow, tried to hide a grin. She knew he was joking, but she didn't doubt that he was an experienced lover. Her stomach fluttered at the thought, and her mouth went dry. She held out her glass for another refill of wine.

Clint uncorked the bottle and filled her glass. "So you like it here?"

"Very much."

"Do you think Alisa likes the Lazy S?" he asked.

"What kid wouldn't? Horses and ponies, a dog that never leaves her side, killer bulls on the hill, a built-in pool—it's pure heaven. Why do you ask? Thinking of taking in stray orphans?"

She was kidding him, but he wasn't smiling. He turned serious.

"You know I like her. Maybe, if she's not adopted right away, she could come and visit," he said. "Maybe she could stay all summer."

"And you'd leave her with Uncle Charlie while you're bullfighting and towing your trailer from rodeo to rodeo? She'd be lonely, Clint. She wants you, and you know it."

He looked into the wineglass as if the answer would be written there in the merlot.

She reached for his hand and held it. "You know, Clint, I waited all my life for my father to come back from his trips. When he was home, I could almost pretend that we were a family, but something was always missing—his commitment to us, I guess. Elaine and I wanted a father. I know Uncle Charlie is here, but Alisa needs you, Clint. All of you—your heart, your love—all of it."

He took a big gulp of wine. "I know. I can't adopt her."

"Were we even talking about adopting?" Susan asked, confused.

"No, I guess not. I just know she's special to me—she's not just another camper."

"Me, too. But neither one of us has the lifestyle to raise a child. Could you change for her, Clint? Could you give up your trailer and live at your ranch for her?"

Clint swore under his breath.

Hand in hand they walked back to the ranch house.

When they got inside, Clint headed for the kitchen to empty the picnic basket and Susan followed. She went over to the sliding door and saw Alisa sleeping on a lounge chair under an umbrella and Uncle Charlie reading a book.

"She's still sleeping," Susan told Clint. "Poor thing must be exhausted."

"She's had an exciting day."

Clint slid the door open, and they walked down the stairs to the concrete patio.

Susan started to pull out a chair from a round table with a purple umbrella, but Uncle Charlie got up and motioned for them both to follow him. He picked a spot away from the sleeping Alisa.

"Clint, why don't you take Susan on a trail ride? Show her the pond and the upper pastures and the cattle. I'm all right here with the little girl. I'm enjoying her company, even though she fell asleep during *Harry Potter.* Can you imagine that?"

His eyes were the same color as Clint's and glittered with amusement.

Uncle Charlie herded them toward the patio door. "She'll be okay. We'll go back to reading Harry."

Clint turned to Susan. "How about it?"

The expression on his face was strangely intense, as if he were thinking about more than a horse ride.

"Let's go," she said.

They were both in the kitchen when Clint whispered in her ear, "Wait a minute. Something's going on. I can tell how my uncle is acting." He led her toward the window over the sink, where they had a perfect view of the backyard.

Clint stood behind her. She could feel the warmth of his breath. All she had to do was turn around…

Alisa lifted her head from the lounge chair and grinned at Uncle Charlie. "Are they gone?"

"Yep. Trail ride to the pond, just like we planned. Just between us, Susan is only the second gal that Clint ever brought home. I think she's special to him."

"Oh, cool. Do you think they'll kiss?"

"Maybe." Uncle Charlie cleared his throat and began reading.

Clint looked at Susan as they headed for the barn. "Seems like we have a couple of matchmakers on our hands, along with Emily Dixon."

"Emily?"

"Emily and Dex have had a couple of successes. Jake and Beth are their biggest coup to date."

"But the two of *us,* Clint?"

"Is it so strange? The CEO and the clown?"

"Bullfighter. You said you wanted to be called a bullfighter." It seemed natural to slip her hand into his. "Well, don't you think it's strange? I mean, we don't have anything in common."

When he stopped and looked at her, it seemed like he could see right through to her very heart. She couldn't move, couldn't exhale, she just waited and wondered what he was thinking, what he was going to do.

He swore under his breath, pulled her toward him and crushed her to his chest. His lips moved on hers, and she felt power surging inside him. She held on to his shoulders to steady herself and could feel his muscles tighten. His tongue traced her lips and she opened for him. Their tongues met in a fierce dance.

He pulled away. "Susan?" he whispered.

She knew what he was trying to ask her. She wanted him, too. Every nerve in her body pulsed with liquid heat.

"Yes," she answered.

He grabbed her hand, and they just about raced to the barn. Clint slid the door open, shutting it behind them and then locking it with a metal latch.

"Tell me that you don't want strings," he said. "No commitment."

In that moment, Susan realized while that might have been true at one time, it wasn't now. She wanted much, much more from him. She wanted him to be a friend, a lover. She wanted to know everything about him. But it was all so impossible. He had his life, and she had hers, and they were thousands of miles apart, not only in geographical distance, but also in the way they lived and worked.

But she'd take the memory of what it was like to be with him back to New York and treasure it always.

Her heart pounded so loudly she was sure he could hear it. She was about to lie to him, and she'd never lied in her life.

"No strings," she finally said.

He took his hat off and hung it on a nail protruding from a thick wooden beam.

Tugging on a blanket that was folded over a stall, he tossed it onto the hay. Taking Susan with him, he fell onto the blanket.

"Take off your blouse," he whispered. "I want to see you. All of you."

She could see the sun streaming through the dusty windows, illuminating them both in golden light. Vaguely she heard the moving of horses in the stalls. She could see a tiny scar on Clint's chin, the little indentation on the side of his mouth. She could smell the scent of the earthy barn and the sweetness of the hay.

It reminded her of the barn at the Gold Buckle, the barn where he'd swept her into his arms and danced with her. She'd bared some of her soul to him there.

There'd be no dancing now.

"You first," she whispered, suddenly nervous.

He knelt and shrugged off his shirt. She saw his scars, the scars from his dangerous job. A job he could lose his life while doing. That was another reason why she couldn't give her heart to him. She might lose him.

Without taking his eyes off of her, he yanked on his belt buckle, loosened his belt and pulled off his boots. He popped the button on his jeans, then started on the zipper.

A fog settled on Clint's brain. He couldn't think for the life of him.

Susan deserved slow and passionate lovemaking, but he was on fire. He'd never wanted a woman so much in his life.

He watched as she undid the buttons on her blouse, tossing it next to his shirt on the hay. She wore a sexy, lacy white bra with a front closure.

"Don't touch that," he ordered. He wanted to unhook it himself.

She smiled and slipped out of her shorts and adjusted the little flowered bikini underwear that she wore.

Looking up at him, she pointed to his jeans. "Take them off. I want to see you, too."

He pulled his jeans off. No sexy underwear for him, just white briefs that were feeling suddenly too small.

He fisted his hands on the front of her bra and unhooked it. Her breasts sprang free, her silken skin stark white against his tanned hands.

He touched, stroked and nibbled, then trailed kisses over her breasts. He teased her nipples with his teeth and tongue. He could taste the wine on her lips, smell the perfume on her skin, and feel her nails on his back.

He stopped himself from tearing off her panties, trying to take it slow, but with Susan he was once again a horny high school junior in the front seat of his pickup.

Finally, they were naked, skin to skin, mouth to mouth. She whispered his name and reached for him. She ran her soft hand up and down his length, until he thought he'd explode. When she squeezed him, he knew he would.

He couldn't reach his jeans, couldn't get to his wallet. He swore.

"Clint?"

He winked. "Don't go anywhere."

Her eyes twinkled. "As if I could." Her voice was low, sexy.

With a grunt, he moved off her, grabbed his jeans, found his wallet. He pulled out a condom and tore a corner out of the packet with his teeth.

Watching Clint unroll the condom over his arousal had to be one of the sexiest things Susan had ever seen. He was hard and long, and breathtakingly masculine.

At least he had enough sense to use protection—she'd never even thought of it.

"You're gorgeous, Clint."

He grinned and pulled her on top of him.

Her tongue made circles on his nipples as her hands explored his chest and stomach.

He cupped her breasts in his hands, his thumbs pressing on her nipples. They peaked under his touch and the warmth of his tongue. She lost all sanity. All she could think of was feeling him move inside her. She wanted him more than ever.

She met his gaze and positioned herself over him. Slowly, she took the length of him inside her, giving herself time to adjust to his width.

He filled her completely, totally. She couldn't move; all she could do was gaze into his eyes. Then she rode him, slowly at first, then faster.

"Susan." His voice didn't sound like his when he whispered her name. "Stop moving or things are going to be over sooner than I'd like."

He rolled over, taking her with him, wincing to hold himself in check.

His tongue demonstrated what he was going to do to her, and she could feel her muscles constrict and throb around him. She moved her hips to take more of him, and he buried himself deep inside her.

They moved together as two parts of one whole, faster and faster until they were both sweaty and spent.

Holding on tight, they drifted back to reality, back to Clint's barn at the Lazy S.

They could only look into each other's eyes and smile as their pulses returned to normal.

Clint kissed her forehead, let his lips linger on hers.

She already regretted their agreement. She could hardly tell him that she'd just had the best experience of her life.

Or that she thought she was falling in love with him.

She'd just given her everything to him. Her heart was lying like a lump in her chest as she thought about how her days in Wyoming were coming to an end. Then Clint would go one way, and she'd go another.

That's just what she was afraid of, losing the people she cared for and missing them every day of her life.

But she'd throw herself into her work, like she always had, and the pain would dull in time.

# Chapter 13

Instead of taking the horses, Clint drove Susan out to the pond on an electric golf cart. He made up some lame excuse about how it was time for the horses to eat.

Actually, he just wanted to sit with his arm around her. What they'd just shared in the barn rocked him to the soles of his boots.

Her mere touch inflamed him like nothing—or no one—ever had. They had fit together so perfectly, and when she met her release…hell, it made *him* feel good just watching her face.

She was nothing like the woman who'd stepped off the plane at the Mountain Springs Airport a few days ago. That woman was a top spinning out of control. The new Susan Collins was calmer, more aware of her surroundings, more appreciative of the beauty of nature.

Just watching her face, flushed with animation and wonder and a hint of a tan, made him feel good that he'd played a part in getting her to slow down.

He'd also take some of the credit for that glow on her face.

He'd never felt as close to any other woman as he did to Susan, not even Mary Alice.

Who would have thought that Clint Scully would fall for a city slicker?

"It's so beautiful here." She pointed ahead. "Clint, what are all those?"

He looked to see a small herd drinking at the water's edge. "Elk." He cut the motor so they wouldn't run off.

"So many of them? Oh, and look at the babies."

"You've never seen elk before?"

"It's not as if they roam around Manhattan and drink out of the fountains, cowboy."

"True."

"Alisa will be disappointed that she missed this."

"She's probably having a ball singing tunes from *The Little Mermaid* to Uncle Charlie."

"That reminds me, I'm going to talk to Emily when I get back. I'd like to pay for Alisa's operation and any expenses. I want her to go to the best hospital and have the best surgeon available, not someplace that Children's Services will send her. Emily said that her operation would be at the end of the summer. I think she should have it done in New

York. I have connections at some of the top hospitals there."

"And who's going to visit her or take care of her way over in New York City? You?" He raised an eyebrow. "Won't you be busy at your company?"

Her eyes widened. Obviously she hadn't gotten that far in her thinking yet.

"I'm assuming her adoptive parents will be with her," she replied.

"And you'll supply the money for them to travel with her?"

"Yes. If they need it."

"And that will make you feel better?" Clint asked, not making eye contact. "By throwing money in her direction, you don't have to get further involved."

"But there's nothing else I…we…can do for her."

"That's not true, and you know it."

He started up the golf cart and headed left around the lake. The elk scattered.

"You wouldn't visit Alisa in the hospital?" he asked. "She'd be crushed."

"Of course I would."

"If you can fit her into your schedule, that is."

"I'll block out time," she said.

"You'll *block out* time?" he said sarcastically. "Isn't that considerate of you?"

"Clint, what's your problem?"

He swung the cart away from the lake. He didn't know why he was so perturbed. It was very nice of Susan to provide Alisa the best medical attention that money could buy, but she still wasn't able to get personally involved with Alisa. She was still comparing her to Elaine.

He'd thought she was over that.

Alisa needed Susan. The girl adored her, and if Susan would let herself, she'd see that she needed Alisa, too.

"Are you scared to go to the hospital because you'd be living Elaine's illness all over again through Alisa?"

"I don't know. Maybe." She looked down at her hands, which were so tightly entwined on her lap that her knuckles were white. "I know that Alisa's condition isn't terminal, and logically, I should stop being such an idiot."

She had such a pained look on her face that he knew she was struggling with her decision.

"Alisa needs you, Susan. You're terrific with her. You know she adores you."

"She adores you, too, Clint."

"That's why I'm going to be there for her, no matter where her operation is. And what do I tell her when she asks for you? That you are too busy?"

"I don't want her to think that." She shook her head. "I just need time to figure things out. To digest everything. I need time to think about my life—past, present and future." She met his gaze. "And *that* is something that I never thought I'd say. I've always tried to stick to reaching my professional goals. I'm detouring into unfamiliar territory here."

Who was he to sit in judgment of her? She'd work through it. She was almost there. He had his own hang-ups. He had a ranch he didn't work. He lived in a trailer that he towed around the country with a beat-up truck. If it weren't for Cletus the Clown and Joe Watley, he'd be broke. If it weren't for Uncle Charlie, he wouldn't have a successful ranch.

His time with Susan and Alisa made him realize that he had the hearth and home, but he wanted a family of his own. That's why he worked with the Wheelchair Rodeo and the Gold Buckle Gang, and visited hospitals. He liked to think of those kids as his own. They were the ones who needed him—kids like Alisa.

He'd like his own kids, too, to ride all over his ranch, to swim in the pond, to play tricks on the ranch hands, just like he had. A baker's dozen ought to do.

Yes. This was what he'd always wanted.

He looked at the woman sitting beside him. Susan certainly didn't share his dreams, and that left a hollow feeling inside him.

Sure, they had great sex in the barn a while ago, but that was just slaking their mutual lust. Wasn't it?

Susan broke the silence. "What happened to Mary Alice Bonner?"

"That came out of nowhere."

"I know. But I was just wondering what happened."

"She left me at the altar, ran off to do her thing in Chicago. She wanted to design her own jewelry. She made a big success out of it, too, and I never heard from her again."

"That must have hurt you."

"Like being gored by a bull. I mean, she could

have told me earlier. Or in person." He shrugged. "But that's old news. It was a couple of years ago."

There had been many eager buckle bunnies in his career, but that was only sex. That's all he'd let himself want.

Until now.

Now he could picture Susan and Alisa on his ranch, riding horses, laughing, swimming in the pool and pond.

But he couldn't get his hopes up like that.

No commitment.

Yes. No. Yes. No. He was driving himself crazy.

Clint cleared his throat. "Let's go see what Alisa and Charlie are up to."

Susan dove into the pool, grateful for the cool, clear water. She came up for air near where Alisa floated on a small pink tube.

"Hi," Alisa said. "Did you go on a horse ride?"

Susan stood and moved a wet strand of Alisa's hair behind her ear. "Clint said the horses had to eat supper, so we went for a ride in a golf cart instead."

A memory of their afternoon in the barn flashed through her mind, and Susan ducked under water to cool her heated cheeks.

Clint came out wearing cutoff jeans. He hit the diving board, splashing them both with a well-placed cannonball.

After they both splashed Clint in retaliation, Susan found a floating lounge chair and leaned back to watch the two of them play in the water.

Clint held Alisa in his arms and swung her around

in the water. They played with a beach ball, played ring toss, and Clint gave Alisa yet another piggy-back ride.

Maybe he'd bought the ranch back to give to his parents, but he'd kept it for Mary Alice Bonner and himself.

She looked at him in a new light. He wasn't just a tumbleweed traveling in his trailer. The Lazy S was what Clint longed for. He'd remodeled his home, added his own touches to it, and if Mary Alice hadn't left him, he'd be here with her now.

She looked at him, stunned by what she'd concluded. Clint was strong and sweet, masculine and yet sensitive. He was great with kids. She marveled at how he was playing with Alisa and listening to her chatter.

Clint would make a wonderful father.

But Clint was no different from her father. He worked the summer programs at the Gold Buckle Ranch, and then he was gone.

He even left his beautiful ranch for others to run, just like her father left her mother to run the household.

Susan said a quick prayer that whoever adopted Alisa would play with her and spend lots of time with her.

Every kid deserved that.

Later, Susan changed into the dry clothes that Clint provided. They settled into pleasant conversation and many laughs around the patio table, filling up on the steaks that Clint barbecued along with a big salad and baked potatoes.

Uncle Charlie started a bonfire as Susan watched the magnificent sunset. Wrapped snugly in the coat that Clint had draped over her shoulders, she could smell his scent lingering on the fabric.

Susan hated the thought of leaving Clint's ranch. She could easily spend more time here with him.

Clint strummed his guitar as Alisa sang her usual songs from Disney movies. When she saw Alisa yawning, Susan called for lights out.

"Time for bed, miss," Susan said, feeling like a mother.

"Aw, one more song. Please?" Alisa begged.

"One more," Susan relented. "But I have a special request if you all don't mind. Clint, will you play 'Home on the Range' for us?"

"With pleasure."

Susan was taken aback when Alisa scrambled onto her lap and leaned her head on her shoulder. Her little hand found hers, and Susan's heart melted. She draped a blanket around Alisa and hugged her close. She could smell the chlorine in her hair, feel her hard metal braces against her own legs, smell the sweetness of melted marshmallows clinging to her.

Susan kissed Alisa's forehead, and Alisa smiled up at her, a beautiful, contented smile.

And in that moment, Susan lost her heart completely.

Clint began to sing. He met her eyes, and it seemed like he was singing right to her. As she listened to his voice drift over his Wyoming land, Susan took great satisfaction in knowing why he loved that song so much.

* * *

"We need to talk about Alisa," Susan said to Clint after they'd put the girl to bed.

"I know. Let me take a shower first and I'll meet you in the living room."

"Okay. I'll do the same."

"We could save water and shower together," he said, eyebrow raised.

She shook her head. "Off you go, cowboy."

Susan took a shower and slipped into a T-shirt that Clint had given her.

She didn't wait for him in the living room as they planned. Instead, she gave a slight knock on his bedroom door. "It's me."

"C'mon in."

He swung the door open, and she saw that he had a towel wrapped around his waist. His hair was still wet and uncombed.

Suddenly, she couldn't swallow, couldn't breathe. She wanted him again.

"I want you naked," she said, not aware that she spoke the words out loud.

"Pardon?"

"Naked. You." Susan stood in front of him and reached for the fold of his towel. It dropped to the floor, and he stood in front of her, gloriously naked and not caring a bit. Smiling, he placed his hands on his hips and raised his eyebrows.

"Now what?" he said.

"Bed," she said, finally finding her voice.

He took her in his arms and pinned her on the bed, the hard length of him pressed against her thigh.

"I want to take it slow this time, Susan."

"No way."

He pulled off her shirt and teased her nipple with his teeth. "I thought you were learning to relax and take things easy."

"Next time, Clint. Next time."

She reached between them, closing her hand over his erection. He was already about to explode. He pulled open the drawer to his nightstand, and with a grunt felt around for a condom.

"Let me," she said.

He handed her a packet. With shaking hands, she managed to get it open. She knelt between his legs, kissing the soft tip of his arousal.

Just as she finished unrolling the condom down his hard length, she found herself under him. His mouth covered hers as he entered her. Their rhythm was furious as they thrust together, meeting each other's pace. Susan found release first, and then Clint let himself go.

They clung to each other, arms and limbs tangled. They stayed that way, dozing on and off, until one of them reached for the other to make love again.

Finally, they relaxed, in a state of bliss, content in each other's arms. But as Susan felt Clint's hand stroke her back, she knew that in a few days, she'd have to figure out what she was going to do without him in her life.

# *Chapter 14*

After a big breakfast that Uncle Charlie had ready for them at his cabin, they headed for the plane. This time they had an extra passenger—Rodeo.

As they got closer to Mountain Springs, it started raining, then the weather got progressively worse.

Alisa thought it was "awesome" to see lightning off in the distance, but Clint concentrated on piloting and didn't say much. Rodeo was curled up on the seat next to Alisa with his chin on her lap.

They touched down at the airstrip on Joe Watley's Silver River Ranch at eleven o'clock in the morning, then they took Alisa to the Dixons' home. Clint carried her inside, and commanded Rodeo to stay on the porch.

"It's organized chaos around here because of the

rain," Jake Dixon said, shutting the kitchen door. "Glad you're all back. We were all worried about you in this weather."

"Looks like some thunder and lightning is headed this way," Clint said.

Emily appeared in the kitchen, looking harried. "Welcome back." She stared out the window. "The weather service said to expect this for the next three days. It's a mud pit out there." She turned toward Alisa. "Did you have a good time?"

"Cheyenne Clint's ranch is so cool." Alisa grinned up at Clint. He pulled out a kitchen chair for her, and she sat down.

"Excellent," Emily said. "I knew you and Susan would love it there."

"We had to cancel the games, which disappointed the kids to no end," Dex said. "Riding lessons were called off. We've added roping lessons and relay races in the dining hall, and we've scheduled a dance. We're going to need you to play, Clint."

"No problem," Clint said.

"Susan, can you take on more craft classes for the week since the outdoor activities are canceled?" Jake asked.

She had a moment of panic, and then remembered all the pot holder loops in the cabinet of her classroom. "I can if someone can teach me how to make pot holders."

"I can," Alisa said. "My mommy taught me."

Susan gave her a thumbs-up. "Excellent. You can show me, and we'll teach the classes together."

Her face glowed. "Really? Me?"

"Really. You."

"Joe made a couple of calls and got us the Mountain Springs arena on Friday, free of charge," Jake said. "We're going to have the Gold Buckle Gang Rodeo indoors there. The arena is big enough for two baseball games at the same time. Joe's bringing in some steers for the roundup."

"And then we could do the logo T-shirt competition. I have a little runway fashion show planned," Susan added.

"Excellent," Emily said. "The kids will love it. Then the volunteers can serve hot dogs and hamburgers. It's not going to be as exciting as a trail ride, but we need to improvise."

"I'll help Joe with the stock," Clint said. "We could always bring horses and let the kids ride around the arena."

"Just what I was thinking." Jake gave Clint a slap on the back that would have sent a normal man flying across the room, but Clint didn't budge. "I need to get going. Don't forget lunch in about an hour." Jake bent over and gave Alisa a tweak on the nose, then tipped his hat to Susan. "Thanks for your help, ladies."

"Uh… Mrs. D, we had a stowaway on the plane." Clint opened the kitchen door and Rodeo walked in, looked around, then immediately went to Alisa's side and sat down.

"Rodeo, I haven't seen you in a while." Emily held her hand out, and he walked over to her. She petted him, and when she stopped, he went back to Alisa's side. Her hand automatically went to the dog's head.

"He's taken a real liking to Alisa," Clint said. "He's very protective of her."

"I can see that," Emily replied.

"He can stay in my trailer with me," Clint said.

"Or in the Homesteader Cabin with me," Susan volunteered.

She jumped at the sound of her own voice volunteering to take a dog. She'd never had a dog in her life and would need detailed instructions on what to do, but she liked Rodeo.

Emily's eyes twinkled when she looked at Alisa's face. "He can stay here just as long as Alisa takes care of him, walks him and feeds him." She tried to look stern but couldn't pull it off.

"I will, Mrs. Dixon. I really will," Alisa promised.

Clint nodded. "I've got some dog food in the truck, Mrs. D. I'll bring it in."

When Susan entered her chilly cabin, she immediately started a fire.

After a long, hot shower, she noticed that she had some aching muscles in places that she never knew could ache. Smiling, she knew it was from her lovemaking with Clint. He could be quite imaginative. Her smile soon faded when she realized that he'd become a part of her life in such a short time. Things would never be the same without him.

*She'd* never be the same without him.

She'd go on as she usually did. She'd throw herself into her work.

A half hour later, she unlocked the door of her classroom and began opening the boxes from her company. Her staff had done an excellent job in gathering everything she needed.

The last box made Susan grin. They'd packed boots, jeans and shirts in her size along with a denim jacket. She giggled at the pink cowboy hat and turquoise cowboy boots.

She put the hat on and looked at herself in the mirror. Awesome, as Alisa would say.

She'd have to give her administrative staff a raise when she got back. What would she do without them? Then it struck her—she hadn't thought of calling Winners Wear in ages.

Right now, her company was the last thing on her mind. She was more concerned about a little girl, a rodeo bullfighter and helping out the Dixons.

She got everything unpacked, stacked the T-shirts according to size, and put the trim in various baskets and bins. Happy that everything was sufficiently organized, she headed back to her cabin to change into her cowboy clothes.

Wouldn't Clint be surprised?

When Susan Collins walked into the dining hall, Clint Scully did a double take.

It could have been the tight jeans or the pastel plaid shirt. Maybe it was the pink cowboy hat or the turquoise cowboy boots. All he knew was that Susan looked hot.

He was at her side in a heartbeat, and couldn't stop staring at her. He tweaked his hat. "Well, hell-o, Miss Rodeo Queen."

"How do I look?" She turned in a circle.

Clint whispered in her ear, "Hot and sexy."

Her face flushed with heat. "You don't look too bad yourself, cowboy."

"I'd like to make love to you right here and now, but this is a G-rated dining hall."

She grinned. "I take my hat off for only one thing, and it's staying on until lights out."

The next morning, Dex Dixon walked up to the stage in the dining hall and welcomed the Gold Buckle Gang campers. He said a prayer, everyone recited the Pledge of Allegiance and he explained the changes in the program due to the heavy rain and mud. There were groans when he said that the events would be held indoors.

But then there were cheers when he said that there would still be horseback riding and other events at the Mountain Springs arena.

After breakfast, the Gold Buckle Gang program would officially start.

Susan had a nine o'clock arts and crafts class. She could hardly eat or concentrate on her conversation with Clint.

"Clint, I want to go to my classroom and go over my notes."

"Sure. Let's go."

"I've never been so nervous in my life," she said, walking around the room, straightening the table coverings.

"They're just kids," Clint said. "And here they come."

Her class filed in wearing raincoats, carrying umbrellas and backpacks.

Clint stood at her side. "You can do it."

"I can do it." She drew upon every bit of strength she had in her. "Good afternoon, campers. Welcome to arts and crafts class. Hang up your coats and take a seat. We have a big project to start today."

Susan had the time of her life. She did two more classes and found that Alisa was a great help. Clint provided individual attention to each of the kids.

Even the boys liked the thought of bringing something they made in camp back to their mothers and/or fathers, even if it was only a pot holder.

They were actually interested in the manufacturing process of clothes and asked questions. Naturally, they couldn't wait to start on their logos.

"Tonight, think about something that would represent what the Gold Buckle Ranch means to you, and we'll get started with the designs tomorrow," she instructed.

As the kids filed out to their next activity, Alisa handed her the pot holder she had made. It was a perfect blue-and-green-striped square.

"I'd like you to have it, Susan."

"Thank you, sweetie. I'll keep it always."

Her light blue eyes lit up. "You will?"

"Absolutely."

"Do you think Cheyenne Clint would like one?"

"I know he would."

"I'll make him one the same color as yours."

Susan walked Alisa back to the Dixons' home after lunch because another couple wanted to meet her.

In Emily's kitchen over milk and cookies, Alisa couldn't have been more gracious, but Susan could tell that she was tired and not up to this again.

Emily took Susan aside. "The Ketchums decided that they wanted someone who isn't facing a hospital stay and rehab."

"I can't believe that they put her through the whole process." Susan sighed. "It's another rejection for Alisa."

"It's apparently the procedure for older children," Emily said calmly.

"What? Trial and error?"

Susan studied the couple sitting on the couch. They were younger than the Ketchums and seemed to be inspecting Alisa as if she were a bug under a microscope. Maybe they were just nervous.

Emily shook her head. "It does seem that there could be a better way, but what can I do? I only have temporary custody of Alisa. Tonight was the only night they could make it this week."

"Another busy couple, I presume."

Emily grunted. "I think you presume right."

Susan looked back at Alisa. At least Rodeo was at her side, keeping her company.

"Good night, Emily."

Susan stepped outside and opened her umbrella. She had no right to criticize anyone's busy schedule.

She'd be just as bad.

## *Chapter 15*

Thursday night, Susan was reading in her cabin when Clint came by with a surprise.

He held up a key. "From Emily. It's the key to the lock on the cover of the hot tub." He grinned. "Emily's still calling it a spa. Shall we try it?"

"But it's raining."

"So? We'll be wet, anyway."

Who could argue with logic like that?

"I'll put my suit on."

"Do you have to?" he asked.

She raised an eyebrow.

"Okay. You're right. Put it on and let's go."

Clint waited for her in the living room while she pulled a pair of navy-blue yoga pants and a hoodie over her suit.

Clint took the two towels she carried and they walked in the light rain hand in hand to one of the caretaker cabins off to the side of the dining hall. The hot tub was around back on a big wooden deck. Three sets of patio tables with umbrellas and matching chairs were positioned around the tub.

Clint unlocked the padlock and removed the top. Immediately, ghostly fingers of steam reached into the air. He flipped a switch on the side of the cabin, and the water churned into a nice froth.

It looked wonderful.

She slipped out of her clothes and put them on a chair under an overhang, hoping they might stay dry. Clint did the same. He wore a pair of dark-colored nylon jogging shorts.

Clad only in her bathing suit, she shivered in the cold rain and even colder air.

Clint held out his hand and helped her up the steps into the tub.

She took a seat, and he sat next to her.

"This is wonderful," she said, looking up at the black sky. In the glow of the outdoor lights near them, she could see the rain coming down like silver shards. The sensation of the cold rain and steamy, hot water on her skin was better than any spa treatment she'd ever had.

Clint added to the heat of the hot tub when he pulled her onto his lap and kissed her. His hand slipped under the top of her suit and played with her nipples.

"Mmm…"

"I know you like it when I do this," he said, his voice husky.

She clung to him, knowing that their time together would end soon.

She was falling in love with him. She didn't know when it started, but Clint Scully seemed to be keeping his side of their agreement. He hadn't mentioned taking their relationship to a higher level, so she kept silent.

Back at the cabin, they took a warm and soapy shower together, content to feel and touch. They moved slowly, letting the water rain down on them just like it had outside. When Clint finally entered her, they moved as if they were in a sleepy dream, prolonging their joining, not wanting it to end.

They moved to the bedroom and talked in between kisses. Then Clint dozed off, and Susan was content to watch him sleep. She wanted to memorize every scar, every muscle and every strand of hair. She inhaled his scent, looked at the laugh lines around his eyes and remembered how he appeared with the breeze ruffling his hair as he looked over his ranch.

She knew she'd miss him so very much.

Getting out of bed, she slipped into her nightgown and her fuzzy socks. She pulled a blanket around herself and went onto the porch. It had stopped raining after they'd returned from the hot tub, but the leaves and needles of the trees were still dripping rain.

She rocked, listening to the night sounds of the Gold Buckle, sounds that would have sent her scurrying into the cabin and under the covers just a few days ago.

She smelled the damp night air, listened to the crickets or whatever else was chirping, croaking or howling out there.

She'd miss this place. She'd been happy here. It had been a hard journey of self-discovery, but with a little help from a wonderful cowboy and a darling little girl, she'd worked through some things that had been bothering her.

She'd met giving, caring people—volunteers from the community and some chaperones and parents of the campers.

Susan had felt like a part of it all. She taught her classes, and held a fun dress rehearsal for the logo competition in the dining hall.

And she'd fallen in love. How it hurt to admit she loved Clint when they'd agreed to forgo strings. Too bad she hadn't known when she'd made that deal that her heart wasn't a corporation.

She only had one more day here. One day to absorb enough of Clint to last her a lifetime. Saturday morning, she'd be leaving.

When she got back home, she planned on sending cowboy shirts, T-shirts, golf shirts and jackets in a variety of sizes for all the staff and campers at the Gold Buckle Ranch with the new logo. It would be her way of giving back.

She'd also send some terry-cloth robes and big beach towels for Emily's "spa."

The Dixons could sell the shirts to cover some operating expenses or give them away, whatever they wanted. She'd see that they got a hefty supply every year.

She'd even told Dex and Emily and Jake that if they ever needed an arts and crafts instructor during the summer to give her a call. She'd be taking more vacations from now on.

Rocking on the porch of the little cabin, she thought about many things in those early hours of the morning. Above all, how hard it would be to say goodbye.

Alisa must have felt it, too, because she'd barely left Susan's side yesterday. Rodeo must have sensed that Alisa was becoming upset, so he'd tried to be even more attentive to her.

Susan heard Clint walking around the cabin, and soon caught a whiff of coffee. After a while, the door opened and a fully dressed and showered Clint handed her a cup.

He sat down next to her, and they drank their coffee in silence, watching the sunrise together, holding hands, content to be in each other's company.

"I'm looking forward to the rodeo today," she said. "Looks like the sun's finally going to make an appearance."

He set his empty mug down. "I volunteered to help Joe get the stock there. I'd better get going." He gave her a quick kiss.

"I'll be riding on the bus with cabins one and two," she said.

"See you later." He kissed her, kissed her again and ran the back of his knuckles down her cheek and under her jaw. "I'll miss you."

She didn't know if he meant that he'd miss her until they saw each other at the rodeo, or after she'd gone. Either way, she'd miss him desperately, too.

If only things were different.

* * *

They sat and cheered for Alisa as she played baseball. She scored two runs, but her team lost. Later, Susan led Goldie around the arena as Alisa rode. Clint volunteered with the boys.

Every event brought her departure that much closer. She struggled to focus on the children, not her own breaking heart. This was their day.

Susan's T-shirt-logo contest and fashion show had been a success, and the four finalists stood in the middle of the arena. The winner, by vote of several judges, was a freckle-faced boy from Kansas City, Mason Detlin, who drew several smiling faces inside a gold buckle. Under it he lettered "Gold Buckle Ranch" in bright colors and "We Try Our Best."

Susan loved the logo when she first saw it, since it fit the Gold Buckle Ranch's theme perfectly. She'd take the T-shirt back with her and have it duplicated by Connie on the computer. From now on, all the merchandise at the Gold Buckle Ranch would carry that design.

When Clint wasn't needed to help, he sat with Susan and Alisa, bringing snacks and drinks and watching the competition.

He'd miss Susan. He'd make an occasional trip to New York when bullfighting took him to events in the northeast, but it wouldn't be the same. It wouldn't be the magic that he'd found with her here.

Could he give up bullfighting and be content to stay home and tend to his ranch and his other ventures?

Could he ask Susan to give up her company for

him, marry him and move to his ranch? Could he ask her to adopt Alisa with him?

When they had been making out like teenagers in the hot tub, he'd wanted to ask her. Whenever they were lying in bed holding each other, he'd wanted to ask her. He never had.

In many ways, loving Susan was as dangerous as fighting bulls—except any damage done would be to his heart. And he didn't think he could stand it if she said no.

Susan needed tall buildings, public transportation, designer clothes and a cosmopolitan culture. She ran a successful company with a few hundred employees.

How could someone give that up for a quiet life at the Lazy S?

While Alisa would love it, Susan would soon grow bored and unhappy. He couldn't do that to her.

As far as she was concerned, he was just another business deal.

The campers left the Gold Buckle Ranch right after breakfast on Saturday. Susan saw them off into vans and busses as they left for the Mountain Springs Airport or waved goodbye to them as they drove away with their families. She'd miss the kids, but she had a fistful of addresses and promised to keep in touch.

Emily and Dex came to see her off. She told them that she'd be sending all the merchandise they wanted, free of charge, and they couldn't hug her enough.

Alisa handed her a white gift box tied with a ribbon. "Open it when you get home," she instructed.

Alisa begged to go to the airport with her and Susan couldn't say no, although she would have liked to have said her goodbyes to Alisa at the ranch, and be alone with Clint. She kept wishing he'd tell her that he loved her. It was perplexing that she had no fear in business situations, but she just couldn't get a handle on her relationship with Clint.

Alisa wouldn't let go of her hand. There was no room for Rodeo in the front seat with them, so he sat behind them. Frequently, he'd let out a little whine.

Susan kept glancing at Clint as he drove, still trying to commit every nuance of him to memory. His strong jaw, his tanned hands on the steering wheel, the little smile lines at the corners of his mouth. She could smell his aftershave, the spice-and-pine scent that was all his.

As they pulled into the airport, she knew she couldn't do it. Couldn't walk in and hand over her bags and answer the security questions with Clint and Alisa beside her. That would make it so much more real. She had to get the goodbyes behind her. Then she could dash for the ladies' room and wash the tears from her face before she had to face the reality of walking onto the plane.

As Susan got out of the truck, tears welled up in Alisa's eyes, breaking what was left of Susan's heart. "Do you have to go?" Alisa asked.

She clenched her fists as she waited for Clint to ask her the same thing, maybe look at her and at least gauge her reaction to the question. Instead, he stayed silent, looking forward.

She cupped Alisa's face in her hands. "I do,

sweetie. I'll miss you terribly, but I'll see you soon. You're going to have that operation in New York City, and I'll be there to visit you all the time."

Alisa wiped her eyes and pulled something out of her pocket. "I made you another one of these."

A pot holder. Red and yellow. "I'll treasure it always, Alisa. Both of the ones you made me." She kissed her cheek and looked away, hurriedly wiping her eyes so Alisa wouldn't see her crying.

She looked at Clint, and he got out of the truck. Leaning into the truck, he said, "Stay here, Alisa. I'd like to say goodbye to Susan, too."

Susan closed the door and blew a kiss to Alisa. The girl was crying slightly, and Rodeo was whimpering with his head on her leg.

Clint stood with his hands in his pockets, leaning against the back end of his pickup. How could she go the rest of her life without seeing him like this, waiting for her?

Susan plastered a brave smile on her face and walked toward him. "Don't just stand there, cowboy. Kiss me."

Just the right touch, she thought, casual and not needy.

He obliged, long and hard.

She wished the kiss would never end; neither did she want to leave the warm embrace of his arms. "Thanks for a wonderful time. Thanks for listening. Thanks for…everything."

She noticed that his smile wasn't his usual grin, and his turquoise eyes had lost their twinkle.

He wasn't going to ask her to stay, but she knew

now that he was going to miss her. Why couldn't he tell her that?

Maybe they'd agreed on no commitments, but admitting that he'd miss her wasn't committing. Maybe she'd read him all wrong.

"I'm going to miss you, cowboy," she finally said.

He took a red bandanna from his pocket and dabbed at her eyes. Then he picked up her hand, kissed the back of it as he often did, and slid the bandanna into the pocket of her blazer.

"If it works out, I'll bring Alisa to New York City," Clint said.

She waited for him to say more.

"It won't be the same, will it?" he said.

*It could be better. It could be forever.*

She couldn't stop herself from touching her hand to his cheek, letting it linger there. God, how she'd miss him. They'd keep in touch for Alisa's sake, but it wouldn't be the same.

She clutched the pot holder in one hand, and the white box that Alisa had given her along with her purse. Clint hailed a skycap, shoved some money in his hand. Susan handed him her ticket.

Just as she began to walk away, she heard Clint say, "Susan?"

Her heart raced, hoping that he'd ask her to stay—might even tell her that he loved her. "Yes?"

He stepped back and hooked his thumbs into his belt loops. "Have a good flight."

Her heart dropped. "Bye, Clint."

Then she turned and walked through the door of the Mountain Springs Airport.

# *Chapter 16*

When Susan got back home late Saturday, she took a hot shower and unpacked. She took out the box that Alisa had given her and opened it. Wrapped in white tissue paper was the bird's nest with the three pinecones in it. Tears welled in her eyes as she remembered the day of their picnic at Silver River.

Three pinecones together in a nest: Clint, Alisa and Susan.

Alisa's symbolism wasn't lost on her, either—home and a family.

The phone rang, splitting the quiet. It was probably the office. They knew she was home and thought she was eager to get back to work. Not true. For some reason, she wasn't ready to jump back into the fray just yet.

"Hello?"

"Susan?"

Her heart raced as she recognized that low, deep voice. "Hi, Clint."

"I just wanted to make sure that you got home okay."

"It was a long flight, but I'm here. How's Alisa? How are *you?*"

"She's been pretty gloomy since you left. Even Rodeo can't cheer her up. She misses you." He hesitated. "So do I."

She couldn't swallow over the lump in her throat, couldn't breathe. "I miss you both, too."

"Bet you can't wait to get back to work tomorrow," he said.

"I don't think so. Tomorrow's Sunday."

"Didn't you tell me that you work on Sundays?"

"Not anymore."

"Whoa! Good for you. Are you sure this is the Manhattan tornado that landed in Wyoming ten days ago, or do I have the wrong number?"

Clint could always make her laugh.

"You do not have the wrong number, Cheyenne Clint. I am a changed woman."

"See what a little good sex can do for you?"

It was more than sex—at least for her. Still, her face heated as she remembered the first time they'd made love. "It wasn't just good, it was great. And quit fishing for compliments."

She heard him laugh, then more silence.

"Clint? Are you there?"

"I really miss you. You know that? And you've been gone only eleven hours."

*He missed her.*

She thought she could settle for seeing him occasionally at the Gold Buckle Ranch, but that wasn't nearly enough. Maybe the three of them could meet somewhere at Christmas.

No. That wasn't enough, either. She wanted to see him every day for the rest of her life, but she'd bargained that away.

"I'll call you tomorrow," Clint said. "Right now, I have to load some stock for Joe. I just wanted to make sure you got home safe. Good night, Susan. Sleep well."

She couldn't wait to talk to him again.

"Give Alisa a hug for me. Say hi to everyone."

"You got it."

She hung up the phone and sat by herself in her apartment. Night had fallen, but she didn't bother to turn on a light. She felt so alone. She missed Alisa singing her Disney songs. She missed Clint's laughter and his company and his touch.

She took inventory of her life. Here in New York she had three friends, an apartment and her business. Those were all good things, but they couldn't compete with what she'd found in Wyoming—family, purpose, love.

She was a different person, and she had Clint to thank. Even if they never saw each other again, she knew that there were some things she needed to change in her life.

She reached for her planner, found the picture of

Elaine, and smiled this time, instead of crying. Then she got started on another list.

The most important list of her life.

She worked on her list on Sunday, too, and set up some time frames for completion. In between, she got hold of her lawyer and told him what she was planning to do.

He tried to talk her out of it, but she stood firm. It was what she wanted.

On Monday morning, instead of going to work, Susan went to the cemetery to visit her mother and sister.

She pulled some of the weeds from around the roses and sat on a nearby bench. The sun was shining through the leaves of the big maple overhead, dappling the two graves with shade.

"Mom, Elaine, I can't spend my entire life at Winners Wear anymore. I need some time of my own. You see, I've finally learned that there's more to life than just work. There's also a lot of this world that I haven't seen. So I'm not going to work for my money, I'm going to let my money work for me."

This time she didn't cry when she thought of her sister. She felt a lightness inside her that she hadn't before. Maybe this was the biggest gift she received from Clint. She was able to unlock all her guilt and remember the good times with Elaine.

She sat for a while, enjoying the peace and serenity and just being outside—things she'd learned to treasure.

She arrived at work after one o'clock. After exchanging greetings with everyone, she made her way to her desk. At a quick glance, there was nothing that needed immediate attention, and almost everything was just tagged "For Your Information." Her former response would be to call a meeting and get up to speed on every piece of paper and every minute that she'd missed.

Instead, she pushed the papers aside and pulled out a box of DVDs from the Professional Bull Riders World Finals that she'd bought at the airport.

She unwrapped the plastic and slid the first disk into her computer. She sat back as it booted up. Then she sat upright and turned up the volume when she saw that the beginning introduction was a collage of bull rides—and Clint was one of the bullfighters. She watched him move, remembering when he moved that way with her, catching his smile.

There were six discs, and she watched one every day at the office. She continued to look for Clint, losing herself in seeing him again, reliving particular moments from her week with him. She only stopped when her secretary called her for the third time.

"Janet, can't Bev or Darlene handle it? I'm really busy here."

"Yes, Miss Collins."

She never would have done that before. She smiled as she turned the DVD back on.

The next morning, Bev cornered her in her office. "Okay, spill it," Bev ordered. "You've been awful quiet about your trip to the ranch. And you're not the same Susan Collins who left New York a couple weeks ago. What exactly happened to you in Wyoming?"

Susan sighed. "I want to thank you again from the bottom of my heart for making me go on that trip, Bev. So many things happened to me in those ten days." She walked over to her briefcase and pulled out a stack of papers. "Call everyone in for a meeting, Bev. I just came from my lawyer's office, and I have something important to discuss with all of you."

She crossed another item off her list.

Later that day, her receptionist, Janet, popped her head in. She was smiling, and Janet rarely smiled.

"Miss Collins, you have a visitor, a gentleman who is insisting that he see you. His name is—" She laughed.

Susan stared at the usually stoic Janet. "Yes?"

"Cheyenne Clint Scully."

Susan froze when she heard Clint's voice. He walked through the door looking hot and sexy in his tight, dark blue jeans, a long-sleeved light blue shirt and a white hat with silver conchos. He had on a thick brown leather belt clamped with a big gold buckle that gleamed in the overhead lights. His boots thumped on the old wood floor with each long stride.

Janet stared with her mouth open, and Susan motioned for her to close the door. With a sigh, she did.

Clint tweaked his hat and gave her a smile as big as the Wyoming sky. "So all this is yours?"

Susan couldn't stay put any longer. She ran toward him, needing to feel his arms around her. His embrace was strong, warm. She gave him a big kiss.

He picked her up off the floor and twirled her in a circle without moving his lips from hers.

Clint finally lowered her to the ground but held on to her hands.

He looked so darn good. "Clint, what are you doing here?"

"I flew up with Alisa."

"Oh, no..." Her throat tightened. "Is she okay?"

"She's fine." A finger gently touched her lips. "You sure have a lot of juice with the children's hospital. They moved up her operation a week. I just checked her into the hospital and told her that I was going to get you."

"You left her alone? Oh, Clint, she's all alone?"

He nodded. "Alisa and I had a discussion on the plane. We made a plan. My part of the plan is coming here and talking to you. Her part of the plan is to get well."

He led her over to the conversation pit and sat down. His gaze shifted to the coffee table in front of him. Susan had brought the bird's nest with the three pinecones in it to work. One red and one blue bandanna of his and the pot holders Alisa had made were also on display.

He smiled up at her. His eyes were as turquoise as she remembered. "You've missed us, haven't you?"

"You know I have."

He picked up a porcelain angel that was on the table. "What's this?"

"It's for Alisa. I want her to have it, to watch over her. It was Elaine's."

"Beautiful." He raised an eyebrow. "So you're all set to visit her in the hospital?"

"Of course."

"I knew you'd come through, but there was a time when you wouldn't consider it."

"I know. I've learned a lot from everyone at the Gold Buckle," she said. "I decided that I have a lot to offer the kids and staff. I had a conference call with Jake and Emily last week, and you're looking at the new full-time arts and crafts counselor for next summer."

"Well, I'll be." He pulled her onto his lap and hugged her. "They didn't tell me."

"It's so good to see you, Clint," she whispered. He kissed her forehead, and a warmth flooded her.

"Susan, I have a business proposition for you."

She thought he was kidding, but the look on his face told her that he wasn't. "This sounds serious."

"It is." He removed several pieces of paper from his jeans, unfolded them and spread them on the table. "This is my net worth."

Confused, she didn't even look at the papers.

"Why are you showing me all this?"

"I'd like you to take a look."

Shaking her head, she gave a cursory glance at the papers, then *really* looked. She couldn't have been more shocked if Clint Scully had showed up at Winners Wear sporting a three-piece suit and tie.

"This is impressive as hell. You never did give me Cletus the Clown's phone number." She pushed the papers back at him. "I still don't know why you're showing me this."

"I want to buy you out."

*"You what?"* Her heart raced. What was he saying?

"Call it a friendly takeover. Call it what you want. The money's yours. If you want more for the company, I'll sell some cattle."

She held up a hand to stop him. "Clint, I don't know what to say, other than I'm astonished. Why do you want my company?"

"I don't want it. I want *you,* but if that's what it takes to get you to leave here, the money's all yours. You can start another Winners Wear in Cheyenne."

"Are you asking me to come and live with you in Wyoming?"

"Susan, I'm asking you to marry me."

That was what she wanted to hear, but only if he loved her. He hadn't said that yet.

"To give Alisa a home?"

"Well, yes. She needs us as much as we need her. I want us to be a family, Susan."

He was almost there, but not quite. She loved them both, but she wouldn't marry him just for Alisa.

He got up and looked out the window, facing the towering skyline. Susan knew that Clint didn't belong here, and at this point in her life, she didn't want to be here, either.

She could see the resolve on his face. "But, Susan, if you want to stay here, I think we should find a place to live with a park nearby for Alisa."

"But I thought that the Lazy S was your dream place. You'd move to New York for me?" She couldn't be more surprised.

"I really hoped you'd like the Lazy S. That's why I flew you and Alisa there. We'd be great parents, Susan. I want us to have more children." He grinned. "The Lazy S is a great place to grow up, and a great place for kids to run—and Alisa *will* run."

He knelt down on one knee, took his hat off and put it over his heart. "I love you, Susan Collins. Tell me you'll marry me."

Her heart soared. Finally. *He loved her.*

She pulled his hands to get him to his feet. "What took you so long?"

"Well, we had that stupid agreement, and I didn't think you'd give all this up. That's why I came up with the idea of buying you out. I thought then you could start somewhere else—like on the Lazy S."

She put her hands on her hips. "Clint Scully, you never asked me to stay. I'd give all this up if it meant being with you and Alisa. Matter of fact, that was part of *my* plan—but only if you loved me."

She walked to her desk and picked up a stack of papers. "These papers, all nice and legal, make Winners Wear into a partnership. I'm going to be a silent partner for a while, or maybe forever, but mostly it'll be managed by three of my employees—the three who've been with me from the beginning. We've all just signed the paperwork today."

He raised an eyebrow. "You did all that?"

"If you didn't get here in the near future, I was going to come to you."

He grinned and he held out his arms. "Well, then, what do you say?"

"Well, there's one more thing…." She looked at

him. This was going to stab him right in the heart. "Your trailer."

"What about it?"

"Do you think that we could get a motor home instead? If Alisa and I are going to travel with you to bull riding events, we want to travel in style." She opened her top drawer and held up a brochure. "I already have one picked out."

"Yee-haw!" He moved her onto his lap and kissed her.

"Think you could give up being a tumbleweed in order to raise a family, cowboy?"

"In a New York minute. Think you could be a rancher's wife?"

"In a Wyoming minute!"

She stepped into his embrace and looked into his eyes. They reflected his love for her, and she could see a happy life with him full of laughter and fun and music.

"Yes. Yes, I'll marry you. I love you, Clint Scully."

"Finally," he said, kissing her.

"Let's just have a minute alone before we go and ask Alisa if she wants us to be her parents. We'll have a lot to learn and—"

Susan put a finger over his lips. "All we have to do is try our best."

* * * * *

WE HOPE YOU ENJOYED
THIS BOOK FROM

HARLEQUIN
SPECIAL
EDITION

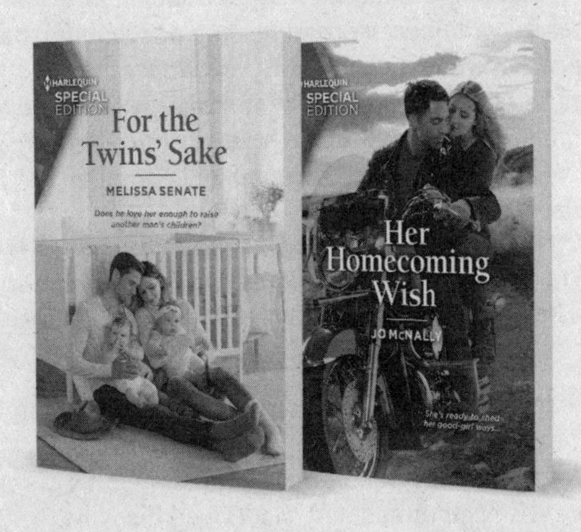


*Believe in love. Overcome obstacles. Find happiness.*

Relate to finding comfort and strength in the support of loved ones and enjoy the journey no matter what life throws your way.

**6 NEW BOOKS AVAILABLE EVERY MONTH!**

HSEHALO2020

SPECIAL EXCERPT FROM

HARLEQUIN

**SPECIAL** EDITION

*When Laurel Hudson is found—alive but with amnesia—no one is more relieved than Adam Fortune. He will do whatever it takes to reunite mother and son, even if it means a road trip in extremely close quarters. Will the long journey home remind Laurel how much they truly share?*

*Read on for a sneak preview of the final book in The Fortunes of Texas: Rambling Rose continuity,* The Texan's Baby Bombshell *by Allison Leigh.*

He'd been falling for her from the very beginning. But that kiss had sealed the deal for him.

Now that glossy oak-barrel hair slid over her shoulder as Laurel's head turned and she looked his way.

His step faltered.

Her eyes were the same stunning shade of blue they'd always been. Her perfectly heart-shaped face was pale and delicate looking even without the pink scar on her forehead between her eyebrows.

Her eyebrows pulled together as their eyes met.

*Remember me.*

*Remember us.*

The words—unwanted and unexpected—pulsed through him, drowning out the splitting headache and the aching back and the impatience, the relief and the pain.

HSEEXP0520

Then she blinked those incredible eyes of hers and he realized there was a flush on her cheeks and she was chewing at the corner of her lips. In contrast to her delicate features, her lips were just as full and pouty as they'd always been.

Kissing them had been an adventure in and of itself.

He pushed the pointless memory out of his head and then had to shove his hands in the pockets of his jeans because they were actually shaking.

"Hi." Puny first word to say to the woman who'd made a wreck out of him.

Still seated, she looked up at him. "Hi." She sounded breathless. "It's…it's Adam, right?"

The pain sitting in the pit of his stomach then had nothing to do with anything except her. He yanked his right hand from his pocket and held it out. "Adam Fortune."

She looked uncertain, then slowly settled her hand into his.

Unlike Dr. Granger's firm, brief clasp, Laurel's touch felt chilled and tentative. And it lingered. "I'm Lisa."

God help him. He was not strong enough for this.

*Don't miss*
The Texan's Baby Bombshell *by Allison Leigh,*
*available June 2020 wherever*
*Harlequin Special Edition books and ebooks are sold.*

Harlequin.com

Copyright © 2020 by Harlequin Books S.A.

HSEEXP0520

**IF YOU ENJOYED THIS BOOK**
**WE THINK YOU WILL ALSO LOVE**

LOVE INSPIRED SUSPENSE
INSPIRATIONAL ROMANCE

*Courage. Danger. Faith.*

Find strength and determination in stories of faith and love in the face of danger.

**6 NEW BOOKS AVAILABLE EVERY MONTH!**

LISXSERIES2020